ALSO BY ANDREA BARTZ

The Spare Room
We Were Never Here
The Herd
The Lost Night

THE
LAST
FERRY
OUT

THE LAST FERRY OUT

A Novel

ANDREA BARTZ

BALLANTINE BOOKS
NEW YORK

Published in the United States by Ballantine Books,
an imprint of Random House, a division of
Penguin Random House LLC, 1745 Broadway, New York, NY 10019.

BALLANTINE BOOKS & colophon are registered trademarks
of Penguin Random House LLC.

Map by Eric J. Hanson

Hardback ISBN 978-0-593-59797-2
Ebook ISBN 978-0-593-59798-9

Printed in the United States of America on acid-free paper

penguinrandomhouse.com
randomhousebooks.com

1 2 3 4 5 6 7 8 9

First Edition

Book design by Elizabeth A. D. Eno

The authorized representative in the EU for product safety and compliance is
Penguin Random House Ireland, Morrison Chambers, 32 Nassau Street,
Dublin D02 YH68, Ireland, https://eu-contact.penguin.ie.

For my nagymama, Marianne Denes, whose bravery, grace, and resilience—especially in the face of grief—inspire me. Nagyon szeretlek.

ISLA COLEL

Lighthouse

Picnic Area

N

NATURE PRESERVE

Paraíso Escondido

trail

Bio Bay

CARIBBEAN SEA

RESIDENTIAL AREA

Playa Oscura

Playa Destello

LUNA RIFT

PLAZA PÚBLICA

MAIN PORT

AUTHOR'S NOTE

This book contains depictions of murder, anaphylaxis, drug use, and self-harm, as well as references to physical and mental abuse, queer-phobia, forced outing, alcohol use disorder, suicide, and drowning. Please read with care.

THE
LAST
FERRY
OUT

B lood hits limestone and splatters for a second before the rain beats it back, diluting it and sluicing it away in pink rivulets. Next a raw scream pierces the air, but the storm waters it down too. A human cry is no match for the roar of rain on rock and the steady pulse of whitecaps beating against the cliff, of thunder rolling around the bay and palm fronds shivering in fear.

There's no chance of anyone hearing it, but the scream isn't a cry for help. It's involuntary, a knee-jerk reaction to the way her skeleton now juts out of the arm that ensconced it moments ago. The bone is a riot of white, like a sharp, bleached tooth, and where it pierces the skin, blood gushes freely.

She managed to drag herself here, through the frothing waves, but the base of the cliff isn't the oasis she hoped. Forty feet of sheer rock stretch overhead. Even if there were a clear path, there's no way she could scramble up with her forearm snapped in two. She's trapped in a bay with no hope of climbing out.

Looking above her and then out at the roiling sea, she sees no sign of the people who are after her. No sign of a savior, either, anyone to help her out of this mess.

Her chest heaves, harder and harder, until her vision starts to blur. She presses her half-shredded palm against the rock and turns to rest her back on the limestone. She looks out at the storm, a tempest strobed in lightning strikes. The foamy water makes her think of a rabid dog.

Blackness tugs at the corners of her vision, an undertow from every direction.

I did my best, she thinks. *I went down fighting.*

Then she closes her eyes and lets the darkness win.

CHAPTER ONE
ABBY

Monday afternoon

Sweat beads on my neck and lip and slithers down my chest. The path is overgrown and steep, sprouting from the edge of town and pushing a mile north from the island's inhabited southern end, into its lush nature preserve. Though there are a few signs of life along the trail—empty beer bottles, a rotting pack of cigarettes, litter I stuff into my backpack as I pass—I haven't encountered another human since I began the climb a half hour ago.

Just as Eszter promised. *Look, I have it all to myself,* she told me, panning the camera around her. Smiling crookedly, sunlight shimmering on her maple-colored hair, tattoo taut on her shoulder. *It feels like I'm the only person on Earth.*

I finish the steep ascent along a coastal cliff, where loose rocks slide under my feet. Thick vines hang off the trees like stiffened rope, and I cling to them as I ascend. To my left, I catch glimpses of the choppy waves and yellowish sea stacks sending up wild sprays of salt water. My heart thrums. I must be getting close now.

The path widens and zags inland, past a patch of fat ferns and broad-leaved banana trees, everything glistening and wet. Was it just this morning that I paced the terminal at Mitchell International Airport, airline announcements garbling through my ears like squawky trombones? A mid-May storm was brewing outside the windows, specks of rain floating on the breeze. I thought my flight might get canceled. Then I'd have an excuse to abandon the whole idea. On the plane, my eyes flooded with tears when a flat-voiced flight attendant droned, "Cross-check completed."

The vegetation drops away and it's clear, abruptly, how close the trail is to the cliff's edge, to its rough rock and deadly pitch. Eszter *loved* this hike—on the phone, she told me she couldn't wait to show me the route to the island's highest peak. My heart thuds against the backpack. I take a step closer to the precipice, closing the gap between myself and thin air, four flights of sheer limestone. Vertigo pulls at my head and knees.

So badly I had wanted to walk this path with her.

This is the spot, then. The highest lookout point on the island that took her. A dilapidated hotel hulks behind me—twisting around, I can't make out the building, but I spot curls of barbed wire peeking through the foliage, perhaps fifty feet inland. There's some sort of abandoned comm tower jutting above the treetops, too, big rusted pipes and dishes. The resort must've been impressive when it was open: a hilltop property rising out of the Mexican rainforest.

I slip the backpack off my shoulders and ease the zipper open. I feel feral, unpredictable. The sea roars and tumbles, calling out to me, somehow. I picture it: My body sinking below the whitecaps, giving in to the undertow, the ocean's impassive yank. Waves slapping my face and worming into my nose and mouth and, eventually, lungs.

It's been four months since Eszter's brother Laszlo called me, his wife's sobs audible in the background.

There's been an accident.

I felt a desperate swoop. *Is Eszter okay?* I asked. My brain flipped through possibilities like a slide projector: car accident, bike accident, hiking accident—

She's—

And I interrupted him. *Tell me she's okay.*

The silence was so long that it took on shape and form, dark and thick and widening by the millisecond, broadening to make room for the dawning horror.

On New Year's Day, kicking off this godforsaken year, Eszter arrived here, on an island where the Gulf of Mexico meets the Caribbean Sea, for a three-week trip. I was going to join her that final week, after she'd made some headway on a big final project she was working on for business school—her capstone. But her brother called before I ever got to the airport. Eszter and I were only just beginning; our time together, a year and a half of dating plus three months of an engagement, should've been a start, not a finish.

I pull the phone from my backpack and leave the bag flopped against my ankle. I open a folder labeled ESZTER PHOTOS and swipe through the last ones she sent me. Smiling from the top of the ferry, hair flapping in the breeze. Sitting in the town square, dark sunglasses shielding her eyes, with a stingray mural over her shoulder. The cute rental she found, even more darling than it looked in the listing, its salmon-pink walls offsetting the white front door. Her toes in the sand, her sparkly ring in front of the marina. And sunsets, so many sunsets, each a commotion of color, lovingly documented like every one was a miracle.

I zoom in on the one picture that's not like the others: Eszter with her arms around some other folks, everyone in bathing suits and cover-ups, cheesing for the camera. *Hey, babe! These are the cool people I met . . . can't wait for you to meet them.* I'd given the heart response, fighting down a flicker of envy, labeling it my own excitement to see her. There was a tall fellow with broad, tanned arms and a salt-and-pepper beard. A pale, round-faced woman who reminded me of an angel in a Renaissance painting: unlined skin, barely-there brows, calflike eyes. An artsy-looking girl with an Afro and hoop earrings. I've always wondered who took the photo. Did Eszter intend for me to befriend them, too?

Only one way to find out.

Eszter never shared their names, let alone their contact info, so I came here to look for them. Reconstruct her final days, understand the place she loved so much. We weren't talking nearly as often as we should've while she was here; I was so busy, so focused on the upcoming investor meeting at work.

I failed, of course. Couldn't get the demo to work in time; didn't get the promotion I was hoping for. So I'm finally doing what Eszter begged me to do a few months ago: taking a vacation.

I rewatch Eszter's video, wind competing with her voice: *It feels like I'm the only person on Earth.* It ends on a freeze-frame, silent. This is definitely the spot. I look back and forth between the screen and the seething water—

A bird streaks past, so near it rustles the air across my back. I startle and step and then I feel it, the disorienting whoosh of losing my balance. The phone slips from my fingers as my arms windmill, and I trip over the backpack at my feet. I call out, joining the cacophony of wind and bugs and waves.

The last thing I see before I hit the ground is my phone bouncing off the rock face and sailing out of sight.

I scuttle away from the edge, icy adrenaline shooting through my limbs. I sit there for a second, my heart a jackhammer, my brain catching up to what just happened. A deranged laugh pops out of me. And then—

Another spurt of cortisol. *My phone.* I crawl forward and peer over the lip of the cliff—no sign of it. A panicky pang goes through me. I'm now alone and phoneless in a foreign country.

Get a hold of yourself, Abby. At least my photos and videos are all backed up in the cloud. A shard of optimism creeps in: Maybe a store on this tiny island sells pay-as-you-go phones? Otherwise I'm out of luck. The next ferry to the mainland won't show up until Thursday, three days from now. I'll be on it, beginning the long journey home.

I spot my sunscreen, then my ChapStick, both strewn on the ground near my feet. My backpack is a few inches from the ledge—unzipped, flipped on its side. I snatch it up and rifle through, then suck in a breath. Eszter's EpiPen is missing. The one rattling in the bottom of my bag, a slim tube I still occasionally grabbed when groping around for a tampon. I should've taken it out months ago, obviously, but something stopped me.

Idiotic, like carrying mace *after* a mugging.

Also idiotic: getting so lost in thought that a single bird almost cost me my life. *See, Abby? This is what happens when you don't focus.*

I scan the area for the EpiPen's yellow case, but it's gone. Another piece of her. I stand.

I undo the clasp of my necklace. The pendant is a tiny gold llama with an emerald chip as its eye—a birthday gift I gave Eszter a couple months before she died. Early in our relationship, she was learning Spanish, and in solidarity, I learned a phrase for her; instead of ending a call with the usual "G'night, love you," one evening I proudly said, "Buenas noches, te amo." But she heard "Te llamo," which (I soon learned) has a totally different meaning: "I call you." Sitcom-y confusion as we sorted it out, and just like that, two inside jokes were born: llamas as a relationship motif, and a hand signal we could shoot each other anytime we wanted to say "I love you": thumb and pinkie out, knuckles near the face, miming talking on an old-school phone.

My chest burns; I remember the last time she did it, before bed on Christmas, the night of our spectacular blowup. I had no idea we were in the final countdown: one last week together. I was still upset and I'd rolled over, pretended to be asleep. I want to reach back in time and shake that Abby: *Grow up, stop it. Appreciate what you have.*

The emerald sparkles in the light. She only wore this a handful of times . . . it glittered on her clavicles at a New Year's Eve party on our last night together. I matched it to her engagement ring, a glittery green solitaire on platinum. I fought to get that back from her parents, but they iced me out. My guess is they pretended not to understand its significance.

"Te llamo, Eszter." I whisper it, then clear my throat and say it again, louder. I wait, listening, as if for an answer, but all I hear is the sea's heady drumbeat.

And then I think of the texts.

Those goddamn texts, the last ones she ever sent me. Words that'll haunt me for the rest of my life.

Why did you say that, Eszter? Why did you open up a vortex of anxiety and pain before leaving me forever?

With a little gasp, I take a step and fling the necklace over the edge. It seems to hang in the air for a second before plunging out of sight. I lean forward and study the tumbling spume. Eszter was only twenty-seven years old. She had so much to say, to do, a huge impact to make on the planet. No one was kinder, more selfless and social-justice-minded. Why, why was her life cut short?

I turn away from the cliff, tense and anticipatory, like I'm waiting for a drug to kick in. Back home, this seemed like a good idea: The mere sight of the necklace triggered nausea, and turning its disposal into a mourning ritual made some kind of sense. Now the whole thing feels . . . soulless, like playacting grief. Another breaker plows into the cliff, banging against it like a million angry fists, and the vibration shoots up the soles of my feet.

Nothing. No tears, not even hysterical laughter. My insides feel hollow and wrung out. I glance toward the abandoned hotel one last time, then turn and begin the slow march back down the mountain.

CHAPTER TWO

This grief isn't anything like I expected it to be. I thought it would be sadness turned up to eleven, a slow-healing heartbreak working through me like a head cold. But Eszter's death has been an eerie absence, ebbing and flowing in intensity but always messing with me in some quiet, corner way. Like when the dentist has numbed part of your mouth and you just . . . can't connect with it, a blank where something ought to exist. *Where is she?* I want to scream. *She should be here.*

My hips and shins cramp as I continue the long descent. A few snail shells litter the ground, flat, perfect spirals the size of a silver dollar. They make me think of Eszter's tattoo, a sketch of Fibonacci's sequence taut against her deltoid, curving lines set inside larger and larger squares. Strategically placed so she could cover it up. Hide it from her parents.

A bit like she hid me.

I pass a knot of gnarled tree roots, a candy bar wrapper that glints like a jewel. Finally, the path spits me out near the beehive of residential streets, and I jump back as a moped zips past, inches away. I could turn toward my rental, but my ritual has an unfinished feeling, and suddenly

I know where I need to be—I know where Eszter would go next. This tiny island has only one main road, so I don't even need a map; by following the setting sun, I should be able to find it.

I walk by a crumbled church, a sun-bleached pink scooter abandoned in a ditch, a dilapidated playground choked with weeds. A small dog heaves itself against a fence, barking so hard he's nearly hyperventilating. Did he snarl at Eszter too?

It was so unlike her—taking off on a solo vacation, spending her winter break alone. She was nervous to tell me, pulling out her little orange notebook, bullet points visible in her small, even handwriting. She always wrote out a script before difficult conversations, a habit I mostly found infuriating; mid-discussion, I'd be reacting, asking questions, and her eyes would slide back to the page in front of her, the words wooden and formal.

Sitting across from me over dinner, consulting her notes instead of meeting my gaze, she pitched this trip to Mexico as a "writing retreat" for her to both practice her Spanish and make major progress on her big final paper for her MBA program. Things were coming together on her capstone project, she said, and it was time to put pen to paper. The project—a school assignment and real-life development rolled into one—seemed brilliant from afar: She was calling it the Haven, a Miami-based long-stay boutique hotel and shelter for refugee families all under the same roof, with the former funding the latter. (Her father, himself a Miami real estate developer and grade A jerk, once referred to it as "half hotel, half halfway house for illegals.")

And, yes, she'd been pulling long weekends in Miami almost monthly to meet with stakeholders and keep the wheels turning . . . but that was different. Three weeks on a random island in Mexico? Unprecedented. Even if she did sell me on it by inviting me to join her for the last week . . . a trip I never got to take.

Finally, I reach the island's narrowest spot, the waist of its hourglass shape, where the main road separates the eastern and western shorelines, visible through the trees on either side. I turn right and push through the foliage onto a small spit of beach. A dozen or so locals are sitting on colorful blankets or standing with their arms threaded across their chests. Waiting for the sunset, their nightly fireworks display. I find myself searching the crowd for her, inspecting the backs of heads. Right after Eszter died, I saw her everywhere, heard her voice in the din, caught glimpses of her in crowds.

I think of the sunset photos she sent me, the most beautiful technicolor skies. *What went on here, Eszter? What did those final texts really mean?* She was good at keeping secrets . . . she waited months to tell her parents about me, and, later, that we were living together, a fact they subsequently pretended not to hear. And beyond that, she was so private, so measured, unable to voice a sentence until she'd beta tested it in her head, unwilling to commit to a decision until she'd poked and prodded it from multiple angles.

Take the Haven—she kept me mostly in the dark about her progress, promising I could read her paper when it was camera-ready. After she died, her parents got her laptop, so I never got to look at a draft. I didn't feel right cornering her childhood friend Shane, whom she always stayed with in Miami, or her beloved advisor, Dr. Patel, at the wake. I did ask Shane if she knew what was happening with the Haven now, if there was any chance of it moving forward, and she blinked twice and murmured something about it being "dead on arrival," a phrase she regretted immediately. So I filed it away in the growing depository of things I'd never know about my fiancée.

Along with whatever the hell she meant by those texts.

The air smells like salt and something grassy—seaweed, maybe. No one's swimming; I was hoping to do a mile or two tomorrow morning, but now, at least, the surf is too rough. To our right are the crumpled remains of a line of houses, once grand, now a mess of cement slabs as jagged as peanut brittle. A wave rams into concrete, sending a spray of white into the air. I think of champagne, of that October night when Eszter and I got home from Lake Mendota and eased the cork from a cold bottle so that bubbles volcanoed skyward. It's so unfair—we were barely engaged for three months, one season, before an allergic attack took her life.

Broad birds dive-bomb the waves; a dog digs merrily in the sand. I see it—I see why Eszter loved it here.

The sunset is one of those hazy, faded rainbows stretched across the sky, peachy pink at the bottom, denim at the top. Eszter explained sunsets to me once, how electromagnetic radiation can paint the sky—two dweebs nerding out over particulate matter and scattered light. I've always loved how equations underpin everything we experience. As a kid, I adored math class, where each question had infinite wrong answers and one right one. It's why I became a data scientist, feeding noisy data into algorithms, coaxing them into making predictions. Data science makes the world reliable, understandable.

I blink back fresh tears. Data science, of course, can't help me now.

The sun sinks behind the horizon, an orange semicircle. Reflexively I reach for my phone to take a picture—another pang, another reminder I'm unmoored.

The crowd ignores me. I could be bold and introduce myself to people—I could ask if they remember Eszter, not her death but her calm presence, her wit, her smile that felt like she was letting you in on a secret. Assuming she talked to locals, that is.

Wait, no I couldn't—Eszter warned me that very few islanders speak English. I figured I'd use the Google Translate app on my phone. The phone I dropped into the ocean. *So much for that idea.*

My eyes flit from stranger to stranger, searching for faces from Eszter's photo. People pop open drinks and shoot the breeze. I feel weirdly muzzled, knowing I couldn't really express myself if I tried. A little toothpick of envy needles my heart—everyone here can *chat,* they can effortlessly communicate, unlike quiet, tongue-tied me. It's not my first time in a foreign country, but it is the first time I've been on my own.

I've always been outgoing; Eszter called it my superpower, my ability to talk to anyone. In some ways, we were so different . . . unlike me, she was shy, discerning, slow to let people in. She exuded low-maintenance calm while I'm a type A control freak. She was thoughtful, her humor a murmured deadpan, whereas I'm jokey and loud, slapping the table and letting quips out as whoops. Physically, of course, we looked nothing alike: Eszter had long honey hair and wore lipstick and purses and crisp, pretty dresses. With my short hair, athletic build, and androgynous wardrobe, I'm occasionally mistaken for a man.

And then, in other ways, we were so similar: two former high school valedictorians, National Merit Scholars, summa cum laude at our respective state universities. Both left-brained geeks who wished we could appreciate modern art but found it kind of boring and samey. Two independent, high-earning women who loved running circles around the mediocre men in our cohorts.

Wait—a guy waves goodbye to someone and turns toward me, and my throat is suddenly parched. It's *him*—he was definitely in Eszter's photo, the guy with the salt-and-pepper beard. It's strange to see him in real life after staring at him on a screen; he's three-dimensional, with a posture and gait and rugged handsomeness I didn't expect.

He lopes closer, closer, and I could say something, I could stop him and introduce myself. I'm staring like he's a celebrity, but he doesn't so much as glance my way as he passes. My heart beats double time. *Tomorrow.* Tomorrow I'll find the people in the photo.

Breathing deeply, I return to the main road and continue east, heading for the opposite shore—Playa Destello. When I reach it, I take off my hiking boots and splash into the shallows; each step sends up a puff of hot murk and the smell of rotting seaweed. Eszter called this the "smelly beach," and I see why.

What's left on the Eszter Memorial Tour? Her Airbnb, one of the only ones on the island—one I was supposed to share with her at the end of her trip. The town square, just south of here, where she snapped a selfie near a stingray mural. And I need to meet those friends of hers. Fellow English-speakers who got to warm themselves by her light, at least for a little bit.

One by one, people pack up and leave as palm-tree shadows slither seaward, carving the beach into yellow-and-brown stripes. When I'm alone, I start to turn, then jump, heart thudding: There's someone in the distance, far down along the same shore. I peer into the fading light; something about the way they're moving, the awkward hustle, makes my arm hairs stand on end. The figure shuttles toward the water, then back, then down again, squatting at both ends.

The silhouette is a woman, I decide, which thaws some of the icy fear. I grab my shoes and head toward her, feet sinking into still-hot sand. She keeps scuttling, crablike, and the world grows darker the closer I get until I'm almost near enough to—

"*Stop!*"

Her shriek hits me like a punch. I can't make out her face, her expression, but I take her in: a fiftysomething with silver hair and an impressive pile-on of loose linen clothing.

"What are you doing?" I holler back. It's weird to be communicating at shouting distance.

"Don't come any closer."

I roll my eyes. Not today—the last thing I need is a stranger yelling at me. "I'm obviously not going to hurt you."

"It's not me I'm worried about." Her accent's not quite British, but close. She points to her feet.

It takes me a second to spot them: dozens of dark circles, each the size of a deck of cards, steadily motoring across the sand. Some kind of crab, or . . . ?

One wanders my way and I crouch. It's a turtle—a baby turtle, with round black eyes and a sweet little beak and skin folded and crinkled like tissue paper.

"Pick it up." The woman grins. "It needs you."

I lift it and it waves its tiny legs. It's blue-gray and perfect, its shell a miniature shield, limbs crisscrossed with wrinkles.

"Floodlights." The woman jerks her head inland, where a lamppost beams. "The artificial light mucks with the turtles' instincts—they have trouble beelining for the water." She nods at the surf. "If they don't make it into there before dark, they'll be food for another creature for sure."

I tip the hatchling into the sea, and it glides away. "That's awful about the floodlights," I murmur. "What eats the hatchlings out here?"

"Dogs, raccoons, seabirds. *Most* hatchlings are eaten by predators." She shrugs. "Rather impressive when one makes it to adulthood. I'm Rita." The *R* sound is a bit soft—Scandinavian, maybe? Even in the dimming light, her eyes are as clear and blue as a husky's, like someone squeegeed the lens in front.

"Abby." I set the next one in the waves while around it, its siblings reach the water, bobbing a bit before being swept out to sea. Oh, there are so many of them, identical and determined, scuttling those duck-billed legs across the sand.

Looking down at them, I feel wonder, quiet awe at the Earth's newest inhabitants—eyes seeing for the first time, virgin snouts sniffing the salty air, leathery skin feeling the moist ocean breeze as they trek home with their brothers and sisters. Tears prick my eyes. *Thank you, Eszter.* I needed this.

The last turtle paddles into the waves, and Rita turns to me. "Care to join me for a drink?" Without waiting for a reply, she pulls two sweating cans of Tecate and an orange Mexican blanket from a sand-covered backpack.

My heart rate ticks up. She wasn't in Eszter's photo, but if she came to Isla Colel before the start of the year, she and Eszter would've overlapped.

We clink cans as the stars wink to light, one by one, like the work of a busy lamplighter. "How long ago did you get here?" I ask casually.

"I washed ashore in February." I'm relieved and disappointed at the same time. "What about you, Abby? I haven't seen you around."

I sigh. "I took the ferry in today."

"Welcome! How long will you stay?"

"I'm heading back Thursday. When the ferry comes again. Then I'm spending two nights in Cancún and flying home Saturday."

"Lovely." She compresses the beer can in her palm. "If you decide to stay longer, though, you can usually hire a boat to take you to the mainland."

"Good to know." I swallow a gulp of lager. "What brought you here?"

Rita's autobiography sounds like something out of an Indiana Jones movie: She's from northern Germany and spent much of her adult life in London, but she came to Isla Colel after a decade of traipsing around the world—South Asia, then South America, followed by Central America and, finally, Mexico's eastern coast.

"When I stepped off the ferry, I felt I was home." She brushes sand off her thighs. "The birds, the waves, the palm trees—it's as if they were all waving hello, like they'd missed me so much."

The ocean laps against the sand, a wet, rhythmic rustle. She doesn't ask what I'm doing here. But I feel a rushing sensation, a need to purge. And Rita—a stranger, someone I'll never see again—is the perfect audience.

I clear my throat. "My fiancée died four months ago. Here, right here. And I came to say goodbye."

"Oh, goodness. I'm sorry."

"Thanks."

No one—*no one* but me knows about the texts Eszter sent me. Just thinking about them fills me with a rush of shame. Everyone who loved us, everyone who squeezed my hand at the funeral or dropped off a frozen lasagna or texted me pictures of their sweet, floofy pets, all thought the same thing: that we were a perfect couple, our relationship marked by honesty and trust, in it for the long haul.

I hear them again, six words that'll echo in my mind forever:

I need to tell you something.

Out of nowhere, a ping on my phone as I was staring at some code. And when, alarm bells looping, I sent back a question mark, she sealed things off: *We'll talk when you get here. Safe travels.*

She died later that day.

CHAPTER THREE

"How'd they pass away? If you don't mind my asking."

Above us, the stars wink in and out through the slatted blinds of palm fronds. "She died of anaphylaxis. In her rental." My voice snags, stutters. "She had severe food allergies, and even though she always kept her EpiPen with her, I guess she couldn't get to it—they found her on the floor in the kitchen."

"Goodness. I'm so sorry, Abby."

"Thanks." I look away, tears streaming. A night bird trills a wild arpeggio. "They found the EpiPen in the living room. It's so odd . . . Eszter was unbelievably careful. Even when she was drunk, even when she was upset, even when she'd barely slept. She had to be; I mean, a lot of people with allergies as severe as hers wouldn't even *think* of living alone or traveling solo. She never let her guard down, not for a second." I don't say the last part: *So how did she wind up dead on the floor of her Airbnb, with her EpiPen twenty feet away?*

"That's awful. I can't even imagine." She shakes her head, her eyes on the horizon.

A spun-sugar cloud hazes over the moon, and something light and quick bubbles through me and comes out as laughter. "One more freaking day and I would've been here—I could've stopped it. I would've grabbed the EpiPen and stuck it in her leg and it would be this wild travel story we'd still be laughing about today."

"Oh, you mustn't blame yourself."

"I know." *I need to tell you something.* For the millionth time, my mind spins: Was it about the wedding? The venue, the invitation list? Something about her parents—had they insulted her again, another microaggression about her being queer, not turning into the woman they expected? Did it have to do with the fight we had on Christmas, a week before she boarded that plane?

And here the theories turn grandiose: Did she have doubts about getting married altogether? Was she rethinking *us*? I'd been the one driving the bus—I got down on one knee, a disaster of a proposal I never thought to view as a bad omen. She'd let *me* spearhead the search for a venue and a photographer, she couldn't articulate what she wanted from the flowers or menu or even a dress . . .

Looking back, I see the proposal as a flex point, the fulcrum when things tipped from wonderful to wobbly. Did I screw everything up by demanding her commitment? Our relationship was so solid before then—why couldn't I just let it be?

"How did your fiancée end up here?"

I swallow. Seawater slaps the shore like a mallet gently striking a timpani.

"Eszter . . . she chose Isla Colel randomly. She wanted to go somewhere quiet to work, and she stumbled across it online. It checked all the boxes: hidden gem, cheap, Spanish-speaking." I push my beer can into the sand. What is it about this hushed, silver-coated beach that's drawing my secrets out like a centrifuge? "She was loving it. But, honestly, her last few days here are kind of a mystery. I was so focused on work, I wasn't keeping in touch as well as I should've, and . . . well, I don't really know what she was up to."

Rita chuckles. "Oh, that sounds like Colel. We love secrets here. We're all escaping something."

I sit up, heart quickening. "What are *you* running away from?"

She clucks her tongue. "That's the cardinal rule, ja? Everyone only shares whatever they'd like to share. Everyone gets a fresh start." Her head rolls my way and she waits for me to meet her gaze. "Even you."

Suddenly the tears are pouring, an avalanche, and Rita lets out a sympathetic tsk.

"I'm okay," I finally say. "It's just—you struck a nerve."

We'll talk when you get here. What was Eszter keeping from me?

"She's here now," Rita declares. "Can you feel it, her presence? Not in a supernatural way, exactly. But if she was here, and you're here now, and time is but an illusion . . ."

I sit up as sobs roll through me like whitecapped waves. Rita loops an arm across my shoulders, and my weeping expands in every direction, sailing into the ocean, sinking into the sand, floating up the ribbed palm trees and into the rainforest behind us. There's warmth in Rita's hug and the sensation reminds me of defrosting, of something solid gaining the tiniest bit of give. When I look up, she whisks a tear off my cheek with her thumb. I take in her wild gray hair, the wrinkles around her eyes. I get the peculiar sensation that we already know each other, social déjà vu.

I exhale. "When she died, they—they shipped her straight home and her dad identified her." I shake my head. "I never got to see her. At the funeral, they—they didn't even acknowledge me as her fiancée."

"Ohh, Abby." Rita looks queasy. "I'm so sorry. I can't imagine anything crueler."

"Thanks." I find the moon's reflection on the water, a white shimmer. "It was awful. We weren't married yet, so I had no legal connection to her, you know? And her parents—they didn't mention me in the obituary, the service, anything." My pulse speeds. "They were up at the lectern, telling everyone what a great daughter she was, and I wanted to stand up and scream, 'You treated her like a disappointment. She couldn't even be herself around you.'"

"They sound awful." She scoffs. "Some people shouldn't be allowed to be parents."

I chuckle in spite of myself. "Do you have kids?" She hesitates and I worry I've overstepped. "Sorry, not to pry. You just seem very . . . nurturing."

"No, no children." She smirks. "I've never liked the idea that even childless women need to be some kind of mom. People said my *work* was my baby, or my *plants,* or my *dog*."

My cheeks blaze. I start to apologize but she stops me. "I'm not upset! It's just an observation. Do you think you'll have kids?"

I shrug. "I was leaning toward it, but Eszter was less sure. I guess I'm scared of missing out on that deep, deep love they say you can only experience for your child."

"I wouldn't put too much stock in that." Her fingers lace behind her head. "I'm wary anytime someone turns 'Kids give *my* life meaning' into 'Kids will give *your* life meaning.' How could they possibly know?"

We're quiet, listening to the insect chorus. "I'm pretty sure my mom would've been happier without us," I say. "I barely think of her and my sister as my family."

The family you choose: For years, I repeated it to myself like a mantra whenever people talked about their families—their siblings and attendant gobs of sticky nieces and nephews, the aunt sending crocheted scarves, the dorky parents leaving fawning comments on every Instagram post.

I lack those relationships, my bloodlines cut off like arteries sliced with a razor. But I have *the family you choose,* kind friends I met through work or school who showed up at my apartment after Eszter died, wordlessly scrubbing dishes and restocking the fridge. I didn't expect Mom and Kayla to come down; neither one has left northern Wisconsin in years.

In fact, I can't remember the last time I expected anything from either.

Whenever I think of them, I feel a pulse of shame. Mom deep in the sofa, watching endless TV. Kayla getting fired from one service job after another for showing up with booze on her breath—or not showing up at all. And then I feel guilty for being so judgmental, so snobby. *You think you're better than me,* Kayla hissed during the one weekend I came home from college. *But at least I'm not a freak of nature.*

It was the only time anyone in our household acknowledged my queerness. When people ask for my coming-out story, I'm bereft—they simply . . . found out. I waited until college and then quietly began dating Jana, a tall, slim music major who practiced cello in her dorm room, making the whole hall vibrate with its rich, mournful tones. One day, I got an email from my aunt: "Your mother said you're gay now. Is it true?"

My whole body flushed cold. I didn't reply, didn't contact my mom for over a week, either. Finally, with Jana's encouragement, I called her.

I heard from Aunt Shelly.

No reply. My heart was a machine gun in my ears and chest.

She said you reached out about—

She cut me off: *We don't need to talk about it, Abby.*

Tears shot straight into my eyes. *Mom, I—*

I don't care if you marry a damn rocking horse, I just don't want to hear about it.

When I recount the story, people chuckle like this was somehow kind: *So she didn't care at all!* But they don't understand how it felt. How, phone clutched in my palm, I got the eerie sensation I didn't really exist, like I could fade into transparency, whiff away like candle smoke.

So, sure, good on my mother for not being overtly homophobic, I guess. (I'd take her reaction over Eszter's parents', when she finally mentioned my existence months into our relationship: tears from her mother, lots of "How could you do this to me?!" from her father.) Mom had plenty of reasons to dislike me; my sexual orientation happened to not crack the top five.

I hate to admit it, but I was relieved when neither she nor Kayla came to Eszter's funeral; I didn't want to give Eszter's parents more reasons to wrinkle their noses at me. Mom met Eszter exactly once, at a brick-oven pizza restaurant while we passed through my hometown to meet a childhood friend's baby. Eszter was the first partner I introduced to Mom, because she was supposed to be my last. The forever one. My chosen family.

"Well, your parents must've had something to do with who you are now," Rita says. "Everyone who comes into your life leaves some kind of impression. They can't help it." She sits up and points. "Like our footprints. We're always leaving things a little bit altered."

I twist around. "Hopefully not for the worse. Like those floodlights someone added."

"Hopefully not."

Rita and I talk on the beach for hours, with me yammering about Eszter late into the night: how she awed me with her intellect and easy grasp of even my techy work problems; how she loved her MBA program and found her classes easy despite the program's notorious difficulty; how she hummed Hungarian folk songs while she cleaned and practiced piano right before bed, so I sometimes drifted off to the sound of Chopin mazurkas and Liszt études. Rita listens, her attention complete and intense. I talk and talk as if someone unkinked a hose inside of me. It feels like an exorcism, the stinging hurt pouring out of me alongside my words.

"Well, I hope being here makes you feel close to your partner." A frog's staccato mating call rings out from the woods behind us. "She picked this place for a reason . . . no one winds up here by accident."

I smile. "Well, sure. The twice-a-week ferry makes it hard to, you know, slip on a banana peel and fall onto Isla Colel."

Rita throws her head back and laughs and oh, I used to make jokes, back before Eszter's death snatched up my sense of humor like Ursula siphoning Ariel's voice into a shell. How, how can I be sitting on a warm beach with a stranger on a planet that *took Eszter away from me*?

"You've got me there," Rita says. "But still, this island—it's a beacon, attracting the most beautiful souls."

I turn to her. "I'd love to meet some of the other expats here."

Her face lights up. "I'll introduce you! The English-speakers have a little crew. Actually, we're having a barbecue tomorrow night, right here on the beach—you *must* come."

I'm gonna do it—I'll meet the people in that group photo, ask questions, get answers. I sit up and lean forward. As I do I feel a falling sensation, like jumping into the abyss. "I'm in."

CHAPTER FOUR

ABBY

December 25, 2023 (four and a half months ago)

Eszter squeezed my palm in hers, then gave it a little tug, a goofy thing we both sometimes did when holding hands to make each other smile. I let out a tense laugh as our arms rested on the car console again.

"We can still bail," I said. "Hit the gas on this Toyota Yaris and go roaring into the night like Thelma and Louise." She smiled weakly and I kept going. "Your parents might be relieved, honestly."

"Look, it's one dinner. We can do this." She sighed. "I'm nervous too."

"Not as nervous as I am." My eyes flicked up. "They're not actively rooting for your demise."

She snorted. "It's not personal. Just your lack of a penis."

"Maybe that's how I'll break the ice. 'Good to see you, sorry I don't have a penis.'"

She laughed and pulled her hand away.

I looked out the windshield. "Remember—you're twenty-seven. You don't need their approval. Okay?"

"I know." We both turned to the mansion in front of us, all white

stucco and cantilevered balconies. She reached for the door handle.
"Let's go."

"A macska rúgja meg!" Dr. Farkas hissed. He was on his hands and
knees in front of the fireplace, and his third attempt at coaxing a flame
from newspaper to log had failed. Eszter and I sat primly on the sofa,
and Eszter snickered.

"What did he say?" I whispered.

She leaned toward me. "Literally, it means, uh . . . 'the cat should
kick it'? But it's like, 'enough, dammit.'"

We swallowed our smiles. I'd met the Farkases once before, when her
father had had a client meeting in Milwaukee, and we'd driven an hour
to sit through a stiff dinner at a steakhouse. But this was my first time in
their sprawling Florida home.

They'd smiled coldly when we knocked on the door a few minutes
ago, neither moving to let us inside. They were both tan and attractive,
Dr. Farkas towering and broad, Mrs. Farkas petite, like Eszter. But then
I pronounced *Farkas* the Hungarian way (FAHR-kash, the *R* a plosive
flick of the tongue, rather than the bastardized 'Farkus' Eszter went by
in normal life), and they'd softened enough to, you know, let us in.

Now Dr. Farkas rearranged the jumble of newsprint and tried again.
Bing Crosby's vibrato rolled around the room. I was initially surprised
to hear the Farkases celebrated Christmas—Eszter's great-grandparents
were Holocaust survivors, and though I knew she didn't practice Juda-
ism, I assumed that was a personal choice. But even in the 1930s, she
explained, her forebears were secular Jews who didn't observe Jewish
holidays.

When her parents immigrated to the United States, they wanted to
seem as American as possible: presents under the tree, caroling in the
fake snow, all the trappings of an agnostic yuletide. Now the lights on
their massive artificial Christmas tree twinkled and the rich smell of
paprika chicken hung in the air and it was all very cozy, very Norman
Rockwell. If only we could relax. If only *Eszter* could relax, and me in
turn.

From the kitchen, Mrs. Farkas emerged bearing a tray with four brandy glasses on top. They brimmed with inky liquor, and balanced precariously in the center was a bottle shaped like a cartoon bomb.

"I have unicum for you to try." Mrs. Farkas lowered it with a clink and turned to her husband. "Istvan? You look like a kutya. Come here."

Dog, Eszter mouthed. Her folks perched on the sofa across from us and we toasted in the center. I braced myself, knowing I absolutely had to not only finish, but appear to *love* the stuff. I knocked it back—a bitter, herbaceous fire that made me think of both licorice and bile. When I opened my eyes, three faces stared back.

"It is for sipping," Dr. Farkas said flatly.

I cast around for one of the few phrases I knew and thanked them: "Köszönöm szépen. And I . . ." Eszter gave me an urgent go-ahead nod. "I'd love more!"

Dr. Farkas remained stone-faced as he sloshed more into my brandy snifter.

I knew today would be uncomfortable; Eszter had never brought a partner home for Christmas before, and her parents were not okay with her dating a woman. But we were engaged now, for over two months, and we'd been living together for over a year, and it was high time they recognized this wasn't a phase and I wasn't going anywhere.

I missed her older brother, Laszlo—he reminded me of a prize-winning racehorse, muscular and sure, and though I'd never been in a room with *all* the Farkases at once, I knew he'd be a good buffer. He lived in Chicago (a pediatric cardiologist, my God) and made it a point to visit his sister a few times a year. But he was spending Christmas in St. Louis with his beautiful wife and their perfect infant son.

I'd already complimented their home and asked Dr. Farkas about his work—two topics Eszter had preapproved. She'd assured me he *loved* waxing poetic about their immigrant success story, how they'd left Budapest in the nineties with nothing but a few thousand forints and the clothes on their back (and, Eszter added pointedly, an uncle in Palm Beach County and her dad's doctorate in mechanical engineering); he then worked his way up the ladder at a hotel conglomerate until becoming a hotelier himself. Decades later, he was a bit of a celebrity in the

Miami real estate scene: media-friendly, multilingual, and cocky in a way that people, bewilderingly, ate right up.

Tonight, though, he was stoic, and Mrs. Farkas followed his lead. We only had to get through dinner—I'd booked an overpriced room at the Hampton Inn, waving away Eszter's insistence that we could stay in one of her dad's hotels for free. But right now, the evening stretched before us, a vast, pine-scented desert.

"Do you have any holiday traditions?" I asked, a wide smile on my face.

Dr. Farkas shrugged. "We do the tree. The decorations. The CD from *White Christmas*. Everything you see here." He lowered his eyebrows, like it was a stupid question.

"What did your family do, growing up?" Eszter asked, rescuing me.

"We always watched *A Charlie Brown Christmas*," I said, "and went to church on Christmas Eve. I liked the caroling service. At the end they'd give us all candles while we sang 'Silent Night'—I'm actually amazed no one burned the place down."

As if mocking me, the pyramid of logs in the fireplace collapsed, snuffing out the entire blaze. Dr. Farkas grunted and went to relight it.

"You've got some nice photos of . . . of Christmases past over there." I gestured to the buffet in the corner, crowded with frames. I smiled. I was fighting for my life.

"Oh, I was going to show you." Mrs. Farkas set her glass down and padded to a bookshelf. She returned with a custom photo book with a toddler on the cover, and I squinted at it for a moment—was Eszter ever that blond, that pudgy-cheeked?

"It's Laszlo," Eszter said tiredly. "Mom, you know that's not me?"

"Of course! But you're in it too." She gestured at the book. "There are lots of photos of you and your brother together."

"And no one thought to make a book for me," Eszter observed, palms high. Still, I started paging through, cooing whenever she appeared alongside him. I paused on a photo of the whole family on vacation somewhere tropical, with baby Eszter in her mother's arms. Even then, Eszter seemed serious, her pale brows slightly drawn.

"You look like someone's trying to talk you into buying crypto," I cracked.

Eszter laughed. "I know, I always looked so dubious."

"Eszter." Dr. Farkas stood, smoothing out his sweater. "Can I talk to you in private, tündi?"

He called her that, *fairy,* far too gentle a pet name for such a harsh man. She trailed him out of the room like a lamb to the slaughter. I watched in alarm until Mrs. Farkas asked me if I had siblings. As we made small talk, I wrestled down my mounting panic . . . what were they discussing in there?

They reemerged fifteen minutes later, and Mrs. Farkas announced it was time to eat, and Eszter met my eye as she passed: *It's fine.*

Then why did she look so stressed?

"What was that all about?" I asked a few hours later, scrubbing my sleeve against the car window, clearing slashes in the fog. We were finally, finally alone together. Our goodbye at the front door had been an awkward affair, with Dr. Farkas leaning close to Eszter and saying, sternly, "Think about what I said."

She sighed. "Can we please go to the hotel? I'm tired."

"That bad?" I laughed bitterly, pulling out into the cul-de-sac. "Was it about me? It's okay, I can take it. Whatever it is, my mom's probably said worse."

I didn't realize she was crying until I heard the sniffle. "What, what'd he say? Is he still being weird about the engagement?"

Raindrops flecked the glass. Eszter made a frustrated noise. "He was just . . . being critical about my project."

"The Haven?" I glanced at her. The last few times she'd flown out here to work on it, she'd come back freckled and refreshed. Though she was secretive about it, I could tell it was going well. "Why is he even weighing in on that? You're doing it without him. Your way. Right? Not his contacts, not his money, not his thing?"

She shrugged miserably and wiped her nose.

I groaned. "God, that man is so controlling. Who's he been talking to? Shane?"

"Look, I think he's been . . . cautious since Coral Gables."

Our headlights stabbed the dark like spears. The incident in Coral Gables had been a tragedy—two workers died when a crane fell on them within hours of breaking ground on a new hotel—but Dr. Farkas had been acting like the real misfortune was how it halted the project. It was squarely his fault: An investigation turned up rushed plans, half-assed permits, and missing insurance.

I couldn't help it: "Ugh, he's such a prick."

Eszter shifted in her seat. "It's not that easy for me, okay? I care what they think. I can't just say *fuck you* to my family like you did."

"*Wow.*" My heart thumped—this was not how we argued, this was not how this was supposed to go. Normally I got louder and louder while Eszter grew mute. Hell, she almost never dropped F-bombs. "Well, that's *one* way to characterize having boundaries around my emotionally abusive mother and alcoholic sister." I could feel her glowering next to me. "And for the record, I would never let my mom or Kayla push me around the way your dad does."

"Thank you. I'm aware you want me to cut him out of my life altogether." We drove in silence for a moment, the only sound the wipers' clunky pulse.

Suspicion smoldered in my chest . . . Was she telling the truth? Had Dr. Farkas said something about me, something so gutting Eszter couldn't even repeat it? There was no denying it—she was dragging her feet on wedding planning.

My voice softened: "Eszter, you don't work for him. You don't need his money or his clout. And we don't have to base our life decisions on whether or not he gives his blessing." I flicked on the turn signal, *tick-tock, tick-tock*. "We're looking at venues, babe. The wheels are in motion."

We were running out of time—and in a week, she'd leave for Mexico, and we'd put planning on hold for another three weeks at minimum. We'd toured our first potential space a week earlier—a darling little wine bar, its backyard all brick and ivy and sweet fairy lights. It was cozy and low-key, nothing like the ballrooms and vast venues of weddings we'd attended. But when the manager chirped, "The ceremony typically takes place right here," Eszter had blanched as if finding herself onstage at Carnegie Hall.

"I'm fine, I'm fine," she'd told me, catching my concerned expression. She didn't say it, but I thought I caught the rest of it: *I know this is important to you.* Guilt had twisted in my entrails like a knife, and I'd thanked the manager and swept Eszter off to brunch nearby, during which neither of us mentioned our nuptials at all.

And now this—their private discussion, plus our dinner conversation that avoided any mention of our future, cutting a swath so wide you could drive a truck through it. That was *panic* inside me, I realized suddenly—not anger.

As I braked, the tires slid over a puddle, just an inch or two, and the thought was like a chatter in my teeth, a whisper in my ear.

I'm on thin ice.

CHAPTER FIVE

ABBY

Monday night

I walk home feeling dizzy. When's the last time I spilled my guts to a new person like that, intimacy pouring out of me like toxins in a sweat lodge? I think back to those early dates with Eszter, two years ago, jumping over each other to go deep on our childhoods, our parents, our eagerness to excel in our respective fields.

I don't open myself up to people all that often. I can be gregarious, the life of a party, but that's different from disclosure, vulnerability. Tell someone the deep stuff and you've shown them where they can wound you. Bare the chinks in your armor, and people know you're weak. But Rita's a kind stranger, someone I'll never see again, someone who came after Eszter left. Somehow that makes her . . . safe.

I wake up mildly hungover, yet—*rested,* rested for the first time in forever.

The sun through the windows is winky and shy. I push the coffee table out of the way for my morning routine: squats, push-ups, burpees, planks. As sweat gathers on my forehead, I marvel anew. I'm *here,* on Isla Colel. Eszter walked the dusty road out front. For months, every corner of my life in Madison—every inch of our apartment, every coffee shop and bar and lake walk—has felt incomplete, her absence a ring-ing bell. But now I'm somewhere *she* went without *me*. This changes everything, in some small, incomprehensible way.

I step into the tiled shower. Today, I'll explore the rest of the island. I've pictured myself here so many times, triangulated every one of Esz-ter's photos so that, as soon as I got off that beat-up ferry, I could drop my suitcase and charge up the hill toward the lookout she loved. I feel like I'm walking around in a dream—a memory that's not even mine.

I'm fifteen hundred miles from Madison, but it might as well be a million. It's still cool there now, the isthmus wind relentless and sharp. And here it's muggy and bright and the air vibrates with light and bugs and the vegetation's hot breath. Tonight, God willing, I'll meet the last people to see her smile, and there's comfort in that.

I carry coffee and my computer onto the front porch. The sight of my hiking boots jumbled on the welcome mat makes my heart ache. Eszter hated how I always abandoned my shoes in front of the door; over and over, she lined them up along the wall for me. I worried she was doing it to chide me, but she insisted she was just being nice. Every week I vowed to fix my messy ways, and every week I completely forgot the second I reached our apartment.

Settling onto a bench, I run my fingers over the stickers on my lap-top, colors fading, edges fuzzed. Late last year, my coworker brought a Bluetooth sticker printer into the office, and we all spent our lunch break playing with it, cropping photos into circles and sending them to the device. I picked out a few favorites of Eszter and me, selfies from vacations, cute coupley shots from various nights out. I smoothed them onto my laptop that night, polka-dotting its chrome surface with the face I loved most.

I turn on my computer and a slew of Slack notifications careens down the screen. (Huh—in all our yapping last night, Rita never asked me what I do for work.) I had to beg for time off this week (*You really want to do that this close to the product demo?* asked my genuinely baffled boss, Tyler), and we compromised with my promise to keep an eye on Slack. Waiting for me are two fresh datasets, five meeting invitations, and a bevy of messages all ultimately asking the same thing:

Figured it out yet? Figured it out yet? Figured it out yet?

I'm failing spectacularly. Less than five weeks remain until demo time, and the function I'm overseeing is a big fat flop.

The startup I work for, TimeIn, is launching an AI app meant to lighten moms' mental load—making meal plans and ordering groceries, booking haircuts and housekeepers and doctors' appointments, that kind of thing. *Intelligent optimization,* Tyler always says. *More time for what matters.*

At first, I loved it: my big, impressive title, the chance to make the world a little better. But lately I've been trash at my job. Nine times out of ten, the scheduler I'm in charge of is creating events for the exact wrong time, and I can't figure out why. It worked perfectly in unit tests and *occasionally* goes off without a hitch. There's a bug I can't find, a needle in the tech stack, and Tyler's made it clear that if I don't figure it out soon, I'll be let go.

Cringing, I answer a few questions and admit I'm having phone issues (to put it mildly). Then, like I do most days, I revisit pictures of Eszter (thank *God* everything synced before I dropped my stupid phone). I start with her shots from here, then move on to our last night together. We were ringing in the New Year at my friend Mei's raucous party, packed into her Mifflin Street apartment, lights low, windows slick with steam. The llama necklace sparkles on Eszter's collarbones, and we look happy, holding up champagne, kissing at midnight. But there was an undercurrent of friction, our chests still tense a week after our Christmas conflict, necks prickly with nerves as we prepared to part ways for two weeks.

I often think of our relationship in reverse, like a filmstrip played backward, the latest moments the crispest and the memories changing shape as they unspool back, back, back in time. Back past our Christmas quarrel, my rocky proposal, our disaster of a third date, up to that first time we met. It was the beginning, sure, but in my memory it feels like an end, a stopper knot at the tip of a rope.

The question sizzles against my ears again: *What did you need to tell me, Eszter?*

A babylike cry makes me jump, and I spot a tabby kitten on the edge of the patio, eyes and ears adorably huge. She mews again and I close my laptop and duck inside, beetles crunching underfoot. When I re-emerge, sunscreened and dressed, I set a piece of jerky on the corner where I saw the cat. She watches from the road, then darts up the stairs as I pass.

I've read everything there is to read about Isla Colel, which isn't much. The island is shaped like a lopsided dog bone, six miles long and about a mile wide. All 250 inhabitants live here on the south end. Behind me, to the north, is the high ground I practically ran for yesterday: a swath of protected wilderness, with sheer white cliffs and thick rain-forest packed, allegedly, with jaguars and condors and candy-colored flamingos.

My skin hums in the warm sunshine. I head for Calle Estrella, just a few blocks from my rental. Eszter's Airbnb was on that street—I have the address memorized, the photos burned into my brain, the spot where I pictured myself joining her. My stomach tightens as I turn left. What was the scene when they found her? Did paramedics rush inside? Did gawping neighbors form a horseshoe out front?

I've never walked this route before, but I know it in my eyes and heart and feet: right at a chicken coop with its walkie-talkie squawks; past a Chihuahua that yips from a balcony, pacing back and forth like a pris-oner; left at a blow-up kiddie pool with cracked dolls strewn around it.

I'm on the block now, and my vision narrows so that the houses I pass on either side blur into a Skittle-colored scroll.

Here it is. Glossy tiles on the front porch and a smattering of Aca-pulco chairs, trim the matte white of a sand dollar, walls the color of a blushing ear. I could draw it with my eyes closed, sometimes see it in my dreams. I studied the little images on the listing like they were a puzzle I could decode.

My heart pounds. This isn't just a house.

For a few hours four months ago, this place was Eszter's tomb.

Was that movement behind the windows? I steel myself and ap-proach the door. My first knock is timid, an apology, and then I overcor-rect and bang. When no one answers, I duck and peek through the windows, pressing my hands against the glass to form a tunnel of shade.

The kitchen comes into view and my stomach makes a sudden, convulsing twist.

I'd figured the kitchen was in the back—in that hazy way you form a mental blueprint from photos—but here it is, the cabinet pulls shaped like semicircles, the tessellation on the backsplash a riot of triangles. Details I viewed on a screen when Eszter showed me the listing, all, *Doesn't this look perfect?*

My guts cramp. Shortly after she died, I made the mistake of googling symptoms of anaphylaxis. Mental impairment is high on the list, anxiety and muddled thinking making it harder and harder to save yourself. But the physical symptoms are the ones that haunt me. And now I'll never scrub from my mind the image of Eszter sprawled on the floor, *this* floor, lips swollen, face ashen, eyes like puffed rice.

The apartment is no longer rentable. Last week I found the Airbnb confirmation Eszter forwarded me in the fall, thinking I'd contact the manager and ask her about Eszter's final days. But her profile had been deleted, and I didn't have an email, phone number, anything. All I could see was a tiny icon: a smiling woman named Marta.

I'll come by again later, I decide, or ask the expats if anyone can connect me with her.

Onward. I reach for my phantom phone to check the map, but no—I know the way. A woman watering her garden waves back at me. In a fenced-in field, cows graze in the grass, gentle giants. It's strange, picturing Eszter leading me around, showing me her routine. When we traveled together, I typically took the lead—buying an eSIM, securing tickets, navigating from point A to B to C.

I pause for a sip of water under a tree that looks like a giant broccoli crown. Taped-up marker drawings beam from the windows of a low concrete building; must be the school. Two hundred and fifty residents—intellectually, I knew that was a small population, but it's only hitting me now how tiny this place is. And isolated, the only inhabited island for miles and miles. What must it be like, growing up here, under a perpetual dome of sky and sea?

I stop at the western shore, where, last night, residents watched the sunset. Playa Oscura, it's called. I'm wearing my swimsuit under my clothes, but it's still too choppy to risk going in alone. My eyes settle on the horizon. Somewhere out there is Luna Rift, a seam in the Earth's mantle where the ocean's depth plunges from fifty feet to close to three thousand. I squint at the water, dusted with its shards of fractured light, and can just pick out the darker blue of the drop-off. Three thousand feet to the ocean floor—my blood pressure rises just thinking about it.

A crab skitters along the sand and crouches in a hole, googly eyes staring. The beach here used to stretch for miles, apparently, wide and tawny, sunbathing tourists stabbing the sand with candy-colored umbrellas. Visitors came from all over Mexico, funneling antlike out of the cities and onto the island's golden shore.

Then, three years ago, Hurricane Diego hit. It gobbled up most of the sandy beach and hurtled the island into darkness and grounded the only ferry in or out. The isle's small tourism industry—already hobbled by the pandemic and, before that, the closure of its only resort—had no hope of surviving. Now visitors, like myself and Eszter before me, are an uncommon sight. And along Playa Oscura, all that's left are small tongues of sand and broken, moldering houses. Twice I reach for my phone, catching myself only as my fingers fumble against my thigh.

I close my eyes and listen to the rhythmic surf.

Eszter, I miss you. Eszter, I wish we were here together, fingers entwined.

I head south and reach the faded town square: a small park with an old band shell and murals of sea creatures. I spot the stingray painting Eszter documented. Spindly coconut trees cast slivers of shade, and three skinny cats sit loaf-shaped in a rectangle of grass. There's a shoebox-sized convenience store, a Western Union. Most of the storefronts are empty, their SE VENDE signs sagging and pale. The last vestiges of English are visible on tattered awnings: SWIMSUITS, SOUVENIRS, a pockmarked TRAVEL AGENCY sign.

The door of the convenience store jingles when I press inside to inquire about a cell phone. I don't speak Spanish (despite a single useless semester in college), so the shopkeeper and I communicate in gestures— I keep making the signal, our *te amo* sign. It's frustrating, being a mime . . . in normal life, I rarely shut up. Eszter would find this entire conversation funny. She grew up speaking Hungarian at home and

English out in the world, and her knack for picking up languages was almost eerie.

The cashier confirms the nearest tech stores are in Cancún, a two-hour boat ride away. I flinch, picturing Tyler's expectant eyes, the Slack messages piling up by the minute. But another part of me is . . . relieved. I make a mental note to email my friend Mei when I get back to my computer, but maybe it'll be nice to not be tethered to a screen for a few days. Perhaps losing my phone was another rung in the ladder toward moving on.

I almost chuckle. When did I start sounding like a New Age influencer?

The sun blinds me as I step back outside. I pass a small restaurant— LA FONDA, per the sign—with a propped-open front door and a leafy side patio where ceiling fans spin lazily. I try to picture the plaza when Isla Colel was still a destination: bustling with out-of-towners, perhaps a weekly market with live music and handicrafts for sale. Now it's . . . not quite a ghost town, but stuck-feeling. Tropical purgatory.

I continue south to the marina, where my feet clank on the metal planks. Was it only yesterday that I stepped off that small, dingy ferry? As soon as Cancún's teeming pier recoiled and then disappeared behind me, alarm roared up my spine. *Turn around; go back.* The journey felt like a bend in the space-time continuum, two hours without cell service or any variations in the blue-on-blue landscape. When I finally spotted Isla Colel in the distance, a green lump, I felt dizzy, drugged, like it couldn't possibly be real.

But here it is; here I am. A few boats bob along the aluminum dock, setting off swishes and hollow tings. Most of the slips are empty— fishermen must still be out. A single panga boat wobbles at the pier's tip, unloading the day's catch. I settle on a bench and watch the man on the boat fling fish after fish, fat and silvery, to a younger guy on the dock, who stacks them in a cooler with metronomic regularity.

Coolers—people left coolers on my doorstep after Eszter died, Styrofoam behemoths packed with meals I was too sad to touch.

Losing someone is like moving to a new country and needing to learn how to live there. How to eat, how to speak. How to be a friend and do my job (though that last one is still touch and go). The world feels different now, like I alone shifted into a dimension just a few degrees off.

I confessed to Mei that I was having the weirdest reaction to the Uber Eats gift cards, flowers, sweet texts, and offers to come over and help. Intellectually, I was so grateful.

On a gut level? The acts of kindness made me ill.

"Well, you grew up in kind of a chaotic environment," Mei said, curled on the couch next to me. *Jeopardy!* was on and it was easier that way, not quite facing each other. "You basically raised yourself, right? Maybe you're not used to all these people worrying about you."

"Dude, I know my friends care about me," I snapped, all grit and bristle. "I'm not some walled-off ice queen." But . . . she wasn't wrong. My most vivid childhood memories are of Kayla getting kicked out of school, Kayla getting caught with booze in her locker, a stranger calling because they'd found Kayla's purse in a snowbank . . . of watching my sister smash through one rock bottom after another.

My mother, at her wit's end, shifted the alleged root of her problems from my father to my sister. And for me, a goal materialized like a rope ladder in a house fire: *Get away.*

"Of course you're not an ice queen!" Mei squeezed my shoulder. "I just mean . . . Abby, you're the most put-together person I know. And that's amazing. But of course it feels weird to have other people see you struggling right now."

My eyes heated with tears. Mentally I was still climbing backward in time, back to our grubby house in Elmridge. Even before Kayla was deemed a "problem child," I was independent, a self-starter. Teachers called me *mature* and *self-motivated* and though neither of my parents kept close tabs on me, Dad liked that: *We're lucky you're such an easy kid.* I could bathe and clothe myself start to finish by the time I was three. I felt hugely embarrassed whenever I had to ask them to sign a permission slip or contribute food to a class party.

So I handled almost everything myself.

Seagulls swirl and squawk, and one lands on the deck in front of me, twisting its neck. Eszter sent me a photo of this very spot, with vessels' snouts like soldiers standing sentry along the dock.

We're lucky you're such an easy kid. What if Eszter didn't feel lucky to have me? What if I did something wrong and came close to breaking everything?

While Eszter was here, we always said good night on the phone, and—after she died, as I picked back over our final interactions like a carrion bird—something felt *off* about one of those calls. In retrospect, Eszter seemed a little squirrely, keyed up. Problem is, I was multitasking as we spoke, iterating on some code and only half paying attention . . . so I didn't ask questions, and now I'm not even sure which night that was. Why didn't I *listen*? Or did I dream up the weirdness after the fact? Desperation, after all, is the mother of invention.

Something snuffles against my calf and I scream, the shriek skipping out over the water. It's a stray dog, a midsize mutt, and I jump to my feet and back away. She sits back on her haunches and stares at me; her ribs look like gills, stretching the skin along her sides.

For a second, my mind spins: Could I take her home? Get her to a vet, find someone to adopt her in Madison?

But it's absurd, obviously. A fool's errand.

"I'm sorry," I whisper, my voice strangled with guilt.

I feel her watching me as I walk back to shore.

CHAPTER SIX

RITA

Last night

hat poor girl. Rita thinks it over and over as she unlocks the front door of her little yellow house, as she fills an orange teapot at the water cooler, as she uses a match to light the stove, *whoosh*, the flame blue and steady. *Poor thing.* Abby looked so sad, so heavy. Dragged down by unanswered questions. To be that young and already weighted by a loss like that . . . at that age, your biggest heartache should be from a breakup, not a tragic death.

Rita detected it as soon as Abby got close, even in the silty light: a glaze across her youthful eyes, her expression haunted and far older than the rest of her. Rita's good at that, sizing up young women's energy and sensing what they need. Abby certainly isn't the first lost sheep she's helped.

Sand clings to Rita's calves and the soles of her feet. While she waits for the water to boil, she returns to the front door and shakes the blanket from her backpack. Sand skitters on the cement as she spreads the fabric over the patio railing. She knew Abby would join her on the blanket and accept a beer. Rita has a nurturing vibe, a penchant for coaxing pain points out of people, then saying the right things to soothe their wounds.

It's innate—a kind of gift. And she relishes it. All her friends here have their own superpower: searing passion; sweet, clumsy openness; smoky, seductive charisma. She'd take her keen sensitivity over any of it.

After all, empathy is power. For a while, it was her entire life.

The kettle shrieks, a shrill whistle that reminds her she hasn't prepared her mug yet. She hurries inside, snaps open the cupboard, and drops a tea bag into a stoneware mug. She had a hunch Abby wanted to confess, and confess she did, the difficult truth pouring out of her like spilled wine. Rita's heart clenched as she listened. Poor girl. *Girls*, really.

Rita leans against the counter, letting the hot mug warm her hands. Abby listened too—she asked Rita about her past and leaned in as Rita shared stories from her tropical escapades: getting stranded in a game preserve in Central India when rain flooded the only road out; fainting during a multiday trek to Colombia's Lost City. And then, sated, Abby didn't ask more questions, didn't reach back any further. As if Rita's story began when she hit the road. As if everything before then had been washed away like ink on dampened paper.

That's true of all her friends here, isn't it? Rap sheets and dark secrets, parents and exes who hover like ghosts. All left behind. Entire histories wiped clean, like they never existed. It's what she loves most about this place, why she's so glad she found it.

She raises the mug, blows on it. Steam wets her chin. She wonders if Abby can experience that here—that reinvention, leaving her old self behind. It's bracing, like jumping into cold water. Like being reborn.

But first, Rita must go digging into the past.

She sets her mug on the counter, picks up the phone, and makes a call.

'm heading up the main road, in the brief no-man's-land between the marina and the town square, when a shout stops me dead in my tracks. It comes from the left, and peering between the trees, I spot another small beach with two kids running in the surf. It's the western shore, a little ways down from Playa Oscura, and the waves are tall and thunderous here too—but the girl and boy show no fear, happily chasing a dented blue boogie board that flops in the shallows like a dying fish. I'm bad at telling children's ages, but they're small—the girl's perhaps a kindergartner, the boy even younger. Is this safe?

"¿Hola?" I call timidly, stepping onto the sand. They turn and stare—eyes huge, mouths open, that naked kiddish curiosity.

"¡Hola! ¿Qué tal?" I jump at a man's voice and then I can't believe I didn't notice him, a burly guy in his fifties or sixties with long eyelashes and a bushy beard. He smiles and keeps talking, with a quick gesture toward the kids, who are presumably with him. Is he their uncle, maybe, or grandfather?

"I'm sorry, I don't speak Spanish—I just wanted to make sure they weren't alone. The waves . . ."

I can't tell if he caught my meaning, but he nods enthusiastically. A huge wave plummets and rolls up the sand, engulfing my sandals. I rush over to grab the girl's pink sunglasses as they skate down the beach. Looking out, I see the ocean's much calmer past these breakers, and it occurs to me: If I was too worried to swim alone, this could be my shot.

"Uh, me llamo Abby." I point to my chest, smile huge.

"Abby," he repeats, like he's trying it out.

"Yep! Is it okay if—está bien if I . . . swim?" I mime dog-paddling. "You're going to be here for a little while? You'll watch me?" As I speak, I point at the ground, my eyes, the sea. This is excruciating—I always sucked at charades. I set my bag high up on the beach and start to pull off my tank top. "It's safe? Not . . . peligroso?"

He waves at the water dismissively. "Sí, sí, adelante, está bien."

"Okay. Gracias. I'll be quick." I hurry into the ocean, bracing myself for every wave. The water's just brisk enough to feel refreshing, and when the next whitecap is about to slam into me, I duck and dive. There's that deep, dreamlike quiet, the cool rush as sweet and bracing as spearmint. I surface and breaststroke past the whitecaps so I can swim parallel to the shore.

I pop my head up and wave at the man, and he waves back before turning his attention to the squealing kids. My thoughts quiet as soon as I start the crawl stroke—hissing bubbles, the steady rhythm of kicks and pulls, my own pounding heart and stretched-out breath.

Swimming has always been my escape; I swam competitively in high school, and it's long been my go-to cardio. And since Eszter died, I've been an addict: swimming lap after lap until the pain in my arms and back and lungs outscreams everything else. Now I pause, treading water, and glance back at the island. From here it looks fake, somehow, this improbable hunk of white limestone and jungle green. Peering down, I no longer see rocks or sand beneath my feet. How close am I to Luna Rift—if I dropped like a stone, how far would I sink?

For a second, I feel it, the isolation: forty miles between me and the mainland coast to my right; nothing but open water to the left, behind me, and on the other side of this lump of land.

How did Eszter even *find* this place? What happened here?

While I'm gazing at the shoreline, a wave rams into me, dunking me under and holding me down. Salt water shoots up my nose, an acrid pain, and it takes me a second to buoy up and reorient myself. This was a bad idea; I got cocky, went too far too quickly. The man is staring at me with concern while the kids sit on the sand, snacking. He gestures for me to come in.

As soon as I get close and stand, another wave scoops my balance out from under me. I stagger the last few yards and accept the man's outstretched hand. I can't understand him, but it's pretty obvious we were both concerned about my imminent drowning.

"I know, I went way too far out." I wipe seawater off my face. "I'm sorry I scared you. But thank you for keeping an eye on me. Muchas gracias. What's your name? Er . . ." Wait, I know this. "¿Cómo te llamas?" *What do you call yourself?* I think of the llama necklace again, somewhere in these same churning waters. A gift that spent more time in a box than around Eszter's throat. Everywhere, another reminder of her.

"Carlos. Y ellos son Camila y Miguel." The kids, hands deep in baggies of treats, both stare. Carlos makes a *phew* sound. "¡Hijole! Qué bueno que estés bien."

As they pack up, I promise not to go back in the water, waving my outstretched palms. I sit dazed for a few minutes while salt water grows filmy on my skin. *That was stupid, Abby.* I think of Eszter, how careful she had to be while traveling, especially solo. What made me barge into the surf like someone with a death wish?

Once I'm dry enough to put my clothes back on, I return to the main road. One more stop: I need a few groceries for my short trip. I head back into town, and the grocery store's smell hits me—pungent and sharp, like musty spices. It's a small cinder block building with a garage-door-like front yawning into the plaza. Two caged parakeets the color of half-ripe lemons hang near the entry, and they hop and cheep as I approach.

Inside, I grab a cracked, sticky shopping basket and head for the piles of produce lining the wall. I lift a golf-ball-sized fruit, bright red and covered in greenish horns. I press until it buckles beneath the pressure.

Eszter must've shopped here; for two weeks, she walked these dusky aisles and placed things in her basket, tortillas and canned beans and candy-bright bags of Mexican snacks. She examined their ingredient lists, showed the grocer a list of allergens, gracious and smiling. The thought triggers an odd swirl of grief and tenderness. Like nostalgia for her time here, as if it were my own.

The woman behind the counter, whose gray-black hair swings down to her waist, smiles like she recognizes me.

"You are on holiday?" she asks as she rings up the dusty cans and packages.

"You speak English!"

"Yes. I like to practice." She accepts my ragtag bills. "My name is Gloria."

"I'm Abby."

"Do you like the island?"

"It's beautiful," I tell her. Which is true. Whether I *like* it feels more complicated. "Have you always lived here?"

She beams. "All my life. I know this island like it's my own child—every plant, every person, I love them all."

My pulse begins to speed—I'm going to do it, the thing I came here to do. "Can I ask you something, Gloria?"

"Of course!"

I lean on the counter. "An American tourist visited four months ago. Eszter Farkas? She . . . died from an allergic reaction here." My voice catches and I clear my throat.

She nods gravely. "Of course. That was so sad."

"Did you ever talk to her? I'm trying to, er, reconstruct her last days here."

She tilts her head. "You know her?"

"Oh, right." I chuckle self-consciously. "She was my fiancée."

"¡Dios mío!" She clutches my forearm. "I'm so sorry."

"Thank you. Yeah, it's been tough. But picturing her here has been . . . nice." I smile. "Do you remember her? She was probably grill-ing you about the ingredients for everything she bought. Because of her allergies."

"Of course! Oh, she was very nice." She nods eagerly. "Always want-ing to practice her Spanish—until it came to talking about her allergies. Then she used Google Translate."

"That sounds right. Not leaving it open to misinterpretation." I'd seen Eszter do the same thing on other international trips. "Do you re-member what you chatted about?"

"Oh, simple things—the weather, what seafood I had that day. Whether Playa Oscura was rough or gentle. She wasn't fluent in Span-ish."

My heart lifts a bit at the thought: introverted Eszter remarking on the big waves or sunny skies. "She didn't . . . buy anything new that day, did she? Something she hadn't eaten before?" I'd always assumed she'd mistakenly eaten something in the cupboards of her Airbnb . . . switched two similar foods, perhaps.

"Hmmm." Gloria thinks for a moment, and then her hair swishes as she shakes her head. "No, I don't think she came in that day. I'm pretty sure she bought all her groceries at the start of her trip. Like I said, we looked at everything she purchased."

"Right." I chew on my lip. "Do you know if there was anyone else she befriended?"

Gloria shrugs. "The gringos."

"Right." I lift my plastic bags. "Well, thank you."

"Gracias a ti, Abby."

She and the parakeets watch me go.

CHAPTER EIGHT

Rita, aware that I'm phoneless, emails to reiterate her invitation to the beach barbecue ("Wear a bathing suit, just in case!"), and I wait eagerly for sundown so that I can join them. I'm doing it; I'm meeting the people Eszter hung out with last, the smiling folks in that photo. *Make a good impression,* I order myself while the afternoon hours slink past. *Don't screw this up.*

As I approach the shallow eastern beach, I smell charred meat and count three figures silhouetted in the sinking light. There's Rita, twisting a corkscrew into a bottle of wine and chatting with someone whose back is to me, and another person kneeling by a squat portable grill.

I clear my throat and Rita turns sharply, then grins and yanks out the cork. Though she's only been here a few months, she strikes me as the group's queenpin—something about that swagger, that warmth and obvious ease.

The guy at the grill smiles through the smoke. I peer at him—nope, he definitely wasn't in Eszter's picture. "Welcome! I'm making us snapper." He has an Australian accent, giddy and round. "I hope Rita told you to come hungry."

"She did! I am." I extend my hand. "I'm Abby. Thanks for letting me crash."

He trips over a browned palm frond, recovers. "'Crash'! Don't be silly. The beach is for everyone, right?" His smile lights up his whole face. "I'm Brady. Pleasure to meet you."

The other man holds out his hand. "I'm Pedro." It's him—the guy I saw last night, rugged and tall with a beard the color of newsprint.

"Abby's from Wisconsin," Rita announces.

"Wisconsin!" Brady enunciates like it's an exotic locale. "That's all dairy farms, right?"

I smile. "I live in Madison, which is a college town. But I grew up in rural Wisconsin, where some of my friends lived on actual farms. Where are you guys from?"

Pedro sticks his hands in the pockets of his tattered shorts. "I'm from L.A. But my parents are from Oaxaca."

"Is that what brought you to Mexico?"

"I actually came for work." He has outdoorsy vibes—tattoos, a gruff voice, gnarled hands with dirt under the nails. "I'm a botanist. USC sent me here to collect some data on old-growth forest, and I never left."

"When did you get here, Abby?" Brady slaps a mosquito on his thin arm.

"Yesterday. I bumped into Rita here shuttling baby turtles into the ocean. She let me help. What about you, Brady—how long have you been here?"

"Two years. I had to flee my hometown." He grins. "I tried Northern California for a bit, but even the Pacific wasn't enough distance for me. Like you, I'm from the boonies—a nowhere town in Queensland. It's like your South, right? All you'll really find is crocodiles and homophobia."

"That sounds like Florida," I crack. "Gators 'n' haters."

"Oh I *like* her," he blurts out, glancing at the others, and my heart swells. There it was, another glimmer of my old self. Chuckling, Rita turns away to poke at the fish.

Eszter, Eszter, Eszter—they both shared space with Eszter. I clear my throat, the questions gathering on my tongue, and my heart starts to race and—

"Snapper's ready!" Rita straightens up. Brady and Pedro hurry to their packs, like stagehands when the lights go out. They pull out plastic plates, a container of mango salsa, a jar of what turns out to be refried beans.

"Are you always this kind to newcomers?" I ask as we scoop heaping portions onto dishes and settle on Rita's orange blanket.

"Just the ones we like!" Brady says merrily.

For a moment, the only sound is the ting of cheap metal forks. I get the peculiar feeling I know them all already, like they're characters in a movie I watched over and over as a child. Once we've polished off the wine, Pedro produces a bottle of tequila and offers me a pull straight from the bottle. There's an easy patter among them, and I work on gathering my courage like it's something spilled on the floor.

"Sorry I'm late."

I turn toward the husky voice and spot a woman with huge eyes and dark, curly hair held back by a rolled-up bandanna—another person from Eszter's group photo. She waves as she lopes closer, her bad posture somehow projecting a cool, devil-may-care attitude. She acknowledges me with a small nod, and my cheeks warm.

"Amari, Abby; Abby, Amari." Rita sweeps her arm.

"Hi." She flings down a tattered towel next to Brady. "Did you just move here, or . . . ?" She sounds American, no obvious accent.

"No, I'm only here for a few days."

Amari brightens. "Oh, you should come out on Pedro's boat with us tomorrow! We're going to the nature preserve." I glance at Pedro and he nods. Amari helps herself to some refried beans. "Cool, I'll text you the info."

"I . . . I actually dropped my phone in the ocean yesterday." A sheepish laugh. "I'm kind of a klutz. But if you tell me where and when . . ."

Brady perks up. "I have an extra pay-as-you-go phone if you want it."

"What?"

"It's got a prepaid SIM card, nothing fancy. I got it a while ago but didn't end up needing it. Been meaning to sell it on PDC."

"PDC?" I repeat.

"Pachanga de Colel." He leans back onto an elbow. "This community website someone made for the island in, like, 2005."

"And it hasn't been updated since," Rita adds.

"Anyone can join," he goes on. "People list stuff for sale, advice, that sorta thing—kind of a hyperlocal Facebook. Some gossip, too. Great for lurking."

"You've got a phone for Abby, then?" Rita butts in, like the headmaster keeping the student on track.

"Right! It's still in the box. Take it, I insist." He sets down his plate. "You can come grab it tonight, if you like."

"That's really nice of you. Thanks." A beat. "Amari, what brought you to the island?"

"I'm an artist. Drawing and painting." She leans against Brady and he pokes her; there's something siblinglike between them. "I was bouncing around Mexico, doing some botanical illustration. And then one day I took the ferry here and fell in love."

I look around the group. Pedro squeezes lime all over his food; Amari plucks a chunk of mango from Brady's plate and pops it in her mouth.

You know how every once in a while, you just *know* a moment is significant? Your body wakes up, shuts off the autopilot, and tells you to pay attention. I felt it the first time I saw Eszter, two years ago, when I turned in to the bar's parking lot and caught a glimpse of her heading for the front door. Not love at first sight, nothing so Disney-fied, but an abrupt knowledge that life had found a seam, splitting neatly into Before and After.

And now . . . I feel it again, as tantalizing as déjà vu. I can't explain it but I *sense* it, how something's about to shift.

"Are there more beans?" Brady asks, popping the feeling like a bubble.

I clear my throat. "There's actually another reason I'm here. My partner, Eszter . . . she passed away on a trip here. She had food allergies and she had a reaction and wasn't able to get help in time." I see the shift—their faces twist with sympathy. "I'm . . . I'm kinda hoping to hear some stories of her time here. She looked so happy in her photos, and when we spoke she went on and on about how much she loved it here. So I'm . . . wondering if you guys have any memories to share, I guess."

Amari sets her plate on the blanket. "Wow. I'm so sorry for your loss. Of course we remember her—what a lovely person."

A little sob ripples through me and I turn away, murmuring an apology. Rita puts her hand on my arm and I can feel them exchanging uncomfortable glances.

"Sorry," I say again with a laugh. "Whew—I really thought I was ready to ask you that."

"Don't apologize," Amari says. "Of course it's hard to talk about. It was . . . really awful. Eszter was awesome. And we were just getting used to having her around."

I nod, sniffling. "It's been cool getting to see this place for myself."

"I remember meeting her for the first time," Amari says. "We bumped into each other on the ferry ride over. I helped her get a ride to her rental."

"She used to bring these cookies to Playa Oscura for the sunsets," Pedro says.

"Orejas." Brady takes a swig of tequila. "That's the name of the cookie."

A fresh gush of tears—yup, that sounds like Eszter. "This is kind of a weird question," I say, "but do you guys know what she was . . . doing, like day-to-day? At the very end." *I need to tell you something,* she texted. *We'll talk when you get here.*

They're all quiet, waiting for someone to jump in. "She came here to work on a big paper about her capstone project," I prompt. "The Haven—this mixed-use project in Miami."

"Huh—she didn't say much about that," Amari says.

"She liked practicing her Spanish." Pedro shifts on the blanket. "So she kinda made friends all over the island. Nice girl." He *ahem*s. "Really sorry for your loss."

"'All over the island'?" I repeat. "Do you know who she was closest with?"

Pedro's index finger bobs between Amari and Brady. A smile spreads across Amari's face. "Well, we gays gotta stick together."

Amari's queer! Some instant, involuntary part of me files this away.

"Well, maybe sometime while I'm here we can . . . grab drinks and pour one out for Eszter." I swipe below my eyes and laugh. "Maybe by then I won't be a complete mess."

"Of course." Amari pats my knee.

"It was really strange," I admit. "Walking around the place where she died? It's almost like I can feel her ghost."

Brady's head pops up. "So you've been up there?"

Confusion strobes through me. "Up where?" I ask.

The air freezes up around us. Brady's staring at me, his bewilderment matching my own. The others are stock-still, too.

I shake my head. "Been up where? She died in her Airbnb."

Brady glances to his left and right. My heart clacks like a train on a track.

"Brady, what are you saying?" I ask.

"Nothing." He shakes his head. "Just wondering if you've been to . . . the rental. On Calle Estrella, right?"

Still frowning, I nod. "I went there this morning. Nobody was home."

Another beat. Amari clears her throat and stacks her plate on top of Brady's. Pedro stands. No one looks at me.

"Where's the lid for the beans?" Rita asks.

I watch them swirl around me. My brain is whirring.

I came here to understand Eszter's time on Isla Colel. Her last few days alive.

So why did the cabin pressure change . . . when I mentioned where she died?

CHAPTER NINE
ESZTER

Then

I *see you.*

She's watching me—curious as a crow, turning away and blinkety-blinking whenever I glance in her direction. She's young, pretty. Tight black curls and a taut white tank, muscly arm slung across the back of the seat next to her. She glances my way and I blush, stupid blood vessels, stupid cheeks. Traitors.

Bam, we hit what feels like a bump in the road. I clutch the armrest, but of course it's not a road, since indeed we are in the middle of the ocean. No, it's a massive wave, unexpected, a worthy opponent for this small ferry, whose nose sniffs and nods and sniffs and nods like we're all on the back of a rocking horse. The inside is dim and dingy, the cracked plastic benches free of people. There's maybe a dozen of us making the trip from Cancún, all sprinkled around the upper deck. For the views, I guess? What views?

Ahoy, I spot it in the distance, *land ho:* Isla Colel, all ruffled and peaked, like a wad of green construction paper crumpled and tossed in the sea. God, that green looks *so green* after two hours of galumphing through the ocean with no cell service and nothing to see but one another and blue sky plus blue water, blue blue blue. Ruffle of movement around me as other passengers spot it too and start to gather their things, all elbows and duffel bags.

Cell service kicks in and I get a text from my mom: "Hi. What are you doing?" She means it in a casual way; after almost three decades in the States, her English is very good, but there's tone stuff she hasn't mastered.

I get a selfie from Abby, too . . . my *fiancée,* a term she's already using regularly, but it keeps sticking in my mouth. Though it's an off-the-cuff selfie, she looks amazing, almost intimidatingly good-looking: cheek-bones like two hacksaws, the sides of her black-brown hair clipped into a fresh fade. Now she's pouting and giving a thumbs-down—her code broke again, apparently. She tells me to soak up some sunshine for her. Poor thing—this is perhaps the first time in her life she's struggled at work.

I *love* Abby, love being next to her, let me count the ways . . . love how she's always the unofficial captain of our trivia team, cool under pressure even as the emcee bellows, "I need your answer sheets! Time is up!" I love how she can surprise me with tickets to the orchestra or ballet, how she'll don a suit and zip me into a dress and we pretend to be all fancy, holding hands as we walk through Overture Hall. I love our inside jokes and morning routine and the easy charm that has crowds eating out of her hand with surprising regularity.

So, why . . . am I doing this, exactly?

The thought makes my chest pinch, but I slam the feeling away, catch it like a fly beneath a swatter, flatten and toss. *Quit it, chest. I won't let your shenanigans ruin this exciting moment.*

The woman catches my eye as she passes. Oh, shit: the gay smile. My face heats for the forty-third time and I look down and cast around for my backpack. I have to figure out how I'll get to my rental. I turned down an offer from the Airbnb host—Marta, that's her name—to book a ride from the ferry dock because I saw on a map that it's only about a mile.

I can't believe I'm here. Can't *believe* it. I'm a woman on a mission, determined and discreet. I keep hearing Dad's voice. *A hazug embert hamarabb utolérik, mint a sánta kutyát: A liar is caught faster than a lame dog.* But this is different from *lying*-lying, right? It's just a phrase; he's got a quietly judgmental Hungarian saying for every imaginable life situation. My parents Americanized the heck out of themselves, but the proverbs? Those they hung on to.

I make my way down the ferry's back stairs and into the hull, where a scraggly line of passengers waits to disembark: three teenagers, a few families. I am the only white person in sight, which is a striking contrast to Madison.

I have this knee-jerk distaste for standing out. As a kid, everything about me felt vaguely humiliating . . . my folks' accents, for one, and the Eastern European food they packed in my lunchbox—dumplings Alexis MacKenzie described as "maggot-shaped," goulash that led AJ Burman to shriek, "Ew, is that puke?!" I occasionally mispronounced words because of my parents' phonetic elocution, to my classmates' glee (hi-po-po-TA-mos comes to mind).

Then there was the EpiPen I carried at all times in a little gray purse (well *hello*, weird first grader with a faux-leather bucket bag). At class-room pizza parties and Valentine's Day card exchanges and, God, every time a classmate had a birthday, cupcakes whizzing around like bumper cars, I quietly busied myself with an allergen free snack bar, wishing the ground would swallow me whole. I can still picture their faces, equal parts pity and fascination, staring at me as if I were an alien.

We plunk against the dock, bounce forward, back. A few stragglers join the line.

It's weird to me how some people don't need alone time. Much as I love Abby, I miss having space to think, to dream. Space to work on my project. Not that I have any idea how to express any of this.

I don't know. Maybe I'm a selfish jerk.

A second, violent thump against the deck, and then we're free to depart. The girl, the hot one, is loitering near the back of the line, one of those polite people letting all the *women and children* off first. Self-consciously, I head past her, back into the daylight, and join the clump of travelers waiting for our bags.

A deckhand yanks them out one by one (wonder if he's ever dropped one, a big wet *CRASH*) and I watch the locals to see if I should tip him. No one does. Thumpity-thump as the bag trails behind me over the planks. There's a stand selling ferry tickets here, red-painted wood and a big sash up top—I think of Lucy's booth in *Peanuts,* PSYCHIATRIC HELP—and beat-up boats of various sizes scattered around the big T of the marina. Contemplating the muddy, carved-up roads vis-à-vis my huge roller bag, I see I was a fool to say no to wise Marta. A few men lean against golf carts and mopeds, smoking and eyeing me warily. I pause, sweating, and I must look helpless because—

"Need some help?" Her smile's friendly, unassuming, unaccented English and an amused glint in her eye.

I grin. "That obvious?" Awkward fumble for my phone. "I'm staying at a vacation rental, it isn't far but with this bag . . ."

She looks it over. "Yeahhh, let's get you a ride. Where are you staying?"

I wonder if she's angling to rob me. Or if she's a serial killer, though that seems less likely. I get that from Dad, I guess, who's perpetually convinced everyone is crouched in the bushes, waiting to screw him over. But my phone's already out, and I pull up the address. "Calle Estrella?"

"Not far. Well, there's really only one residential area. C'mon." She approaches one of the men with a golf cart and asks, in what sounds to me like pretty broken Spanish, for a ride. Finally, she turns. "Jorge wants two hundred pesos. It's a little steep but he can tell you're fresh off the boat." She grins, white teeth gleaming. "You can show him the address—or a picture of the house, if you want. He'll know where to go. Where are you from, by the way?"

"Wisconsin." Jorge's already hoisting my luggage into the back. "And thank you. What about you?"

"Toronto, originally. But I live here now." She murmurs something to Jorge and gives his shoulder a friendly slap. "Well, I'll see you around."

"You aren't coming?" In the loud, confused second after I say it, its stupidity rolls around us, like I was inviting her home with me or something. Who's the serial killer now? "I just meant—"

"No, I have errands to run. But I'll bump into you. The island's small." She hitches her bag up her shoulder and turns away.

"I'm Eszter." Jorge fires up the engine and it judders over my words. She glances back. "Amari. Welcome to Isla Colel."

CHAPTER TEN
ABBY

Tuesday evening

The sun must've set on the opposite shore, because abruptly, we're all coated in darkness. Now I wonder if I was just being paranoid. Did I imagine all the weirdness when Brady looked at me sharply: *So you've been up there?*

People reach for their bags and I feel it—the quiet rustle that indicates the night is wrapping up. Something hinges open in me, a vacuous *no*. My night with Eszter's friends can't be over. Not only that: This is the first time I've hung out with new people since she died. I forgot how energizing it can feel. Particularly with Amari, whom I keep stealing glances at.

"Isn't the night still young?" I keep my voice light. "It feels early to me."

They glance at one another, weighing—the loaded pause when the server asks if anyone wants dessert.

"Should we go to Veta Bay?" Amari has one of those low, nonplussed voices that makes you feel squeaky in comparison. She looks out over the star-freckled sea.

"Oh, I dunno if I want to get all wet," Brady groans.

"We haven't been in forever," she replies. To me: "You've got a suit under that, right?" When I nod, she turns around. "Let's show our new friend!"

"Amari's in!" I clap.

"We really shouldn't be messing around so close to the reserve," Pedro says.

"We'll go." Rita steps forward, like a judge handing down a verdict. "We'll show Abby." She begins to walk north along the beach and Brady hurries after her. Amari saunters their way, and Pedro sighs and hoists his bag onto his thick shoulder.

We walk in silence for a few minutes, the only sound the drone of insects. Amari ambles next to me and I focus on not stepping on any shells.

"You're going in the water? On this side?" I finally ask.

"I am," she says. "And I bet you'll want to, too."

"But the water stinks over here. It's all sludgy."

She snickers. "It's worth it—you'll see."

When the rainforest pushes onto the beach, we slide out of our sandals and splash into the shallows. The bay is bathtub-warm and squishy, and the air smells like seaweed and salt. Near my ear, a mosquito whines. Where are we going?

"Here we are." Rita stops in a splotch of sea that looks identical to the ocean before and after it. She slides her caftan over her head and the others begin to disrobe.

"I don't get it," I say. "Why here?"

"Go on in." Rita waves her hand. "You'll see."

I peer into the black water. My pulse ticks in my neck; water slaps my anklebones. "Are there jellyfish?" I ask. "Or stingrays?"

"Watch for a second and see," Amari replies. They're all grinning and I hate it, I'm out of the joke, are they making fun of me?

What was that? A streak in the water, greenish white, sails past like an arrow. I shriek and jump back, but now light strobes around my feet.

This doesn't make sense—am I seeing things? I take another step and green pulses again, and then a laugh erupts out of me: "Oh my God, a bioluminescent bay?"

They cheer at my revelation and Rita surges into the water, brightness flashing around her, then dives. The others follow, churning up clouds of green. I cup my hands around an oval of water, and up close the specks blink on and off. I raise my palms so the sparkles rush down my forearms. I'm glittering! My chest fizzes. How is this real?

Amari yells my name and I step out of my tank top and shorts and toss them onto the sand. Luminescence billows around me as I breaststroke out. When I reach her, she's untying the bandanna around her head.

"Grab these corners." We hold the kerchief flat and lower it just under the surface. "Now lift it—slowly." The whole cloth is aglow, teeny lights racing over the fabric. I glance up and catch her smiling at me.

"Isn't it magical?" I jump—Rita's right behind me.

I twist around. "It *is*. I had no idea this is here."

"It's kind of a town secret," Pedro says. "It's on the edge of the nature preserve. And they don't want it to turn into a tourist destination—that would destroy it."

"But it's okay that we're here?" What I mean is: *What makes us so special, like the rules don't apply?*

"Every now and then." He grins. "A local showed it to me years ago. We respect the bay. More than we respect tourists."

"I prefer the term *traveler*," I joke. Weren't they all tourists at some point?

"Believe me," he replies, "we wouldn't be taking you here if you were a sunburned American who just stepped off a cruise ship." I roll my eyes—what a snob—but it's hard to focus on his contempt when every wiggle of my fingers conjures fresh light. I can't believe this is the same beach I wrote off as smelly and sallow. A minnow streaks past, leaving behind a comet trail.

I marvel: Yesterday I was crying alone on the edge of a cliff. Now I'm swimming in the night sky.

My fingertips wrinkle and plankton pools in the raisin-y creases. I'm not ready to leave; I could stay here until the morning sun mutes the bay's secret brilliance. But eventually, everyone else trudges out and towels off.

"You coming?" Amari calls.

The water's coolness kisses my scalp. "No thanks, I'm never leaving."

"Great, enjoy your new life aquatic!" Rita volleys. "C'mon, I'll walk you home."

I lope ashore and we begin the shivery walk back. As we near the residential neighborhood, Pedro and Rita peel off with friendly good-byes. My heart clutches at the casualness, the kind of farewell you give an old friend you'll see again soon.

"Thanks for taking me here," I say to Amari, squeezing seawater out of my hair.

"Thank you for pushing the issue!" She's walking close to me and . . . I don't mind it, I clock the inches between us.

I clear my throat. "Did . . . did you ever take Eszter here?"

"I don't think so." A knowing smile. "She wasn't much of a water baby, right?"

It's true; Eszter liked the beach but rarely got into the water. I feel a weird frisson, like this is proof Amari really knew Eszter—that Eszter wasn't squarely mine. "Right," I say.

Amari and Brady start to bid me good night, but I turn to him: "I'd still love to borrow that phone, if you don't mind."

He blinks, like he forgot, then nods. "Of course—come on!"

We fall into lockstep. "Looking forward to the boat ride tomorrow?" I ask.

"Mm-hmm. Pedro always takes us to a really nice part of the nature preserve." Brady shivers a bit, goosebumped in his wet clothes. "You'll like it—it's got loads of wildlife."

I smile. "How do you know I like wildlife?" They're all acting like I've been here forever, and it's . . . well, it's nice.

He counts on his fingers: "Let's see, turtles, a joke about alligators . . ."

We hook around a corner. "Bioluminescent plankton," I add, "which is arguably—"

I stop short. A fat iguana is in the road, gray with black stripes and a line of spikes along its spine. Its dark eyes flicker in Brady's phone flashlight.

"Is it dead?" I ask.

He watches it for a second, then shakes his head. "Just resting, I think. Iguanas are dickheads, always bunging up the road." We circumvent it and he leads me up a short path to a two-story building, its cement walls the color of key lime pie. Fat wind chimes jangle near the door as Brady stoops and pulls a key from beneath a bright purple welcome mat. "Here we are! I've got the ground floor."

When he flicks on the light, I stop short: The place is a pigsty. Pans are piled on the stovetop; dishes clump in the sink. Fly tape dangles from the ceiling, pocked with bugs.

"Do you mind if I change?" He disappears into the bathroom, then comes out wearing blaze-orange joggers and a patterned shirt.

"Speaking of gators," I say, pointing at the little reptiles covering his shirt.

"I'm not from Florida, mate." He grins. "These are crocodiles. Y'know, 'crikey,' et cetera. Now, where is that phone?" He rummages through his chaotic closet, then holds out a box.

"Whoa, it's a smartphone?" MOTO G, it says. I turn it over in my hands.

"Oh, no worries, it's still a piece of shite. Five hundred pesos, if that."

"Still. Thank you. I'll give it back to you before I go."

He waves a hand. "You're unburdening me. A bottle of tequila and we'll call it even. Let's make sure it works, right?"

Together we navigate the Spanish manual. "You were right about it not being an iPhone," I tell him, admiring its curved back and bubble of a camera. "This has gotta be, what—one megapixel? Say cheese!"

He tenses; the screen captures him half turned away. "Sorry, no photos," he says.

I lower the phone. "Are you a celebrity or something? Big in Japan?"

"No, nothing like that. Just . . . don't want my face out there. Here, let's test the SIM card."

We cheer when his text reaches the—*my*—phone. "Seems like cell service is pretty decent on the island," I observe.

"It's fine unless the grid is down. Apparently the carriers never both-ered with backup generators or batteries on the towers here."

"So when the power goes out, cell service does too?" Eszter surfaces in my mind—she didn't call for help, but even if she had . . . "What if there's an emergency?"

He shrugs. "There's a satellite phone with a battery near the old hotel. Gloria—she owns the grocery store—she said that when that big hurricane hit a few years ago, some people had to hike all the way up the mountain to call for help. But normally, the power's only out for an hour or two. Oh! I'll add you to a group thread with the other expats." His fingers fly across his phone. "You're going to regret this. Rita texts like a boomer and Pedro is always sending blurry pictures of . . ." He pauses, concentrating on his screen.

"*Pictures of what?*" I cry, and when it clicks, he lets out a birdlike laugh.

"*Plants*, Abby, get your mind out of the gutter! Jesus, the man's a botanist!"

Giggling, I drop the phone into my bag. "Is everyone here really this nice?" I narrow my eyes. "You just straight-up gave me a phone. I'm a Midwesterner, and *I* find it suspicious."

"I dunno what that means. But yes! Kindest people you'll ever meet." He fixes the wall behind me with a dreamy gaze. "I can't put it into words. How lovely it is here, right? How at home I feel. After all those years of . . . of awful things." He stiffens, then smiles. "Oh, look at me, the sissy my dad accused me of being."

"Don't say that! You're not a sissy."

"Well, now you see what I was so eager to get away from." He flumps onto a kitchen chair and I scrape one back and sit.

"I'm sorry your dad called you that."

He blinks hard. "Thanks. He was a real douchebag."

A moth taps on the window, drawn to the light.

I take a deep breath. "My dad took off," I say. "When I was thirteen. My sister was ten. I remember him being an amazing father, but I sup-pose that can't be right."

"Oh, I'm sorry, Abby."

"Thanks. It's strange—when you lose someone, it's like their absence becomes this presence. Like, the silence is deafening." Eszter—this is my opening. Time to figure out if his weirdness around her was real or in my head. "Actually, speaking of—"

"I want to show you something." He stands and marches into the living room, then rifles through his backpack. "Here we are." He hands me a dog-eared paperback of *The Year of Magical Thinking*. "The seminal book on grief. Have you read it?"

"I've read other Joan Didion books, but not this one." I lift the cover; there's a bookplate on the first page, FROM THE DESK OF BRADY KING, the *B* and *K* large and serifed. I flip forward; notes crowd the margins.

"Oh, you can't look at it!" He swipes it back sheepishly.

"Sorry!" I raise my palms. "I thought you were lending it to me."

"My bad. It's the one and only thing I brought all the way from Australia—I'd never go anywhere without it." He's clutching it to his chest, like I might lunge for it. "I figured you can order it for yourself when you get home."

I tap my chin. "I wonder if I can buy a used copy off . . . what's the website you were talking about? PVC?"

"PVC is vinyl, mate. It's PDC. Pachanga de Colel. You could try, though I doubt you'd have much luck."

"The island's not big on reading?"

"Not big on English," he says, and I blush—duh.

He slides the book back into his bag. "This book . . . I lost a parent. My mum. When I was fourteen." His head ducks. "She always saw the best in everyone. And unfortunately, that included my arsehole dad. You want to know the *real* reason I moved halfway around the world—that's it. The only family I had left was an alcoholic with anger issues." He looks up. "Sorry, I don't normally talk about this."

"It's okay—I get it." *More than you even know.*

He laughs bitterly. "That's why I won't let anyone take pictures of me—I don't want him knowing anything about me or my life."

I set my palm on his arm. "I'm so sorry, Brady."

"Thanks." He stares at my hand. "Leaving Queensland—it felt like the first time I took action. Because whenever he'd get violent, I'd freeze. Like in a bad dream when you tell your body to move and it won't listen."

"Oh, Brady." He digs his knuckles into his eyes. "When my dad left," I say, "it was hard not to blame myself." Part of me floats up and watches with detached interest as I keep spilling my guts. I've been so closed off since Eszter died; this feels like part two of the exorcism that began last night, yanking a cork from my throat. "Like if I'd just been a better daughter or something, he'd have stayed."

"You poor thing."

I sigh. "That was the beginning of everything falling apart: My mom injured herself on the job—she worked at a factory—and started drinking. My sister fell in with a bad crowd and started drinking too. They're both still struggling."

He shakes his head slowly. "Fuck alcohol."

"Totally." I think back to the February day when Kayla almost drank herself to death, chasing sleeping pills with cheap booze in what she later insisted was simply an attempt to fall asleep. After I got the call, I ducked into my boss's office, tears stinging my cheeks, and told him I had to go—my sister was in the hospital, unresponsive, and they weren't sure she'd make it.

Of course, Beckman, get out of here, Tyler said, sitting up straight, all magnanimous. And when I started to turn: *Just push the code you're working on to GitHub before you go.*

It was a three-hour drive to Elmridge, and I panicked the entire way. I'd left Eszter a voicemail as I sprinted to my car, and when she finally called me back, she was baffled that I'd set off without her.

This is my problem, not yours, I told her. Every part of me recoiled at the idea of her being saddled with this, sullied by it, this dark and shameful piece of my identity.

I'm your partner, Abby, she said. *You don't have to deal with this alone.*

And I'm not proud of it. But right then, I murmured, *I'm about to lose service . . .* and hung up.

"I get why you needed to leave Australia," I say. "I was so deter-mined to get the hell out of my tiny rural town. It felt like working hard and getting a scholarship was the only way out." My heart thunks. "Can I ask you something?"

He nods. "Sure."

"Before, when I asked about Eszter . . . what did you mean when you said I'd been 'up there'? Where she died?"

His brow crinkles. "The residential neighborhood is north of the beach, right? I was . . . surprised you'd want to see the site, that's all."

My belly clenches. "How did you find out?"

"What, that she died?" He shakes his head. "Everyone was talking about it. Nothing ever happens here, so it was . . . big news." He pushes a hank of damp hair out of his eyes.

I tilt my head. "A random visitor's medical emergency was all anyone could talk about?" I can't seem to wrap my head around this island, the pace, the population density—they act like I'm the first new face they've seen in months yet complain about tourists.

"On the island, sure. I doubt it made the nightly news on the mainland or anything, but we'd all gotten to know Eszter. It was a shock. A horrible one."

"Right." I dab my eye with the back of my hand. "Maybe this is naïve, but I thought I'd feel a huge weight lift off me when I got here and saw the island for myself, you know? Instead I just felt . . . weird." Brady clicks his tongue sympathetically and I shake my head. "But then tonight, when we were all in the bio bay, it felt like . . ." I look away, blushing. "This sounds dumb, but it almost felt like she was smiling down on me. I felt close to her for the first time since she died. It was . . . comforting."

I smear away tears. "Maybe the only way to actually move on is to confront it head-on," I continue. "I guess that's what I'm trying to do here. For four months, I've been, like, trying to soldier on as if everything's fine. But it's not fine, and it won't be, and maybe I've got to accept that, you know? Face it down like it's a demon and then . . . I don't know, maybe I'll be stronger for it." I glance up. "Maybe *we'll* end up stronger."

He looks so sad right then that I lean forward and grab his arm. We catch eyes, laugh sheepishly. "Well, this turned into a real trauma swap!" I say.

Maybe that's the magic of an expat community. When everyone's a stranger, transient—well, why *shouldn't* I open up to this guy I'll never see again?

"I hope being here helps you." He smooths his crocodile-print shirt. "Gives you closure and all that."

"Thanks." I squeeze his bony wrist. "I'm glad I found my way here."

I cry on the way home, a good cry, emotions leaking out with the salty tears. The wind rushes to and fro, cooling my tear-lined cheeks. I'm almost to my rental when a crackle behind me makes me turn, and I jump: Someone's at the end of the block, motionless, silhouetted in the patchy beam of a foliage-filtered porch light. But then a fresh gust of wind makes the greenery creak and chatter, and when I look again, no one's there.

At home, eager to distract myself, I open my laptop to a gush of work messages. I spend a few minutes trying to sync my new phone; I get Gmail and Google Photos to work, but there's not enough data for a translation app. My new number is Mexican, obviously, and I can't connect this phone to my work email or Slack because of their security measures. My chest tightens. My boss is *not* going to like that.

As I brush my teeth, the scene replays in my mind: *It was really strange,* I said. *Walking around the place where she died? It's almost like I can feel her ghost.*

And Brady snapped to attention: *So you've been up there?*

The nature preserve, the cliff? It could be nothing. But the way the air bristled around us, that animal instinct that something wasn't right . . .

In the morning, a cymbal crash of thunder jolts me out of a tangled, jagged dream. Rain is throwing itself against the screen like a dog desperate to be let in. I stagger over to slide the pane closed and push a towel against the wet sill.

I reach for my phone, blinking a little at its foreign shape and weight, the unfamiliar screen. There's one text, from 3:04 A.M.

Brady's words soak the whole world in a high-pitched hush:

"You deserve to know the truth about Eszter. Meet me at the fonda tomorrow. 9 am."

CHAPTER ELEVEN

ESZTER

Then

"Did anyone bring snacks?" Brady, propped on his elbows, looks around hopefully.

I sit up on my beach towel. "I have orejas. One sec." It had been a whole ordeal, going item by item through the ingredients with Gloria, the chatty grocer; there were a few options, all in similar-looking bags, and only one kind of cookie contained no eggs or peanuts. I worried I was taking up too much of her time, but the customers behind me smiled patiently as we worked through the list. I tried one at home, nibble-nibble with my Benadryl and EpiPen at the ready, and thank Jesus, these passed the test.

"I brought Dos Equis," Pedro adds.

"And I have weed!" Hilde giggles boisterously, waving a vape pen like it's a magic wand.

The gang's all here, all the expats lined up on blankets, facing the setting sun. Sure enough, I bumped into Amari my very first evening here, night before last. And look, I told myself I was *not here to make friends*, in the parlance of those hilarious dating reality shows Abby and I like to watch all snuggled on her couch on cold winter nights, sipping red wine while the icy wind rattles her old windows (*our* windows, she'd remind me, *yoursandmine*). I've got an agenda and "enjoy nightly sunset" isn't on it.

But . . . there's only so much work I can do in a day. And Amari was so convincing in that devil-may-care kind of way. *Everyone's cool, I'll introduce you,* her tone the audio equivalent of a shrug. How could I resist?

So I met the whole crew: Pedro, the cranky tree hugger; Hilde, the apple-cheeked Swede whose tote bag jangles with sparkly crystals; and Brady, Amari's bestie, a delightful twink from Australia. Pedro makes me a bit nervous, but the others seem eager to let me into their happy little expat world. If anything, they're a bit *too* friendly. What's their endgame?

I snap a picture of the sunset's first blush, the undersides of the clouds violet and fuchsia. I study it for a moment, then send it to Abby. She replies with the hang-loose emoji, i.e., hand-as-phone. It triggers a splash of guilt and I stuff the phone deep in my bag.

We pass around my heart-shaped cookies and Pedro's sand-speckled beers. Some locals have shown up for the celestial pyrotechnics and we smile and wave and raise our drinks. I confirm that my hosts, Marta and Carlos, aren't present before taking a hit of the vape pen; they're such a sweet, warm couple, parental, and I don't want them to see me break the law. A couple kids barrel into the warm water, which gleams pearly gold and indigo like an oil slick.

The sun hits the horizon and a strip of ocean glows orange; in Hungarian, there's a word for that lit-up reflection, *aranyhíd,* literally "golden bridge." Birds plow below the surface beak-first, *splash,* and my brain, for once, shuts up, until my whole body feels like a smile.

"Wow," Brady says softly. "That pink—I cannot fathom how the sky can be that shade."

"Particulate matter," I murmur.

Four faces turn to me—*Huh?*

I laugh. "Picture the Earth as a tiny bead rolling away from the beach ball of the sun." I point at the horizon. "Sine waves of sunlight are still beaming up through the atmosphere, right? Particle pollution—y'know, dirt, dust—it scatters the sine waves so we see psychedelic colors."

"Trippy," Hilde says after a shared reflective silence.

"Nerdy," Amari adds good-naturedly.

"Oh, for sure." I stretch. "I like how science explains the entire world. Like, pretty much everything comes down to a simple algorithm. The universe follows rules and that makes it . . . I don't know. Predictable." I accept the vape pen again and take another small hit before passing it on.

"'Predictable'? Psshht." Hilde waves her hand. "Personally, I love not knowing what'll happen next. I just follow the unfolding."

"You been using that hoja alma again?" Brady cracks.

Hilde smiles, her eyes trained on the horizon. "It's interesting. Eszter looks at nature and sees equations. Pedro sees the names of things. I see wisdom—things unfolding as they should."

Pedro snorts. "I hate that everything-happens-for-a-reason bullshit. Ice caps melting, sea levels rising, hurricanes and droughts getting deadlier by the month—is that all part of some *divine lesson* for someone's *personal evolution?*"

I'm glad he said it. I like Hilde (I like all of them!), but they seem a tiny bit . . . allergic to personal responsibility. I take another pull from the vape pen.

"That's not what I mean." Hilde exudes patience. "People have lost touch with their divinity, sure. Maybe that'll be our downfall. But nature?" She nods. "Nature is as wise as ever."

Pedro rolls his eyes dramatically. A wave fizzles up the sand, slapping and sucking.

"Oh, c'mon, Pedro," says Brady, impish. "If you didn't come for the sunsets, what the hell are you doing on Isla Colel?"

Something I've been trying to figure out snaps into place: Pedro reminds me of my dad, but like, a funhouse-mirror version. They share a rock-solid conviction that they're right and anyone who doesn't agree is stupid. But their actual beliefs couldn't be more different. Oh, they would *hate* each other.

When I was tiny, whenever people asked me what I wanted to be when I grew up, I'd say, "My dad." It was cute—a little girl not quite grokking the question—but in the moment, I meant it. He was brilliant, that was undeniable. Hardworking, strategic. I watched him hopscotch up the company ladder, engineer, lead engineer, charming the right people, racking up success after success. He had the kind of charisma li'l Eszter could only *dream* of. And dream I did.

"Guys, look!" Amari shouts, pointing. We stare at the horizon and for a few seconds there's nothing, just the sapphire band where the ocean meets the sky. But then I spot a lump poking out of the water, and right as I'm beginning to doubt myself—

"Dolphins!" Hilde cries. Now they're showing off, leaping out of the water in beautiful arcs. I've never seen the creatures in the wild and I tear up at how *dolphiny* they are, their curved silhouettes like the ones in coloring books, dorsal fins like arrow fletching.

"The water's getting cleaner so the fish they feed on must be coming back," Pedro says. "I hate to say it, but the two best things to happen to Isla Colel were COVID and the hurricane."

I smile. "I know you're a plant expert—marine biology too?"

"Oh, I like animals almost as much as plants. It's humans who depress me."

Hilde sits up. "Humanity is beautiful!"

Pedro groans. "I take it you haven't been to Señor Frog's in Cancún. Look, the reason our island is such a haven for wildlife is because people have a relatively small footprint here."

Our island, he called it. Claiming ownership, as if he didn't wash ashore like the rest of the expats.

I think of my folks again—they were my age when they gave up everything to come to the United States. No one called them "expats"; no, they were *immigrants*, with their choppy accents and pungent, paprika-y dishes. Other than the fact they all left their homelands, what do my parents have in common with this group?

When Mom and Dad emigrated in the nineties, Hungary was taking the final, halting steps to liberalize its economy: ballooning debt, plummeting standards of living, strikes gumming up the streets. They both had grandparents who'd survived the Holocaust and who repeated horror stories like macabre fairy tales. *They didn't live through that,* my parents said, *just for us to make nothing of our lives.*

That's what Abby doesn't get—there's a *reason* they're so hard on each other, and Laszlo, and me. In Florida, they worked their butts off, Dad rising through the corporate ranks, Mom teaching piano lessons all over town. It's mind-boggling, honestly; they were hustling before they could even speak the language. *Aki nem dolgozik, ne is egyék,* Mom used to say—*those who won't work shouldn't eat. Az becsüli a pénzt, kinek körme kopik utána,* Dad often added—*those who appreciate money broke their nails for it.* Basically: Put your head down and work.

And *keep* your head down, while you're at it—don't stick your neck out. It was their overarching mantra as they studied and emulated American culture, sculptural furniture and *Seinfeld* and moss-green sponge paint and stuffed-crust pizza: *Fit in, fit in, fit in.*

Laszlo *nailed* the assignment. He made it look easy, striding down one of the few acceptable paths away from the family business: pediatric cardiology. Day in and day out, he fixes kids' broken hearts—even Dad can't criticize him for that. But now, looking out at the aranyhíd, it occurs to me that it couldn't have been easy; Laszlo too had a choice, he flicked away the opportunity to rebel, felt that pressure to never mess up.

And here are these iconoclasts smoking pot on the beach, all *What, me worry?* Where's the in-between?

"Whatcha thinking about, Eszter?" Brady asks. Whoops, he's been offering me the vape pen again for a few seconds, unbeknownst to me.

"Sorry. Just thinking about my parents." Nobody reacts. It's weird to even *picture* their parents, thousands of miles away, left behind. Everyone in this crew—kinda like Abby, now that I think about it—was like, *Adiós, mi familia.* Why would these perfectly nice people run away from their loved ones, their home countries, the lives they were born into . . . ? I feel a gentle rocking, like the ocean's inside of me.

Oh, right—cannabis.

"Mine were super strict," I continue, as if anyone egged me on. I'm floating, following the thought like it's a bird midflight. "My dad was the disciplinarian, but . . . I'm just now realizing my mom *let* him be a tyrant. Let him run the show. It makes me, like, not respect her."

Awkward shimmy-shake and shuffle to my left and Brady's rising to his feet, brushing sand off his swim trunks. "I'm going in."

He staggers into the surf and then ducks below the water, T-shirt and all. Now he's bobbing in the aranyhíd, his head like a black buoy. The other three won't look me in the eye. Shoot, I'm high.

"What . . . just happened?" I say, hanging on to the question like it's a reed basket in the Nile and I'm baby Moses. (What?)

"He'll be fine," Amari says. "You didn't know. His parents are a sore spot, that's all."

"Oh, no." Guilt streams through me—I hate this, I'm so distressed that I distressed him, upset that he's upset. Stressed, a mess. Messy Eszter.

Stop.

"Didn't his dad kill his mom?" Pedro says bluntly. I stare at him in horror.

"Is that true?" Hilde lifts another oreja. "All I know about his dad is that he's the heir to the third-largest mining company in Australia."

Amari nods. "That's him. Absurdly wealthy. And Brady cut all ties."

"That makes me respect him even more," I say moonily. "He has integrity."

"Well, he told me he moved here with the money his grandfather left him, so." Pedro waves his hand, like, *Make of that what you will.*

"I feel awful for bringing it up," I announce. "I had no idea."

Hilde sits up straighter. "How could you?"

I hear it the accusatory way first, and then it slides into place, *click*. I turn over the idea like it's a rock with a message on the bottom: Hilde's telling me not to feel terrible about hurting Brady's feelings since I truly had no way to know. Because I'm not a mind reader. This feels revelatory.

"He'll be okay. Just needs to feel his feelings." Amari lifts a palmful of sand, lets it drip through her fingers in silky ribbons. "I'll walk him home, just to be sure."

"Can I come with you?" I ask, warmth bulging in my chest for both of them.

She smiles. "I'm sure he'd love that."

CHAPTER TWELVE

ABBY

Wednesday morning

call Brady right away, letting the phone ring and ring and ring. I text him that I'll be there. *The truth about Eszter*—he even spelled her name right. The expat group thread is still active, though Brady hasn't contributed since adding me. Amari asks if we'll need to rain-check the boat ride; Rita tells her to have faith. *The boat ride.* I forgot all about it. Is Brady still planning to go?

My pulse thuds in my temples, like I've just begun a long swim. I don't have time for my morning workout; instead I grab my laptop and head toward town. The rain has lightened to a drizzle and the air has a still, heavy feel, silvery and cool. On the road, water pools in broad divots, turning hardened soil into mud.

I pass a copse of dead trees, their gnarled limbs reaching for the sky like monsters emerging from the underworld. A few blocks later, I freeze: The iguana we passed last night is still in the road, but now a tizzy of flies buzzes around its black eyes, *on* them. Dead, then.

I step inside the fonda and pause, blinking, while my eyes adjust: laminate tables, old wooden chairs. There are paintings on the walls, big daubs of paint on unframed canvases. The nearest is of a horse midrun, specks of orange and red and purple somehow forming a tousled mane and velvety muzzle. A man's sitting at the bar; the young woman behind the counter waves and (I think) tells me I can sit anywhere. I check out the side patio, scanning the tables eagerly.

No sign of Brady.

I choose a shaded corner of the terrace and text him again. I ask the group chat if anyone's heard from him. Amari says no; Rita adds that she assumes we'll see him at the shore.

"He stood me up for breakfast," I add.

No one replies.

I connect to the Wi-Fi, read an email from Tyler asking if my phone's not working: *I don't think my texts are going through.* Swallowing, I reply that my cell broke but I'll be on Wi-Fi as much as possible. I alert a few friends that I'm temporarily phoneless. The minutes crawl: 9:05, 9:10. The concern eddies and widens, like a curl of smoke.

Relax, Abby. Is this now a lifelong curse? Anytime anyone fails to reply right away, I'll think back to Eszter, to that growing sense of panic, and assume the worst?

You deserve to know the truth about Eszter. It's eerily familiar: *I need to tell you something.*

Blobs of sun now speckle the patio. From the corner of my eye, I think I see someone entering the patio, but when I glance up, I'm still alone. My chilaquiles arrive and I drown them in hot sauce. I try to ask the server, a late-teens girl with a glossy crown braid, if Brady already came in that morning, but she shakes her head. I'm not sure if she's answering the question or indicating she doesn't understand me. Another mushroom cloud of frustration that I can't open my mouth and make myself understood.

Tense voices make both the waitress and me look toward the town square. I could swear I see Rita and Pedro sweep past, voices low, hostility like a cloud around them. I can't make out the words, but I *think* they're speaking English. I check the time; the boat ride isn't for another hour. Where are they off to?

My phone buzzes. *There he is,* I think, relief rushing through my veins.

But it's Pedro: "Told you the weather would turn around. All aboard at 10:30. Be on time, please."

Rita texts next: "The whales wait for no man." Are they together still, both on their phones?

Then Amari: "Whales have no patience for male nonsense? I KNEW I felt a kinship with them."

I frown. No one even acknowledged my text about Brady being AWOL. That must mean I'm overreacting . . . right?

I drop my laptop at home, then hesitate—should I stop by Brady's house and check on him? But it's already 10:20 and Rita seemed to think he'd be on the boat ride. Perhaps he forgot he even sent that text? It was three in the morning, after all. Maybe he'll be waiting at the beach, freckling in the sun, skinny arm waving hello.

The main road's spotlit by the now-scorching sun. A bird trills overhead, its squeaky song like a finger on wet glass.

You deserve to know the truth about Eszter. What truth, Brady?

At the beach, I shade my eyes and slump—no sign of him. No sign of *anyone*. I *think* this is the pad of dry sand Rita identified as our meeting spot. This one's a cove, less churned up than most of the western shoreline. Small, gangly seabirds cross the sand on stiltlike legs, their footprints a trail of backward arrows. The waves are calmer today, and I drop my things and approach the surf.

The first step feels cool, and foam sucks at my toes, my ankles. The sun blares on the surface, so bright it makes me squint. A clump of seaweed drifts by, convulsing like a beating heart.

I press my eyes closed. I'm on vacation with Eszter that final summer, standing in the rocky shallows of Lake Novak.

You have to hold still, babe, she said, grinning. *You have to stop squirming.* We'd been holed up in the Airbnb cabin all weekend, waiting out the rain, and it was our first time in the water.

You seriously think the minnows will swim over?

And she grasped my hand tighter. *Yes! They'll come to you as soon as you stop moving.*

I funneled all my energy into keeping still; I even held my breath.

There they are, she whispered. *Don't move.*

My heart pounded. They darted over, a dozen tiny minnows, metallic and moving like hummingbirds, rushing this way and that. They came closer, closer, daring one another . . . and then one shot forward and nibbled my pinkie toe.

It was the gentlest tickle but I screamed and jumped away, and we laughed and laughed until I swore I'd hold still again. They flocked to us. One pecked the top of my foot, another the big toe. We doubled over in giggles. Eszter ducked and scooped a palmful of water my way, and I kicked a spray of water back, and—

"Hello, hello!" Amari calls from behind me. I whip around as she scuffles through the sand, platform sandals dragging.

I wave. It's like my heart's a soldier and the sight of her makes it stand at attention. She gives me a quick hug.

"You haven't heard from Brady?" I ask.

"Nope." She spreads a towel and plops down on it. "You said you had breakfast plans?"

I nod. "He . . . he said he had something to tell me. About Eszter?"

She's fishing in her backpack, and for a fraction of a second, she pauses. "Huh." She slides out a bottle of sunscreen and I wonder if I imagined it. "Those two were BFFs, so maybe he thought of another story he wanted to share. He said something about getting to the mainland this week, so I bet he found a ride. I wouldn't take it personally." She squirts a blob on her arm, then offers me the bottle.

BFFs—I file this away for later. "You two seem close," I say casually.

"Oh, he's like my little brother." She slathers lotion on her chest. "We . . . figured out we have a bunch in common. But even I'm in the dark about his whereabouts most of the time. He's a freewheeling guy."

I nod. A pelican thrusts its long beak into the water, then sits back, a fish wriggling in its balloon-like bill. *Gulp.*

I check the time: 10:42. "Where is everybody?"

"Oh, they're always late. Here, if you're on time, you're early."

"But Pedro's text . . ."

"Oh, that's Pedro being Pedro." She snickers and lies back, hands behind her head. "He's, like, a disgruntled uncle."

My antennae go up, but I keep things light: "A 'disgruncle,' if you will. What's his deal?"

She shrugs. "What's interesting is that he *could* assimilate with the Coleleños. But he feels more kinship with us. I dunno, maybe that's given him all this internal conflict." She smiles. "He's a big teddy bear at heart, but it drives Rita crazy. She—"

Though I desperately want her to go on, I swat her arm as Rita emerges from the trees.

"What did I tell you? Perfect day for a boat ride!" She tips her floppy sun hat. "Where's Pedro?"

As if in answer, the toot of a horn makes us jump. On the water, a white panga boat with a blue canopy approaches. It pauses at the mouth of the cove and Pedro hops out, splashing into the waist-high waves.

"I thought we were taking *Red Rum*," Rita murmurs. When I raise an eyebrow: "That's Pedro's boat. I suppose it'd be a little small for all of us."

"Get in!" he calls.

I look around. "We're leaving without Brady?"

Rita waves and starts swashing out toward Pedro. "He's an odd one, Brady—might just be feeling antisocial today. If he isn't getting back to you, he doesn't want to talk."

Amari shoots me a look: *See?* I glance back at the shore and trail after them; Rita climbs in first, then Amari. She offers her hand and I clutch it tight as I step onto the wet, wobbly surface. I settle next to her on the molded bench, and stray drops soak into my shorts.

The captain—Esteban, a mustachioed man in a baseball cap—starts the engine and the boat slaps against the waves. Amari and Rita make their way over to a cooler, chatting in low voices. I glance back at Pedro, who's already opened a Modelo.

And sure, this is probably the kind of breezy community where people float in and out, devoid of firm schedules. I know that; I tell myself that. But I can't help clocking it.

Pedro didn't ask about Brady.

In fact, no one did.

CHAPTER THIRTEEN

"You deserve to know the truth about Eszter. Meet me at the fonda tomorrow. 9 am." I keep rereading the text, like it'll morph in front of my eyes.

I send yet another desperate reply: "Where are you?"

"You're missing the views!"

Rita's smiling over me. I slip the phone into my pocket and rise from the bench. The breeze prickles at my scalp where the hair's shorn close.

"Sorry, I was trying Brady one more time."

"Still worried about him?"

I nod. "His last text . . . he was—" Something clicks. He contacted me at three this morning. *Tomorrow* could mean tomorrow, Thursday. Otherwise he would've said *this* morning. The thought mellows the cold concern. Hell, if he was up at that hour, he might still be asleep.

. . . Right?

"'Views'?" I join her at the railing.

We're passing Playa Oscura, the unofficial sunset-viewing area, and next to it, the once-grand houses, now broken and graffiti-blotched. The flat roofs of several slump into the water; the windows and doors are gone, empty eyeholes and screaming mouths. I catch glimpses of waterlogged furniture, tile work furred with algae, and nosy vines clinging to rebar.

"Why haven't any of these been repaired?" I point. "That's from the hurricane, right?"

Pedro shrugs. "They're all owned by families on the mainland. They haven't bothered fixing them."

"Why not?" I ask.

"Maybe they're worried about another hurricane." He waves his hand. "Some were probably empty before Diego hit. The tourism industry ground to a halt when the resort closed in the early 2000s."

The coastline ducks away as we reach the narrowest part of the island, and then we pass the residential neighborhood, its colorful casitas like toys on a shelf. Rita points to the sudden blare of white rock along the coast. Greenery frosts the top, with the tip of the radio tower poking out like a cocktail pick.

"The ruins of the hotel are just up there," Amari says.

"Surrounded by barbed wire," Pedro adds. "Nobody should be up there."

"I thought there was a path up to the cliff," I say innocently, omitting the second part: . . . *a path I hiked two days ago.*

"There are so many rare plant species growing there now," he replies. "Anyone walking around up there is part of the problem."

I turn away, blushing. A *disgruntled uncle,* Amari called him. "Were people bummed when the resort closed?" I ask. "It must've been the engine of the economy here."

Pedro shrugs. "Some people felt that way. But this isn't Cancún; we don't need spring breakers getting drunk and making a mess. Outsiders don't treat the island with respect."

The cliff looks terrifying from here: eggshell-colored, sheer. Waves batter the base like a bloodied boxer, relentless and cruel. My phone, the necklace, and Eszter's EpiPen are down there, decomposing in the salt.

"Has anyone ever fallen off?" I ask.

"From the cliff?" Pedro considers. "Not that I know of. When the resort was open, there were deck chairs at the top for people to sit and watch the sunset. Now it's pretty overgrown." He sets his beer down. "Technically, there's a scramble to the bottom. Someone marked it with blue paint. Teenagers will try it at low tide to take pictures on the sea stacks. But it's dangerous. A local boy drowned a few years ago."

We solemnly watch it spool past. "It definitely doesn't look climbable," I say. "So steep."

"Pedro, tell Abby about the rock," Amari prompts.

"The limestone?" Pedro nods at it. "It's made up of millions of years' worth of crushed-up shells and bones." He's serious when he talks about nature, focused. "Imagine how thick with life the ocean used to be—packed so tight you could almost walk on the water."

"Leave it to the rock climber to worship rock," Rita cracks.

"You rock climb?" I ask.

"Used to." Pedro nods at the crag. "That's actually how I got into botany. I spent some time climbing in Thailand. Met a retired arborist who told me there's an entire *world* up in the canopy. I was sold. I could get paid to climb trees and sit two hundred and fifty feet in the air with rare endemic species? Yes, please."

"Pedro prefers plants to people, if you couldn't tell," Rita says in a stage whisper. He smirks. Was that really them I glimpsed arguing in the town square?

"Do you miss doing research?" I ask. He seems young to be retired—late forties, maybe.

He shrugs. "I got fed up with the corporate side of things—even if we reported rare species, somehow the companies always managed to tear up whatever they wanted. A bunch of the politicians here are corrupt as shit. I mean, as they are everywhere. It's actually shocking the preserve's in good shape."

His words are perfectly timed: We pass the final signs of civilization, and then the island is an impenetrable tangle of green—palm fronds stretching ten feet from stem to feathered tip, mangrove trees squatting at the shoreline, their roots forming a gnarled web.

The corporate side of things. Isn't that, ultimately, what almost every job boils down to? It's strange that this boat ride is a vacation activity for me but a regular Wednesday for them. My chest clutches at the thought of work—the broken code hanging over me, which my brain returns to like a tongue poking at a missing tooth. *Why won't the scheduler work?*

Man . . . when I first got the job at TimeIn, I felt so lucky—behold, a dream role at a buzzy startup with a feminist mission. I was highly paid and high-powered, so remarkably young and nonmale that when a local magazine profiled the company, I got my own sidebar: *Meet the Data Scientist Making AI Work for Moms*. If only.

Eventually, we reach the island's northern tip and curve around an old lighthouse. The water is calm here, gentle sine waves instead of the wild surf we've been cutting through. Esteban eases the boat to rest on a sandbar.

"We'll have lunch here," Pedro announces.

"There's a picnic table in the shade," Rita adds.

My eyebrows lift. "Isn't this protected land?"

Pedro slips off the back of the boat. "I wouldn't call it true protected land, unfortunately. Shit's lax here. But no nesting grounds or endangered species right here, so it's fine."

They splash toward the shore, but I hang back. Esteban has seated himself in front of a blue cooler, and as I watch, he opens it and pulls out a huge fish, eyes bulging, scales glinting pink. He flicks the cooler closed and plops the fish on top, *smack*, then slides a toolbox out from a cubby near his ankles.

I hear the silvery sound of the group's laughter on the beach behind us, but I can't look away. Esteban plunges a knife into the fish's head, slides it along the spine, and hacks off two thick filets. He throws parts overboard as he works, and blood pools on the cooler in melon-colored moons.

He jumps when he notices me.

"Sorry, didn't mean to scare you," I say. "Perdón."

"Está bien." He says something else I don't understand, waving the glistening blade at the shore: *Go have fun with your friends.* I lower myself off the stern, feeling that fresh zip of cool water, and vow to get in some rhythmic breaststroke before we depart.

Rita lounges in the dappled shade, letting the camo-patterned sunlight dry her. I feel a wistful, twisting kind of envy. Opting out of being a contributing member of society to splay in the sun—it's just not something I could do. Not with my lack of a safety net, anyway. But you have to admit, this is . . . nice.

"Abby!" Rita slides her sunglasses down. "Come sit with me."

I pad through the sand and drop onto the edge of her towel. The breeze smells like seashells and brine. I squint at the ocean, white from refracted sunlight. Dead seaweed and knotty mangroves fringe the shore in either direction. I notice a faded beer can caught in the roots and rise. "What happened to Amari and Pedro?" I duck to pluck out the trash. "Did they go inland?"

"I'm sure they're fine."

A Styrofoam plate flaps a few yards away, and then the litter seems to multiply: bits of plastic and aluminum, humans' gross detritus. I shuffle along the shore, cleaning as I go. A seagull screeches; another bird lets out a series of scratchy, hooting coos. I cock my head—was that a voice, low and tense?

I follow the sound into the thick brush and spot them in a clearing, Amari with her back to me, shoulders tense. I crouch a bit to see them better through the palm trees. Pedro leans in close, mouth a defiant line, finger in Amari's face. They're—if not *arguing,* certainly having a tense discussion. But I can't catch their half whispers from here.

Amari starts to turn away, and Pedro grabs her wrist, snarling, "Hey, I'm talking to you."

I flinch and a twig snaps beneath my sandal. Pedro freezes and Amari whips her head back—spotted. I raise the litter in my hands and smile bigly: "Just doing a beach cleanup!"

Amari slackens as soon as she sees me. "Nice. Is the ceviche ready?"

I watch their faces; Pedro's slides into a neutral expression, then a grin. "Esteban makes the *best* ceviche." He's back in hosting mode. "We'll be there in a sec."

I nod and wander off, heart thumping. What was *that*? The argument I thought I glimpsed in the town square this morning—was that actually Pedro and Amari, not Rita? On the beach, our captain is scooping ceviche into plastic bowls while Rita pops open a bag of tortilla chips.

Pedro and Amari appear a moment later, both at ease again, and we sit around the weatherbeaten table.

There are carvings on its surface, names and dates scratched into the wood. All implying the same message: *We were here.* I scan for Eszter's initials, but of course, I don't find them.

I think of the picnic table in Madison that bears my etching: *EF + AB,* enclosed in a heart. We're both rule-followers, and we giggled as I dragged the jackknife's blade against the wood. *Vandal,* Eszter called me. *Scandal!* I replied. I wanted to commemorate our engagement there. After the proposal went so wrong, I needed *some* piece of it to be under my control.

The ceviche is bright and tart and fresh, bursting with jalapeño and citrus. Both Amari and Pedro seem normal, but I notice they never look at each other when addressing the table. Esteban crunches silently, brown eyes trained on the ocean. I look at them one by one. Their dynamic isn't the *least* bit thrown off by Brady's absence?

While Rita finishes a story about fishing for gigantic arapaimas in Brazil, Amari leans over. "I'm mortified you saw us arguing."

My cheeks heat. "Sorry—I wasn't trying to eavesdrop." I catch Pedro eyeing us.

Amari smiles. "You just missed me?" Then her gaze shifts to something behind me. "Whoa, hello there!"

A pigeon-sized bird, iridescent black with a swoosh of scarlet on its head, hops onto the table. Pedro throws his arms in front of Rita's and my chests, like in a car accident.

"Holy shit." He lets out a wild chuckle. "Holy *shit*. Who's got a camera handy?"

Amari grabs her phone and starts snapping.

"What is it?" I murmur.

"That's a red-capped grackle." He's nearly whispering, his face aglow. "They haven't been seen this far east in . . . I don't know, decades. Amari, don't post that!"

The bird lifts off and Amari sets her phone down, eyes wide. "Wait, why?"

"Last thing we need is for this to become a birding destination. They'd be coming in droves." He's downright giddy. "You know, I thought—I thought I saw one a few months ago. But it was in a tree so I figured I must've been totally off base. I was with Eszter, actually."

Coldness shoots through my veins. "You were?"

"Yeah, at the fonda—she asked me to meet, but . . . I never really figured out why. She left kind of suddenly."

Esteban starts collecting bowls and I lean forward, pulse ticking. "When was this?"

Pedro's eyes are still on the trees, scanning. "I dunno, January?" He turns to me and shrugs. "She got out this orange notebook and opened it and closed it and said she had to go. Seemed pretty distracted."

The notebook. "What?" I press my hands on the table, ignoring the bustle of cleaning around us. "What did she want to talk about?"

He lifts his palms. "No idea, hand to God!"

Esteban says something in Spanish and Pedro turns. "Esteban's asking when we want to head back. The wind's picking up and it'll make the ride back choppy."

"We can get going," Amari says.

"Oh, let's stay!" Rita says. "We came all this way. Abby, what do you say?"

I glance at Amari. "Well, I did want to swim. The water's so calm here."

Rita says something to Esteban, then beams. "Great, now we don't have to rush."

As we clean up, my head spins: What on Earth did Eszter want to talk about with Pedro—what would merit the help of her difficult-conversations notebook? Just the sight of that thing, pumpkin-colored and ragtag, gave me heart palpitations; it was the canary in the coal mine, a surefire sign that a wrenching discussion was imminent. I'd seen her use it with me; her father; her best friend, Shane . . . people she knew well, people with whom conflict was an inevitable part of the relationship. But . . . Pedro? What the hell?

You deserve to know the truth, Brady said.

Does that mean everything I know now . . . is a lie?

CHAPTER FOURTEEN

On the ride back, I stand near the bow and stare at the horizon, chasing waves with my eyes, looking hard for dolphins and whales. They had to cajole me out of the water when it was time to go—swimming my slow backstroke, marveling at Pedro's casual admission, I lost track of time.

Glancing down, I spot a jellyfish bobbing near the surface, its top a full moon. The beauty of this place is unspeakable, something Eszter's photos couldn't grasp. Our—or *their*, maybe, or Eszter's—own little world.

"Careful," Pedro says, startling me. "If you drop something here, it's thousands of feet to the ocean floor." I shuffle back, suddenly dizzy.

The beach we departed from comes into view, a few brushstrokes of white sand and leafy green. As we gather our things, I thank Esteban and slip him a tip. He's so surprised he drops it onto the wet floor, drawing everyone's attention as we both stoop to grab it.

While Rita and then Amari slide off the boat's hull, I corner Pedro. "How much do I owe you for our outing?" I fish around in my bag. "I think I have more cash."

He waves his hand. "Don't worry about it."

"I insist! I know I was a late add."

Pedro shakes his head. "You're good."

It's my turn to slide off the boat, and disaster strikes: Gravity catches me before I'm ready, and my knee snags on the propeller. Everyone rushes forward as I right myself in the thigh-deep water. Fantastic.

"Typical graceful dismount." I bow slightly. "I'm fine, I swear."

"Abby, you're bleeding." Rita points. "Have you got bandages?"

"Um . . ." I steady myself on her shoulder to flamingo my leg. A scrape, wide but not deep, scores my kneecap.

"I have some at my place, but they're small," Amari notes.

They're crowding me, three stricken faces, and I try to lighten the mood. "I'm all right, guys, I'm not that fragile! Could someone point me in the direction of the nearest drugstore?"

"There's a little clinic and medical supply shop near the plaza pública," Pedro replies. Mercifully, he heads for the beach and we start moving.

"I'll take you!" Rita trills. "It's easy to miss."

"See you tonight for the sunset?" Amari asks as we reach the road. When I blink at her: "We meet to watch it at Playa Oscura most nights."

"Sure! Sounds great." I force a smile; my stinging knee is becoming more insistent. "Hasta la vista."

"C'mon, then!" Rita sets our pace and we walk in silence for a minute.

"Was I supposed to pay Esteban for the outing?" I finally ask. "I figured Pedro hired him."

She shrugs. "Esteban probably owed him. This whole island runs on the favor economy." She grins. "It's a delicious break from capitalism, really."

"People seemed happy to take my money at the grocery store and café and everything." I pause to blot my knee with the beach towel. "I didn't get the impression the island is, like, a communist utopia."

"That's true, I'm exaggerating." She chuckles. "I just meant . . . well, people aren't so addicted to the grind here. It's much less of a rat race."

I chew on this. "What do you guys do all day?" My eyes widen. "Sorry, that sounded so judgmental."

"It's a fair question! But we all have routines. Amari's very diligent about her art, of course, and always going back and forth to Cancún. Pedro works with the island council on conservation efforts. And Brady likes helping out the locals, especially the aging ones—yard work, that kind of thing. He's a bit hapless but so well-meaning."

Given the chaotic state of his apartment, I can't picture him meticulously maintaining someone's lawn. But then again . . . do I know Brady at all?

"What about you?" I ask.

"Me? I'm the least industrious of us all, I confess," she says. "I'm detoxing from the corporate world."

"You don't get . . . bored?"

She smiles. "There are many things much worse than boredom. Here we are." She stops in front of a windowless concrete building on an otherwise residential street. I assure her I can take it from here.

But the man behind the counter—is he a medical professional, a pharmacist, simply a cashier?—asks something I don't understand and, when I nod, tells me to sit. Before I can stop him, he kneels and starts to bandage the knee himself—a dab of carrot-colored iodine, a rectangle of gauze, his eyes and gloved hands gentle as he winds the roll around my leg. To my great humiliation, tears spring into my eyes.

Everyone here is so dang *nice*. This place really is a kind of paradise.

So how could it have taken the love of my life from me?

I reach my rental and key in the door code, then step inside, drained and dopey from the sun. After a glass of water and a moment in the cool stillness, I decide to venture back out and check on Brady myself. Rita implied he might be hiding out—abstract references to his mental health—and I want to make sure he's okay.

That's a reasonable, responsible thing to do, right? I'm not selfishly tracking him down to find out what he wanted to tell me.

I backtrack a few blocks, skirting a dog that pants at me from the side of the road. The lime-green duplex is gaudier in the sun; a gecko zips up the wall, then disappears around the corner. The wind chimes sway, and today their peal sounds ominous, dissonant.

"Brady?" My pulse doubles as I approach the front door. I rap on it, then peer through the window.

For a second, I think I'm at the wrong house. This one is impeccably clean, kitchen gleaming, cabinets closed, books lined up on the shelf like soldiers in a battalion. My heart thuds. *This isn't right.*

The practical voice pipes up: *So he finally cleaned his house. He's had plenty of time since you stopped here last night.* Maybe the mess was the anomaly; maybe this is Brady's natural state.

But . . . what if something *is* wrong? My fist pounds on the window as I yell his name into the glass. I picture Eszter gasping for air a quarter-mile away, spied only by the spiders and beetles. If I'd been there, if someone had heard her struggling or spotted her through the windows . . .

The purple welcome mat is slightly askew in front of the door. "Screw this," I murmur, stooping to grope below it. My hand closes around the key and, fingers shaking, I let myself in.

The floor tiles sparkle and a sickly clean smell permeates the air, bleach and artificial fragrance. I call his name a few more times. I poke my head into the bathroom—spotless—and the bedroom in the back. The bed's neatly made and in the closet, clothes dangle from wire hangers. The casita looks like it went through a Marie Kondo makeover, so tidy it should send my blood pressure plummeting.

So why is my heart still thumping against my ribs?

I pull out my new phone—*his* phone—and tap Brady's name. Tilt my head, listening hard. A clock on the nightstand ticks; through the window, the trees rattle and sigh. The buzz of a bug pierces through like someone strumming a washboard.

Wait—that's not a bug.

I pad farther into the living room and call him again. It's unmistakable this time, the *bzzzt* of a vibrating phone. I rush around until I spot it: his phone cowering below the sofa, facedown. My name's on the screen, and then it switches to a tally—five missed calls. I tap, but I don't know his password.

So he headed out and chose to leave his phone behind, a voice argues, the pragmatic one, slow to panic. *He's not tech-addicted like the rest of us. He cleaned his home and ditched his devices and he's out enjoying this beautiful day, and when he reappears he'll crack up at my freaked-out expression:* Crikey, Abby, you look like you've seen a ghost!

But the house feels all wrong, like someone's scrubbed away any trace of him. I set his phone on the coffee table and head for the front door, then freeze with my hand on the knob.

Shivering, I approach Brady's bookshelf. My eyes slide along the titles; they're mostly in Spanish, yellowed paperbacks from the eighties, presumably in the apartment when he moved in. I'm about to give up when I spot it, its spine cracked and wrinkled like an elephant's hide: Brady's treasured copy of *The Year of Magical Thinking.*

My pulse bangs as I press a finger to its top and slide it out. *It's the one and only thing I brought all the way from Australia,* he told me. *I'd never go anywhere without it.*

I step back and my heel snags on something, and for a split second, I see it: my foot thudding against the contorted form of Eszter on the floor, her hazel eyes glassy, skin flushed, hands and feet all shiny-swollen. My tongue freezes midswallow as if my own throat were constricting, and the book slips from my hands, bouncing off my foot before coming to rest splayed open on the floor.

I stumble backward, hands pressed to my mouth, the realization so awful it knocks the wind right out of me.

I asked him about Eszter.

He said he had something to tell me.

And a few hours later—he disappeared.

CHAPTER FIFTEEN
ABBY

October 7, 2023 (seven months ago)

This wasn't right.

I'd sketched out every detail—it was a simple plan, sure, no frills, but I'd been watching the weather for days, excitement brewing in my chest, relieved we'd have a sunny October Saturday for my nonsplashy proposal. As we approached the key spot of our hike along Lake Mendota, though, dark clouds slipped across the sky, steady and sure, like a stadium's retractable roof. The wind picked up, stirring orange and brown leaves, and Eszter grabbed my hand.

"It's fine," she said. Obliviously. "We'll pick up the pace."

But we couldn't because this was the spot, *our* spot, a clearing with a storybook view of the lake. We'd eaten so many lunches here, sandwiches and artisanal sodas on a weatherworn picnic table.

"Let's pause." I set my backpack on the bench. "I brought orejas. Hopefully they aren't too crushed." (They wouldn't be crushed. I'd packed them meticulously.)

She frowned. "Don't you think we should head back?"

I swallowed my frustration. "We'll make it quick."

My pulse thundered in my ears as she shrugged and leaned her hip against the wood. I took her in: thick, golden-blond hair and full eye-brows, a sharp nose and chin, and lash-fringed eyes that drifted to the side when she was thinking. Features I loved; features I knew as well as my own. God, how could someone so spectacular exist? And want to be with *me*? Behind her, sailboats skidded across the blue water, white sails shiny and taut. They seemed to be hurrying back to the shore, also sensing a cold autumn rain.

You can do this, Abby.

I reached into my bag again, and my fingers closed around the velvet box. I took a deep breath and cleared my throat. I'd just started to pull it out when—

"Fuuuuck, look at those clouds!"

We whipped around to see a trio of undergrads heading toward us, two guys and a girl, eyes reddened and glassy. Oh, come *on*—pothead intruders? *Now?*

"Do you guys think it's going to rain?" asked a girl with long pigtails sprouting from a knit cap. She wandered over and a skunky smell wafted off her clothes.

"Are you asking us?" Eszter said after a confused second. They turned, blank-faced and blinking like three owls.

"Why—are you, like, meteorologists?" The guy in a massive denim jacket presented it as a genuine question.

Eszter glanced down at the table, where the orejas still sat. She winked at me, then turned to them. "Hey, would you like some cookies?"

I shot her a puzzled look—*No, I want them to* leave. The three zoomed toward her like fish converging on chum.

"What are they?" the girl asked.

"They're called orejas," I said.

Denim Jacket turned to me, thunderstruck. "That means 'ears.'"

Eszter thrust the container into his chest. "They're delicious. Take them home and have them with hot chocolate and listen to the rain."

Their eyes lit up and they exchanged giddy grins.

"Thank you!" He grabbed the plastic tub and took off. The others followed, like they feared we'd change our minds. We laughed as they disappeared between the trees, and then the first drop of rain hit my face. Eszter was like that—generous in a way that felt so natural, so second nature. She brought me coffee in bed and folded my laundry with that same gentle sureness. I was still getting used to it, slowly letting go of the part of me that panicked over being unworthy of her kindness.

"Should we head home?" Eszter said again.

The show must go on. "Just a second. There's something I wanna do."

I fished out the ring box and dropped to one knee. I felt the Earth's chilly crust through my jeans. Eszter froze, eyes wide.

"Eszter . . ." I began.

And then, *right freaking then,* a boat blasted its horn, cutting me off like a censor. I let out a frustrated howl and Eszter laughed, pulling me up to stand.

"Are you asking me to marry you?" She could be so hard to read, not overjoyed, not turned off, just . . . alert. Certainly not certain.

"I am! I mean, it went a little differently in my head. But I love you. And I'm asking you to marry me."

She looked around. "Is someone filming us?"

"No. It's just us."

"And everyone we know isn't about to pop out of the woodwork and cheer?"

"Of course not. You'd hate that." I stepped forward and kissed her, smiled against her mouth. "Gimme a second to cancel the flash mob, real quick."

She cracked up, whacking me gently on the shoulder. Her eyes dropped to the box. "The ring is stunning. I love it."

Is that a yes? I slipped it out of its case and onto her finger. She held it up to the gray light, watching it sparkle.

"Where did you get it from?"

I grinned. "I'm glad you like it. I actually ordered it online— I googled 'sustainable, cruelty-free emeralds' and found this awesome woman-owned startup in Portland."

She shook her head, amazed. "And just like that, you had a ring?"

"Why drag my feet?" I replied.

We often joked about how quickly I could pick things out; while she could spend weeks researching, say, couches, I could find a this'll-do sofa in two hours flat. She taught me the Hungarian phrase for my pro-active approach: *Az idő pénz. Time is money.*

The rain was a three-dimensional drizzle, like being in a cold steam room. "I hate to further sully this magic moment, Eszter, but you still haven't answered." I laughed nervously. "Is it because I leave my shoes in front of the door? It's because of the shoes, isn't it."

She smiled. "It's not the shoes. I love you. I don't have any doubts about that."

My chest constricted as I squeezed her hands in mine. "But?"

She looked away and I couldn't help it—I started monologuing. "What we have is special. We're such a good fit. You make me more pa-tient. Kinder. You—you got me into yoga and barre and classical music. And I got you into hiking, right? And . . . hopefully have had some other positive impact in your life?" She chuckled, but her posture didn't relax. "We could have a beautiful life together. I've loved living with you this past year. In spring you'll finish B-school, and then we can go anywhere, do anything . . ." I lowered my hands to her waist. "What is it?"

She looked away. "The idea of a wedding . . . it makes me nervous."

"I know. You hate being the center of attention. But we can keep it small. Or do a courthouse thing. Hell, we can elope if you want." I brought her hand to my lips and planted a kiss there. "I promise, I really thought this through. We can decide together how it'll go down."

She nodded, thinking. "My parents . . ."

"It's your life, Eszter. Not theirs."

She leaned away—a fraction of an inch, but I felt it, and a dark, cold panic started swirling in my belly.

"Eszter," I said urgently, "this isn't about them. We don't need to do it in one of your dad's hotels. We don't need their money. We don't even need their blessing. This is about *us*."

Her eyes dropped. "The thing is . . ."

"Are you worried about making me compromise?" My voice rose— a protestation. "Yeah, I said I wanted a big wedding with a photo booth and live band and everything. But that was before I really knew what I wanted. It's not about the wedding, you know?"

She swallowed. "You shouldn't have to settle."

I waited for the full blast of her eyes. They seemed to change color depending on the lighting—now, in the steely drizzle, they were greenish gold.

"If you don't want to do this, that's okay," I said slowly. "And if you want to take a while to think about it, that's okay too. But I don't care about some big party. I'm ready. I love you. I love our life together and I'll wait as long as I need to."

She hugged me tight. "I hate feeling like you're accommodating me. Like I'm messing things up for you." She nestled into my neck. "You should have everything you want and more."

"Look—you're my family. All I care about is marrying you."

The wind rattled dry, crispy leaves and then she sniffled. *Oh God, is she crying?*

"But you . . . you *love* being the center of attention," she said.

I laughed. "I know! I love the spotlight. But you know what I love more?"

She pulled back to look at me. There was an entire world in her eyes—words trapped behind them, maybe, something she didn't want to say.

"What?" she said.

And I answered, "Loving you."

A slow smile stretched across her face and I nearly melted with relief: She was going to say yes. Thunder cracked and rain poured over us, like it had been collecting on a tarp in the sky this whole time. We grabbed our bags and hurried to the trail, ducking as drops found us beneath the trees.

"I brought champagne!" I called over my shoulder, laughing. "It's getting all shaken up." We burst out of the woods and paused at a red light. "Man, I had a whole plan. A simple one, but a plan nonetheless."

"Okay, control freak." Eszter's hand found mine. "Isn't the important thing that I'm saying yes?"

I turned to her, glowing. "Really?"

She nodded, giggling.

I kissed her in the cold downpour. "It's the most important thing by far."

CHAPTER SIXTEEN
ABBY

Wednesday afternoon

I pick up the paperback and, after a moment's hesitation, shove it deep in my bag. Something about the way he pulled it from his backpack and then ripped it away, clutching it to his chest, stuck with me; what did he want me to both see and not see? I shudder and head outside, then find the stairs in the back of Brady's building. On the second floor, a petite, wrinkled woman answers the door.

"Sí, Brady," she says, after watching me point and signal and repeat his name with my hands cupped like binoculars. "No lo he visto."

I catch her meaning and bite my lip, rummaging through my paltry vocabulary. "¿Qué pasa?" I try. "Qué pasa with Brady?"

She shrugs, shakes her head again. I'm the obnoxious white woman, spraying English her way: "When did you last see him?" Her palms open, like, *I got nothing,* and I thank her and turn away.

On the road, dried leaves and beetles crack beneath my feet. *Be reasonable, Abby.* I hold still for a moment, ferreting around in my own psyche. I barely know Brady. Am I overreacting?

I need to tell you something, Eszter said. A window cracked but never closed. And I clung to it . . . in order to keep our interactions, our *rela-*

tionship, open-ended. A mystery smoldering at the center of our love. But I know Occam's razor; the simplest explanations are uncomfortable, sure—walking back the wedding, even breaking up—but also most likely to be true. Her secret, her medical emergency, Brady's intel, his sudden ghosting . . . there's no reason they should all intersect.

But no matter how many times I turn it over, it doesn't make sense. The stepping stones of logic are right there: He was about to deliver some smoking gun, something about Eszter's final days here or even her death, and someone . . .

It's too ridiculous to put into words. What, someone shut him up? This isn't a mob movie; there was *nothing* suspicious about Eszter's death.

Except that she died at all. It runs through me again, that quill of suspicion. Eszter never lost track of her EpiPen, never ate something she wasn't sure about, never let her guard down.

I cross the street, narrowly missing a fat frog flattened by a tire, poor thing. Even if I lend the situation the least-sinister interpretation (Brady wanted to share a cute memory and intended for us to meet tomorrow), that doesn't explain his sterilized apartment or the phone and book he left behind. Something is off, though I have no idea what.

Think, Abby. It's a small island. If he's still here, he shouldn't be hard to find; if he left of his own volition, like Amari suggested, someone must know about it. I turn toward downtown, then groan. My barebones phone can't handle a translation app, and my old one is twenty thousand leagues under the sea. I can't do much info-gathering when I don't speak Spanish.

Rita answers the phone cheerily.

"Any chance you feel like being my translator?" I try to sound breezy. I hate being dependent on people, but I don't see another way around it.

"Sure! Why?" There's that German directness.

I kick a chunky stone out of my path. "I tried to check on Brady. And his apartment was spotless, like someone had something to hide, and—"

"You went inside his apartment?"

"I . . . I wanted to make sure he's okay." Flash: Eszter crumpled on the linoleum, face puffed, chest red. "His phone was on the floor—isn't that a bad sign, too? Who forgets their phone and doesn't come back for it?"

"If anyone would do it, it's Brady," she says. "But that *is* odd. Have you checked the main square? He's often in the fonda."

"Well, that's why I wanted your help. I'd like to ask around."

The line hisses between us. I've reached the iguana again, and I zero in on its frizzled feet—like slivered onions left on the stove too long.

"I'll help you," she finally says. "Meet me at the fonda. Try not to worry—he probably had some errand to run on the mainland." Before I can ask her more, she hangs up.

My ears hum as I make my way down the main road. *You deserve to know the truth about Eszter.* Talk about unfair: I came here seeking clarity on her ambiguous text . . . and instead received an even more baffling one.

I'm splotched in sweat by the time I burst into the restaurant. There are a few more customers now than in the morning, but still, most of the tables are empty. The pretty server with the braided updo offers me a greasy menu, its lamination peeling around the edges.

"Hello!" Rita calls, her tone all *Yoo-hoo!* "No sign of Brady, I take it?"

I shake my head. "I thought maybe someone here could tell us if he chartered a boat out."

She takes in the café's patrons. "Let's go across the street. That's where the fishermen will be."

"'Across the street'?" I repeat, following her out.

She motors through the plaza to what looks like a regular casita: sandstone walls, postage-stamp windows. But there's a tiny sign next to the door: CASA HERRERA.

"This is a locals-only joint," Rita explains, rapping on the door. "They won't be thrilled to see us, exactly, but we'll be quick."

A man holding a Dos Equis answers the door, looking polite but confused as Rita explains why we're here. Even to my foreign ear, Rita's accent sounds Germanic, *ähm*s peppering her sentences, *R*'s deep in her throat. Still, I'm impressed—she keeps smiling and gets through it. Learning languages has never been a skill of mine; I hate doing things I'm bad at, and butchering a foreign tongue brings out my rare shy side.

Finally the man replies and opens the door wide. A few faces take us in as we step into a living room sprinkled with chairs and two folding tables. On one, dominoes form a strange, many-limbed monster. A cat bathes itself on a floor pillow near the window, and cumbia music leaks from a stereo.

"He said almost all the fishermen he knows are working today," Rita reports. "They went out late because of the rain and won't be back for a few more hours."

But I spot our boat captain drinking a Jarritos and wave. "Let's talk to Esteban. Can you ask if he knows if someone took Brady to Cancún?"

He listens to her politely. After a moment, she turns to me. "He's not sure, since no one's back yet."

I tilt my head. "Is he saying they *wouldn't* have taken him? Or that we'll have to wait until they get back to find out?"

She turns, clarifies.

"I think both. Someone might've done it for the right price. But he hasn't heard of anyone taking anyone to Cancún."

At my urging, she asks Esteban to let us know if that changes—if word gets out about a scrawny Australian man being shuttled ashore.

We pop into the convenience store, the medical clinic with its kind-eyed employee, sheepishness plastered on my face as I stop empty-handed at registers and prompt Rita to ask: *Have you seen Brady? The short, blond man from Australia?* Gloria, her yard of hair in a fist-thick ponytail, greets us at the grocery store, and I'm hugely relieved to be able to ask without an interlocutor. But her answer is the same as all the shopkeepers', and my chest squeezes tighter with every no.

We pause in the center of the town square. "I'm sorry that didn't bear fruit." Rita lingers, like a kid waiting to be dismissed.

"Rita, there's something else." I tell her about my trauma swap with Brady and show her the text he sent early this morning. "My gut is telling me something's very wrong," I conclude, eyes flushing with tears. "Doesn't it sound like Brady knew something about how she died? Like it wasn't as cut-and-dried as I thought?"

She looks horrified. "I'm sorry, Abby. That must be so . . . destabiliz-ing."

I nod, lowering my sunglasses over my leaky eyes.

"You said he opened up about his parents?" She waves me over to a bench. "I'm going to tell you something private and ask you not to repeat it. Brady's wonderful but troubled. Well, you know—he told you how he lost one parent and is estranged from the other. There's a mental health clinic in Cancún that he's checked himself into a couple times when he felt . . . overwhelmed."

I lean forward. "You think he's there?"

"I don't know. He didn't say anything to me. But talking about his parents is hard for him, so if that prompted him to disappear . . ." She taps her temple, like I gave her the idea.

I don't believe you. The thought shoots through me before I can stop it. But . . . but the adult part of me is the one that replies. "Got it. Thanks for telling me. I know I'm grasping at straws here."

"Don't worry. He'll turn up. If I had to guess, this all has nothing to do with Eszter."

My insides contract. "You think?"

"It's very human," she says kindly, "to look for patterns—see connections that don't exist. Whatever you seek, you find." She points to a vine slinking up the trunk of a palm tree. It's foaming with fuchsia blossoms, each like a tiny firework. "Take the sómbravid. I didn't notice it for months, and then Pedro pointed it out one day; apparently the petals are full of tannins, good for getting a cut to stop bleeding. And as soon as I started looking for it, well . . ."

She sweeps her arm around the plaza and it's like she's brandishing a magic wand, because now, the blooms are *everywhere:* shinnying up the trees, stippling the path, winding around ferns and shrubs and bushes.

"Apparently it flourished after the hurricane," she says, "because so many trees lost their leaves or even limbs—so it could take over all that real estate. Hearty little things."

"Sómbravid," I repeat. "What does it translate to?"

"'Shadow vine.' But I don't know why it's called that—look, it's thriving in the direct sun here." She shrugs. "Pedro would know: *It's obvious, Rita, you just look at the root system. Even a child knows that.*"

I'm taken aback—Rita does a surprisingly good American accent. She snickers. "He knows more about plants than God, and he loves prattling on about them."

I think back to their taut voices. "I know it's none of my business," I say, "but this morning, before the boat ride, I was at the fonda, and . . . I thought I heard you and Pedro arguing in the town square."

She leans back. "Ohh, it was nothing. Suffice it to say he's kinder to the island than the people on it."

A cold tingle climbs my neck. "What do you mean?"

She waves it away. "Just that he's a . . . what's the word? Mansplainer."

I peer at her for a moment, then smile. "Amari called him a 'disgruntled uncle.' "

Rita snorts. "She's not wrong. I probably shouldn't tell you this, but . . ." Her eyes glitter. "Gloria—she runs the supermarket? Well, she knows everything and everyone here. And she told me that when Pedro first arrived here, he fell in love. Pretty girl, a local. Couldn't wait to get married. But then . . . as soon as she got her green card, she was off to America. He was gutted."

"She left him? It was all a ruse?"

Rita screws up her mouth. "Or he couldn't bring himself to move back with her."

I tilt my head. "He's head-over-heels, but he won't even consider following her?"

Rita smirks. "Weren't we just talking about how much he loves this island? Still, he was devastated."

"And that's his villain origin story?" I say.

" 'Villain'!" She laughs. "From what I hear, he already had a checkered past. Not that . . ." She fades out, like she's overstepped.

"What do you mean?"

"No, sorry." She shakes her head. "It's like I told you the other night—on Isla Colel, everyone gets a fresh start."

My chest flushes with shame, like I'm a bad person for prying. But wasn't Rita the one sharing bygone gossip? A bird whips by, so close I can hear the dry slap of its beating wings. I didn't push Brady off the island, did I? Bubbling up his trauma by bringing up my own?

I thank Rita and tell her I'll see her at sunset. I hesitate—I'm the outsider, pestering an established group—then text Amari: "Do you think it's weird that Brady left his phone in his apartment?" I sit there for a few minutes, hungrily watching people trickle past, willing one to be Brady, open-faced and cheery, ready to spill his guts.

CHAPTER SEVENTEEN

Data, Abby—you need data. This is what I do: process noisy data and draw conclusions. But where to find it? I rise and head north and scan Playa Oscura, where the waves are once again ferocious. I cross the island and survey the span of Playa Destello, where I first encountered Brady cooking snapper to a crisp. I walk along the coastline, looking for the bio bay that we approached like ducklings, all in a row, but by day the entire eastern coastline looks fetid and flat. I stare at the tide and wonder if, late tonight, it'll light up like a switchboard.

The thought tickles my brain, like there's an idea just out of reach. Another avenue I haven't tapped yet. But what?

I head back through the neighborhood, then down the dead-end road leading up to my place, calle sin salida. Biting flies and winged roaches speckle the front porch, like they're waiting for me.

Inside, I turn on my laptop and ask my friend Mei when she can talk. When I close the messaging app, the window behind it pops to the forefront: new Slack alerts from my team at TimeIn. My stomach twists; if I fall too far behind on work, I'll become a jobless loser too. As I scan through the messages, the laptop explodes with noise—Mei with an incoming video call.

Her face bobs as she holds her phone up, walking. "Abby! What's up?"

I try to explain, but I keep starting at the wrong place, talking in circles. My eyes heat with frustrated tears.

She stops on a street corner. "Take a deep breath, Abby. I'm listening."

She's hitting me with her most earnest listening face and I nod. Mei is . . . one of the best people I know. We met volunteering at a girls' coding camp right after college, and she has the distinct ability to put anyone at ease. She's sort of a Debbie Downer, always saying what everyone else is thinking ("So that networking event was a huge bust, huh?"), but somehow it's disarming instead of demoralizing—like I can be *real* with her even when everyone else expects the Best Me. When I got the big job at TimeIn, amid the tidal wave of congratulations and *You must be so excited!!!*s, Mei tilted her head: *Damn, Abby, that job sounds like an ass-ton of work. Are you nervous?*

I try again: the expats from Eszter's photo, Brady's text, Brady's mysterious absence, and everyone's bewildering nonchalance. When I'm finished, she peers at me for a second and then starts walking again. "Babe, I know you like to carry the entire world on your shoulders. But this isn't your battle."

I sit up straight. "It is, though. Eszter—"

"Right, I know—you'd give anything for some clarity there. But it sounds like you've made finding Grady—"

"Brady."

"—Brady your responsibility, and it's not."

I blink away tears. She's right. "But what if he had something important to tell me? And that's why . . ." I can't finish the sentence. It's ridiculous. Someone, what—kept him from squealing?

A police siren whoops behind Mei. "Sounds like he's on the mainland, getting the help he needs," she says. "Maybe he, I don't know, drunk texted you because he and Eszter had some disagreement and he wanted to talk shit. And then he slept it off and was like, *D'oh, I need help*. I don't know. It's really not that surprising to me that a backpacker who rolled in from across the world floated away in the middle of the night. But whatever it is . . . I'm Team Abby. What does Abby need?"

To talk to Brady, I think, but I look away.

She furrows her brow. "You really want to find him."

I nod.

Mei sighs. She's against a brick wall now, a glass door visible behind her. "You could try to track down the facility," she says, "although they probably can't give out the names of whoever checks in."

I drum my fingers along my jaw. "I wonder if there's another way to figure out what happened when Eszter was here. I mean, that was my stated purpose for coming: I wanted to piece together her last few days. Other than talking to people, I mean, since . . . now I don't have Google Translate on my phone."

"Right. If only you could click 'show in English' IRL."

This knocks loose the idea that tickled my brain a half hour ago: PDC. *Kind of a hyperlocal Facebook,* Brady told me. *Great for lurking.*

"There's one thing I can try," I say. "I should let you go." I promise to keep her posted and send her off with my hands folded into a heart.

Here it is: PachangaDeColel.mx. I make an account and start to scroll, and Brady wasn't kidding: It's like an even-less-refined Nextdoor or Reddit, with people posting questions or topics and others replying below. It's almost all in Spanish, but my browser translates it with a single click.

Xavier is selling a kiddie pool. Rosa wants to buy a sewing machine. Hector is complaining about wet, brimming potholes after a hard rain, the same pools I circumnavigated this morning.

My pulse ticks like a time bomb. I search for *Eszter:* nothing. I try alternate spellings, *Esther, Ester:* still nothing. *American, gringa, allergies, medical, emergency, anaphylaxis, rescue* . . . I read through all the posts that pop up but none are right, none are even close, and none of the dates are anywhere near Eszter's death.

There's an Advanced Search function in the corner, and I set the date range for the week of and following Eszter's death on January 14. I hit Buscar and my laptop buzzes, like it's exhausted from the effort.

January 13: Manuel was setting up a greenhouse in his backyard and recommended hiring Carlos if anyone needed help building one too. Blurry pictures backed him up.

And then a jump, a time warp in the feed—January 20: The entire community was invited to Julieta's daughter's quinceañera. I scroll up and down, up and down, then I refresh the site, because I can't believe what I'm seeing.

Someone scrubbed from the site the entire week of Eszter's death.

Nothing on the internet truly ever disappears, so I check for cached versions, visit Archive.org. No dice, since you need to log in to see the posts.

Fingers shaking, I tap out a message: *I'm trying to find a post from January 14, 2024. Does anybody know why all posts from January 14–19 were deleted?* Translate, copy-paste, post.

While I wait for a response, I return to the home page. Maybe Brady used this very site to plan his escape? A search for his name yields nothing. Frustrated, I try everything related to planning a private egress: *boat, mainland, captain, charter, ferry*. I pick at my nails. He said he was a lurker . . . did he truly never post? Where are you, Brady King?

King. I search for the Spanish word, *rey,* and there he is: *ydarbrey.* It's his first name backward and his last name in translation and I can't click on his profile fast enough. There's his dorky little photo, a far-off, full-body shot of him from behind, donning what appears to be a seersucker suit. The screen fills with his comments, newest at the top, the translations a bit garbled from going from English to Spanish to English again:

Does anyone have a grill brush I can borrow?

Adriana, I can care for your hamster while you are away!

Have you tried OK Kayak Cancún?

Historically, he posted a few times a week. But his latest is six days old. Nothing telling or suspicious, just dead silence since then. I rub my forehead, a headache blooming. What am I even looking for?

I scroll back, back, back, his comments and replies and cheerful exchanges all turning into a blur. I stop at random: In November, he thanked Silvana for sharing a flyer about a holiday market on the mainland. In August, he tried to organize a community cleanup of the smelly seaweed along Playa Destello. I go back in time, further and further, watching him crowdsource the region's best hot sauce, search for the owner of a sweatshirt he found in the town square, offer up homemade kombucha after he brewed too much (zero replies) . . .

This isn't working. I search for Pedro and Amari—no hits. Are they not on the site, or are their usernames creative as well? I find an account for Rita, with a few recent posts. Gloria, the grocer, makes an appearance too, announcing store closures and answering questions about their holiday hours.

I can't wait any longer—I return to the home page, check for replies.

Wait. This isn't right. I refresh, refresh again.

Other posts appear, ones newer than mine. Xavier is selling a laser printer. Gabriela's giving away new cat treats rejected by her gatito.

It's undeniable. I gasp and lean away from the computer.

My post about the week in January is gone.

CHAPTER EIGHTEEN

My heartbeat echoes in my ears. I submit the post anew, checking a box so that any replies will be emailed to me—maybe someone will help me before a mysterious admin deletes it this time.

I post a second message, shot through Google Translate: *I'm trying to find Brady, a short, blond Australian man, who hasn't been seen since yesterday. Has anyone seen him? Did anyone with a boat help him get off the island?*

I roll the mouse back and forth over the time gap, January 13 abutting January 20, zero acknowledgment of the chasm between. Rita made a joke about the site being out of date, possibly glitchy—is this absent week a coincidence, one of several missing chunks? For a second time, I start scrolling backward. Every day there's a fresh crop of posts, a drumbeat of timestamps I syncopate in my head: 13, 12, 11, 10. I reach the February day when TimeIn was supposed to have its first live demo, my original deadline, the date by which I'd promised Tyler a workable product. A lie—I wasn't actually close to rooting out the calendar bug then, and I'm no closer now.

I scroll through winter, fall, summer. So far, not a single day is unaccounted for; not a day went by without at least one post, mundane things—the quotidian favor economy that, like Rita said, keeps a small community humming. I slow as the one-year mark appears. If there isn't an innocent explanation . . . all that's left are sinister ones.

My stomach feels like a rock. I close the window and the screen pulses with Slack messages. *When are you back? Can you make it to this meeting?* Cringing, I drop something vague into the #announcements channel about getting back to everyone ASAP. I text Rita to ask for the name of Brady's clinic, then google *inpatient mental health facility Cancún* and call a few. The receptionists all speak English, but as Mei suspected, they can't share patients' names.

I get up and make myself a snack, then wash a few dishes in the sink. The hiss of the faucet, warm water and porcelain and bubbles against my skin. I could scream.

Brady's book stares at me on the kitchen table, its pale yellow cover like the sun on a hazy day. *I want to show you something.* He smiled as he rummaged through his bookbag. Relaxed, not like someone on the verge of a breakdown.

"'The seminal book on grief,'" I murmur. I started doing this after Eszter died, voicing inane thoughts as if there were still someone around to hear them. I flip through the paperback's browned pages, searching for clues in Brady's small, even lettering, neat as the speech bubbles in a graphic novel. I feel a bulge of guilt—*Oh, you can't look at it!*—but the notes are remarkably unremarkable. Underlines and brackets and five-pointed stars, a few sentence fragments that make my heart ache: *tyranny of distance, forgetting = another death, time as circle.*

Toward the end, a flash of white. There's a piece of paper tucked deep inside. I unfold it, and it takes me a second to make sense of the squiggly lines and small letters: a hand-drawn map of Isla Colel. It's a bit messy and pockmarked, like it was copied on a dirty Xerox pane, and I squint to read the annotations: *Playa Oscura. Playa Destello. Plaza pública,* i.e., the town square, populated with little rectangular businesses, and the tiny port, complete with a cartoon ferry. The bio bay with (I squint) a miniature crescent moon next to it. The main road up into the residential area, with a burst of blocky casitas along the beehive of streets there. I do it without thinking, the way you search for yourself in a group photo: My vacation rental is . . . there, an unmarked spot on an unnamed drive.

I flex the sheet's creases. The handwriting looks different from the notes in Brady's book. Who made this, and, more important, why is it here?

There's a whirl of red ink in the center of the page, where someone—Brady?—circled a point of interest. It's the dilapidated hotel I keep hearing about, Paraíso Escondido. *Surrounded by barbed wire,* Pedro warned. *Nobody should be up there.*

The fridge clunks on. A gray gecko skates up the wall. I glance at my new phone, see that no one's texted me, no replies or updates or expressions of additional concern for Brady. Old, blackened blood peeks through the gauze on my knee and sand prickles my toes and calves. I look back at the map.

Then I stand, determined, and beeline for the front door.

I fling it open and shriek—someone's there, *right there,* nearly barreling into me. Amari. She takes a few steps back and tugs at a curlicue of hair.

"Whoa, sorry. I was about to knock."

Despite everything, the observation zips across my mind: *God, she's pretty.*

"It's okay. What's up?"

"Should we sit?" A small smile. "I like your patio. I've got the *one* casita on the block that doesn't have a front porch . . . just a soggy backyard."

"How did you know which house I'm in?"

She grins. "You think I don't take note when someone hot shows up on my street?"

My chest fizzes again. *Don't be ridiculous, Abby.*

"It's the only vacation rental left," she adds.

"*Your* street? You're here too?"

She throws her hand out. "Yeah, a couple doors down. So listen." She lowers herself into a chair. "I saw your text. You went to his apartment?"

I nod. "Which was *impeccably* clean today, unlike when he had me over."

She studies me. "You went inside?"

"I . . . had to make sure he was okay." I frown. "You haven't been?"

"I went by too, but he wasn't there." She drums her fingers on her thigh. "I really thought we'd have heard from Brady by now. I guess he can't contact us if he doesn't have his phone."

I feel an illogical spurt of guilt for taking his burner phone. "You think something's wrong?" I realize, abruptly, how much I was relying on everyone else's nonchalance to sand the edges off my panic. It's like when you argue and argue and argue and then the other person comes around and suddenly, *snap!* Everything changes, *wait, let's not be too hasty . . .*

"I don't know." She crosses her legs. "I was just downtown. Gloria said you and Rita asked about him."

"Right. We talked to a bunch of people, but no one knew anything." I lean forward. "Should we be trying to find him together? No reason to duplicate efforts." I cringe—it's a term Tyler's always using at TimeIn.

She nods. "Do you have any theories?"

I peer at her for a second. "Well, he did seem kind of upset on Tuesday. After the bio bay."

"Right," she says. "The last time any of us saw him."

Us. Like I'm one of them. But I'm not; I get the feeling this group knows how to circle the wagons, and I am definitely outside that ring.

I swallow. "When I was at his place, he told me about his parents. We were talking about loss and . . . people unexpectedly leaving your life. Which is ironic, I guess, since he promptly disappeared." I chew my lip. "Rita mentioned Brady deals with depression."

She nods. "But it's not just that. Also self-harm and . . . and suicidal ideation."

"Oh, jeez."

"Yeah. I mean, I don't want to assume the worst." She picks at her fingernails. "I just wish I knew where he was."

I play the conversation back in my mind. He told me about his abusive father . . . and how his mom died, which spurred him to pack up and leave . . .

A circuit connects. "Wait, was his mom . . . did his dad . . . ?"

She nods. "That's what he told me. The official story was that she tripped and fell down the stairs. His dad's some corporate bigwig and made the whole thing go away."

My fingers curl into a fist. The entitlement of high-up men—I know it well. My boss, Tyler; Eszter's father—they wield power in this casual, comfortable way, grabbing it like a pen whenever their reputations are threatened, sniffing, nonchalant, *Oh yes, that's mine.*

"That's awful." She hasn't mentioned the mental health clinic Rita brought up. Amari and Brady are close—practically siblings, she told me—but did he withhold this from her? I can relate . . . I told both Rita and Brady things I was too ashamed to share with Mei in Madison.

I sit up. "What should we do? Should we file an official missing person report?" I hate that we have to have this conversation, but . . . there's some forward momentum to it, someone to brainstorm with, someone who isn't looking at me like I'm out of my mind.

"I thought about that. But then there will be an official record that he's here."

I frown. "Which is a problem because . . . ?"

"He has a no-photos rule. He doesn't want his dad to know where he is."

"It's not like he's off the grid. He had to use his passport to enter Mexico, right?"

"Sure, but that's different—you can't just ask every country's border patrol to give you a heads-up if your son passes through. Even if you are as rich and powerful as his father." She takes a deep breath. "Brady agreed to see his dad in San Francisco a couple years ago. He was even considering reconciling. And it went . . . very badly."

"What happened?"

"Well, first of all, his dad sent these private detectives to track him down at home, which was obviously scary—strangers following him and whatnot. Then they dropped off a note from his father saying he'd be at such-and-such restaurant on such-and-such date and wanted to see him. The note made it sound like he wanted to patch things up, so Brady was considering it—he showed up to the restaurant late and was, like, working up the courage to approach him."

I tense for what's next: "Then what?"

She sighs. "I guess his dad was drinking . . . and he decided Brady had stood him up? And he *freaked out*. Screamed at the waiter, broke a glass. Brady was outta there."

I whimper. "Poor guy."

"I know. So that's when the no-photos thing started. And when you report someone missing, the first thing they do is try to get the word out, right? 'Have you seen this man?' They'd be blasting his name and face far and wide."

I look away. "If we could even *find* a picture of him, that is." We're quiet for a moment. A chicken moseys across the street. "Do you think his dad is involved in his disappearance?"

She shakes her head. "Probably not? Obviously he's a real asshole. But I don't know how he would've known Brady's here. I'm more worried that he . . . hurt himself."

"He didn't *seem* suicidal," I say. But then again: How would I know? So often, it's part of the headline: Someone hid their depression so well, no one knew they were close to killing themselves. I suck in a breath. "Brady's probably fine." It's like a tic, the normal, rote response to this unfathomably huge worry. "We just need to find him." *You deserve to know the truth about Eszter.* He typed those words and hit Send. I'd give anything, do anything, to hear what he wanted to tell me.

Amari looks away, and my stomach contorts; her eyes shine with worried tears.

"We could go to the mainland," I say. "Rita said there's a mental health clinic he goes to sometimes. Do you know it?"

She wipes her cheeks and nods. "I tried calling, but they wouldn't tell me anything over the phone."

"I called a few places too," I say. "But maybe if we show up in person? I was gonna take the ferry to Cancún tomorrow anyway; I'm staying there until I fly home Saturday."

Her brow creases. "I've visited him at the clinic before. The front desk closes at six, and if we take the ferry, we won't get there until seven at the soonest."

I tap my chin. "Could we hire someone with a boat?"

I picture all the vessels lined up along the marina; is this what Brady did, tapping a local to shuttle him ashore? Amari stares at me for a long second. She's probably thinking what I'm thinking, the error in our algorithm: If Brady hitched a ride off the island, as we're trying to do, why isn't there a record of it?

Finally, she nods. "Okay. Let's try. I . . . I don't know what else to do." Her voice cracks, but she recovers. "And it'll give me an excuse to ask everyone with a boat if they know where Brady went." She sniffs. "It'll probably have to be tomorrow morning, since the sun's setting soon; they don't like leaving this late because then they have to come back in the dark. I'll keep you posted."

"Okay. I was gonna . . . go walk around and look for clues, but I'll keep an eye on my phone." My own words surprise me—I wasn't planning to hide my visit to the hotel grounds from her.

"Sounds good." She clears her throat a few times, then starts to cough. I think of the wet clicking noise Eszter made when her mouth began to itch, an involuntary reaction to the first creeping signs that peanuts or eggs had somehow breached her defenses. I wave Amari inside for a glass of water, and she leans against the kitchen table as she gulps. Her eyes fall on Brady's book.

"Did he give you that?"

"No, I . . ." I catch the question in her furrowed brow: *Did he say you could take it?* "Whoa, does it look like I went into his house and, like, *stole* his favorite book?"

"Isn't that . . . exactly . . . what you did?" She metes the words out slowly, and after a frozen, wide-eyed second, we both start laughing.

"That never crossed my mind! Oh my God, how did I *burgle* someone?" I press my palms together at my chin. "Should I put it back?"

"A *second* B-and-E? I think not, no." Our laughter is incredulous, almost hysterical.

"Fair point. Okay, well, hopefully he's grateful we're so concerned about him. And not mad that I let myself in. I can compliment him on how clean he got it before heading out." We're both giggling too hard, the way you laugh nervously while sharing something awful.

She shakes her head. "I'll keep you posted about getting to Cancún." She starts to stand, slipping from her pocket a set of keys with a purple turtle key chain.

"Oh, one more thing!" I lean forward. "I was on PDC earlier. To see if Brady was trying to charter a boat out of here, right? I didn't find anything." I swallow. "But I did notice something weird. There's a chunk of time missing from the forums—an entire week in January. Any idea why that would be?"

She frowns, thinking, then shakes her head. She's either a very good actor or genuinely clueless. "I don't use it, so I can't really say. But you could ask Pedro." She swings the turtle key chain around her pointer finger, all casual.

"Why?"

She shrugs. "He's an administrator for the site. When something gets deleted, he's usually behind it."

CHAPTER NINETEEN

After Amari leaves, I lace up my hiking boots, then step inside for a water bottle. On the way back out, my feet tangle in the Teva sandals I ditched in front of the door. *This is why Eszter hated when I did that.* I stomp past them and catch myself before I fall, leaving them in even worse disarray on the doormat.

As I set out for the nature preserve, I give Pedro a call. A nearby insect is clicking, the steady *tick-tick-tick* of someone clipping their nails.

"Abby! ¿Qué tal?"

I—whoa, I wasn't expecting him to pick up. I half trip over a root. How can I ask him about this without letting him know I'm suspicious?

Focus, Abby. Though I'm the opposite of helpless, I also know how to strategically wield girlish ineptitude when necessary. So I take on a gentle, vaguely ditzy tone as I request his help with PDC: *Poor Abby's posts keep disappearing, and I noticed a whole week's worth of threads from January disappeared—gosh, what could've happened?*

He's unmoved. "Honestly, that sounds about right. The site is glitchy as hell."

"And that would lead to an entire week going poof?"

"Sure. Sometimes the caching fails and entire dates don't get copied to the server. It happens maybe once a year or so. Same thing back in . . . hang on, I'll find it." The tap-dance sound of a keyboard. "The February before that. I mean, we don't have sophisticated servers here. It's a miracle the site works as well as it does."

"Hmm." I navigate around a sunbathing orange cat. I wonder what Pedro's thinking. What I'm thinking is: *With those very same clicks, you could've trashed that February week to make January look like less of a one-off.* "As for all my posts disappearing . . . ?"

"Like I said, glitchy."

"Right." I clear my throat. "Um, in other news . . . I take it you haven't heard from Brady?" What I want to ask is: *Why aren't you more worried about him?*

"No, I haven't." But then he catches me off guard: "And frankly, I don't want to know where he is."

Coldness pools in my stomach. "What?"

"It's not our business if he doesn't want to tell us. People have a right to their privacy."

"I guess that's true," I manage.

"Look, it's really not that weird to have someone up and move one day," he says. "There was this Swedish writer, Hilde, said she never wanted to leave, but she kept having digestive issues from the water— I mean, you try to avoid it, but I guess her system couldn't handle it here. So one morning she got on the ferry and never looked back. And this guy from Singapore before that, he'd been here longer than any of us, and then suddenly—"

"You think he's gone *forever?*" I interrupt.

A beat. "No, I'm just saying. With an expat community . . ."

"Right, it's transient," I finish. "Made up of . . ." My brain sticks on *vagabonds*, which feels unnecessarily judgy. ". . . a revolving door."

"Exactly." I picture him raising his eyebrows, impatient. My heart thumps. Rita and Amari discussed the psychiatric facility, but Pedro's the first to suggest Brady's absence might be permanent.

"But, Pedro, he left his phone. His favorite book—all his stuff. That doesn't worry you?"

His chuckle makes my blood heat—so patronizing, all *Little girl, let me tell you how the world works.* "I might be concerned if it'd been more than . . . what, a day? I think it's a bit early to send a search party."

"I guess so."

"Anything else?"

I waffle for a second—should I quit while I'm ahead or reveal that I heard some things I shouldn't have? I navigate around a gargantuan palm frond, brown-tipped and corkscrewed. I'll be off the island with Amari soon; might as well go for it. "Sorry if this is a weird question, but . . . what was going on the morning of the boat ride? I saw you in what seemed to be intense discussions with Rita and then Amari."

He kinda chuckle-scoffs, a quick exhalation. "Oh, it was nothing," he says. "Not worth explaining."

The seconds tick by, one after another. Finally I clear my throat. "Right. Well, thanks for your help."

"Anytime."

I open my backpack and toss in my phone, which yesterday belonged to Brady. I picture him in an inpatient facility, skinny legs popping out of a hospital gown. My fingers find the folded map in my back pocket, and I pick up the pace.

After a half hour of hiking, I reach the rock ledge where I stood just two days ago. And then this morning, I gawked at these white cliffs from a boat, picturing my possessions swirling at its base. Now I have a front-row view of the sunset, and I think dully of the crew's invite to watch it on the beach with them. The sky is a riot of magenta, and below me, the ocean is as thick and sudsy as the head on a bad pour of Guinness, fracturing the sunset into a spumy, bloodlike mass.

It's dangerous, Pedro said. *A local boy drowned a few years ago.* I picture it, so real it's almost a hallucination: a body poking through the froth, the flash of an arm, a desperate hand, and then the back of a head, bobbing like driftwood. The surf pounds and stutters and I scream his name into the cacophony: *"Brady!"*

The only answer is the sea's steady pulse.

Shoot—I need to hurry. Night's coming on faster than I expected, and I have to get back down before it's dark. I turn around, I should probably rush right down, but . . . I glance inland and I'm close, so close. It's a straight shot through a strip of overgrown forest, and then, here it is: Paraíso Escondido.

A chain-link fence, topped with coils of razor wire, surrounds the property, along with shiny metal signs I don't need Spanish to understand: PROPIEDAD PRIVADA and PROHIBIDO TRASPASAR and LOS TRANS-GRESORES SERAN CASTIGADOS. They're reflective and threatening, and I pause, watching a spider skulk across one. I brace myself and head for what must've been a pedestrian entrance, a swinging gate hanging at a wild angle. As I push past it, I think of a broken jaw.

There's a fountain inside, ten feet across and now bubbling with greenish muck. Behind it a brick building looms, a sprawling single-story structure with white walls, fat columns, and holes where there were once doors and windows. Sómbravid vines lean out of them like passengers on an old-timey train, flowers fluttering in the breeze.

Goosebumps sweep along my arms and scalp; something about this place feels familiar, though I've never set foot on the island before. I swallow and pass through the double-wide maw that used to house the front door and pause in the lobby.

The furniture's gone, but remnants of the resort's former glory remain. Blue paint clings to cement columns, freckled with mold and spindly weeds. Though most of the floor is dirty concrete, matte black tiles stick tight in the corners.

Unease thrums in my chest like a guitar string plucked. Darkness seems to be crawling out of the corners, retaking the ruins. The back of the lobby opens into a courtyard, now an imprisoned chunk of jungle that's fighting its way out. Vines and shrubs and even a defiant tree, bursting like a green firecracker, blanket the space, nosing into rooms and up the balusters. The empty door and window frames watch me like black, ghostly eyes. There's a sunken circle in the center—a plunge pool, I presume—now furred with that same blue-green slime. Stone benches hulk in the corners, reclaimed by ants. This place feels quiet, sad, watchful, like an empty restaurant that seems to gaze at you as you pass.

I pull the map from my back pocket, struggling to read it in the dusky light. Brady marked the entire compound, and now I don't know where to turn or what I'm looking for. I do a quick lap of the courtyard, peering into hotel rooms as I pass. In one corner, limey stalks crowd the bowl of an ancient toilet; the broken porcelain sink is on its side, shards spread like confetti. I study them as if they're tea leaves, seeking answers in the debris.

At some point, Brady must've come here. There's a reason he circled this resort.

I pad from room to room, heart snapping like fingers. I pass a bit of graffiti: a scribbled shark on a far wall, the anarchy symbol above a door. I turn left and spot spray paint that makes iciness spider up my spine: an arrow toward the foot-high hole in the corner of a hotel room and sprawled English: JOIN US. A few doors down, a second jagged hole with a big arrow above it: C'MON. Something chitters from the ceiling—a bat; no, dozens of them—and I hurry back into the open.

I picture the resort as it once was, tropical and neat, couples and weary parents reading in lounge chairs while children bumper-car'd around.

Did Eszter ever come up here? Did she stand right where I'm standing now?

I pull out Brady's map and tilt it in the waning light. Darkness is descending quickly now, like someone dialed down the exposure. What am I missing? I need to head back before it's too dark to see the path. Suddenly all four sides of the courtyard look the same. Which way did I come in? Adrenaline shoots through my hands and feet. Some young, desperate part of me sounds the alarm: *It's a trap. Find the exit.*

RUN.

I hustle to the nearest door frame and poke my head inside, trying to be rational, methodical. There's an opening on the opposite wall, but this isn't the lobby; it looks like a onetime restaurant, tables overturned, rusted appliances on their sides. Through the empty door frame—once an emergency exit, maybe—I spy the base of the comm tower. While most of it's decrepit, creepy dishes and pipes atop a pyramid of decaying metal, I spot a black square the size of a shoebox: the satellite phone Brady mentioned.

I return to the courtyard and force myself to breathe, to think. It's like someone's pouring India ink over the grounds, and it's pooling in the corners, blackening the space.

West—the front doors must have faced west for that spectacular sunset view. I turn toward the brightest part of the sky and race across the courtyard, and my rib cage loosens when I find myself back in the lobby.

My eyes fall on the check-in desk, with a smattering of blue and yellow tiles on the wall behind it. There's an ancient brochure holder on the floor, I notice, its once-clear plastic cracked and yellowing. I cross to it and pull a pamphlet from the stand. It's faded from time and warped from the humidity; the graphic design is clearly nineties, all pastel patterns and geometric shapes, but the image on the front is still impressive: Paraíso Escondido rising up from the rainforest, columns pristine, fountain gleaming white.

I ease it open and it splits along the crease. The copy's in English—*Welcome to your hidden tropical paradise!*—with nightly rates and a long list of amenities. On the back, one panel shows smiling couples lounging on beach chairs and clinking piña coladas, while the next is meant to appeal to parents, with kids and families playing in the pool and grinning in the courtyard.

I'm prepared to fold it back into thirds and slip it into my backpack when . . .

Wait.

I sit back on my heels and feel my heart thumping in my chest. I fumble for my phone and turn on the flashlight, hand shaking. Slowly, I turn the brochure right-side up and ease it open. I zero in on the back panel again, smiling tots and babies, a family resort in its prime.

No.

I squeeze my eyes closed and pop them open again. It has to be a trick of the light. Any second now, I'll correct my mistake and go back to life as I once knew it.

Eszter chose Isla Colel randomly. That's what I told Rita two nights ago; that's what I've told myself for months now, ever since Eszter showed me the pink Airbnb she'd found, smiling shyly. *She wanted to go somewhere quiet to work,* I said, *and she stumbled on it online—it checked all the boxes, hidden gem, cheap, Spanish-speaking.*

And that's what makes this brochure so baffling.

On Christmas, not even half a year ago, I sat on the Farkases' sofa and paged through a photo book dedicated to their eldest son. And I paused on a picture from a family trip: tiny Eszter bundled in her mother's arms, palm trees framing the four of them. White columns and tall windows that meant nothing to me at the time.

But they mean everything now. I look up. I'm just a few yards from them.

The Farkases' vacation photo . . . is on the back of an old, tattered brochure for Paraíso Escondido.

CHAPTER TWENTY

ABBY

February 6, 2023 (one year and three months ago)

"**Q**uit it, you keep making me laugh!"

"What am I doing?!" I leaned back on my stool, eyebrows high. "I'm just looking at you!"

"Yeah, like an *otter*." We both giggled. When we'd rented a lake house Up North a few months ago, every time we sat on the dock, an otter—the same one, we decided—would pop his head out of the water and stare at us intently. We named him Otto, and even now, to be silly, we'd randomly fix each other with his round-eyed stare.

"I'm not trying to be Otto! I'm just listening." I waved my hand. "Go ahead. Whenever you're ready."

Whooping followed a wooden clack behind us, and we turned toward the pool table's rowdy crowd. A dive bar had seemed like a low-pressure place for Eszter to practice a high-pressure speech, but we hadn't banked on it being quite this full.

She took a sip of beer and looked down at her orange notebook. I still couldn't quite believe she literally wrote out a script for certain talks—it felt fake, or like something seventh-grade girls do before calling their crush—but hey, whatever it took to get her to set some boundaries with her sleazy father.

"Okay. So. Dad, as you know, Abby and I have been dating pretty seriously since—*stop!*" She smacked my shoulder.

"Ow!" I uncrossed my arms and relaxed my posture. "I was trying to sit like him. Give you an authentic experience."

"Oh my God. Maybe I *shouldn't* have moved in with you." She grinned mischievously.

"You can't use mail forwarding forever." I tapped her notebook. "Less joshing, more rehearsing."

She took a deep breath. "Dad, you know that Abby and I have been dating since May."

"Do you think you should . . . go right into it like that? No easing into it?"

"Oh, definitely. Az idő pénz." Even I knew that one: *Time is money.* She brought her thumb and forefinger almost together. "His patience has been about *this thin* since they bought that Coral Gables site. When I call them, he keeps yelling at my mom for taking too long to get to the point: 'Siess, Olga. Hurry up.'"

My eyebrows flashed. "Okay, wow. Resisting the urge to comment on that."

"Thank you." She cleared her throat. "Abby's an amazing partner and we get along really well. We actually . . . we've decided . . ."

I dropped my voice a few octaves: "Tündi, are you cutting me out of your life and never speaking to me again?" My attempt at his accent came out vaguely Russian. She chuckled weakly and I leaned forward. "Sorry, bad joke. He's obviously not going to say that." I swallowed the impulse to add: . . . *not that it would be the worst thing.*

"I know. He'll get over it." She took another swig of beer. "Okay, next point. By living with Abby, I'm saving a lot of money, and I'm closer to campus so I can spend more time getting to know my classmates. I know those are two important principles of success: frugality and networking."

I patted her knee. "Maybe there's a way to say it that's a little less . . . stiff?"

"He responds to directness. Subtlety is lost on him. When I was a little kid . . . ooh!" The bartender set down two greasy baskets: onion rings and fried cheese curds. "Thank you!"

The food was the temperature of molten lava and we both huffed and fanned our mouths. Finally Eszter swallowed and stuck out her tongue. "I don't think my mouth will ever recover."

"Pity." I slid off the stool and slipped my arms around her shoulders; reflexively, her hands found my waist. "You have the prettiest mouth. It's like art."

We kissed. "Thanks for helping me," she said. "I know my parents . . ."

"They'll, what, hate that we're *living in sin*?" I plucked an onion ring from the pile and waved it in the air. "Well, in that case, maybe we should . . ."

It was a joke, one I hadn't even thought through—*If our unmarried status is the problem, hey, here's a ring*. But the look in her eyes made me freeze on the spot. I shook my head. "I'm sorry—man, all my attempts at comedy are falling flat tonight."

She kissed me again. "No, you're good. I'm just nervous."

"About your dad?"

"Yeah. But it's fine." She picked up the notebook and smiled. "Shall we take it from the top?"

CHAPTER TWENTY-ONE
ABBY

Wednesday evening

No. *No.* As the seconds tick by I become aware of a battering sensation in my chest, like a frog between a kid's cupped palms. I keep staring at the brochure, hoping each fresh blink will turn the four tiny figures into strangers, make this whole thing make sense. But the longer I look, the surer I am. That's them. That's the Farkases, a hundred feet from where I crouch.

Already, none of the pieces fit together, and now they're even more confounding. My ears buzz. I thought Eszter had no particular connection to Isla Colel. What does this mean?

The ferns shiver behind me, and I turn sharply, surveying the horizon. It's dark, too dark, and I fumble with the burner phone as I rise to my feet. Ugh, the flashlight's barely bright enough to light my path. Lord knows I'm clumsy enough in broad daylight.

I retrace my steps down the mountain, swinging the dim light around me, jumping a mile at every rustle. By the time I reach the neighborhood, the streets are empty, lit only by a silver coat of moonlight. A dark lump near the road makes me freeze, but then it lifts off—a big black bird. As I continue past, a chill goes through me: Light glints off a rodent's skeleton, its leg bones little zigzags.

I glance up and around me, sure the vulture's got its eyes on me still.

It's a little after eight when I reach my rental. My fingers shake as I key in the code and fling myself inside. The apartment smells musty, that wet tropical funk. I lunge for my computer, then freeze—did I close my laptop before I left? I'm in the habit of leaving it open, letting the screen go to sleep . . . it bothered Eszter, who claimed that hackers could theoretically co-opt the built-in camera and spy on us. (I suspected that that fear and related habits—always using incognito mode, keeping her phone's location services switched off—were all paranoia inherited from her dad.) But now my MacBook's sealed and flat and six tiny Eszters look back at me, smiling from those golf-ball-sized stickers. A cold tingle slides up my neck as I take in the constellation of happy moments.

Frowning, I hinge the screen up and start to email Eszter's brother, whom I haven't spoken to since the funeral. There, he hugged me close, told me to let him know if I needed anything—but then he stiffened as his parents came into view, and then he turned away, and then I felt a harpoon of pain I'll never forget.

My email is brief and overly polite. *I must've misunderstood why Eszter chose this place,* I say. *I didn't realize you took a vacation here.* I add her father to the CC line, then remove him at the last second. I start to email Eszter's best friend, Shane—and then freeze, midword, the full force of the humiliation hitting me. Here I am, begging for scraps about a fiancée who chose, *chose,* to keep this weird detail from me. What else did she withhold? How much pity accumulated on me like dust in the two years of our relationship? Why didn't anyone *say* anything?

What happened here, Eszter?

I google the hotel, which brings up a handful of results, the hyperlinks purple because I clicked on them a few months ago in one of my late-night internet spirals. I thought I knew everything there was to know about this island, no rock left unturned. Once again, all I find is a single photo from a travel blogger's listicle ("The 17 Creepiest Abandoned Hotels in the World") and a few newspaper articles about the resort's closure in 2003. No bombshells, no smoking guns. I open PDC, but a search for the hotel yields nothing. I'm not surprised to see that my new comment about the missing week has disappeared, too. My question about Brady remains—no replies.

I close the browser and Slack pops to the front; Tyler wants answers, and everything about TimeIn feels like it's from a dimension totally distinct from this one. As I spit out some lines of code to convert PDFs to plain text, my head spins. *Eszter had a connection to this place.* So what? Am I like my machine-learning model—taking in data and drawing the exact wrong conclusion, taking the wrong action next?

I text the group: "Sorry I missed the sunset. Anyone still at the beach?" Amari and Pedro spent time with Eszter. Amari called her "lovely." Maybe Eszter told them why she picked this place—her personal connection, what the resort was like back in the day. It's worth a shot, anyway.

No one answers, so I set out for Playa Oscura, making my way south through the residential neighborhood. On lit-up balconies, drying clothes flutter like prayer flags. I stop by Brady's house as I pass—it's dark, locked, exactly as I left it—and call his number, pressing my ear to the door. But the walls are too thick, the jungle too loud—I can't tell if it's still buzzing on the table.

As I approach the beach, I'm a salmon swimming upstream against the trickle of islanders heading inland, sandy towels dangling from their arms. I get a text right as I pop out onto the sand: Amari's already home, sorry, and still working on our boat ride. The pulse of disappointment this evokes surprises even me. Was I . . . hoping to see her again?

I shove the feeling aside and glance around. Pedro's on the sand, hunched over his phone, and I gaze at him for a second—brow clenched, hair falling into his eyes.

After a second, he senses my stare and turns. "Abby! Just saw your text." He smiles as he shuffles over, which catches me off guard. He didn't seem thrilled when I called about PDC a few hours ago.

"Yeah, I . . . lost track of time." I can't tell him I went to the hotel when, just this morning, he made an impassioned plea for everyone to steer clear. "Hey, can I ask you something?"

"More questions!" He grins. "What, are you a PI?"

"Nope! But this one's actually about Eszter. I told you how I'm trying to, uh, learn about her time here."

He nods, his eyes attentive and neutral.

I clear my throat. "Did she ever talk about coming here with her family? As a baby?"

A surprised chuckle. "Really? She never mentioned that! Did they stay at the resort?"

"Yeah. They . . . their picture's actually on the brochure."

"Huh! I had no idea." He shakes his head, amused. "You going into town?"

He moves toward the main drag and I know I have more to ask him, though I'm not sure what. "I'll keep you company," I say brightly. "I've got a few more questions."

"Sure thing, Detective." A black cat pads a few yards behind us, its tail a stub.

You deserve to know the truth about Eszter. What could Brady have meant? I guess I could ask Pedro head-on, but a part of me presses on the brake pedal. That PDC business was suspicious, and even if Rita hadn't referenced his "checkered past," her gossip painted Pedro as a sad man, scorned. The most dangerous kind, in my experience.

"Eszter sent me this great photo of all of you." I fumble with my new phone. "Where was this?"

He pauses to take it in, wrinkles branching over his brow. "Esteban took us out for a whale-watching tour. Hilde—that's her there—she insisted the whales would swim up to us if we blasted house music. Something about the bass. I thought she was out of her mind, but then they headed straight for us. It was insane." His smile drops. "Eszter didn't tell you about that?"

I shake my head. "It was right before I was supposed to fly here, and I was so busy with work—I told her to save everything for when I got there." I frown. "Was Hilde close with Eszter? Is she still in Mexico?"

"Nah. She's in Goa, last I heard. I was surprised she wanted to visit India after she kept getting sick here. But no, I think Eszter and Brady and Amari had sort of a crew."

"Right." We've reached the edge of the town square, with reddish lamplights spilling onto the cement. "Were you here . . . when she died?" Nausea rises through me like bubbles in seltzer. This isn't what I came here to ask—these aren't the memories I planned to mine.

He sags. "Again, I'm really sorry for your loss." He runs his fingers through his beard. "I was on the mainland when it happened, but everyone was talking about it. It was big news, obviously, an American passing away on our little island. I mean, we hardly get tourists, period."

I stare across the plaza, insides heavy. "The person who ran her Airbnb called the police, right?"

"I assume so? Marta. Like I said, I wasn't here." He turns to me, like he's wrapping this up. "Hey, that's cool that she had a connection to the island. From childhood. You said she really liked it here, right? It's a pretty amazing place."

"It is. Thanks for, you know, fielding all my questions."

"Anytime." He says good night and disappears into the convenience store.

As I look around the town square—*plaza pública* on Brady's map—the painted sea turtle, dolphin, stingray, and whale all seem to watch me in the streetlamp's dusky glow. The grocery store's pull-down door is at half-mast and I beeline for it. There's one local I can communicate with: a born-and-bred Coleleña with institutional knowledge of the island, someone with whom I don't need an interlocutor. *I know this island like it's my own child,* Gloria the grocer told me. *Every plant, every person.*

I reach the store, with its caged parakeets, and duck inside. "Hello?"

Gloria, ponytail swinging, lights up at the sight of me. "Hola, Abby! I'm closed now."

"I'm so sorry to ask, but could I bother you for two minutes?"

She grimaces. "I'm sorry, I am trying to close the store."

I spot a broom leaning against the wall. "Can I help so we can talk at the same time?"

"Sure!" She goes back to stocking boxes of cereal.

As I sweep, I tell her I'm still trying to track down Brady. I slide the map out of my pocket and set it on the counter. "Do you recognize this?"

She peers at it, then purses her brow like I'm an idiot. "It's Isla Colel."

I let out a surprised laugh. "No, I know. Have you seen *this map* before? Or do you know whose writing this is?"

She inspects it again, then shakes her head. "I'm sorry. But I can ask around. Can you give me your number?" She takes a picture of the page, then adds me to her contacts and calls me so I'll have her number too.

"Thanks. Another thing . . ." I tap the red mark on the map. "I was just up there, and I found a brochure for the hotel with a photo of Eszter on the back. My fiancée—the one who died. But I had no idea she came here as a baby."

Gloria tilts her head. "Let me see the picture."

I spread the brochure on top of the map and point.

She examines it. "I don't recognize them, but the hotel was a busy place for decades. So many tourists came in and out." She shrugs. "If she visited Colel as a child, it makes sense she came back. No?"

My finger taps the counter. What am I missing? "Were you here when they found her?"

"Yes. I was here, opening for the day."

"What happened?" My stomach tightens. "Were there police cars, sirens? Did you find out right away, or . . . ?"

She frowns. "She was already dead, right? And it was very early in the morning. I think they tried not to draw too much attention. Out of respect."

I think back to how Brady's head popped up like a meerkat's last night: *You've been up there?* "So there wasn't a big scene?" I ask. "People standing around and watching her get carried out or anything?" I'm rushing, trying to get the words out before I can process them. The grocery store feels small, stuffy with the smell of raw potatoes and onions.

"Not a big scene, no." Gloria shakes her head. "Marta found her, I think; she lived right above that rental."

I nod. "I noticed it's not on Airbnb anymore."

"Yes. I don't know how they could afford it, but she stopped running the Airbnb almost right away." Gloria grimaces. "It's not great for business when a guest dies in your home."

She doesn't mean to sound callous, but my stomach drops all the same. She turns away and lifts a half-empty box of avocados—my cue to go. I linger, squeezing my hands around the broom handle.

"Um, can I ask you one more thing?"

"Of course." She smiles pleasantly, chucking vegetables into a bin. God, she's patient.

"Are you . . . friendly with Marta? I really want to talk to her, but assuming she doesn't speak English, I'm not sure . . . how I'll . . ." I look down, cheeks hot. "Basically, I'm looking for a translator."

She peers at me for a moment, then turns and plucks a bulb of garlic from the onion bin. "Sure, I know Marta. Her place is on my way home. Let me text her. If she's home, we can talk to her as soon as I finish up."

I set the watchful parakeets in the back office, then wait while Gloria scrapes the metal grate to the ground and slides a lock into place, sealing the store like it's a citadel. Together we head north, and fluffy chickens scatter as we enter the residential area. Free-range, indeed.

Eszter walked this road four months ago, knowing she'd have the island to herself for two weeks before I showed up. I was always coming after her, always certain my proactivity was the glue holding us together. That fateful call we had just a few months into our relationship, the discussion that changed everything while I slinked along U.S. 12—was *that* the flex point? Did I push too hard and push her away?

The wind whips around us, no longer playful, now feral. A snarling dog throws itself against a chain-link fence and I startle, heart erupting with beats. We turn on Calle Estrella and I spot it in the distance, lit up by a porch light: carnation-pink walls, bone-colored door.

Gloria climbs the front steps and I hover behind her. Once again, I picture Eszter sprawled on the floor on the other side of this wall, struggling to breathe as her body betrayed her. My determination to find

Brady, to hear what he wanted to tell me, to *figure out what the hell is going on here,* billows up like a kite catching air.

The woman who answers the door is older than I expected—middle-aged, with long black hair, a mole near her lip, and pretty, tired eyes. *Marta.* That's her—a match for the little icon on the Airbnb exchanges. She *communicated* with Eszter, ushered her inside. Dealt with the questions and chaos after she found Eszter dead.

My heart slams in my chest as I trot out all the polite Spanish phrases I know. They both look at me expectantly.

"Gloria, can you please ask what it was like hosting Eszter?"

As they go back and forth, I can't help nodding along, as if I have any idea what they're saying. Marta keeps using the word *Airbnb.* Finally, Gloria turns to me, a whisper of confusion on her face. "She said Eszter was very nice to Marta and her husband. And . . . she was the reason they were going to stop using Airbnb."

"What?"

Gloria frowns. "Eszter said she wanted to stay for the whole year. At Airbnb rates, so Marta was over the moon. She canceled all her bookings and took the listing down."

I shake my head, mystified. "A year?"

Gloria turns sharply to Marta, a quick game of telephone: "¿Un año?"

Marta nods, then whirls around and disappears into the house. Gloria and I exchange a baffled glance. From inside, I hear the rattle of metal filing cabinets.

"Aquí." Marta reappears with something in her hands. "Mira."

She hands me a shiny green folder, and I find a legal document inside. At first, it's gibberish to me, lines and lines of Spanish broken up into numbered sections.

Then things start to jump out.

This address, 42 Calle Estrella. *El depósito, la renta.* Dates that make goosebumps sweep up my neck and arms despite the oppressive heat: January 15, 2024, through January 14, 2025. A legal document that won't expire for another eight months.

Though I can't read it, I've signed enough of these in my time to get

the gist: *CONTRATO DE ARRENDAMIENTO DE VIVIENDA.*
Most chillingly, there's a line at the end and, in blue ink, a scribble I
recognize instantly.

The looping *E,* the *F* like an unfurled flag.

It's a one-year lease . . . signed by Eszter.

ABBY

October 3, 2022 (one year and seven months ago)

"How much longer?" Eszter's low voice shot out of all the car speakers at once, surround sound.

"No idea," I said. "I haven't moved in, like, ten minutes and it's bumper-to-bumper as far as the eye can see."

She replied with a sympathetic groan. Though we'd been dating for five months, we still hadn't figured out how to time the drive between us. She lived on the west side of Madison, near Middleton, and I on the east end, and the commute time ranged wildly from twenty-five minutes to the better part of an hour.

A beat. "I'm sorry, Abby. I told you I'd come to you."

"No, it's not your fault. I'm—*whoa!*" I slammed on the brakes, bouncing forward and leaning on the horn. Though Eszter's patience in gridlock dwarfed mine, she hated driving, so I girded my loins and came to her most of the time—that was my decision, a small price to pay for getting to see her.

"What is it, what happened?"

"Adrenaline tingled in my veins. "An SUV came within an inch of plowing into me." My heart thrummed against the seatbelt. I flipped off the driver, now directly in front of me. "I can't keep doing this."

A long silence. "What are you saying?" she asked miserably.

For a second I was lost, and then I laughed. "Wait, you thought I was breaking up with you? Over the *drive time*?"

"I mean . . . you *really* hate traffic."

"I do. But actually . . ." Waze suggested a new route, shunting me onto the next exit. I turned on my blinker. "I don't know, should we move in together?"

Tick-tock, tick-tock, tick-tock.

"You mean after your lease is up in a year?" she asked.

"Why wait that long?" Excitement surged through me. "You know how much I love waking up next to you. I love having you in my space and cooking with you in the kitchen and loafing around in the living room. Your lease ends next month, right? What if . . . what if you moved in with me?"

I gave a grateful wave to the hatchback that let me slip in front of him. One more lane to go.

"You think I should move into your place?"

"It wouldn't be *my* place anymore. It would be *our* place. Our home. I mean, you moved into that unit sight unseen—Eken Park makes more sense." It felt like a given: My apartment wasn't just closer to campus; it was also larger, with a grassy backyard and a sunny office in the front. We couldn't cohabitate in her studio, but my apartment was more than spacious enough for the two of us.

"No pressure," I continued. "But I really think it would be fun." Excitement was piling up in my torso like snow. Things had been going *so* well—the more I got to know Eszter, the more twinkling facets I discovered, the more I loved her. I wanted to be my very best self around her, smart and strong and kind. I pressed my palms into a dramatic prayer and smiled at the truck driver to my right; he waved me over.

"I've never lived with a partner before," she said.

"Neither have I. And I know it's kinda fast. But I also know how much I like hanging out with you. And I think it'd be even better if we got to do it all the time."

"The only thing is . . ."

And suddenly I knew what she was going to say. "Your parents, right?" A motorcycle zipped up the shoulder beside me. "Listen, I get it. I know they'll be weird about it and I know that's hard for you. But . . . you're almost twenty-six years old, Eszter. You're in the driver's seat. Not them. You. Aki mer, az nyer." *He who dares, wins*—it was one of the few Hungarian phrases I could repeat back, since Eszter lobbed it my way so often, admiring how I barreled after whatever I wanted.

I *liked* that, unlike me, Eszter didn't dash headlong into things. The only decisions she took lightly were the small, joint ones, when she didn't have a strong opinion either way: where to go for dinner, which bottle of wine to order, whether the seven-fifteen or eight-thirty screening was better. *You care more,* she always said. *I'm good with whatever.* It was part of what made our relationship click—we both hated conflict and felt grateful for the steady, predictable peace.

So I tried to avoid pressuring her on big things. But right now, I was twelve feet from the exit, ten feet, eight. It was free of cars, a wide-open escape route. In the backseat, a bouquet of hydrangeas rocked against a box of orejas—Eszter's favorite. Every foot got me closer to her, to the glass front door where her voice would crackle through the intercom, and then the third-floor hallway where I'd knock on her door, grinning. Seeing her always felt like a revelation, a mix of coziness and elation. *There she is.*

"I'll help you practice telling your dad," I said. "You're strong; you got this." She was quiet and I kept my voice light: "I'll be way less messy if you're there too! I promise. Those shoes I'm always leaving in front of the door? A thing of the past."

"No more booby-trap boots?"

"Cross my heart."

She laughed, and it was the best sound, my favorite sound in the world. "Let me think about it," she said. "But . . . I think you're right. It could be really good."

I grinned. That was all I needed to hear—that *probably* would soon be a yes.

"Great. Take all the time you need." I coasted down the off-ramp and reached the light right as it turned green.

CHAPTER TWENTY-THREE
ABBY

Wednesday evening

My fingers go lax and the pages skitter to the floor, ruffling around us. We all duck to pick them up, a race against the erratic breeze. I stand up too fast and press my hand to the wall, blinking hard as my vision fuzzes.

"Are you all right?" Gloria touches my arm.

I manage to nod, though I'm not all right, not at all.

Eszter was planning to stay? For a *year*? And she didn't think to tell me?

How long had she been planning this? Everything about it seems wrong: Eszter took forever to make major (even minor!) life decisions. So who the hell was the Eszter Farkas who signed the contract clutched in my shaky hands? Had she done it under duress, somehow? Had someone forged her signature?

I need to tell you something.

Was she planning to invite me along?

"Gloria." I straighten up. "Can you ask if Eszter said anything else? About why she was staying, or if she . . . if she thought anyone would be joining her?"

The hope is like a bubble: *Oh yes, she said her fiancée would live here too.*

Gloria stares at me for a second, her eyes sympathetic, then turns back to Marta. Sure enough: "She doesn't know why Eszter was staying. And as far as she knows, it was only her in the apartment. But she didn't ask about a roommate. Eszter paid for the year up front, at Airbnb rates, so Marta was thrilled."

I still remember the price: $400 a week, less than $60 a night, a true budget vacation. But $1,600 a month is Madison rates. And how did she drop $20,000 without blinking? She had a trust fund, thanks to her father, but she was always careful with her money.

Marta says something, tucking the folder against her chest, and Gloria turns to me. "Do you want to ask anything else?"

I palm the sides of my head, like I can stop the way my brain is whirring. There's *so much* I want to know, but I'm not sure what—or how—to ask. I'm crying again, more out of exasperation than anything else.

Focus, Abby. Don't fall to pieces now. "How did Eszter seem?" I say. "At the end, I mean."

Marta shrugs and even I can understand the first words out of her mouth: Normal. Bien. She seemed excited about staying, Gloria translates, but nothing seemed extraña—odd.

My stomach turns to stone as I ask the last question, for a third time today: "What happened when Marta found her?"

It's a quick exchange, with Marta hooking a thumb over her shoulder. Her face is pained; she's listing away from me, her hand firm on the door. I catch the end of her answer: Fría, fría, fría.

"She saw her through the front window." Gloria keeps her eyes on the casita. "She called the police, then ran upstairs and got the key." She swallows. "But it was clear there was . . . nothing they could do. She was . . ."

"Cold," I finish.

They both look at me, their creased brows like question marks. A kid's birdlike cry wafts out of the house, and Marta turns. She's ready for us to leave her alone. Ready to stop talking about the stranger who brought this darkness into their home. A distant bug clacks like a met-ronome.

I thank Marta, and she backs inside and closes the door with a thump. Gloria, eyes round with pity, tells me to call her anytime before leaving me to make my way back in the darkness. On the trudge home, I make a short list of people I need to contact, people who might have an answer to the million-dollar question: What the hell was Eszter planning to do for a year on Isla Colel? Business school buddies, Laszlo (whom I emailed earlier), and of course—most gut-wrenchingly—her parents themselves. I can't imagine they'd be cool with her extension—missing classes and all.

Unless . . . unless breaking up with me was part of the package. Un-less they knew she was about to end the relationship, and that was enough sugar to make the medicine go down.

I reach my front door and slump against it—that can't be it, can it? They didn't like me, wouldn't have liked anyone other than a tall, football-playing, all-American male, but would that really outweigh their desire for her to finish her degree and graduate at the top of her class?

I'm typing the door code into the keypad when a twig snaps, then another. I twist around, glancing up and down the darkened street. There's a tangle of dark shadows below a neighbor's trees and I could swear someone slipped into it as I turned. I squint at the black knot, heart thwacking in my chest.

"Hello?" I call. Silence. A breeze coaxes the trees into a hissing, shushing chorus. After another moment, I whirl around and close my-self inside.

There, my imagination gets to work, twisting the facts like they're parts of a complex puzzle. Why would she stay? Was she in a jam in the States and decided to flee the country? Did something go terribly wrong at business school? Was she finally planning to cut her parents out of her life, as I'd been encouraging her to do for so long?

I flick on a light. *No.* No, she would never do that to them.

Only to me.

There it is, Occam's razor, the answer with the fewest wild leaps: She was going to break up with me in person and send me back home to Wisconsin . . . alone. It sounds unspeakably cruel, but maybe she thought she owed it to me to do it in person—dust off the orange note-book, say it to my face. A headache throbs at the back of my eyeballs and I drop onto the sofa, crying.

Why would Eszter do this? Did I know my fiancée at all?

Classes—she'd miss the all-important start of the spring semester. Surely she'd tell her beloved advisor, Dr. Patel, right? I find an email from him deep in my inbox—Eszter, thrilled, had forwarded me a rare instance of praise—and scroll down to the signature.

I pause. The last time I saw him was at the funeral . . . he clasped my hands in his and smiled sadly.

What a brilliant mind, he said. *Always full of surprises.* I took it at face value, admiration of her keen intellect and creativity. Now the compli-ment feels more loaded. *Surprises.* Had she told him something unex-pected right at the end . . . ?

I copy his phone number and call him from my laptop.

He clears his throat a few times after answering.

"Ajay Patel," he finally intones.

My heart pounds as I introduce myself. He's quiet. "Sorry to be call-ing so late," I add. "I . . . thought this was your office number."

"No, my cell. I wouldn't have . . . sorry, I thought you were my daughter's friend's mom."

The beat stretches out between us. Finally: "Well, can I take a min-ute of your time?"

"Yeah, no, sure," he says. "Shoot."

"Um, I know this is out of the blue," I say, "but I recently learned that Eszter was planning to stay in Mexico this whole year. Did she talk to you about missing classes or making up schoolwork? Or"—hope flickers like a candle flame—"did she not need to be on campus while she finished her capstone?"

An awkward silence. "You didn't know?" he finally says.

My stomach clenches like a fist. "Know what?"

"She . . . she put her enrollment on hold. At the end of the semester. Said she wasn't sure when she'd be back."

Nausea swarms my belly. "Eszter . . . dropped out?"

"I mean, it's Eszter, I wouldn't call her a dropout." A sharp laugh. "I was hugely disappointed—she was a brilliant, brilliant student."

My insides are contracting, pulling away from my skin.

"Such a hard worker," he continues. "And it was so sudden—just popped into my office one day."

It's an effort to speak. "Do you know why?"

"She didn't say. Just apologized and said there was something else she had to focus on. Seemed genuinely worried about, y'know. Having taken up my time."

That last part sounded like Eszter, at least. *Something else to focus on? What the hell?*

"What about her capstone? The Haven? The . . . the mixed-use shelter and hotel?" She sent photos from her Miami trips—things were moving along. Why wouldn't she finish her degree at the same time?

"No idea. Like I said, she just put her enrollment on hold."

"When was this?" I ask.

"Ohhh, let's see. After Thanksgiving, I think. Early December, maybe?"

My pulse throbs in my ears. "You don't have any idea what it was about? Did she seem . . . was she in trouble, or nervous, or . . . ?"

"She told me not to worry, that everything was fine." I can almost hear him shrug. "But that's Eszter, right? Able to shoulder the world on her own. She seemed, I dunno . . . determined."

I genuinely can't think of anything to say.

"I'm not one to pry with my students, y'know?" he finally says. "They all have their own stuff going on. So I wished her the best and told her to let me know if she ever needed anything. That was the last time I heard from her. I'm really sorry, again, for your loss."

"Thank you," I say softly.

"She was one of the best students I've ever worked with, y'know. A real shining star."

We're both quiet and the line between us soughs like wind in the grass.

Eszter lied to me. Eszter didn't even tell me she'd quit school.

"Thanks so much for your help," I finally say. When he hangs up, I calmly stand from the table, walk into the bathroom, sink to my knees, and vomit.

Sometimes, in my dreams, Eszter and I are doing the most mundane things together: sipping lagers at a dive bar, walking around Lake Mendota, driving Up North. Even the banal stuff was better with her. The first time we went to Trader Joe's, I thought it in that voiceover way: *Grocery shopping shouldn't be this fun.* Her little sardonic comments, the way I had to bring my A game to make her laugh. For months, my REM sleep has funneled me back there, to the in-between moments that added up to everything.

Whenever I woke from one of those dreams, I'd hang in that liminal space for a few seconds—the plane where Eszter still existed. And then I'd remember, my own mind the bearer of terrible news. And I'd feel that awful crash all over again.

Now I stare into the toilet bowl. I didn't think *anything* could top that blow; nothing could pierce me deeper. But here I am, a secret dancing at the edges of my vision. Everything Eszter told me about school—her plans, her capstone—was a lie. What else wasn't true: our relationship, our shared future? Did she ever even love me?

My stomach cramps again, and I spit. "Eszter," I whisper. "What were you up to?"

I rinse my mouth, then reach for my phone to call Eszter's childhood friend Shane. But of course, she's not in my contacts; when I snatched up Brady's burner, I didn't consider how unmooring it would be to lose my saved numbers and old text threads. I email Shane, then Eszter's brother, Laszlo, asking both to call me. I'm not even sure what I'll ask them: *Did you know this, did you know* I *didn't know this, what the hell was going on?!*

My phone chimes with a new text from Amari: "Found us a ride @ 11am tomorrow. Soonest I could get . . . everyone's fishing before that. Meeting place TBD."

I thank her and eye my luggage—guess I should pack up. It feels . . . odd to be leaving this place. I arrived so eager to love it, to understand how it captured Eszter's heart. To find the people she bonded with and connect with them too. And I did, at least at first. God, the beach-blanket beers with Rita, that trippy hour in a bay that made me glow: How could I not feel some of what Eszter must've felt?

I open my suitcase and . . . that's weird, I don't remember leaving it quite this messy. I fold my tank tops into rectangles, pile them inside. I can't believe I'll be back on the mainland tomorrow. Not on this lit-up speck in the middle of the ocean. Like a single fleck of bioluminescent plankton, dark until disturbed. What did Rita say that first night? We leave everything we encounter a little bit altered, for better or for worse?

I stuff my sports bras into my suitcase's pocket. My chest tingles at the prospect of seeing Brady, of grabbing his shoulders and nearly shouting: *What do you know?* I'm missing my sandals—oh, right, I left them on the front porch, tripped over them spectacularly. I fling open the front door, flick on the light, and—

Wait.

I remember my quick stumble, how my toes tangled in the Teva straps. My muscles recall the sensation, flying forward, heavy-footed, then righting myself, leaving the booby-trap sandals in even wilder disarray. *I don't want us tripping on them,* Eszter always said. *It's like you're trying to kill us both.*

And that's why the sight in front of me makes no sense. I stare and stare as the realization rushes through my veins: As usual, I left my shoes in a jumble.

But now they're perfectly lined up, parallel and precise, next to the door.

Like someone stood in them to guard the entrance . . . and disappeared.

CHAPTER TWENTY-FOUR

ESZTER

Then

I kneel and hold my phone out to focus on a row of sómbravids climbing up a coconut tree, pretty as Christmas ornaments. I'm adding a phone-fingers emoji, *te amo,* when Brady claps my shoulder.

"You must be quite the photographer," he says. "Always zooming in on interesting details. Do you want one of you on the cliff?"

"Um, sure!" I take a few steps back and pose awkwardly.

"C'mon, we're almost there!" Amari waves her hand as she passes, and we follow her onto the trail. Vegetation scrapes and scratches at my calves. Amari points out a butterfly, flitter-fluttering like an airborne flower. "Did you know a group of butterflies is called a kaleidoscope?" she says.

"And three or more queers is a gay-gle," Brady adds, without missing a beat. The sun blares down but it's breezier up here, the hot, wet air darting around us like it wants to play tag.

I've only been here a few days, but they're travel days, which work like dog years. Already, Brady and Amari feel like old friends. They have this near-reverence for the present moment—what we're doing, how to wring any activity dry. But not in an efficiency way, not like Abby is in

Madison, queen of the *Wait, if we get off an exit earlier we can stop at Trader Joe's and not have to make another trip,* all optimize, optimize, optimize. This is different. Like: We're doing X now—how do we block out the world and let X be all there is?

It sounds obnoxious, the way I'm describing it: privileged and puerile, puke. *Nem mind arany, ami fénylik,* Dad would say—*all that glitters is not gold.* But . . . I felt butterflies in my stomach when I asked them to take me up here this morning, and when they agreed (with gusto!), I could've floated an inch or two off the ground.

It's occurred to me that I don't *really* know them, that this might be incredibly stupid—they might take this opportunity to, I don't know, steal my wallet and push me off a cliff. There was that huge story a few years back about those girls—fellow Wisconsinites—killing not one but two unsuspecting backpackers in far-flung places. But sometimes you have to trust your instincts. Brady shrieks and claws at a spiderweb he must've walked into, *Eeeeeeeh!,* and yeah, this guy does not present a clear and present danger.

On the bright side, even a couple days without Abby have made me miss her. I guess I acclimated to her sureness and wit, plus the beautiful bubbliness that draws strangers close like moths to a porch light. Being away from her has underscored it all, so that I catch myself expecting her zippy jokes and that social acuity—the way she can make any conversation flow.

I'm excited to see her again. An eight out of ten on the excitement scale . . . and that's saying something because my eight is most people's ten. I see other people (like Abby!) get *thrilled* and I want to believe they're faking it but I know it's just me, my set point topping out early, anxiety edging out the scale's peak.

And then, at the same time, I feel a nervous squeeze in my chest at the idea of seeing her. But I guess that's okay. *Soha szerelem sóhajtás nélkül édes nem lehet. Love without sighs can never be sweet.*

Mom used to say that all the time when I was dating men. She never met them—they never made it to that level of realness—but God, she had a slew of sayings about why love is supposed to suck. The implication? The issue wasn't my sexual orientation but rather my unwillingness to put up with misery. *A szerelemben több a keserű, mint az édes: In love, there's more bitterness than sweetness. Hideg kéz, meleg szív: Cold hand, warm heart.* And the real coup de grâce, *Ha nincs ló, jó a szamár is: If there ain't a horse, an ass will do.* I sometimes wonder how she truly feels about my father (who, to be fair, can be a real ass).

We wade through more overgrown vegetation, and then Brady stops, points dramatically: an old chain-link fence with barbed wire on top. In the center, a rusty gate creaks in the breeze. I feel . . . *nervous* to see it, a little zippy undercurrent of first-date energy.

"Paraíso Escondido," I read on the decaying sign.

"I thought it meant 'paradise *lost*' at first," Brady says.

"But it's actually *hidden*." Amari slaps my back as she passes.

I squint into the greenery wrapping itself around old rebar and crumbling walls. "From the looks of it, I'd say it's both."

"It must've been gorgeous when it was a resort. Wish I could've seen it." Brady leads us past a tangle of flowers and weeds in the shape of a big fountain. "I still think it's so special."

I start to reply, then stop myself. "So this wasn't always a nature preserve?" I say carefully, pointing to the fern-choked ground. "It's wild there was a business right in the middle of it."

"I think the hotel predated the preserve," Amari replies. "Pedro would know. But they only formally protected the land in . . . the late nineties, I think? So the property had a special land-use permit or whatever."

"See what I mean? A bummer we missed our chance." Brady crosses his arms, smiling. "She must've been a beaut."

"No one will mind that we're trespassing?" It's a joke but kind of not, because I'm not about breaking the law in a foreign country.

"I assume it belongs to the preserve now," Amari says. "But don't tell Pedro we came here. Unless you want to get chewed out."

I know it's dumb; I'm no longer the eight-year-old who bawls because she got in trouble in class for talking after the teacher had signaled for quiet. Which was a real thing that happened, when I didn't realize Mrs. Marriott had shushed us. Dad still grounded me when I brought home the pink slip for him to sign.

My parents were like that, standards skyscraper-high: I remember showing him my third-grade report card, the first time we got letters instead of checks and pluses. Dad glanced at it below his glasses. *Why are there two A-minuses?*

I managed a true 4.0 the next semester, thanks to him. Dad took us all out to Applebee's to celebrate and even let me order a chocolate shake for dessert.

Brady spreads his arms as we burst out of the crumbling lobby and into a courtyard. "Worth it, though, right?"

I take it in and it's like someone popped open prosecco inside my chest: It is *glorious,* a word I'd never freaking use, only that's what it is, glorious. It's eerie and still and Jurassic and wild and *hold on to your butts,* we have reached a nine on the excitement scale.

I have zero memories of being here—I was just a baby—and I couldn't find much online about the property's former glory or current state of decay. But these ruins . . . they're speaking to me in some charged, zappy way.

They both giggle at my awestruck expression. Amari tugs my wrist. "C'mon, I'll show you the creepiest part." She crosses the courtyard and skirts what looks like a motel-esque row of rooms. I trot through the weeds and find a second, smaller courtyard on the far side, a square of guest rooms around it. Amari's in an empty door frame, a flash of color in a rectangle of black. She waits for me to see her, then steps back and disappears.

I blink. Trail her to the doorway, pulse picking up as I near. One step up onto a cement patio—flower petals and fronds crushed underfoot, a frog hopping steadily—and I poke my head into the room that swallowed Amari whole.

It swallows *me* whole, this hole, the darkness strangely dampening, like soundproofing for light. But there's a weird depth to my left and right, like I'm looking down a long hallway or tunnel. And no sign of Amari. As my eyes adjust, the hotel room, strewn with bits of old furniture, comes into focus, logic following a split second later: The rooms were all linked, and with the connecting doors missing—where'd they go, how did this old mattress outlast a *door?*—it's like being inside a long train.

"See 'em?"

I jump—Amari is in the corner, motionless.

"See what?"

She raises her chin slowly and I mirror her, gasp: bats, dozens of them, hundreds, knobby and still, dangling like black chrysalises.

"It's always dark in here," she murmurs. "Even at noon. And it's always *packed* with bats." She walks toward me, gazing up at them. A tingle works up my spine. She leans in close. "You know, the Mayans believed that bats bridge the heavens and the underworld—above and below."

They're so still, they seem inanimate. I can make out their veined, spindly wings, like folded umbrellas, and the texture of their brown-black fur, fuzzy—

"Why are we whispering?"

The sibilance is so close to my ear that I scream and jump right into Brady, who somehow snuck up behind us. He shrieks too and now the bats are agitated, stirring, making strange little chirps. They flap and chitter and churn through the air like a velvety tornado and Amari bolts for the door and the three of us tumble out into the daylight.

Amari bursts out laughing. "You weren't supposed to wake the bats!" We join in, nerves bubbling into hysterics.

"This can't be good," Brady adds, between guffaws.

But it is, that's the thing. I can't explain it, but I know it with certainty.

This is good.

CHAPTER TWENTY-FIVE

ABBY

Wednesday night

*E*szter *was here. Eszter moved your shoes.* I can't stop the thought from coming. As I stare at the sandals, a gecko skims by, its skin an alien silver-blue. A bark of laughter shoots out of me, and then I grab the Tevas and close myself inside.

Get a hold of yourself, Abby. Nothing supernatural is going on here. Which means . . . what, that someone walked up my front steps and moved them?

But . . . my laptop. Closed and waiting, Eszter beaming at me from the top. And my suitcase, the piles inside messier than I remembered. Did someone come in here? Why? My heart patters and I catch my reflection in the window: wide-eyed, alone. Suddenly tomorrow can't come soon enough, tomorrow and the boat and the escape route from this island.

Suddenly I don't want to be alone.

I step into my sandals and let the front door slam. Amari's words echo in my ear: *I've got the* one *casita on the block that doesn't have a front porch.* Blocky patios jut from the first few I pass. *A couple doors down,* she promised.

Something brushes my ankle and I scream—but it's only the kitten from my first day. The whole street's empty, dim lights leaking from windows, people closed up in their houses, each a colorful fortress. I squint into the darkness. Is someone out there?

My heart detonates with beats and I hurry down the block. This has gotta be it: the one house without a front porch. The walls are seafoam green with a seashell mosaic around the door. There's a covered carport housing a flip-top trash bin and an old station wagon. The garbage lid catches the breeze and bangs against the wall. I get out the burner phone: "I'm walking by your place. (I think.) Up for some company?" Blood chugs in my ears as I hit Send.

Fifteen seconds go by without an answer, thirty, and I wish I could take it back. Am I even at the right house?

Then the door pops open. "Abby? What are you doing here?"

My resolve crumples a bit, but I square my shoulders. "I . . . wondered if you felt like hanging out. I was . . . sitting at home stressing myself out." Suddenly, the sandal thing is too ridiculous to say aloud. What, I convinced myself I was visited by a laptop-closing, shoe-straightening ghost?

She nods. "About Brady?"

I meet her huge, calm eyes, and the desperation deepens: *She can't know how pathetic I am.* Eszter's school deferment, the lease, even the baffling family photo on the back of a raggedy brochure—each is another mortifying blow. Proof I barely knew the woman I wanted to marry, the woman who, at every turn, put up barriers to setting a date. How big of an idiot am I?

"Right," I say. "You're not feeling anxious?"

"Oh, I'm a mess." Her eyes dart upward. "I'd invite you in, but my landlady . . ." She shakes her head and holds open the door. "It's fine. We'll just be quiet. Hey, I'm glad you're here. I was sitting there twiddling my thumbs."

I enter the living room, which must double as her painting studio: paint-spattered drop cloths rumpled on the floor, bright Mexican blankets covering the TV and slung over the sofa, books and used coffee mugs scattered like curios.

"Nice place you got," I say.

"Thanks. Do you need a drink? I need a drink. I think I have some rambutans."

"Rambu-what?"

She waves me into the kitchen. "Kind of like a lychee." She shakes open a cloth bag and it's that shaggy red fruit I saw at the grocery store. She peels one and takes a bite, then lifts the other half, white flesh and a black pit winking from the center. "Try it."

It looks . . . luscious, almost vulgar. My senses sharpen as I behold it, this sweet dripping thing that just touched her lips.

I catch the thought and wave it away. *We're just friends. Amari is simply a magnetic person.* I pop the fruit into my mouth. It's soft and floral with a bit of acidity. "Delicious."

"Wait till you try it in a Gibson. Here, help me peel some."

The resulting cocktail is crisp and just tart enough to make my lips purse, my mouth water. She serves our drinks in juice glasses—blue along the rim, Mexican blown glass—and the cloudy white cocktail seems to glow in the base.

"It's like drinking a full moon." Gin blooms pleasantly in my stomach. "It is, look!" I point at my glass from the top and she leans in to look. She laughs her musical laugh and then our faces are somehow close and our eyes meet and time pauses for one second, two.

"Sorry." I shift away, cheeks reddening.

"No, you're good." She picks up her drink again.

"I'm, uh . . . having a weird day. I found out some stuff about Eszter that left me reeling."

"Oh, no! Like what?"

My stomach pretzels. Three sips of a cocktail and I'm close to spilling my guts. The humiliation is still neon and fierce: *My fiancée told me lie after lie.* "I don't want to get into it. Let's just say I'll be leaving tomorrow with more questions than answers." A loamy breeze wafts through the room. "You know what's wild? I keep wanting to *ask* her. To tell her about this bizarre situation I'm in. She was the smartest person I've ever met. I could come to her with any dilemma, any puzzle, and . . . oh, no." Amari's eyes are so earnest that a laugh-sniffle pops out of me. "Don't give me that look of pity, I can't take it."

"Pity?" Her brows lift. "Has it occurred to you that it's empathy?"

I shake my head. "*Sympathy*, maybe. Unless . . ." She fixes me with a look. "Oh, gosh. You lost someone, too?"

She nods. "My boyfriend. Years ago, in Tanzania. I fell for this guy—he was really into this psychedelic drug, iboga." Her eyes glaze over. "I did it with him once. It sounds crazy, but you basically leave your body and meet your true self. But then you have to come back and if you don't have the support to, like, anchor yourself, it can be . . . bad." She peeks at me. "One time, he did this big dose and was in a weird headspace already and . . . it was too much for him." She looks down. "He died by suicide a few days later."

"Wow. I'm so sorry."

"Thanks. I was so lost. I left Africa and bummed around Mexico for a few months in this deep state of depression and shock. Ironically, it was plant medicine that helped me feel like myself again; I did an incredible peyote retreat. And then somebody at a hostel mentioned Isla Colel and . . . as soon as I set foot on it, I knew it was right." She smiles. "This place . . . it's a creative well, you know? Connected to the Source. It's been super healing for me. Brady too."

"He said something like that." We're quiet, listening to the insects and frogs. No wonder she's worried about Brady; losing another loved one to suicide would be a nightmare.

"Brady once called this place the Land of the Lost," she muses. "It draws a certain kind of person."

Amari and I lost our partners; Brady lost his mom. Pedro lost the love of his life, as Rita told it, but of course that was *after* he washed ashore.

I frown. "What did Rita lose? What's she getting over?"

Amari sips her cocktail. "I'm honestly not sure. Hey, want to hang out in the backyard? I'll bring bug spray."

"Sure." I follow her through a softly lit bedroom and out a screen door. There's a rough half-moon of mismatched deck chairs and we each settle onto one. Birdsong rolls around us: three solemn hoots, like someone blowing on the top of a beer bottle.

"Oh, for tomorrow," she says, "supposedly there's a big storm coming. The boat captain texted me about it right before you came over. So we're still on for now, but we'll keep an eye on the weather."

"Got it. Thanks for handling that. I'm all packed." I look down at my drink. "Hopefully Brady is happy to see us."

A smile flickers on her lips. "Hear, hear."

I take a long sip. "Pedro said it's not really our business where Brady is."

"Well, not everyone knows about Brady's . . . you know, mental health history."

"Rita's been fairly blasé about it, too."

She shrugs. "They don't know the extent of it." She snickers. "Wow, for once they're on the same page about something."

My ears perk up. "That reminds me . . . before the boat ride on Wednesday, you were gonna tell me something about Rita and Pedro. How they drive each other bananas. Do you remember?"

She looks like an owl, eyes wide, head tilted. "Sorry, I don't know what I was going to say." She sips thoughtfully. "They have really different energies. They get under each other's skin."

I shake my head. "Okay, but right before that, I heard Rita and Pedro arguing in town. Neither one would tell me why."

Amari busies herself with her drink. "Probably one of their little squabbles."

But the gin makes me bold. "Why do I feel like you're not telling me something?"

She sits up, and it's that thick, barbed moment when someone's about to tell you something—no going back, no pretending it's not hanging between you. I flash to being in bed with Eszter, streetlights silhouetting the window blinds, staring at the ceiling as I prodded her, the pain unpleasant but irresistible, like tonguing a canker sore: *Just tell me what's bothering you. Is it your thesis? Your parents? Did I do something?*

"What?" I prompt again.

Amari sighs. "Okay, you know how you found Rita helping baby turtles reach the water? Per Pedro, that's actually bad for them. They need to imprint where they're gonna return to lay their own eggs. Plus it stresses them out, and bacteria from human hands can make them sick."

I rear back. "I had no idea."

"Me neither!" She throws her arms out, all earnest. "But he was upset and confronted Rita about it. He wanted to yell at you too, but she didn't want him lecturing you during your first group outing. So then, when I got to the beach, before Pedro showed up with the boat, Rita seemed . . . off."

"She did?" *Perfect day for a boat ride,* she called, hand on the brim of her floppy hat. *Did* she seem distressed? Then again, I'd known her for thirty-six hours at that point. It hits me again: I don't know these people at all.

"Yep. When we were setting out, I asked what was up, and she told me what happened with Pedro. And then . . . when he and I finally got a moment alone together, I . . ." She itches her nose, then clutches her hands together. "I told him to leave you alone, that it wasn't your fault. There was nothing you could do now and it'd only make you feel bad."

So *that's* what she and Pedro were arguing about in the trees: me. I'm disappointed on multiple levels; I was hoping it had something to do with Eszter, some new, key intel. "That sucks. I never meant to hurt the turtles."

"I know. That's what I said." She looks away. "You were only trying to help."

Now it's obvious why Rita didn't tell me—she felt bad and knew I would too.

"Thanks for defending me." I drain the last of my cocktail. "Even if I'm an inadvertent turtle murderer."

She touches my knee. "Oh, manslaughter at best."

"Turtle-slaughter? Nope, that's worse." We're giggling again and I start to relax. Of course the two arguments I witnessed had nothing to do with Eszter . . . or even Brady.

Amari wraps both hands around her glass. "Rita has this, this *motherly* energy. We all naturally started deferring to her. And Pedro didn't like that, out of . . . I don't know, seniority? Misogyny? Obviously this is all subtext." She shrugs. "She can't help that we adore her. She's, like, our house mom."

I raise my eyebrows. "Was that a *sorority* reference?!"

She smacks my arm. "I'm aware of how the Greek world functions, thank you. And yes, in my youth I attended some frat parties."

"Is that what turned you into a big ol' lesbian?" I joke.

"Sure didn't make me straighter!" She chuckles again. "No, I had a girlfriend in high school. My parents were super supportive—they're, like, aging hippies who were marching for gay rights before I was born."

"That's awesome." An ember of jealousy: *Must be nice.*

"I know, I'm lucky. But then they got really confused when I started dating a dude in college." She runs her fingers through her hair. "It's pretty wild that, once you come out, you're, like, contractually bound to stick with it forever."

"True." I hadn't felt even a flicker of desire to date men after I kissed a girl in college, but I saw her point. "I mean, it's weird that we have to come out in the first place. We expect fourteen-year-olds to sit down with their parents and say, *Hello, here's who I want to bone.*"

"Totally." She grabs my hand; the pressure zips up to my heart. "It's not anyone else's business." I squeeze her hand back. These drinks are deceptively strong. "I could make us margaritas," she says, "or . . . would you rather have another Gibson?"

I chuckle. "We're playing Would You Rather now?"

Her eyes sparkle. "What is life if not a big game of Would You Rather?"

I shake my empty glass. "I'd rather have another drink with you than go home right now." My stomach flutters as I follow her into the kitchen. What am I doing?

We volley as we juice the limes: I'd rather have horns coming out of my head than stegosaurus plates along my spine. She'd rather wear a tuxedo every day than a coffee sack.

Finally she hands me a drink and we head back onto the patio, where the wind whips like it's fighting its way out. I sit close to her, and when our knees touch, my chest fills like a water balloon.

"My turn." She takes a gulp. "Would you rather have your pinkie cut off or, every ten minutes for the rest of your life, randomly smell some leftover Chinese food?"

I cock my head. "Do I get to choose which pinkie?"

A flick of laughter. "Sure."

"Can other people smell the takeout?"

She whacks my knee. "You're overthinking it."

"I can't help it, I'm a data scientist!" My heart's thumping, effervescence growing in my ribs. "Hmm, I wonder if you could write an algorithm to calculate the net impact of either situation."

"Oh, please. The game's not Which Is Objectively Better." She narrows the gap between us. The breeze feels crackly, alive. "Stop thinking logically! Turn off that big brain of yours for a second." She's so close I can see individual eyelashes. "And don't say something dumb like, *Without any cortical tissue, I couldn't generate neuronal activity.*"

I clap heartily. "That was good!"

She slides invisible glasses up her nose. "*According to my neural networks—*"

A sudden whoosh of rain makes us leap to our feet.

"C'mon." I grab her hand and start to head for the door in the sideways downpour.

But to my surprise, she pulls away. Grinning, she turns on her heel and dashes into the center of the lawn. She yells to be heard over the storm's roar: "Would you rather go inside or dance in the rain with me?"

The seconds fan out so that, for a moment, I feel water beading on my skin and inching through my clothes. I see Amari in slow motion, arms outstretched, head tilted back to let the rain splash down on her.

The storm thrashes against my ears as I chase after her. She grabs my hands and coaxes me into a twirl. Rain soaks into my scalp, through my clothes, every bit of me slick like I jumped into a pool.

Amari opens her mouth to drink the rain and before I can think, I do something wild, so unlike me, the Abby I never am in Wisconsin.

I grab her face and kiss her hard.

CHAPTER TWENTY-SIX

MARTA

Tonight

What killed her? Marta will never know.

But she thinks about it regularly. *What happened to you?* Qué pasó to Young Marta, the carefree girl, springing with energy, trusting things would always feel this way? Now she yanks open the back door and reenters the house, a basket of clean laundry tucked under one arm. Behind her, clothespins cartwheel on the line.

A few minutes ago, she tucked Camila back into bed—why does her granddaughter have nightmares whenever she spends the night here?—and from a window upstairs, she spotted forgotten laundry snapping on the line. As she gathered it, she noted the strawberry stain still clinging to her favorite blouse—*Thanks, Miguel,* with his perpetually sticky, chubby hands—and somehow that thought cracked something open, the awareness that she's old and boring, that her zest for life slipped away without her noticing, like a single sock evaporating somewhere between the washing machine and clothesline and drawer.

She dumps the clothes on the sofa and calls out for Carlos, who stands heavily from his armchair and comes over to help. She and Carlos were high school sweethearts, fools in love, and when they finished school and found work—her at the hotel, Carlos as the apprentice to the island's carpenter—life on Isla Colel felt just about perfect.

The island was so lively then. There was a steady influx and outflow of visitors, boomeranging like blood in a beating heart—fascinating people who chatted with her by the pool or at the front desk. Carlos took over for his boss and Marta hung out her own shingle: She set up cruises for tourists, whale-watching tours, sunset sails, fishing expeditions that ended at the fonda, where sun-sleepy travelers ate their own catch of the day.

Customers loved it, well-heeled folks from Guadalajara and Mexico City cosplaying at island life. Paraíso Escondido named her a preferred vendor and business boomed. Carlos's services were in demand, too, and he went from home to home, renovating kitchens, erecting chicken coops, rescuing sagging carports and damaged roofs. They had a small wedding in the church and then drinks and dancing on Playa Oscura, where the sunset was like a grand stained glass window. For a few happy years, Marta thought: *I could do this forever.*

Then—it's hard to pick out a date for the tombstone: RIP, CAREFREE MARTA. The hotel closing was the biggest hit, of course. It dumbfounded her when some Coleleños called it a blessing; a heart attack, that's what it was, cutting off the island's lifeblood. Once, tipsy at Casa Herrera, she got into an argument about it with Pedro, that smug transplant. *Do you realize how self-righteous and patronizing you sound?* she finally snapped. *So you like the island better when it's poorer—how virtuous of you.* Carlos jumped in: *I think it's time to get you home.* Like *she* was the problem. The disdain in Pedro's eyes—she's never forgotten it.

Even before the hotel shuttered, of course, Marta gave birth to Ximena. Oh, how things changed the day she became a mother—she couldn't have pictured it, the strange sensation of watching her own heart exist outside her chest; staring at the sweep of little Ximena's cheek and knowing there was nothing, *nothing* she wouldn't do to protect this girl. She felt different then, but not old, necessarily. In a way, Ximena made her feel like a child again. Fresh eyes on everything, blinking with wonder.

Through the window, the sheets strung on their neighbors' balcony billow and flap.

"I heard a big storm might hit us tomorrow," Marta says. "Wonder if it'll affect the ferry."

As if in response, a long, low peal of thunder vibrates through the house. Next to her, Carlos flinches.

"When did you get so jumpy?" she teases. She crosses to the window and yanks down the sash as rain smacks against the glass.

Once Ximena was in school, Carlos helped Marta start another business—they turned their ground floor into a studio apartment and started renting it out to the trickle of tourists still enamored with Isla Colel. Airbnb launched and Marta signed up pronto. Years passed, eras that only grew distinct after they'd ended. Ximena met Tito, may God rest his soul, and had little Camila, then Miguel, making Marta an abuelita. And now she feels . . . *older,* stiffer, a different skeleton scaffolding her skin.

Lately, Ximena's been talking about moving to the mainland; she says she's sick of her teaching position at Isla Colel's tiny school. She calls the island stifling. If only she could've seen it when the hotel was open, sophisticated polyglots coursing through the plaza pública.

Marta sees her daughter's point; it *is* quiet now, and Ximena wants her kids to have opportunities she didn't. But Marta can't help taking it personally, like Ximena *resents* them for raising her on this beautiful drop of paradise. Marta doesn't know what she'll do if her daughter and sweet grandchildren move away.

It's been a rough year, overall. There was that horrible business with Eszter, of whom both Marta and Carlos had grown rather fond. When Eszter's girlfriend stopped by the house an hour ago, it took Marta far longer than it should've to sort out what was going on. (*Eszter was a lesbian?* she thought dully, taking in this new girl's huge brown eyes and close-cropped hair.)

She'd been making herself a snack and Gloria the grocer, the island's resident busybody, was blinking at her impatiently and, well. Marta was too caught off guard to offer anything other than the truth, without considering how much whipping out the lease might hurt Eszter's girlfriend's feelings. What a tragedy that was, a nightmare; after Eszter's death, Marta couldn't even *think* about welcoming more Airbnb guests into their home. It was like that part of her personality had withered to nothing, the side that loved being in hospitality. (And it was, of course, a blessing that Eszter had paid for the year up front.)

So they stopped renting out the studio. They spread out, turned the den into a playroom for the grandkids. And Carlos's business has picked up lately. She joked that he must be drumming up business by sabotaging the island's golf carts and ATVs with wire cutters.

But Carlos's shoulders puffed. *I would never betray my community like that. You can't buy the kind of trust I have.* She tried one more joke— *Sounds like you're practicing for a stump speech;* he was always talking about running for the island council—but he just rolled his eyes.

She's lucky to have him, and so blessed to have sweet Ximena and beautiful Camila and Miguel, whose giraffe-like stares and peach-fuzz ears and sweet round bellies fill her with a wonder so intense, she almost can't bear it sometimes. But every once in a while—especially as Camila gets bigger; when did she become a miniature teenager?!—Marta glimpses herself in her granddaughter. The old Marta, the *young* one, full of boundless vigor.

It's funny—back then, all she wanted was for nothing to change.

And now, not always, not every day, but on occasion . . . she wishes everything would.

CHAPTER TWENTY-SEVEN
ABBY

Wednesday night

Amari smiles before kissing me back, her fingers finding my jaw and sliding up into my hair. Rain spills down both our faces and mingles with the kiss; it's sweet and charged and tastes like gin and rambutan and rainwater, tart and bright. She pulls away and looks into my eyes, and all I can see around her is a vertical torrent like we're standing beneath a waterfall, and there's that pulsating moment when anything is possible . . .

And then the thought zips through my consciousness: *This isn't right.* Kissing Amari—the way her lips taste and mouth moves aren't *Eszter,* my Eszter, and what am I doing?

"What is it?" Rain spatters across her eyebrows, down her cheeks, over her collarbones. She's beautiful and I hover on the precipice; I could lean forward and tumble over the edge.

But instead, I step back. "Sorry, I'm . . ." I shake my head. I'm everything at once: inconsolable about Eszter, ashamed of today's humiliating discoveries, anxious about my grip on reality, and, strikingly, embarrassed to fall apart at a sweet, single kiss.

"Don't apologize. It's okay." She stretches a tentative hand toward my arm but I pull away. Her face changes—like a spell is broken. "No, *I'm* sorry. I know you're still working through everything with Eszter."

"You didn't do anything wrong." We cross the lawn. "But yeah, it's . . . a lot." She holds open the screen door and I step inside, rainwater pattering off me.

She crosses to her closet. "Do you want to borrow some clothes?"

I raise my eyebrows. "You're not kicking me out?"

Grinning, she tosses me a towel. "Stay as long as you want. No funny business, I promise. I just . . . like hanging out with you."

A fly bumbles through the bedroom, bumping into things. I smile. "Then I'll stay."

She lends me a dry tank top and sweatpants and I change in the bathroom. They smell like her—her conditioner or lotion or something—and my stomach flips. I like her; I really like her. Is it selfish of me to let that attraction distract me from all the real reasons I'm here?

Men are just a distraction—that's what Mom used to say, rolling her eyes from the couch. I didn't date at all in high school, didn't have any interest. I now see that my queerness was a key reason, but at the time, I told myself it was because I had better things to do: a GPA to maintain, a varsity swim team to lead to state finals, college applications to sweep me away from Elmridge, Wisconsin. Why bother dating? Nothing could beat the high of being the best, the hardest-working, the winner.

After Eszter died, I thought I'd return to that mentality. *Never again.* Back to what even teenage Abby knew was the safest way to be: strong, buffered, self-reliant. So that nobody and nothing could make my life grind to a halt again.

But here's Amari, a beatnik artist who skydived out of her own comfortable existence. I won't even *see* her again after this trip. What am I doing here?

When I come out, she's on the couch in the living room.

"Have a seat." She pats the cushion next to her. A chorus of frogs and insects twangs against the windows.

But instead I cross to the easel, currently empty, a pane of air where a painting should be. There's a jumble of canvases stacked against the wall, all turned away from me, their wood-framed backs flecked with paint.

"Mind if I look at these?" I sink to my knees and tip one forward.

It's beautiful, an off-center portrait of a lolling cat, in a pointillism-esque technique that's somehow both realistic and technicolor. Wait, why is this so familiar?

"You did the paintings at the fonda! Right?"

"Guilty as charged!" She chuckles. "It hasn't led to any sales, but I thought the place could use a glow-up."

The canvases thunk against one another as I rifle through: a rambu-tan, a cluster of those sómbravid flowers, a spiderweb studded with pearls of dew. I admire a portrait of Rita: It really looks like her, with sparkling eyes and shallow wrinkles like a topographic map.

Brady. The next one is pitch-perfect, the kaleidoscope of strokes and dots somehow capturing his poof of hair, splatter of freckles, and goofy smirk. I hold it out, feeling the braille-like daubs beneath my fingertips. The canvas is encrusted with a tender, gentle love you can't fake. Some-thing she said before the boat ride comes back to me: *He's like my little brother. We . . . figured out we have a bunch in common.* They both lost someone, someone very, very precious to them. I know that pain, how it builds up in your bloodstream, marking you in some quiet, permanent way. How it colors every interaction, every moment, for the rest of your life.

"These are incredible," I say.

"Thank you," she says. "I need to go through and pick some to sell at the market in Cancún next week."

I flip to the next one and everything around me darkens, like my view is a photo and someone's playing with the vignette settings. It's another portrait, lovingly rendered, every detail just right.

Here—in painted form, light glinting on her hair and eyes, naked to where the frame cuts her off below her collarbones, and smiling that smile I thought was only for me—is Eszter.

"Wow," I say softly. "This is really impressive."

Something high-pitched and strange flutters in my chest—jealousy, discomfort at the idea of Amari observing her so fully. My insecurity takes the wheel: Amari's charming and beautiful, and—if I'm being honest—more Eszter's type than mine. But I always knew with certainty that Eszter wouldn't cheat on me. She was so loyal, so principled, that the idea seemed as ridiculous as her, I don't know, sprouting a third arm.

But that was my *idea* of Eszter. The Eszter who told me the truth. And not at all, it turns out, the Eszter who walked the streets of Isla Colel.

"Thank you—I was really happy with how that turned out." Amari leans forward, plants her forearms on her knees. "Yeah, I painted that . . . the second or third time she came to Colel."

CHAPTER TWENTY-EIGHT

ESZTER

Then

A mari sashays onto the restaurant's patio, eyes glittering.

"Guess what I have?" Silver keys dangle from her fingers. They jingle and jangle and spangle in the sun.

I stand. "Motorcycle? Golf cart? Scooter?"

Brady bounces on the balls of his feet. "Treasure chest? Lockbox? Mysterious storage unit that hasn't been opened in forty-three years?!"

"Better." She slams her palms on the tabletop, *clank:* "*Red. Fucking. Rum.*"

"*Red Rum!*" Brady's arms shoot up, touchdown! Other people in the fonda turn to stare.

"Pedro's motorboat," Amari explains. "It's just a little aluminum fishing boat, but it's fun for zipping around."

Pedro's gruff and grouchy in a vaguely endearing way, but I can't imagine him handing over his boat keys.

"He's letting you borrow it?" Brady's incredulous too.

"He lost a bet." Amari grins. "And he knows I'm responsible. C'mon, let's put our swimsuits on and meet back at the marina." She turns to me. "It's the *perfect* way to spend your last day here."

"Last day *for now*. I'll be back in all of . . . what, a month?"

Brady shakes his shoulders. "Don't worry, Eszter. We won't have too much fun without you."

Oh, what a few days it's been. This morning, as I hung out in Pigeon Pose on a yoga mat in my Airbnb, a memory surfaced, an early one. Dad had taken Laszlo and me to the famous Venetian Pool in Miami. Mom had refused to go—she hated getting her hair wet, and eventually I decided I don't love being in the water either—but at the time the pool felt like paradise: arches and fountains and grottos and caves, curly wrought-iron fences and the happiest sunbathers I ever did see.

While other parents lounged around the deck, Dad splashed in with us, carrying us around his thick middle, tossing us up in the air and into the water. I wonder now what put him in such a good mood—his playful spells were infrequent and memorable. As exhilarating as Class A substances.

Two boys asked if I wanted to play a game with them, then mocked me for not knowing the rules for Marco Polo. A few minutes later, I was sitting on a lounge chair with Dad, crying my eyes out while he wrapped a towel around me and asked what was wrong: "Mi a baj, tündi?" I looked out at Laszlo, already horsing around in the deep end with all the big kids. Like he belonged.

But then—I made a decision and sat up straight. "Nothing. We're having a good day and I won't let anyone ruin it." I looked up at his face, at his hooked nose and square jaw. "Thanks for taking us here, Dad. Let's go back in the water."

His eyes twinkled with delight, and even now, a quarter-century later, I can still feel my high-pitched glee. "That's my girl," he told me. "Maybe it's time for some ice cream?"

Now I signal for the waitress, Silvana, and hand her a fistful of pesos. "Disfruten su día," she says. *Enjoy your day.*

I know we will.

When I get back to my rental on Calle Estrella, my phone pings with a photo from Abby: It's a gym selfie, her arm flexed, delt popping. I send back fire emojis, because damn, she is hot. She follows up with a text: "Safe travels today! Can't WAIT to see you and hear about your progress."

My ribs flood with ice and for a second, I can't breathe. I feel cold and crampy and a little sick, doubled over with guilt. But . . . this will all be worth it. Abby will understand. I step outside and carefully position myself in front of a palm tree and send a selfie back.

Elvágyódás—a word I've never quite been able to translate for Abby. She thinks it means "wanderlust," and that's *close*, but it's not quite a concrete desire to travel. No, it's less zesty, more ennui-adjacent: absence, longing, homesickness for something you're not sure where to find. I can't remember ever *not* feeling it. I thought it had something to do with being first-generation, i.e., not sure where I fit in. But here, on Isla Colel, something incredible happened: The feeling shrank and shriveled like a puddle in the sun.

It's sweeter too because I wasn't expecting it. I came to Isla Colel with my armor up, prepared to keep a safe and healthy distance between myself and these free spirits who might not actually love that I'm here. But then: They were wonderful! ¡Adiós, elvágyódás! It's beautiful. And agonizing. Because soon I'll be home in Madison, and October in Madison is cold and gray and brittle, and now my flip-flops slap against the hot road as I make my way south.

"Eszter!" Hilde waves from across the town square and jogs to catch up with me, blue eyes sparkling. Last time I saw her, she mentioned she's a freelance writer, and something about the idea of airy-fairy Hilde as a journalist cracked me up. "Where are you heading?" she asks.

"To the marina. What about you?"

"Same!" she says. "I'll walk with you. Are you going to the mainland?"

"Not yet. But I'm taking the ferry this afternoon—time for me to head home."

"Such a quick trip!" she says. She's older than us, though it's impossible to tell by how much. She's got one of those bright, ageless faces, thirty-one or forty-two or, who knows, fifty-three.

"I know. But I'll be back soon. What are you heading ashore for?"

"Acupuncture and Reiki," she replies. "If I don't go twice a week . . ." She shakes her head gravely, hand on her belly. This rings a bell—Amari said something about how Hilde's system is really struggling here and how she needs to avoid ice and fresh veggies "with the same intensity as you with your eggs and peanuts." Which irritated me at the time—foodborne illness, much like food intolerances and dairy aversion and gluten sensitivity, does not equal food allergies. But I let it go, because it was nice of Amari to remember my restrictions. Even people I've known for years still occasionally offer me trail mix or bring Snickers pie to my potlucks.

"Do you know what Reiki is?" she asks.

"It's, like, energy healing, right?"

I curse my lack of a poker face as she bursts out laughing. "It's okay—I can tell you think it's bullshit." She pushes her white-blond waves over her shoulder. "I used to mock people for believing in things they couldn't see and hear and touch. Not anymore. Take the energy here, on the island—this is such a special place. When you come here, all your shit comes up. Colel draws it out of you like a washing machine. You feel that, right?"

For a split second, everything around us seems to dilate—the dock below us, the ocean around us, the birds overhead and people milling around the marina, are magnified, crisp, like the island's demanding my attention, *Knock knock, anybody home?* I feel a strange, shivery exuberance deep inside.

A boat horn blares, and Hilde waves to someone in a speedboat.

"¡Hasta luego!" She breaks into a jog.

"Good luck!" I call after her.

I sit down on a bench. Amari and Pedro are always unhurried, *island time,* they call it. It's almost unbelievable that I'll board a plane in Cancún tonight and end up in Madison. The last few days have felt like a break from my life, and once I see Abby, all the real stuff will kick in again, like a motor, *kachunk.* Our brand-new engagement. The second half of the semester. Eventually talking to Dr. Patel about my capstone.

Capstone. Dr. Patel casually mentioned it's an archaeological term:

the big flat rock plopped on top of a megalithic tomb. A coffin lid, in essence. So on the nose.

Actually, you know what? I just figured something out. A big part of what makes the expats, and Amari and Brady in particular, so great is that they don't give a hoot about all the things that make me "impressive." They barely asked what I'm studying or what I did before biz school. They scarcely blinked when I told them I'm engaged. The things that normally get people all excited, all *Congratulations good for you!!!*, hardly register with them. You'd think it'd make me feel invisible, but, paradoxically, not hiding behind that stuff has left me feeling . . . well, *seen*.

Abby likes my palm-tree selfie. "You doing anything on your last day?" she texts.

I hesitate. "I'm just walking by the water," I tell her, like the truth is a wild animal I must approach inch by inch.

"Send more photos so I can live vicariously!" It's so nakedly cheery my stomach folds in two.

I turn and send her a photo of my pretty engagement ring, nothing but blue-green water behind it.

Right then, Amari appears, footsteps ponderous on the metal pier. I wave and put my phone away, Wisconsin forgotten.

I only see Abby's reply hours later, when I'm salt-glazed and sunburned and beer-tipsy, exhausted and happy from the day: "You're killing me."

CHAPTER TWENTY-NINE

ABBY

Wednesday night

My eyes fill with TV static and I sit back on the floor. I can't control my breathing; my heart beats so fast I'm sure it'll burst.

"What is it?" Amari, alarmed, crosses to me. She crouches and touches my back. "What's going on?"

"She's . . . I'm . . . oh my God." I start laughing, a manic, miserable squawk. Finally I stop and squeeze my eyes closed. "What the hell is going on?"

"What happened?" She sits next to me. "You seemed fine a second ago."

I get myself under control. "I thought . . . Eszter told me she only came here once. The trip where she died . . . that was the first time she visited."

"What? No!" Amari leans away, as if blown back by the force of the revelation. She shakes her head, mystified. Again, a tingle of suspicion: Is this feigned or genuine? *What is real?* "I met her the first time she came here. We were on the same ferry over. It was . . . October, I think."

"The first time *that you know of,*" I say shakily. "Did she say it was her first time? Because that was a lie, too. Apparently her family came here when she was a baby."

"Really?" Amari's eyes are two big question marks. "She didn't tell me that."

I swipe at my cheeks. "When did you see her here? What other dates?"

She cocks her head. "I guess it was three times—pretty close together. October and then I think once in . . . late November maybe? But those were quick trips, like long weekends." A corner of my brain begins to bristle, itching for my attention quietly at first and then with growing intensity. Dr. Patel's words strobe in my mind: *There was something else she had to focus on.*

"And then the last time was the one in January," she says. "I'm pretty sure October was her first time as an adult, though. I introduced her to everyone—including Pedro, who's been here for a long time—and no one seemed to know her."

The itch is a full-on inferno, fire ants inside my skull. I push my fingers into my temples. "When in October?"

"The end of the month. I remember because I had a meeting with a gallery owner in Playa del Carmen and I spotted her on the ferry back."

"Okay," I say slowly. "Late October, late November, and January."

"Right. I'm—God, I'm sorry, I had no idea you didn't know that."

The humiliation soars through me like an arrow. Well, no sense keeping it from her now: "I also found out she signed a lease. She was planning to stay here a whole year. Do you have any idea why?"

Amari's eyes flare, and then slowly, she shakes her head. "I'm sorry. That's really odd. She definitely didn't tell me she was staying." She presses her lips together. "Did she want it as, like, a vacation destination? Was she planning to go back and forth?"

I feel instantly idiotic for not thinking of this. But my brain was so firmly on the she-was-leaving-me track . . . could Amari be right? *I need to tell you something.* Maybe Eszter figured when I saw the island for myself, with its lush jungle and blue water and friendly inhabitants . . .

My phone starts to ring, and though I don't have the number saved to my phone, I recognize the 305 area code: Miami. I excuse myself and duck into Amari's room, closing the door behind me.

"Hello?"

"Abby, it's Shane. Are you okay?"

It's weird to hear her voice, just like it feels strange to see marketing emails in my inbox and get Slacks from my TimeIn coworkers here. Does the rest of the world still exist, outside my island biodome? I think vaguely of my own best friend, Mei, her life chugging along as usual in Madison. Unfathomable.

"Thanks for calling, Shane." I sit on the edge of the bed. "I'm on Isla Colel, actually, and I'm trying to figure out some stuff about Eszter."

"Oh, wow. How can I help?" Though I only met her a few times, I always liked Shane—the kind of person who's so unbelievably *nice,* you feel like a mediocre human in comparison.

"Her capstone project," I say. "The Haven? She . . . sorta stopped updating me on it in the fall." Shane doesn't respond, so I press on. "I talked to her advisor and he said she wasn't going to return for the spring semester. But she cared so much about this project, you know? She wasn't *only* doing it for school . . ."

I trail off. The jumble at the bottom of Amari's closet seems to stare back at me: a flock of bras, a shoebox brimming with crinkled tubes of paint.

"I'm confused," Shane finally says. "The project . . . it's been off for a while."

My pulse thrashes in my ears. "Since she died?"

"No. Er . . ." She makes me wait, like she's stringing together the sentence. "Eszter abandoned the project long before she died."

The room whooshes into a sudden, cottony silence. My blood bangs against my rib cage, down both arms, rushing in and out like a pounding surf.

But then . . . another part of me, beaten down, embarrassed, isn't surprised at all. "So she wasn't staying with you in the fall," I say flatly.

"When I thought she was in Miami working on the Haven. October and right after Thanksgiving."

"Wait, when? No. I . . . I didn't know you thought she was with me." A sharp intake of breath. "I'm sorry, she asked me not to say anything when she told the team the Haven project wasn't going to happen. She wanted to tell her dad on her own time. I mean, you know Istvan. She was worried he'd, like, shame her."

"Right. Or gloat." I swallow. "When, exactly, did she stop working on it?"

"The first or second week of October, I think."

I stare at my feet. Right around when I proposed, then. "Why'd she give up?"

"She couldn't get the numbers to work. Contractors in Miami are *so* expensive. A grant she was really counting on fell through, and then, even though her dad's connections were cutting her these big discounts . . . there just wasn't a way to make it feasible."

A rock forms in my stomach. Eszter had promised, *promised* me she'd do this on her own—without taking a single penny or introduction from her dad. I blink back tears. "Do you think that's why she dropped out of school not too long after? She couldn't finish her capstone and couldn't graduate without it?"

"It could be. I didn't know she withdrew." Shane sounds miserable. "I'm sorry, Abby. She didn't tell me anything else. I . . . I really wish she could've opened up to us."

I unpeel a thought I've been avoiding: Eszter didn't seem to struggle with depression, let alone suicidality, in all the years I knew her. But she was a perfectionist. A huge setback like this . . .

But no, that doesn't make sense; why would she have signed a lease? What was she doing *here*? Was she simply hiding out from all of us, licking her wounds?

I thank Shane and begin hunting for the calendar app on my phone, but it's not synced to my account. I change back into my damp clothes, still drying on the shower rail, tell Amari I need to head home, and trudge back in the rain.

———

Inside, after a moment's hesitation, I shove a chair under the doorknob, just in case. On my laptop, I confirm exactly what I suspected: Eszter's two latest trips to "Miami" spanned October 26 through 30 and November 30 through December 4. So she was *here*. Lying through her teeth.

I dig in my Photos app for images she sent me during that time. A selfie in front of a palm tree. A portrait-mode shot of what is, I now realize, very clearly a cluster of sómbravids. A picture of her hand, engagement ring sparkling, with a nondescript ocean in the background. I feel hollow, boneless. This was an elaborate ruse. What was her plan? What did she think would happen when I stepped off the ferry on January 15 and learned she'd been here so many times, she was practically an expat herself?

I swipe up on a picture to see more data, but of course, below the date and time and iPhone camera used, there's only an "Add a location" button . . . privacy-obsessed Eszter always kept location services turned off. But there are clues. August—that's the last time she sent me photos from Miami, *actually* Miami, the road signs in English, restaurant names legible in the background. She'd given me zero indication the project was teetering on the brink. She even sent me a selfie from the site they'd identified, an abandoned middle school in Wynwood.

I squint at the photo. Something's bothering me about the construction site behind her. There isn't much to see, just a barricade with a smattering of signs on it: NO PARKING and PRIVATE PROPERTY and NO TRESPASSING, all shiny and bold, with a faded LOT FOR SALE sign still hanging crookedly. "Big day!" she'd texted.

It clicks—the signs Eszter put up around what was supposed to be the Haven are the same shiny, holographic metal I spotted on the fence near Paraíso Escondido. Which . . . is strange, come to think of it. If the hotel closed more than twenty years ago, wouldn't the signs be rusty and old-looking? And if they're new, why would somebody . . . ?

All hail Google and the article I unearth in seconds: *Here's how to find out who owns a house or land in Mexico*. It leads me to the Public

Registry of Federal Property, where I fill out a form, entering Paraíso Escondido's old address. I hit Submit, praying the auto-translate did me right, and I wait. I know what's going on under the hood: APIs hitting endpoints, retrieving data, all in a fraction of a second.

Holy crap—someone started to buy the property in November. *Sale pending*. A corporation called Izmos Construction Inc.

My pulse thrums. I open another tab and search for it.

These are results for gizmos. I click on *Search instead for izmos* and sift through the results. Finally, a hit.

In a Hungarian-English dictionary. *Izmos*, apparently, means "muscular" or "strong."

My heart's like a jackhammer. I try "Izmos Construction Miami" and this time I get a result from a .gov site: Florida's Division of Corporations database.

> *IZMOS CONSTRUCTION INC. (DOS #6443339) is a Domestic Business Corporation in Miami-Dade registered with the Florida Department of State (FLDOS). The business entity was initially filed on October 13, 2023. The current entity status is Active (current). The registered business location is at 1345 Brickell Ave, Miami, FL 33131.*

But it's the last line that really makes my throat dry:

> *Corporate officers: Eszter Farkas, Istvan Farkas.*

Then

"Got it, will do. Thanks, Dad." I hang up and set the phone down next to my notebook, where I jotted notes throughout the call: *chain of title* and *special-use permit* and *design and access statement*. Already, he sounds different when he talks to me. Even-tempered, respectful. The tone I've heard him use with investors and bigwigs.

I can't help it—I let out a happy yelp.

I tiptoe into the living room and look out at the street—half-lit from the freshly risen sun, spidery with palm-tree shadows. Though I'll be a few minutes early, I decide to head for the fonda. I've got a standing date with Amari and Brady, who hugged me hello yesterday as if a month hadn't passed since my October visit.

The air is still today, soupy, no breeze to keep the tropical heat moving. I reach the restaurant and wave hello to the waitress, Silvana, who seems to always be here, shiny hair in a perfect plait. She greets me warmly—this is what I mean, how is everyone here so *nice*?—and sets a steaming mug of coffee on the counter before I can even ask. She knows a little English—understands it better than she can speak it, she tells me—and we make small talk for a minute, me stringing together my syncopated Spanish, her coming to the rescue when my limited vocabulary fails.

"I like that you try to speak Spanish," she says, all slow and deliberate while I concentrate, churn through the foreign syllables . . . then nod in excited comprehension.

"The other gringos don't try?" I ask.

She shrugs. "A little. Pedro is Mexican and Brady is always using his translation app. But"—and here she says something she needs to repeat a few times, in different words, until I grok her meaning—"the expats mostly keep to themselves."

I try to picture it, can't. If I lived here, you *bet* I'd become fluent. Not to assimilate, exactly, I'd never be a Coleleña, but because language is a decoder key—the way to *literally* understand a place and its people. When my parents first came to the States, they enrolled in night classes to learn English, and once Laszlo was old enough to start baby-jabbering, they refused to let him use Hungarian, even though they spoke it at home.

(Thank God, they'd relaxed the rule by the time I came along three years later. Even today, while Laszlo has no trouble following the conversation, he sometimes struggles to retrieve the right Hungarian word. Speaking Hungarian is—and I can't stress this enough—the *one,* single-dingle way I outshine him.)

And then . . . here are Brady and Amari, having a loud English conversation I catch floating in from the back room. It's a sittin'-pretty privileged decision—straight-up *existing* in a foreign place without trying to assimilate.

But then I tread through the dim interior and spot them, sweaty and relaxed, empty mugs and plates slick with bean juice scattered on the table. Brady says, "Morning!" as I approach, and Amari raises her glass of OJ and *gahhh,* I don't despise them, not even a little.

"I thought I'd be early!" I slide into a seat.

Amari chugs her juice and slams the glass on the table. "Not today— I've got a date with Hilde." She checks the time on her phone. "I'm taking five thousand photos and doing some sketching so I can paint her portrait. Brady, I'll let you know when I need you." She grins at me. "I'm doing a portrait series of all the expats."

"Cool!" Big, broad smile but I feel a twinge of envy. I know I'm not an expat; I know I'm not like them. They're freewheeling and bohemian, mysterious and manic. Curvy question marks that make me feel extra square.

And I can cosplay their boho lifestyle, sure. They still think I'm here as a devoted traveler, someone with airline miles to burn and a penchant for quiet destinations. I'll tell them about the project when the time is right, though. I'll sit down with my orange notebook, write out a script, and practice the conversation in the mirror, murmuring the lines under my breath like a big, anxious weirdo. I'll make them understand what a boon it'll be—an eco-resort, totally self-sustaining. Raising money for conservation efforts and drowning the island in funds. I'll do it right; it'll be a net positive, they'll see.

But then Amari brightens. "Can I paint your portrait too, Eszter? I know you're not a permanent resident, but . . ."

"I would *love* that."

"Great." She stands and hoists her bag onto her shoulder. "You can come by my place later."

"You owe me for brekkie!" Brady calls after her, and she spins around, flashes a huge grin, and is gone.

Silvana stops by the table and I order tamales. "Brady, you'll wait with me, right?"

He opens his palms. "What else have I got to do?"

We chat for a few minutes, but I can tell something's up. Silvana sets my plate down right as I call him on it.

"I'm a bit distracted." He sighs. "An old mate emailed me today. Someone from primary school. Said he's eating his way across Mexico and he heard I'm somewhere in Quintana Roo. I asked who told him that and . . . he hasn't replied." He shrugs. "It's probably nothing. But . . . y'know, I'm quite invested in staying off my father's radar."

"I'm sorry." I set my fork down. "Has . . . has your dad been trying to contact you?"

He nods. "He tracked me down when I was living in San Francisco.

Sicced some private investigators on me. Anyway, I got a letter in my mailbox—no postage, someone delivered it by hand. It was from my father; said he'd changed, he wanted to see me, he'd be in San Francisco for work in a week. Gave me a date and time. And, oh, I was torn . . . I was really, really torn."

He looks away, face red. My eyes skirt the room—diners and tables and painted ceramic bowls and pretty blue enamel spoons.

"What did you do?"

He cringes. "I thought about it—I came close to sitting down with him, I really did. But in the end . . ." His gaze floats beyond me. "I couldn't."

My heart cracks. "I'm sorry, Brady. Do you . . . do you actually think he wanted to reconnect?"

He shakes his head. "People don't change. Relationships don't change. I've never once seen a shitty parent stop being shitty to their kid."

Nice work, Eszter. That's how Dad wrapped up our call this morning. I heard his smile through the phone, could picture that toothy grin he so rarely aimed at me. "I'm not sure that's true," I say carefully. "Obviously every situation is different, but my dad and I have had a tricky relationship for basically my entire life . . . and lately, we've been getting along really well."

His eyebrows lift. "What changed?"

"We're . . . doing a project together. And it's actually pretty fun. I mean, not saying you should start working for your dad or whatever." I laugh. "I just mean, it feels different now, when he's not treating me like a little kid. We're relating like adults. And maybe . . . I don't know, if your dad went to all those lengths to see you . . ."

Brady tilts his head, considering. "What's the project? Out of curiosity."

Butterflies—no, *bats* in my stomach, chittering and swirling like the ones we disturbed at Paraíso Escondido last month. *It must've been gorgeous when it was a resort,* Brady said, spinning in a slow circle. *Wish I could've seen it.*

I lean forward. "Can I tell you a secret?"

His eyes glitter. "Can you ever."

I grin. "I'm trying to reopen Paraíso Escondido!"

"You're kidding!"

The waitress leans over to refill my coffee, and I thank her.

"An eco-resort," I continue. My heart is thumping; I can't believe I'm doing it, I'm letting him in on it without notes, without a rehearsal, just me and my excitement and my own tippy-tapping pulse. "Brady, it's going to be so amazing. I remember you were like, 'It's a bummer we missed our chance to see it in its prime.' Well, it'll be even *better*. We'll have breathwork, meditation retreats . . . yoga, obviously . . . really celebrating the specialness of the space. Of the *island*."

Brady's eyes are enormous. "Wow."

I can *see* it, Paraíso Encontrado—"Found"—airy and chic, rising like a phoenix from the ashes. "I'll find a Mexican architect, of course," I continue, speaking quickly. "Mexican everything. Interior designer. Contractors. Chefs."

"'Chefs,' multiple?"

I shrug. "I don't know, maybe there'll only be one restaurant. But a retreat center needs food. Local, sustainably sourced, lots of fresh seafood. Oh, I should have them include a vegetable garden! Or a mini eco-farm?! I should talk to Pedro . . ."

But then I catch his face, the very picture of surprise. I grin. "Sorry, I'm getting ahead of myself. We've barely even started looking into it."

He nods, then drops his chin onto his fist. "Huh. That's quite an idea."

"Who knows if it'll actually happen," I say, modesty muscling to the surface. It's the knee-jerk instinct to downplay anything that seems to be going well. "I was working on this other project before—without my dad—and it kinda crashed and burned. But my point is . . . I mean, your dad loves you. We only get the one set of parents, right? If he wants to reconnect . . . I don't know, maybe it's worth exploring."

I fork a bite of tamale into my mouth.

He takes in a breath, then shakes his head. "You might be right. Maybe I will get in touch." He smiles weakly. "And hey, I'm glad you and your dad are patching things up."

"Thanks. Hey—could you do me a favor and not mention the hotel thing to anyone? Not even Amari." I drop my napkin on the table. "It's suuuper preliminary at this point. I want to get my ducks in a row."

"You've got it." His phone jolts on the table. "Speak of the devil. Shall we head over to Amari's?"

As I slip my wallet out of my bag, I spot my notebook in the bottom—closed, unused. I'm gobsmacked: I did it, I broached a sensitive topic on the fly and didn't get tongue-tied in the process.

With a final wave to Silvana, I follow Brady out the front door, smiling.

CHAPTER THIRTY-ONE

ABBY

Wednesday night

I stare at the screen until the letters start to blur: *IZMOS CON-STRUCTION INC.*

I feel gutted, a fish being prepared for ceviche: like someone stuck a knife in my belly and yanked out my entrails. Eszter was doing *exactly* what she promised me she'd never do. She lied to me every step of the way.

Did I even know her? Was any of it real?

Something connects: How . . . how goddamn reticent she was to commit to me. To marrying me or even living together before that. Like she knew a bright future couldn't possibly be in the cards. It was her parents or me, and she made her choice. And, for reasons unknown, she kept stringing me along, a sucker.

It's not that easy for me, okay? she said on Christmas night as we drove through a steady Miami downpour. *I care what they think. I can't just say* fuck you *to my family like you did.*

By then, she was months into her double life. Kissing me goodbye before driving to the airport and—I marvel anew—getting on a plane to Cancún. Sending carefully framed photos, letting me think she was admiring the Florida sun. Eszter was one of the most principled people I knew; she hated telling anyone, especially her parents, even the most innocent fibs.

Or so I thought. *What happened to you, Eszter? What the hell was going on* here . . . *and what does it have to do with Brady?*

A brand-new construction company, headquartered in Miami, purchasing the land and slapping up NO TRESPASSING signs on the fence around Paraíso Escondido. They were planning to build there, right? A hotel makes the most sense . . . either rehabbing the original or demolishing it and building a new property on its site. I think of the brochure, tiny Eszter staring shrewdly at the camera. Reopening their favorite vacation spot, I suppose.

I might be sick.

I find myself returning to the question I've asked after every detonating bombshell: Who else knew? Who was privy to this knowledge painstakingly withheld from me? Shane seemed to be in the dark as well, and Laszlo hasn't answered my emails. I think of her parents sitting across from me at Christmas, watching me sip disgusting liqueur and making small talk about holidays past and knowing, the entire freaking time, that I had no idea what was really going on, no idea that they were in cahoots.

Oh, of course. *Can I talk to you in private, tündi?* Dr. Farkas asked, rising to his feet. They had business to discuss.

Amari texts to ask if I'm okay, and the facts rearrange themselves again: Wait, who knew about her plan . . . *here?* The expats keep joking about loving the island more than almost anything . . . did someone try to stop her? I think of Pedro, his steady potshots at tourists. Would he . . . ?

I do a split-second calculation: Should I tell Amari? What do I have to gain from keeping this from her? I need data, and my quickest route to answers is by asking, point-blank.

My pulse stammers as I call Amari. "Did Eszter tell you she was going to reopen Paraíso Escondido?" My voice comes out strangled and raw. "Or—or build another hotel in its place? Did you know?"

"*What?* What are you talking about?"

Once again, I find myself thinking her shock and ignorance seem genuine . . . no one's that good of an actress, right? I tell her about the corporation, the in-progress purchase of the ruins. The abandoned Haven project.

"Jesus," Amari mumbles. "So you think she gave up on the refugee thing to do this instead?"

"I do. And I'm pretty sure whatever she had planned for here wasn't a shelter. Her dad hated that project from the start—he probably wanted it to fail." As the words leave my mouth, I blink. He wouldn't have sabotaged it, would he? Even he's not that much of a monster.

"Well, I haven't heard anything about it, and that sounds like the kind of gossip that would be all over the island. So maybe they were trying to do everything on the DL?"

"Do you think Pedro knows?"

"Oh my God, if he knew, he'd be, I don't know . . . chaining himself to a tree up there."

I picture him on the boat ride, eyes glued to the cliffs.

"I'm gonna ask him," I announce.

The phone line fizzles with static. "It's late," she says. "He goes to bed at, like, nine-thirty. You might have better luck tomorrow."

Goosebumps track up my neck. Is she being helpful . . . or trying to buy some time?

"Thanks for the tip," I finally say. "I'll keep you posted."

As Amari warned, Pedro's phone is off, so I get ready and climb into bed. As I stare at the ceiling, my thoughts churn. For four months, I wrestled with the jagged ache of not-knowing, repeating Eszter's last texts like a mantra: *I need to tell you something.* But now that I'm here—now that I have more of the puzzle pieces—I'm more confused than ever.

Moonlight lances my bedroom, shivering as the palm trees outside sway in the night breeze. I'm getting out of here tomorrow; I have until eleven A.M., and then I can get the hell off this island, something Eszter never got to do. Twelve short hours until I'm on a boat with Amari, bouncing over the waves and back toward reality.

My cheeks heat as I flash to that moment in her backyard. Boldness rushing through me, that sudden urge—no, *need*—to press my lips against hers. For a second, the newness felt amazing, like the frenzied high of submerging myself in that sparkly bio bay.

And then . . . the foreignness took a turn. *This isn't Eszter.* The wires crossed, pleasure and pain, *How bad is it that this feels good?* And, feelings tangled, I pulled away.

Eszter. I kissed her so many times for so many reasons: sympathy, passion, gratitude, pride, to cheer her up or calm her down. Simply because I loved her, planting a peck on her lips as we rode the escalator at Target, her one step above me so her face was at the right height.

I thought I'd never have a first kiss again.

Focus, Abby. Twelve short hours. I need to make tomorrow morning count. What am I missing?

I sift through the pieces again, shuffling them like a deck of cards. There are too many strange, unexplained details yawning open: The missing islander. The scrubbed week on PDC. The marked-up map of the island I'm stranded on, feet stuck tight to a dumbbell of land in a shining vat of deadly water . . .

A rooster's sudden yodel yanks me back into not-my-bedroom, back to Isla Colel, the place that took her from me. I blink my eyes open; light gushes around the curtains.

What am I doing here?

I look at not-my-phone. No missed calls, no voicemails. No replies in my inbox, either, nothing from Laszlo . . . my only notifications, in fact, are from impatient coworkers on Slack. On my laptop, I push some new code, then leave it to run.

I call Pedro one more time. As the phone rings and then goes to voicemail, I remember something odd he said: Eszter met him at the fonda, orange notebook in hand, then proceeded to discuss . . . nothing. It's a bizarre story, to be honest. It would make more sense if she did tell him something—something he inelegantly snipped from the narrative.

But then . . . why bring it up at all?

My mind whirs as I rush through a quick HIIT routine. If Pedro won't talk to me, the only other option I see is a pipe dream: I'll walk to the fonda and wait for Brady there, even though no signs point to that first, innocent explanation, that Brady's "tomorrow" is now today. I have to try.

The wind feels frenzied and something crowlike caws at me from the treetops. I look up at the sky: still blue above me, but in the distance there's a gray slash with a hazy curtain dangling below it. Is that rain?

I'm almost to the fonda when another conversation breaches—Rita musing about Pedro's villain origin story. I pause to tap out a text to Amari: "This is random, but Rita said something about Pedro's 'checkered past.' Do you know what she meant?"

I order. Push huevos rancheros around my plate. Picture Brady meandering through the door, all smiles, resplendent in his orange joggers and crocodile-print shirt. I ask the pretty waitress if she knows anything about Brady, anticipating the shake of her head but disappointed all the same. It's a *Groundhog Day* repeat of yesterday, when I peered at everyone who walked in, begging them to be Brady.

I pay and rise, then stop short: Pedro's stooped over the bar, his finger tapping on his phone. There's a half-empty bottle in front of him and from a distance, I think it's beer. It makes me think of my mom, and how the decision to open a single bottle—unthinkingly, *pop!*—could keep her so stuck.

Thunder rumbles, so deep and fierce that everyone in the café looks around and murmurs excitedly, like when a plane hits turbulence.

As I cross to Pedro, sound bites from the last few days echo in my ears:

We respect the bay, he told me as we splashed into strobe-light water. *More than we respect tourists.*

We don't need spring breakers getting drunk and making a mess, he sneered on the boat ride. *Outsiders don't treat the island with respect.*

As we ate lunch on the preserve, somewhere we weren't even meant to be: *Last thing we need is for this to become a birding destination. They'd be coming in droves.*

And finally—the clearing on the nature preserve, his hand clamped on Amari's forearm: *Hey, I'm talking to you.*

If he did know about Eszter's plans . . . how far would he have gone to halt them?

"Mind if I join you?" I slide onto the stool next to him.

"Sure." He shoots me a dark smile. "Ready for the storm?"

But I get right down to business. "Random question: How many times did Eszter come to Isla Colel?"

"Let's see . . . three, I think." His eyes widen. "Why, how many times did you think it was?"

I ignore the question. "Do you know why she kept coming back?"

"Because she liked it?"

"And that's it?" Pedro's not an idiot; if Eszter was here laying the groundwork for a hotel renovation, wouldn't he know?

He shrugs. "It's a nice island, okay?"

"But you hate tourists."

Something snaps against the window—the first few specks of rain. "I don't *hate* anyone." It feels like a lie. "And I liked Eszter."

"That's right—she asked you to help her with something. You met her here."

"Yup. Never figured out what that was about. Maybe the answers are in that little notebook of hers." He shrugs again. "We sat down—right over there, in the corner—and before she could start talking I got distracted—I told you how I saw that bird. When I finally turned back to her, she . . . it's like she lost steam." He spins the sweating bottle—Coke, it turns out, Mexican Coke.

"I have a theory," I say. "About what she wanted to talk about."

"Shoot." He lets go of the soda and it jangles before balancing upright.

"Did Eszter say anything to you about opening a hotel on the grounds of Paraíso Escondido?"

A surprised laugh hiccups out of him. "What?"

"Fixing it or building something new. Opening it to the public." I swallow. "Her dad's a hotelier, you know. He could make it happen."

He crosses his arms, forearms bulging and threaded with veins. "You can't be serious."

"I'm not making this up. They were working on it. I saw the record online." I study him. "Someone hung new signs on the fence around it. You didn't notice?"

When he looks up, antagonism flashes like lightning in his eyes. "No one's reopening the hotel. That would never happen."

My mouth goes dry, but I keep pushing: "No? You said yourself that the local government can be shady. Someone comes in with deep pockets, promises to revitalize the economy . . ."

"No. Absolutely not." A mirthless *ha*. "This is one of the last pure places on Earth. No fucking way is some outsider gonna come here and . . ."

BANG—his fist slams onto the bar, and the entire restaurant falls silent, staring. The whole room sharpens, like a photograph filtered into a vividness that can't be real.

After a moment, nearby noises begin to swell again: clanks and murmurs, sipping and chewing, the bottoms of glasses ringing on tabletops like little bells. Pedro glances at me sideways and sweeps a calloused palm over the nape of his neck.

"No fucking way," he says again.

I feel my phone vibrate. While Pedro collects himself, I slide it out to check.

An answer from Amari. One that makes my ribs contract.

"Before he got here, Pedro was in and out of jail."

send back three question marks, pulse thumping, then look up at Pedro. He's staring at the back of my phone sulkily and I slip it into my bag.

Answer, Amari, I beg silently. *Answer me, damn it.*

"Well, obviously no one's doing anything around the hotel now," I say. "Um, in other news. Amari let me know about the baby turtles. How Rita and I were actually hurting them? I'm really sorry." He nods seriously, as if it isn't weird that he's accepting an apology on behalf of the hatchlings. "I know you wanted to talk to me too and Amari . . . went to bat for me."

A glimmer of confusion in his eyes. "'Went to bat' for you?"

"After you chewed Rita out. And wanted to yell at me too? That's what you were arguing about on the nature preserve, right?"

"Ah." He nods and scrapes at the corner of the bottle's label. It might as well be on a marquee over his head, lights blaring: PEDRO IS LYING. But before I can ask more, my phone begins to ring.

I dig out the burner: It's Rita. "Excuse me," I murmur, slipping off my stool.

"Abby!" Rita chirrups. "Listen. I have a friend here—"

"Sorry to interrupt, but can I ask you something?" I curl over myself, as if Pedro will hear me from twenty feet away. "Amari mentioned that Pedro's been in and out of jail. Do you know for what?"

A few seconds pass. "I don't want to dredge up anyone's past without their permission," she says, a touch of consternation in her voice, even though that's exactly what she did when she told me about his green card sweetheart. "The penal system's so problematic, especially for people of color like Pedro. But I will tell you it was all nonviolent crimes. Just him standing up for what he believes in."

I think on this. "Like, protests, sit-ins, that kind of thing?"

"Right."

My head throbs—she assumed this intel would put my mind at ease, but if anything, it proves Pedro's comfortable crossing lines and breaking the law for his convictions.

Rita's already chattering on: "As I was saying, I have this friend who used to be a volunteer firefighter. He thinks we should report Brady missing, but I'm not sure if that's a good idea. Because Brady's so intent on keeping a low profile here, you know."

"Amari and I talked about that—we're not even sure we have a photo of him to provide." I swallow. "We're gonna go look for him in Cancún in, like, an hour." A gust breaches the windows and sends cheap napkins flying.

"Oh, good! That's reassuring."

I play her words back in my mind . . . *a volunteer firefighter,* she said. I.e., a first responder.

"Your friend here—do you think he could tell me anything about Eszter?"

"Like what?"

"I don't know. What happened when they found her." She starts to say something, pauses. "What is it, Rita?"

"Well, I did ask him about it after that first night, when I met you on the beach—I was curious, you know, since it happened before I got here."

My right ear fills with rhythmic churning, the way it sometimes does when I'm swimming. "Wait, was he the one who got the call about her?"

A puzzled second. "No, I—I hadn't asked him about it before, but I knew it happened at his house."

"*What?*" This conversation is making less sense with every sentence.

"In Eszter's Airbnb. Downstairs from him and Marta?"

"Marta ran the Airbnb with someone?"

"Well, no—Marta ran it alone, Carlos has his own shop. But they're married. Have you met Marta?"

I press my fingertips into my forehead. The more time I spend on this island, the more convinced I am that no one's telling the truth. What did Rita tell me that very first night?

We love secrets here. We're all escaping something.

"I met her, yeah, but I didn't meet her husband. Although . . . Carlos, that name sounds familiar."

"Oh, he's lovely. A very caring man."

Carlos, Carlos . . . *Me llamo Carlos.* We met near Playa Oscura that first full day, when I strode into the waves and nearly drowned.

"Well, what'd he say when you asked him about Eszter's death?" I ask.

"Just that Marta spotted her through the window in the morning and by the time they got inside, she was gone. I'm sorry, Abby. I didn't mean to pry."

My eyes rim with tears. "Do you think he would talk to me before I go? I'd like to hear it firsthand."

"I can ask! I'll text him now."

A thrill runs through me. "Thanks, Rita. Let me know when you hear back."

The man from the beach co-owns the house on Calle Estrella . . . how, for lack of a better word, *random*. Though not that surprising, with an island this small, I suppose. Lowering my phone, I spot a new text from Amari: "Yeah, he kept getting charged with ecoterrorism . . . he does NOT like talking about his time behind bars tho (understandably lol)."

Ecoterrorism—that sounds more serious than the occasional protest. I'm still processing when another text from her buzzes through: "I just heard from the fisherman, he doesn't want to take us until after the storm. Should we take the ferry this afternoon and try the clinic Friday am?"

Ugh, another setback—why is it so hard to get off this damn island? I tell her I'm downtown and will try to get her a ferry ticket—I already have my round-trip fare. I glance out the front window, where raindrops polka-dot the cement ground. My stomach flips as I make my way back over to Pedro. He's pulling pesos from his wallet—leaving so soon?

I plop onto the stool. "As I was saying about Eszter . . ."

"I'm sorry, but I gotta get going." He folds a wad of bills in half. "Look, you should be asking Amari about Eszter, not me. She spent *way* more time with her than I did."

There it is again, the needle of jealousy. Well, no sense holding back now: "As friends?" I ask.

He freezes, his nearly empty bottle an inch from his lips. "As far as I know." He takes a final swallow. "Why, do you have reason to think otherwise?"

My heart thunks like a generator. "Not really, no. But . . . I dunno, I keep hearing how close they were."

He stands, sliding his wallet into his pocket. "She did seem really upset and distracted right after Eszter died." He shrugs. "I know what that's like—you meet someone on the other side of the world and feel like they're your new best friend. Happened to me all the time when I was backpacking in Southeast Asia."

A feeling is pouring through me like paint, bright and cold and strange. Vacation friends are one thing . . . is he talking about something more? Something that—even if it only lasted a few months—might've felt like *everything*, dopamine spurting, chest bubbling, hormones and chemicals clouding their judgment and making them half-drunk with lust?

Amari's charisma sucked me in like a tornado . . . less than twenty-four hours after we met on the beach, I grabbed her in the rain, unable to resist. Maybe Amari turned the charm on for Eszter. Maybe she fell for it too.

I picture Amari's painting again . . . Eszter staring straight on, mid-laugh, tucking her hair behind her right ear with sweet, open intimacy. That wasn't a look she gave to just anyone.

"Talk to Amari," he says again, like that's the end of it. "If Eszter told anyone what she was up to here—it's Amari."

Outside, the rain has paused but the air is still and silvery, with a metallic ozone tang. I'm finally face-to-face with an explanation I've been trying to outrun: *Eszter might have cheated on you with Amari.* My whole stomach twists and I double over, my hand on a tree trunk for support.

Deep breath in, deep breath out. *Keep moving, Abby.* As I trudge toward the marina, I rewind through our relationship in my mind, moving back through the months and years, searching for the signs I missed, the pulled threads in the fabric of our love. When will I find the root? How far back does the deception go?

When I reach the ticket booth, its plywood walls stop-sign red, I feel a dropping sensation, like I'm being sucked down into a pneumatic tube.

A handwritten sign in blue highlighter: FERRY CANCELADO.

Tears bite at my eyes, a hot mix of exasperation and fear. Forget Brady for a second—if I can't get off this island, I'll miss my flight home, too. Shoulders slumped, I turn—away from my home continent, away from the landmass stretching up, up, up all the way to Madison, to my life. To safety.

I share the bad news with Amari, noting the ribbon of relief I feel at not having to see her . . . not having to picture her lips against Eszter's, her muscled arms around Eszter's waist. How, *how* did the inconceivable become possible in a few short days?

Ferry cancelado. Just my luck. My walk home has a strange, surreal quality, like I'm trapped inside a stress dream. Gulls caw; a dog with a limp follows me for a few blocks, never getting too close, staring impassively whenever I turn to face him.

I'm almost back to my apartment, headache pounding, when the burner phone starts to ring again. I pull it out of my bag hopefully—did

Carlos agree to chat with me? Did Laszlo finally see my emails?—but the screen shows a blocked number. I stare at it, unsure what to do, and then the ringing stops. A robocall? A wrong number? I slip it back into my bag and keep walking.

But then it beeps, and when I dig it out again, there's an alert on the screen: *1 new voicemail.* I pause on my patio and hit Play.

For a second, there's only breathing.

"You can't be here," a low voice whispers. It could be male or female, but I think the accent's American. It sounds familiar and a shiver creeps up my spine.

"You have to get out of here," the voice continues. My pulse speeds—what the hell?

"I mean it." Every hair follicle on my body contracts. Because—on some level much, much deeper than my consciousness—I do recognize that voice.

I heard it next to me, late at night, on the pillow next to mine. Mumbly. Soporific. Talking in her sleep. It's impossible, yes, but I know that voice, I freaking *know it*.

More breathing, long enough that I think that might be it, that the caller might have thought they'd hung up. Then a sharp, sudden in-breath and a final command that makes my blood turn to ice: "Get out of here, Abby. *Run*."

CHAPTER THIRTY-THREE

ESZTER

Then

"Look, I have it all to myself!" I Ken Burns–pan the camera from the massive ferns out to the ocean—a huge bird dives with kamikaze confidence—then down to where the cliffs have whipped the water into a frothy mass. Now for the big finish: I turn so the ocean's behind me and shoot my face. "It feels like I'm the only person on Earth. I think this is my favorite spot on the island—maybe on the planet. Can't wait to show you in four short days, babe! Love you." Phone fingers, *te amo*. Send!

It's weirdly thrilling to be texting Abby photos and videos from Isla Colel with aplomb—the faded murals in the plaza pública; the marina's long dock narrowing in front of me, boats nosing its sides, the departing ferry a white blob on the horizon.

My heart practically kaboomed out of my chest when I told her that I wanted to come here. *I'm thinking of getting away*, like I'd written in my notebook and rehearsed in front of the mirror. It came out tight, high-pitched. *To work on my capstone, I mean.* And then the part that truly felt like lines in a play: *I found an Airbnb on this random island in the*

Mexican Caribbean . . . it looks really quiet and the reviews say there's good Wi-Fi.

She knitted her eyebrows at me. I almost threw my hands into the air right then. *Just kidding, of course I don't want to leave you alone in the Madison tundra for multiple weeks!* I'd sing it like my mom used to: *Smile, you're on* Candid Camera*!* Mom liked watching daytime television when I was small, studying it with the seriousness of an anthropologist, trying to follow the English, asking me to translate words she didn't catch.

Abby was supportive, of course, all *That's a great idea!!!,* but she couldn't exactly say no, could she? She wouldn't—she loves me. She *trusts* me, an opaque, all-encompassing trust that wraps around me like a boa constrictor.

Once she's here, once she sees this place for herself . . . please, God, let her understand. I've turned it over and over in my head and I keep getting the same result: If I tried to explain it from afar, if I showed her pictures and projections and tried to make her see that this is *my* project, *my* way, not another soulless Farkas development . . . it wouldn't work.

It will all be okay. *It will all be okay.*

I hopscotch over some rocks and head for the hotel. Yesterday I asked Amari and Brady to join me on this hike, but they said no. Which—it's ridiculous, I know, taking it personally. But I feel like they've been a tiny bit different on this trip? Cooler?

There's an itchy question in the back of my skull: Should I not have told Brady my plan last time I was here? Dad swore me to secrecy, and I keep reassuring him I haven't spoken to anyone without his permission. I get panicky if I think about it too hard. Like when I was a kid and spilled nail polish on my dresser; I moved a lamp on top of the stain and waited in terror for the inevitable reckoning.

But . . . I trust Brady. And I'm glad I let him in, I think; on this trip he asked how it's going, and it was nice to open up about my fear of messing it up or alienating Abby. He said he hasn't told anyone, and I believe him.

I reach the chain-link fence and pause . . . these PROHIBIDO TRASPASAR signs are new. My stomach twists. Maybe it's a good thing Brady and

Amari hung back. On Christmas, Dad pulled me aside and assured me the application will sail through once we have a detailed proposal; he knows the right people and will make sure of it.

I reach the courtyard and head for the sloped part in the back. There I settle on a bench and the coconut trees swish like town gossips, *psst-psst-psst*. That tense, low-voiced conversation at Christmas scared the crap out of me: Dad was back in taskmaster mode, all *Stop dragging your feet, stop insisting on environmental impact reports. You're slowing things down. We'll just buy up carbon offsets, tündi—it'll be fine.*

This needs to go flawlessly, he reminded me, murmuring because he knew I still hadn't told Abby. *Not one snag, not even a stumped toe.*

Stubbed—he meant a stubbed toe. Of course I didn't correct him.

More than once, Abby's called my dad a know-it-all, but she kinda missed the point: He *does* know, like, way more than the average person. He is exceptionally smart and exceedingly well-read. In Madison, we call our trivia team the Polymaths, a joke with our friends who are in a poly*cule,* but Abby's not that much of a polymath, really . . . her knowledge tends to go deep instead of wide; if she can't master a topic, she's not interested. Unlike Dad, who knows passable Spanish, French, and Russian, and can speak intelligently on almost any subject.

I remember one late night, driving home in the rain from a day at Devil's Lake, a rhythmic thumping erupted from the car's floor. We pulled over and determined the front tire was approximately three billion degrees and reeked of burned rubber. Abby wanted to drive to a hotel and find a mechanic in the morning, and she turned purple—no, *apoplectic*—when I insisted on calling Dad for advice.

Well, he correctly diagnosed the whole thing (stuck caliper!) and told us to call a tow truck: "Do not keep driving on that thing."

Abby was so irritated, like I "chose" him over her. But, uh . . . he knows cars, and she does not?

Here's what I think it is—Abby doesn't know what it's like to have a parent who wants to help you. I mean, I know her mom loves her, but Abby can't (and shouldn't!) rely on her. Whereas my parents *really, really* want to see me succeed. We sometimes disagree about what that looks like (things that thrilled them: my full ride to business school, my interest in the hospitality industry; things that did not thrill them: the Haven, my falling in love with Abby), but in the end, they're cheering for me, you know?

We'll just buy up carbon offsets, tündi—it'll be fine. I'll figure it out. I'll do loads of research to make this a net good for the locals—I won't be some obnoxious B-school outsider busting in to mess up their island. This'll revitalize the economy, raising funds I'll reinvest here.

Plus: Soon I'll have Abby on my side. *By* my side. She's said it herself a hundred times, with something like envy: Almost a third of her company works remotely. Or maybe she'll finally admit that TimeIn isn't a good fit and find something new. Hey, maybe she'd even consider working with me—as even Dad begrudgingly admits, the need for a digital advantage in the hospitality space grows stronger every single day.

One way or another, we'll figure it out. And everything will be better. After all, she's the brightest, boldest, most can-do person I know.

A bird lands on the ground a few feet in front of me—pretty thing, feathers the color of an oil slick with a brushstroke of red on top. It looks like the one Pedro pointed out the other day, all excited, *No* way *is that a red-capped grackle!* I tried to squish flat whatever feeling his excitement evoked in me, a spiny orb of anxiety and guilt.

"Hey, buddy." I find orejas in my bag and toss a few crumbs on the ground. "Hola, pajarito." It tilts its head at me, like it's questioning me too.

When I first met the other English-speakers in October, I was prepared to dislike them. After all, I figured what bound them together wasn't the normal friend-glue stuff, generosity or friendliness or a shared sense of humor . . . no, it was their collective decision to parachute out of their previous lives. A choice I didn't—couldn't—fathom.

Well, that and the need to speak the language we think in. Those first couple days in October, loudly swapping English as if the Spanish around us were background noise, I thought: *Would any of these people even be* friends *if they met in "real life"?*

But then . . . I did like them. Amari and Brady in particular. As I got to know them, I witnessed this genuine love and fuzzy tenderness and stiff loyalty among 'em that, goddamn, was as heady as a big bottle of Mom's inky unicum liquor.

And then . . . on this visit, I'm back on the outside. Maybe I'm imagining it.

Doesn't mean it doesn't hurt.

I can't take it any longer—I shoot Brady and Amari a message, "What's everyone up to today?" I'm wandering around the open casket of a swimming pool when they reply: They're eating breakfast at the fonda, Brady says, and I should come hang.

Little burst of left-out-ness that I wasn't invited from the start, but I fight it. No matter that I've already eaten. They confirm they'll still be there for a while, and I begin the descent.

I spot all four of them on the patio, Hilde and Pedro and Amari and Brady. Amari jumps up and drags over a chair for me.

"Thank you!" I drop into the seat. Pedro's eyes slide right past me, around me, like I'm blocking his view at a concert.

I feel awkward after our nonmeeting here; as Dad waved away my environmental concerns with talk of carbon offsets, I wanted to subtly ask Pedro about the ecology research that brought him to Isla Colel. As soon as we sat down, though, a fleeting thought from my first visit echoed in my head: *He reminds me of my father.* I chickened out on the spot. And now he sips his Coke calmly, like he has zero curiosity about me.

I clear my throat. "How's everyone's day going?"

Their gazes zap, a quadrangle, and I feel a prickle in my neck. Why'd they invite me if they're here telling secrets?

Finally I laugh self-consciously. "What?"

"Just discussing a little business," Hilde announces, and everyone snickers.

I'm a dumb doll with a bewildered, wide-eyed smile plastered on my face. "What, what is it?"

Amari takes pity on me. "Sorry, we're being weird. We were . . . obtaining a local medicinal plant from Pedro."

I frown. "Weed?"

They shake their heads and Pedro stretches his arms back. "It's called hoja alma."

"'Soul leaf,'" Brady translates, like a little kid at show-and-tell.

Pedro nods. "It's similar to peyote, if you know what that is." (I don't.) "It's, you know. Mind-expanding."

"Like mushrooms?" I ask.

"More like ayahuasca," Amari says. Seeing Pedro's raised eyebrows: "Its effects, I mean. Genus-wise or whatever, I have no idea. *He's* the plant taxonomist."

Pedro grins. "And they're totally unrelated."

"It's a beautiful drug," Hilde says.

"It is." Amari nods. "I was skeptical at first, but now I've done it a bunch of times. It's quite lovely. Like being held."

"Is it local?" I'm both impressed and intimidated. They're so casual about it, like this is a super-normal way to start a Thursday.

"It grows on an island a few miles from here," Pedro says. "One of only a handful of places where the conditions are right. There's a certain kind of bee that thrives on the preserve here and makes the trip over to pollinate it. Rare stuff—obviously it's pretty hush-hush so people don't come and cut it all down."

"The stuff he brought us is cultivated, though." Brady nods proudly. "Pedro knows we can keep a secret. We aren't about to tell anyone."

"Other than her!" he jokes, pointing. I get that odd frisson when someone talks about you right in front of you.

"Eszter's cool." Amari locks eyes with me and I have to look away.

"How do you take it?" I ask. Surprising exactly no one, I was always a Goody Two-shoes; in middle school, my parents found a cigarette in my backpack that I'd been too afraid to smoke and grounded me for two weeks, and in college, I didn't touch alcohol until my twenty-first birthday. Then I was too scared to buy pot off anyone (a drug deal, me?) and *then*, when Abby and I got together, she was so uninterested in any controlled substances other than marijuana, I forgot all about them too.

"You can smoke it, but I like it in a tincture." Amari presses her palms together. "Why, do you want to join us? We're gonna take it to-morrow."

That frozen moment, high-pitched and charged and *eeeh*, when someone makes an offer both intriguing and terrifying. I could say yes and take advantage of being here all by myself. Live a little. Abby won't arrive until Monday . . . this could be my one shot.

But . . . what if something goes wrong? My heart rat-a-tats and they're all looking at me and I start to defrost as the words come out of my mouth: "Thanks, but I don't think I should."

Relief and disappointment flood my stomach all at once, like the de-cision left a void—a vacuum in the space-time continuum as the alter-nate future collapses, *shhhoom*. I could've done something wild, but I passed. Life marches on as usual. Why disrupt the status quo when it's served me well for so long?

"You're sure?" Brady's eyes sparkle.

"Don't pressure her," Pedro breaks in.

But now they've all clocked the uncertainty on my face. My pulse accelerates again. "Is it dangerous?"

They perk up. "We're gonna do the teeniest, tiniest doses," Amari says. "Like, the minimum viable dose."

"And it's much quicker than an ayahuasca trip," Hilde adds, as if that were my top concern. "Are you sensitive to medications or anything?"

I shake my head. "Not really, but you know I'm allergic to peanuts." My egg allergy seems less relevant.

"No relation," Pedro says. A taxonomic botanist—what luck. "Pea-nuts are in the *Fabaceae* family. This is *Apocynaceae*. Totally different." We stare at him and finally he shrugs. "I'm not a doctor, don't look at me. I'm just telling you. No peanuts."

"So go nuts!" Brady whoops.

"Eszter, what do you say?" Amari smiles and they're all looking at me, eight eyes, and I feel like a shaken-up bottle of Sprite. Can I do this? Should I?

"I have a better question." Brady sets his hand on my forearm. "Do you want to?"

Tutyimutyi. My older cousins in Budapest, far cooler than I, lobbed the insult my way when I was a teenager and unwilling to steal lipstick from the drugstore or flirt with boys at the diner or sneak out with them after dark. Sort of a goody-goody and a wimp rolled into one: weak-willed, indecisive, terrified of making mistakes.

Do you want to? Time stands still. Then it explodes out of me, *whoosh*, cap's off the bottle: "You know what? Yeah. I do."

CHAPTER THIRTY-FOUR

ABBY

Thursday morning

The voicemail ends with a click and I stab at the screen to replay it. I blast the volume as I listen to it a second time, then a third, waiting for this to make sense.

You can't be here.
You have to get out of here. I mean it.
Get out of here, Abby. **Run.**

I feel less certain with every replay—it sort of sounds like Eszter, but it's so few words and no voice at all, only whispering. By the fourth listen, I'm not even convinced it's a woman. But more important, the words feel urgent.

I look up at the frenzied, flapping palm fronds above me. What is going on?

I reach my front door and start to key in the code, and my eyes fall on the spot where the Tevas sat perfectly perpendicular to the door. So far, there's been a reasonable explanation for everything: I must've lined up my shoes unthinkingly. I shut my laptop while I was distracted. I left my suitcase messier than I realized. The simplest answers, therefore probably the right ones.

But this? This is different. And everyone knows I'm staying in this apartment; I'll be a sitting duck inside its cool walls. I turn on my heel and head back into the street, walking with purpose.

I'll help you, Rita said. And while I'm not *sure* I can trust her, she has a huge advantage over the other expats: She got here the month after Eszter's final visit. If something strange was going on when my fiancée died, Rita could not have had anything to do with it.

Unlike Pedro, with his criminal history and ferocious protectiveness for the island.

Unlike Amari, with her effortless charm and artsy sexiness—and the closeness with Eszter no one can explain.

Unlike Brady, whose whole demeanor changed when I brought up Eszter.

Hell, unlike Marta and Carlos and even Gloria. All the locals probably roll their eyes at the way the gringos, the actual immigrants, pretend this island is theirs. *Expats*—what a privileged, puffy term, as diaphanous as cotton candy.

My brain moves a million miles an hour, and my footsteps nearly match my heart's woodpecker pace. And I keep it together, jaw set, eyes dry, the entire way. I reach the house Rita pointed out the first night and ring the bell.

She answers the door . . . and I fall apart.

I blame the way Rita smiles at me—warm, happy to see me, eyes brimming with empathy. That full-fledged gaze as she sees me, really *looks,* her attention clear-eyed and complete. It cracks me wide open, and I fall into her arms, sobbing.

"There, there." She pats the back of my head like I'm a toddler. "Let's get you inside."

She ushers me into the living room and deposits me on the couch. Her little ranch has tiled walls and folk art paintings on the walls— loopy, candy-colored images of tail-feathered birds and vibrant foliage. I accept a cup of water and sip it as if in a trance.

"I don't know how I'm going to get home," I announce. "The captain bailed on Amari and me, and they canceled the last ferry out." The air in Rita's house feels thick and stale, like a held breath. Through the window, a wind chime gives a sudden, fervent jangle.

Trapped. I can't believe I'm trapped on the island. What kind of karmic BS is this, winding up stranded on the island that took my fiancée from me?

Rita clucks her tongue as she settles onto a love seat. "You can charter a boat as soon as the storm passes." She leans forward. "What's going on, Abby? I'm sure we can get to the bottom of it if we put our heads together."

From anyone else it would sound patronizing, but her words are like a balm. I start by playing her the voicemail from the blocked number. When I begin to explain that I thought it sounded like Eszter, I realize how ridiculous it sounds—like something out of a low-budget horror film. It must be that face-in-the-crowd phenomenon, the way I keep seeing her, hearing her, thinking she's still around.

Rita takes the phone from me and listens on her own. Finally, she shakes her head. "I don't recognize it, unfortunately." She rests the phone on her thigh. "Whoever left it, he must have really wanted to spook you."

"You think it's a man's voice?" Possibilities flicker: Pedro, Eszter's dad or brother, Brady . . . an islander . . . ?

She listens to it again. "I'm sorry, I really can't tell. Who would do that?"

I groan. "That's not all." My voice is thin and dyspeptic as I tell her about my strange new bombshells about Izmos Construction and Eszter's plans to put off school and turn her Airbnb into a long-term stay.

"Paraíso Escondido!" She shakes her head in disbelief. "What an idea. I wonder what the locals would make of it."

Goosebumps pop along my spine. "You think they'd hate it?"

"I'm not sure." She tilts her head. "From what I hear, its closing crippled the economy. But the folks here now—they like how quiet it is. There's always talk of what happened to Tulum, you know. A cautionary tale."

We're quiet for a second. "You haven't heard from Carlos yet?"

"He hasn't texted back," she replies. "I mean, when I asked him about Eszter's death the other night, he assured me: nothing strange about it."

I almost laugh. *Nothing strange?* About my partner, my fiancée, secretly planning to move here and be her father's foot soldier? The more Rita insists Eszter's death was the innocent tragedy I once believed it to be, the more convinced I am that someone is keeping something from me.

"I need to figure out who else here knew about her plans for the hotel." I look up. "Who could help, do you think?"

She stares at me for a moment. A rumble of thunder seems to envelop us, and after a still, breathless second, rain heaves itself against the window. "Carlos is the only person I can think of in construction around here—maybe he'll know who to ask. I'll try calling him this time."

She ends up leaving him a voicemail, and then we both sit, waiting, listening. On the coffee table, her cell lights up with a news alert. "Severe storm warning," she tells me. She sets it back down and I squint: The wallpaper on her phone is a group shot, four people, and it looks like two adults and two kids. Goosebumps whisk up my neck . . . she told me she didn't have a family. So what's this?

"What's your lock screen?" I attempt to sound casual.

"Oh, this?" She taps again and I almost laugh—it's the expats, Pedro and Rita standing tall, Brady and Amari hunching in front of them. That tracks.

But then . . . wait.

Coldness plunges through me. Is this the same day, the same background and outfits, as the photo Eszter sent? Did Eszter take this photo—was Rita here with her all along? Has she been lying to me from the moment we met on the beach—spotting me, meddling with my trajectory like we did to those poor, defenseless hatchlings?

The screen blackens again and I lean forward, trying to play it cool: "Can I see that?"

She holds it up and no, this isn't a match . . . it's a different outing, clothes instead of bathing suits, and they're in front of the marina, not the beach. *Relax, Abby.* Rita didn't overlap with Eszter.

That might make her the only person I *can* trust.

A blast of lightning whitens the space, and the lamp flickers but stays on. A power outage is the last thing I need; Brady warned me even cell service halts when the grid is down. Rita looks around the room, her eyes like full moons. "Let's hope this passes quickly."

Another moment of tense silence. "Carlos is on Calle Estrella, right? Can we go see him?"

"We can try. He might be home and not looking at his phone. I have rain ponchos."

Though it was my idea, I hesitate. Yes, here's something to *do,* a step toward answers.

But . . . there's another part of me running its own calculations. Questioning if my type A approach to, well, everything will actually serve me here. Rita could still be lying. Maybe all of them overlapped with Eszter. After all, every one of the expats is either seeking or running away from something.

Or both.

Wind hauls another curtain of rain against the windows. I clear my throat. "Good idea. Let's do that."

Rita stands, happy to have a plan. "I'm going to run to the toilet. Then we'll go."

She disappears and I wander into the kitchen to fill my cup at the water cooler. As I sip, I look at the jumble in an open drawer—her junk drawer, as far as I can tell. Paper clips; a lighter; three pads of sticky notes, each bowed into a gentle C. And something burgundy and matte, partially hidden, that I recognize as a passport.

A lightbulb blinks on: I can find out exactly when she got here. Confirm, once and for all, that she ferried onto the island after Eszter. She said she came to Mexico from Central America, so there should be a stamp in the back.

With a glance toward the bathroom, I slide the passport out. I flip through the back pages, past a colorful smattering of rectangles and ovals, black and blue and red, the occasional triangle. There: It's a big green stamp, SECRETARIA DE GOBERNACIÓN, with the date in red in the center.

My shoulders droop with relief: 13-02-24. So she wasn't lying. So she had absolutely nothing to do with Eszter.

I really can trust her.

I'm about to toss the passport back into the drawer when the picture page, stiffer than the others, catches my eye. I hesitate for a second as a fresh peal of thunder percusses the floor like a subwoofer.

I don't know what makes me look at it. Curiosity, I guess, the way you peer at a friend's old driver's license when their wallet lolls open, laughing at their outdated haircut. I press the passport open and the page's metallic bits catch the windows' light, which is gray and alien as the storm gathers force.

My stomach drops like a pebble in a pond.

Next to Rita's smiling photo is a name I've never heard before: *Petra Amelia Siegel.*

CHAPTER THIRTY-FIVE

ESZTER

Then

You're an idiot.

Last night I lay in bed silently screaming at myself. Why did I say I wanted to try some unlicensed, illegal drug on a remote island far from paramedics and hospitals and, like, all the things that keep us alive when disaster strikes? I decided then and there to call it off: *Sorry, guys, I have to wuss out.* But now it's the morning and I'm undecided, waltzing into the day curious what Eszter will do. Like it's a movie I'm about to watch. Choose your own adventure!!!

I was so sketchy on the phone with Abby last night—twitchy and off. Usually she calls me out when I'm being weird . . . she's the hyperverbal one, silver-tongued, always eager to *talk it out, talk it out, talk it out.* Normally I hate it; she speaks so quickly, over me, pontificating and making points, and it's like my brain goes blank, curls up like an overwhelmed kid. But last night, for once, I *wanted* her to push me.

I wanted her to talk me out of it.

But then the sun sloshes in and I turn on my phone and Amari and Brady are beyond excited. Hilde is having GI issues again, I learn, but not to worry; Amari had a "prophetic dream" that the universe has wisdom to download to all three of us. Brady adds that he can tell our "gay-gle" will create the just-right vibes.

Sometimes it's that simple—if you think I should do drugs with you, I will; if you want me to keep your existence secret, I won't ask questions. And if you want us to get married, well . . .

Wisdom from the universe: It's a tantalizing promise, dripping like a peach. I'm petrified of what I might discover, but also . . . hey, if someone told you all the answers were in a sealed envelope, you'd open it, wouldn't you?

In Amari's pretty living room, we splay on her rainbow rag rug. Chitter of bugs, roosters' boastful caw. My stomach gurgles; though it's not a vomity drug, Amari warned us not to eat beforehand. That way it'll be quicker and more predictable.

They take theirs first, all at once, *glug*. My heart's pounding and my teeth are chattering; I'm so tense that I'm not sure I can open my mouth and dump it down the hatch. But if I wait, our timing will be off.

So I flatten all the panic in my head, the voices chanting *nonono,* and swallow.

Amari puts on some airy-fairy spa music and flumps onto the ground. We lie there. Every time my thoughts start to skate off like water bugs on a pond, I tense up: *Is this it? Am I tripping?!*

And then . . . it hits.

At first, I resist. Like my brain is coasting down a bobsled run, picking up speed, and I'm sticking out my arm, my heel, anything to stop the momentum.

Look, I know it's boring to hear about people's drug trips. *How will I put this?* It's my final coherent thought, the last time I'm in this world, skin against rug, Eszter stretched between the crown of my head and ten pink-painted toenails.

Now . . . off we go.

I'm in a vast black space, no walls, no floor, no ceiling. It feels amazing. Not that *I* feel amazing, because there's no *I*, no Eszter, just this open expanse, free from those pesky labels we slap on everything. Tenderness swells for Eszter, my idea of *me*, and for all the humans bravely toddling around, all white skeletons and soft skin and hardworking mitochondria.

Humans! Another wave of affection so strong it makes my heart puff. For Abby. Oh, I love her so much, with her thick eyelashes and husky voice and swift mind. And suddenly, *blink*, we're in the outer-space-like blackness together. And—how do I put this?—our relationship is this *thing* between us, a billowing, three-dimensional mass.

And then I grasp it all, like there are subtitles spelling it out.

Abby and I are different—of course we are, *az ellentétek vonzzák egymást, opposites attract*. But not only in the ways I thought, Abby all type A and badass and a bit bossy, me all quiet and chill and happy with whatever everyone else wants to do. That's how I always saw it, yin and yang, but now I see *why*, the reasons underneath, like they were on the back of something I never thought to flip around.

Abby got out of Elmridge, Wisconsin, by *grinding*, each accomplishment another stepping stone out of the center of the monsoon. No wonder she can't sit still, always optimizing, adapting, decisive. She makes a choice and barrels ahead in a way that looks impulsive—no, *petrifying* to me. And it attracted me to her: that heady certainty, a sixth sense for making stuff happen.

Then there's me . . . scrambling to be perfect, agreeable, for everyone to like me. I'm a chameleon hyperfocused on everyone else's convenience. And again—how did I miss it?!—it's obvious where this came from.

Mom and Dad were *proud* of their strictness, proud of how disciplined Laszlo and I were even as toddlers—well-behaved at restaurants, rule-following, always *a pleasure to have in class*. They ruled with iron fists. *Hideg kéz, meleg szív: Cold hand, warm heart.*

And it didn't start with them. I picture Nagymama and Nagypapa on the couch, liver-spotted hands gnarled together, voices tautening as they recounted *their* parents' stories of huddling in basements while air-raid sirens shrieked, of neighbors' bodies lumped on the street, of hiding in cupboards, my great-grandfather's fingers locked around the pin of a grenade while Nazi soldiers moseyed around the house. One even tried the piano.

We were to be perfect—model first-generation kids, never rocking the boat or stirring the pot. Laszlo pulled it off: Mr. Perfect, handsome and popular, straight A's and straight hair and straight white teeth.

Then there's me. Very much not straight. Of course they were horrified.

The revelation booms, like it's been waiting impatiently for me: *I don't have to be who they want me to be.*

I feel a pull, like the moon tugging on the tide. My body calling me home. I slip back into every cubic inch, the way your fingers poke into a glove, ahh, a perfect fit. I start to laugh as words return to me, the voiceover piping back up in my head, *ha,* that's my skin, and those are my eyelids flicking open, and bit by bit, I come back into the space my senses construct for me.

There's giggling around me and I steep in it, letting it bubble pleasantly, and finally the last bits of the trip whiff away like smoke and we're on the floor, all three of us, laughing so hard we cry.

When we've finally calmed down, Amari announces she has to pee and then starts tittering from the bathroom.

"What is it?" I call, picking up her contagious laughter.

"It's just so funny." She's gasping for air. "I touched divinity. And now . . . I'm peeing!"

"Something so banal," Brady agrees, but he mispronounces it so it rhymes with *anal,* and we're in hysterics again, prompting me to breathe, "Stop, I'm gonna pee my pants!" which sets off a third wave.

"Paraíso Escondido," Amari announces after the comedown. Like it's the answer to a question someone asked.

"What of it?" Brady asks.

"We should go," she replies.

But I barely notice. The words have sent my brain spinning off in another direction. It's obvious what I need to do—so obvious, I must have known all along. *But what about . . . ?* part of me asks, but that's Old Eszter, Scared Eszter, that's Eszter Before.

I feel alert. Alive. No longer a tutyimutyi, I now feel energikus, fully charged. Izmos, even.

And sure, some folks will be disappointed. But—and I cannot stress enough how revolutionary this feels—that's okay.

It's a funny word, when you think about it: *dis-appoint*. Deprive of a position of power. Snatch back the car keys to my life.

I stretch my arms above me and smile.

The new Eszter knows this is going to work out beautifully.

CHAPTER THIRTY-SIX
ABBY

Thursday, late morning

They're liars. Every last one of them.

Rita—Petra, whoever the hell she is—emerges from the bathroom, snatching up her phone and prattling about how she can't seem to find her rubber boots, and we can try Carlos's wife too, but she stops short when she sees me in the kitchen. I've slammed the passport back inside the drawer, but it's too late.

"You were looking at my passport, ja?"

"I . . . I was checking when you got to Mexico. I'm sorry, I know that sounds crazy. I wanted to . . . confirm you definitely got here after Eszter . . ."

There's a glitter of annoyance in her eyes, but it ebbs just as quickly. "Okay. I understand. No one could blame you for being on high alert."

"Right." The moment tightens. Will she bring it up? Does she know I know?

"I take it you peeked at the first page, then?" She smiles. God, she's good at reading people. "I go by my nickname, that's all. Now—shall we?"

My arm hairs rise as I search her expression—brow smooth, face open and calm. I know I saw something there, anger like a passing cloud, but now I wonder if I imagined it. It chills me, how quickly she can slip in and out of character. Is she faking more than her composure . . . is she obscuring her true identity, too?

"All right," she says decisively, as if I've answered. "I need to find those rain ponchos." She sets her phone on the counter and starts digging in a closet. I take a few steps closer to her.

Check it out. The research instinct is strong, the almost palpable pull of more data. No more taking these expats' words at face value.

But my loyalty to Rita tugs at me too. She definitely arrived after Eszter's death—I have proof of that now. Maybe it really is a nickname, nothing more?

"You'd think I'd keep them somewhere accessible—God knows I need one often enough." Her head's deep in her closet, muffling her voice.

And then—a phone buzzes on the coffee table, its whir so familiar that I still think, knee-jerk, that it's mine. Rita's screen lights up with a text, and I read the words as they careen down from the top.

It's from Amari, and it makes my blood run cold: "Just heard from Pedro. Are you with Abby?"

Jesus Christ, they're working together. Of course I can't trust this woman. Rita whirls around, triumphantly brandishing two plastic ponchos still in their packaging. "Catch!"

She tosses me one and I snatch at the air a second too late. My mind races. I need to get out of here—must get away from her.

"I'm going to swing by my apartment first. I"—and here I struggle for a second, why else would I need to get home?—"uh, I need to . . . use the bathroom. My digestive system's not doing so great with all the stress. I'm feeling pretty awful, actually." I plant my hands on my stomach for emphasis. "Can I meet you on Calle Estrella?"

"You poor thing! Of course—let me know when I should meet you there. Hopefully the storm will pass."

I follow her out the front door and gaze up at the clouds, an eerie shade of bruise, greenish on their swollen bellies. The rain has abated a bit, but I can't help thinking the worst is yet to come.

———

My eyes dart across my apartment; I feel exposed here, on display. I race around, drawing the curtains, hurtling the room into silty darkness. Next, I lunge for my laptop and type *Petra Siegel* into a search bar. It's a common enough name that I have to sift through the results, but soon I spot her in a ten-year-old photo—standing at a podium, nearly unrecognizable in a bright suit and red lipstick.

The caption explains she's speaking at a women-in-business conference, and from there it doesn't take long to uncover an entire empire: books, business consulting services, personal coaching, even seminars and retreats, all aimed at young women trying to lean in, climb the corporate ladder, shatter the glass ceiling. My frantic brain strings this into an alarming image: someone rushing up a ladder, reaching a thick pane at the top, and, by breaking it, finding herself beneath a shower of glittering, deadly shards.

Materialize: That's the name of the company and the eponymous brand, some mangled play on both "material girl" and showing up, making yourself visible, and I hate it, I hate this pink-washed version of feminism.

This? *This* is my Rita, the statuesque, silver-haired hippie who just a few days ago told me time is an illusion and Eszter is here now? The first person whose hug made me feel comforted, seen, in months?

A bellow of thunder makes me jump, and beyond the windows rain gushes like someone tipped over a bucket. A text from Rita: "This storm is no joke. Let's wait to pay Carlos a visit."

I pour a glass from the water cooler. I listen to the rain drumming against the glass.

Amari texts me as well: "How'd it go with Pedro? And are you ready for this epic storm?"

Thunder shakes the house like it's shaking me, like it's grabbing my shoulders and hollering: *Enough*. I'm so tired of this. I'm tired of running around and letting people lie to me.

Ugh, what I need to do is obvious. It's time to put on my brave face and talk to Amari, in person, head-on. *Aki mer, az nyer,* Eszter used to say. *He who dares, wins.*

As soon as I think it, I feel a bright shift, like when music changes key: I'm gonna do it, I'm gonna get to the bottom of this. I'll ask Amari straight up if anything happened between her and Eszter. No more circuitous asking around, because the shortest distance between A and B, between the truth and me, is to stop messing around and talk to the woman who knows.

I tap out a reply: "Can I pop over?"

A few seconds pass. "In the downpour?"

"Hurricane party!" I reply. Here I go—right into the eye of the storm.

The rain is a thick, steady pour, as if God aimed a showerhead straight down onto Isla Colel. The drops are so loud on the hood of my drippy poncho that they seem to shake my skull. Murky brown pools, their surfaces churning, dot the dirt road, and I give up on avoiding them, instead letting my sandals and toes squelch in the mud.

A bang of thunder rocks the ground and travels up my legs, and I stop short, like I somehow caused it. I'm a few feet shy of Amari's house when nerves kick in; what am I doing? How strange will it be to see her after I ducked into her room to answer Shane's call and then took off like a shot? Worse yet—what am I going to do if Amari tells me the last thing I want to hear: that Eszter didn't just lie to me, she cheated on me too? The rain intensifies and I dash beneath the carport and huddle between the wall and a rusted ATV.

The wind gusts and something slams behind me. I whip around and spy the small dumpster belching black bags of trash. The breeze flipped the lid open, and now it's reeking at me.

"¿Puedo ayudarte?"

I jump and turn around. A woman has joined me under the carport, middle-aged and heavyset, with a thick band of silver in her dark, wavy hair. She's clutching a set of keys; maybe this is Amari's landlord, hurrying home in the storm.

I smile broadly. "I'm looking for Amari." I think back to the last time I showed up on Amari's doorstep, how her eyes had slid skyward, *I'd invite you in, but my landlady . . .*

She shakes rain from her umbrella. "¿No hablas español?"

"No. Perdón."

She sighs and pulls a phone from her pocket. After a second, she holds it up and speaks into the base.

Can I help you? the computerized voice says cheerily.

A translation app. I start to answer but she holds out her phone and I step closer. "I'm looking for Amari," I say into the microphone.

Did you try the door?

My cheeks heat. "Oh, not yet—I was going to text and make sure she's around. I'm . . . sorry for showing up like this." I stare at the phone as I speak. "Amari said you don't like when she has visitors."

As Spanish comes out of the speaker, the landlady's expression changes. From her tone, I grasp her reply even before it's translated.

What are you talking about?

I clear my throat. "I must have misunderstood. I came over pretty late, so maybe Amari just didn't want to wake you up."

Were you here with her Tuesday night? She looks at me evenly. Tuesday, the night of the barbecue, the bio bay, the last time any of us saw Brady. My pulse begins to accelerate.

"I wasn't with her, no," I say. "I came over last night. On Tuesday, we . . . had a cookout and got home around ten-thirty."

She shakes her head. As she talks into the phone my head seems to float, and when she finishes there's a moment of latency before the app responds.

No, late that night. I heard the door slam at three A.M. and again around four.

The air around me seems to tauten. "Three A.M. . . . . Tuesday night, Wednesday morning?"

She listens, nods. *The next day I told her to be quiet if she is out so late. That's what I thought you meant.*

I feel woozy, off-kilter. The night that Brady disappeared . . . right after he texted me . . . someone slammed Amari's door. And slammed it again an hour later.

I need to figure out why.

I thank the landlady and busy myself with my phone until she disappears inside. Rain drums on the aluminum roof of the carport, louder than a heavy metal concert. The dumpster's lid bangs against the wall a second time, and, holding my breath, I lean toward it to thump it closed.

A cloud of flies rattles in protest as I reach for the top. But then—my eyes flick across the contents. The drawstrings of the stinking bags yawn open in various aperture sizes. My attention snags on a bag at the top— its tie haphazardly knotted, a flash of fabric peeking out the hole.

I frown and lean closer, so the stench stings my eyes and invades my lungs no matter how tightly I hold my breath. Water slip-slides down the carport's open sides, enclosing me in clear, shimmering walls. What the . . . ?

I reach a shaking finger into the dumpster and nose it into the top of the bag, dilating the hole. I snatch up the fabric and start to pull it through the fist-sized opening and it comes and comes and comes, like a scarf unfurling from a magician's sleeve, and wait, that's what it is, a *sleeve* that now gives way to the rest of the shirt, *pop*, and I step back, coughing, and shake it out to behold it.

Speaking of gators, I said to Brady three days ago, pointing at the tiny reptiles marching steadily across his chest.

I'm not from Florida, mate, he replied, eyes glinting. *These are crocodiles. Y'know, 'crikey,' et cetera.*

It's his shirt, no question. But that's not what makes my pulse thud in my ears.

That would be the big dried blotches, irregularly shaped, like a map of the world.

That would be all the blood.

CHAPTER THIRTY-SEVEN

ESZTER

Then

Make it stop. The thought is a command from everywhere at once, from my heart and lungs and brain and hands, fingers tingly and strange, tongue puffing up against my palate. It's a distant siren at first and then it's louder and higher and faster, the difference between an ambulance at the foot of the block and right in front of you, *wee-ooh wee-ooh*, its siren joggling your skeleton.

My breath sounds like an accordion: creaky tones, squeezed air. Panic is rising through me, swamping my lungs, making it harder to stand, focus, *think*. But think I must. I shift my weight and nearly fall, then catch myself.

Think, Eszter.

Then: *Move, for once in your life.* The thought's a shout in my ears, in Abby's voice, of all things: *Do something!*

My spine straightens and then, mercifully, my legs cooperate. The clouds part: EpiPen—I need my EpiPen. I stagger to my bag and rummage around inside. Where is it? My windpipe grips tighter and tighter and the pins and needles in my hands make it hard to slide things around: phone, water bottle, wallet, hand sanitizer. I let out a frustrated groan but it comes out like a grunt, throttled by my own throat.

It's not in here. Shit. I staked everything on it being where it belonged.

"Where is it?" I ask. I sound like another species, an animal with a larynx unlike ours, meant for growling and roaring, its own language. A memory flashes in my mind: Abby and me in a silly mood at home in Madison, stumbling onto the observation that it's *so weird* parrots can speak human languages with their little beaks and black tongues and we don't talk about that enough, *how are we all okay with that,* giggling and giggling and giggling. My vision begins to fade and another spear of consciousness pierces through: *Your brain isn't getting enough oxygen. You need help now.*

Action, action, action, find the EpiPen find the EpiPen find the EpiPen. As I take a few staggering steps, it's like Abby's here now and pushing me on, but wait, someone *is* here, why isn't—

But then I spot my thin jacket with all its roomy pockets and I funnel my energy into rifling through them, c'mon, c'mon, c'mon. Red welts that first appeared on my chest are rushing down my arms now, and my fingers are fat sausages, and my arms too, wrists shiny and soft. I search, search again. Where the hell is it?

I can't breathe. I can't breathe and it's the scariest sensation, like a monster on my chest squeezing tight tight tight, and I need help, I need an ambulance, I'm running out of time.

And then I spot it.

My eyes lock on to its yellow edges poking out from beneath a foot, a foot belonging to someone who's been kind to me, someone I thought I could trust. My gaze travels up to my not-friend's face and what's there is a confusing muddle: tears and fear but determination, too, and resignation, like this moment was unavoidable.

I take two staggering steps forward, reaching for the EpiPen. I crash onto my knees.

I did my best, Abby, I think, with a sudden rush of peace.

Then I collapse.

CHAPTER THIRTY-EIGHT

ABBY

Thursday, midday

My fingers pop open and the bloodstained shirt falls to the ground. I snatch it back up and ball it into my fist. I turn my head wildly—who's around, what should I do? And then I think to lean over the dumpster again, and *oh God oh God*, there's more fabric beneath it, and I'd recognize that hunter orange from a mile away.

I start to tug it out too but the bag's binding hinders me. I reach down and rip the black plastic apart, letting its contents spill out. It's mostly wadded paper towels but they're tie-dyed pink, and bile ratchets up my throat while I yank out Brady's joggers, covered in erratic bloody splotches.

Amari just . . . *left* these here? Tossing out murder evidence in a loosely tied trash bag? My stomach convulses—she doesn't even care. Out of, what—arrogance? Confidence in the island's quiet anarchy?

Through the roar of the rain, I hear a door snap open. I duck behind the garbage—someone's coming down the outdoor steps, moving quickly. I sink down even farther, nearly gagging from the smell, and spot Amari ducking low beneath a broad umbrella. She reaches the street and turns left, then stops short, looking down. Nervous sweat pricks my forehead and armpits. Oh, no: I left the top of the dumpster wide open, and the wind has scooped up a piece of pink-stained paper towel and deposited it at her feet.

She stares at it for a second, watching the rain turn it into a glob, then swivels her head my way. *Shit.* I flatten myself against the wall as she approaches the carport. She passes through the glistening waterfall at the carport's edge and her shoes crunch on the gravel as she moves toward me.

She's fifteen feet away, ten, five. All the air exits my lungs so that there's nothing in my chest cavity except a machine-gun heart.

Bang—the lid crashes down, and out woofs a fresh cloud of stench. Her footsteps recede, then she disappears behind the veil of rainwater. The wind—she thought the wind heaved the garbage lid open. I'm still clutching the bloody clothes, which smell of onions and banana peels and sickly-sweet rot, when I notice my phone buzzing.

A text from Amari, two whole minutes ago: "Realized I'm low on supplies so I'm running to the grocery store. Back in 20!"

I feel like my blood's been swapped out for battery acid. It all lines up: Amari poisoned Eszter—out of jealousy, a love affair gone wrong, a fierce need to halt the Paraíso Escondido project, who knows—and then, when Brady got close to telling me the truth, she killed him to keep him from squealing. This morning's huevos rancheros threaten to come back up. Did she sneak into Brady's home and then, afterward, scrub it from floor to ceiling? Or did it go down here and she slipped outside in the middle of the night to . . . my stomach convulses . . . what, hide the body? He's tiny, sure, but could she even do that on her own?

I hear a motorbike approaching, and my muscles tense on some primal instinct: *Move.* After a moment's hesitation, I stuff the fabric back inside the dumpster, snap a photo, and take off running.

Get out of here, Abby. RUN. I was so sure it was Eszter's voice, Eszter's warning. Well, I'm running now, and rain seems to surround me like I'm in a dunk tank, dumping on the crown of my head, worming into my eyes. My feet slap and splash in the claylike road and *shit*, this is bad, this is really, really bad.

I have to key my door code in twice to get it right, and then I fling myself inside, lungs heaving like bellows. Dripping water forms a pedestal at my feet, and when lightning strobes, the lights all shimmer. I say a silent prayer—if the power goes out, I'll lose all contact with the outside world.

Think, Abby. Idiotically, I pull out my phone and start to scroll through my contacts—but of course, there's no one but liars and ghosts, those who've hidden the truth and those who've disappeared altogether. What is going on on this island? How do I get off of it? *What do I do?*

A text from Amari: "Not sure if you've left yet, but the storm is legit scary. Might want to wait until it blows over?"

That's right—she's expecting me. And she sounds casual, normal. Is it carefully calculated or does she really not know I suspect anything? My hands shake as I reply with a thumbs-up. God, she said he was like her little brother—is she a sociopath or something? I rub my forehead. I can't believe I grabbed her last night. Slid my hand along her jaw. Can't believe my next first kiss was with Eszter's murderer.

Okay, I need to tell the authorities. I can't prove she killed Eszter, but now there's proof of what she did to Brady. But no one's officially reported him missing, as far as I know, and since he's an Australian citizen, will the policía even care? The burr of a bug crescendos on the wall, and it brings to mind a rattlesnake, ready to strike.

I dash to my laptop and try to figure out if there's a police station on the island, even though Rita's talk of a volunteer responder suggests the answer is no. One search result from Yelp makes my heart skip a beat—*Best Police Departments in Isla Colel*—but when I click, all of them are on the mainland. God, is the nearest emergency dispatch really two hours away by boat? I think of Eszter, her desperate need for a hospital. Without her EpiPen, she didn't stand a chance.

I find the local emergency number: the familiar 911. I type in the numbers—this is a burner phone, can they geolocate a burner phone?—and hit Call.

The ringing tone is a single, low-pitched *beeeeeeep*. The phone jolts in my fingers, but I ignore it, *C'mon, dispatcher, what's taking so long . . . ?*

And then the lights twinkle and—with a buzz—the power goes out.

Shit.

Three taunting tones confirm that the call dropped, and I press the phone onto the table, tears clouding my eyes. "Eszter," I whisper, "what do I do?" Lightning blasts through the windows, catching the yellow paperback still face-up on my kitchen table.

The Year of Magical Thinking. My insides seem to writhe. Is that what these past four months have been, an extended period of delusion?

Since January, I've told myself a story: Outstanding, exceptional Eszter, mere months away from sharing her secretive but surely spectacular capstone project, went on vacation, kept to herself, ate something mislabeled, and died on her Airbnb's cold tiled floor—period, end of story.

In my telling, she's excited to see me, can't wait to marry me. Eager to return to our life together in Madison, with its cold winters and warm meals, our shared future rolling smoothly like a dropped ball of yarn.

But now I know at least some of that is complete fiction.

I glare at the book. What if it was *all* a lie? What if the real Eszter was a stranger? What if the Eszter walking around this island—?

Something glimmers, calling out from my lizard brain. I freeze in place, finger on my lower lip, like if I stay still it'll swim up to me like a minnow—

And then, *bzzzt,* my phone pulls my attention. That's right—a text came in while I was trying to call the police, and I forgot to read it. This must be the second notification, two minutes later.

Now the stillness is too loaded, too eerie.

I pick up the phone like it's a poisonous spider. *New message from Amari.* When I read it, the bottom drops out: "I just got a call from Rita. Call me back, okay?"

Thunder like an earthquake makes dishes rattle and a cabinet door spring open. And then, right then, I realize she sent *two* texts, one after the other: "Actually, hold tight. I'm going to come to you."

CHAPTER THIRTY-NINE

Slivers of lightning slice the room like slim blades. Do I hide? Barricade the door? I'm not safe here; Amari's on her way, and everyone knows I'm inside, cowering from the storm.

My eyes fall back on the Joan Didion book. There was something there, something scratching at my consciousness. I follow the thoughts backward like they're a filmstrip I uncoiled, back to questioning who the real Eszter was, back to my season of magical thinking—

The book. *Brady's map.* What did I do with it? I feel around in the dark, check the tabletop, the kitchen counters, shoving things around, flipping over whatever's in my way.

It's in my back pocket, dampened by my sprint here so the paper's wavy and suede-soft. I squint at it through the dimness, taking in the meandering coastline, the sweeping nature preserve, the tangle of streets like tunnels in an ant farm. The fat red circle, decisive, an answer.

The hotel—the hotel has a radio tower, and on it, a satellite phone with a battery backup. I can use it to call for help. I can tell the cops that Brady's missing—his fear of his father hardly seems to matter now—

and his bloody clothes are in the trash outside Amari's place. And I can wait out the storm until someone gets me off this godforsaken island.

Amari will be here any second. I peek through the curtains and then gingerly let myself onto the patio. I lace up my muddy hiking boots and glance up and down the street—no one—then slip Rita's dripping poncho back over my head. Rain pounds the roof like a drumline as I cross the covered porch. Then I turn in the direction of Paraíso Escondido and break into a run.

The road is a fast-moving river now, with slippery mud passageways encircling dishwater-brown pools. I circumvent them when I can, grabbing on to trees, but still lose my balance, crashing forward with a squelch. My knees scream with pain and the mud sticks to me, suctions me to the ground, pulling on me like hands stretching up from hell.

I reach the edge of the preserve and start to climb, setting my soles onto gnarled roots and spiky rocks, moving as quickly as I can without stumbling again. The overgrown path is like an endless staircase that makes my heart speed, my breath catch, sweat steaming inside the plastic poncho. I clutch at thick vines as I hike higher, higher, closer to the heavens, to Paraíso Escondido. Through the breaks in the trees and giant ferns, I glimpse ferocious waves and spindly sea stacks needled from above by pouring rain.

The quivery foliage drops away, and I pause for a second. I'm once again at the spot where Eszter made me a video. The spot I first visited . . . was that only three days ago? Staring down into the watery abyss, tears muddling my vision so the ocean and rocks became one mottled blur.

Now I peer over the edge, thinking about the EpiPen that quietly rolled away from me, the necklace that lit up like Christmas-tree tinsel, the phone that bounced twice before disappearing over the ledge. I tip my face up to the bloated clouds and let fresh tears mingle with the raindrops, soaking my cheeks and slithering beneath the plastic hood, a cool wash of confusion and pain.

"Abby!"

I startle and turn back toward the jungle.

No. It can't be. What I heard defies all logic.

No way did I just hear Eszter calling my name.

"Who's there?" I yell, my voice high and wavering.

I swing my head desperately, but there's no answer. My pulse sounds like a jackhammer. All around me, the downpour makes leaves patter and shake, rattling the air with a wild drum solo.

And I start to tremble too, my whole nervous system shot through with cold. I think back to the last time I was up here, watching the sunset dye the water an angry red—how I felt like someone was watching me, like the rainforest was alive and vigilant, setting my teeth on edge.

What if it wasn't the trees at all . . . what if someone was really there? Eszter . . . it's absurd to even put the thought into words. Hell, her parents had her body sent home to Wisconsin, presumably in a large container with HUMAN REMAINS stamped on the side.

That's how I pictured it, anyway. Because they didn't want me around. We weren't married; I had no rights. Her parents boxed me out.

I never did see the body, did I? There's no way Eszter has been . . . here, alive, for all this time?

I squint into the rain, looking around wildly. I take a step back. "Who's there?"

"Abby?" the voice calls again, and then—Amari, it's Amari who staggers onto the path, chest heaving, soaked from head to toe. Her clothes are darkened and heavy and her hair hangs in limp tendrils.

My ribs go cold. A spiky ball of panic starts in my hips and then grows and grows and grows, taking over my stomach and chest and limbs and loudening into an earsplitting roar as we stare at each other across a wall of water, both breathing hard.

"Don't come any closer," I warn, taking a step back.

She tilts her head, still coming toward me through the rain. "What?"

"How did you find me?"

She keeps coming; why won't she stop? "When I got to your apartment I noticed your hiking boots were missing next to the door."

I keep inching away from her. "I . . . I know what you did to Brady."

She freezes. "Brady? Did you find him?"

A javelin of confusion soars through me. Lightning flashes and the ground shakes a second later—that bolt found the ground, maybe a tree? Or, oh no—the radio tower. The rain intensifies like someone turned up the volume dial.

"I know you did this!" I yell. "Do you think I'm stupid? I know you did something to Brady."

She takes another step toward me, her hands balled into fists, and all the sound drops away, the world sharpening like a snapping finger.

"You've been lying to me," I say. "What was it—were you in love with Eszter? Were you having an affair? Did she reject you? Or—or were you trying to stop her from reopening the hotel? With your whole 'this place is a creative well, connected to the Source.'"

Amari shakes her head, tears pouring down her cheeks. "No, no, that's not what happened."

"So you killed her. Right? And you killed Brady to keep him from telling me. And now, what? You're going to kill me too?"

She moves toward me, distraught. "I didn't kill anyone. Eszter had an allergic reaction and died!"

"Because you poisoned her! And Brady knew, didn't he? He was going to tell me. Why else would you hurt him?"

The downpour crescendos like a snare-drum roll. The seconds pan out. And then . . . it happens so quickly, and yet in slow motion, each tiny sensation blaring into a shocking frame of a stop-motion film. As I list away from her, my right heel catches on a rock. My leg kicks back to catch me, but the hook eyelet near the top of my boot, protruding next to my ankle, snags on the lace of my opposite shoe. It's too late—I've lost my balance.

For a split second, my gaze meets Amari's and our eyes lock like horns. Her brows lift, and then—*nonono*—she rushes forward, arms outstretched.

I twist away as her fingers graze my shoulder. My arms windmill, grasping for anything as my body lists farther and farther away from vertical. My fingers close around a fern, its fronds fringy and wet, and it breaks away with a soft pop.

My vision tips up, up, up, to the undersides of the giant ferns, the slim trunks of the coconut palms, past the tallest treetops, and finally reaches the last thing I'll see: the curdled gray sky, pouring down on me with full force. I'm no longer on the cliff's edge.

For a second I seem to hang in midair, supine on an invisible mattress of rain and atmosphere.

And then . . . I fall.

CHAPTER FORTY
ABBY

June 10, 2022 (one year and eleven months ago)

"How's that for a third date?" Eszter cracked. Her caramel hair spilled over the pillow, haloing her pale face.

I stood a little ways back from the hospital bed, not sure of my role. "I'm gonna sue that restaurant," I said. "I feel so bad that I took you there."

"It's okay. I looked at the menu—I thought it'd be fine." She shrugged. "Normally I'd know right away if something had egg in it. I don't know why that snuck up on me." A brave little smile. "Maybe I was distracted by your beauty."

Okay, we're joking. I can joke. "If by 'beauty' you mean 'fresh new fade' . . . " I stroked the velvety nape of my neck. "Maybe it's the barber we should sue."

She chuckled, then turned serious. "Thanks for coming to the hospital. I . . . I meant it when I said you didn't have to, but I was hoping you would."

"Of course! Did you seriously expect me to leave?" I lifted my arm. " 'Bye, Eszter! Have a great life assuming you don't die!' " Once the words were out I worried I'd gone too far, but she just laughed again.

"You'd be surprised. I've had partners dip out as soon as they realized this is a real, lifelong thing."

"Well, lucky me." Emboldened, I took her hand. "Those folks were idiots."

Slowly, I bent to kiss her cheek. Her eyes caught mine as I pulled back and, after an electric second, I leaned closer to give her a proper kiss.

"You didn't eat any of the rolls?" she whispered, her mouth a millimeter from mine.

"Not a bite," I replied as I pressed my lips to hers. Then I grinned. "Honestly, it was one of the most memorable dates I've ever had. Dare I say . . . exciting. Driving you to the ER? I mean, what's on the agenda for our next date—a police ride-along?"

She giggled. "Ki tudja, mit hoz a holnap?"

"What's that?"

She repeated herself. "It means: 'Who knows what tomorrow will bring?' One of many Hungarian phrases my parents repeat endlessly."

"I like it," I said. "And I think I have the answer. Assuming you get out of here . . . and I'm not coming on too strong . . . we could make dinner and watch a movie at my place. Certified allergen-free."

"I'd like that."

My chest felt effervescent. "I'm glad you're okay, Eszter."

"I'm glad you're here." Her eyebrows flashed. "And I'm glad you know how to use the EpiPen now."

"Miss Farkas?" A nurse knocked on the doorframe and my cheeks heated as I stepped away. I watched as the woman checked Eszter's vitals and jotted something down on a clipboard.

I want to make you feel safe, I thought. *Unlike those jerks who took off when you revealed yourself to be human, I want to stay and make you feel taken care of.* I had enough sense not to say it aloud, but I could feel it then, how this could really work. How this might be real and for the long haul.

When the nurse said she'd need to draw blood again, Eszter's eyes darted to me: "You don't have to stay for this if you don't want to."

"Do you want me to leave?"

Her mouth curved into a small smile. She shook her head.

So I didn't.

CHAPTER FORTY-ONE
ABBY

Thursday afternoon

twist a bit in the air and for a moment, I'm flying. There's rain above and below me, pressing in on every side, no up, no down, just me weightless on the wind.

While my life doesn't flash before my eyes, I do feel a profound surge of sadness. It's the aching pull of saying goodbye to all the things I won't do again: dance at a concert and stare up at the stars and step on a pile of crunchy leaves and make eye contact with a dragonfly and sip a foamy cappuccino and argue about a buzzy TV show and watch a spider dangle in midair and cry and orgasm and *be*. I get one clear pulse of an image—an early date with Eszter, our first kiss on a hospital bed. It's like all my neurons are firing at once, and in them, those experiences are stored, past, present, and future, and I relive them all for one final, bittersweet moment.

And then—a frigid crash as I hit the water.

My feet get the worst of it, a burst of pain like the blare of a horn. It spritzes up into my ankles and I'm transported back to childhood, that odd fountain of pain when you hit the grass after jumping off a swing at its zenith.

I topple sideways and my flailing arm makes contact with something solid—a deep, internal snapping sensation in my forearm. It's fast, too fast to comprehend after that: All of me is wet, underwater, ice-cold and tangled in the poncho.

I'm in a washing machine, the current somehow pushing on me from every direction. My feet kick and stir like eggbeaters. Useless, useless, useless. The undertow flips me around again, slinging me over like a wrapper in a storm drain. Bubbles and darkness, the sound against my skull a deep roar. My lungs begin to burn, blades pushing at the insides of my ribs. I can't tell which way is up, I can't see through the white churning bubbles, and though I'm fighting like hell, this really is the end.

Then, salvation: I spot a tangle of greenish black and that's seaweed, oh my God, it's floating and that way is *up*. The water slackens its choke hold as if it knows I've outwitted it, and I'm kicking, kicking, my ankles screaming in pain. I breach the top and gasp for air before another wave slams my head back under, and it's like there are people trying to drown me, hands pushing on my shoulders and crown, clutching my ankles and yanking me away from the surface.

Water streams into my eyes and nose and ears and still I fight, churning, until my functional arm scrapes against something and *yes, that's a sea stack*. The tide boomerangs me away from it and I want to scream in frustration but I find the white rock again, its pebbly side my salvation.

I surface.

Groaning with pain and exhaustion, I smack a hand onto its slippery top, then my other elbow, ignoring the strange angle of my arm below it. Rain fills the space around me as I push myself up and twist to get my hips onto its slanted surface. My tiny island is triangular, an arrow pointing at the sky, with one longer side sloping gently enough that I can sit on it.

My cough coaxes seawater out of my nose and lungs. I reposition myself to face the shore. It looks impossibly far away. Twenty-five feet, maybe, with several more sea stacks dotting the expanse of churning water between. The storm shows no signs of slowing.

I could die out here.

I lie still for a while, taking stock. Miraculously, I haven't hit my head or injured my spine. I somehow banged up my right knee, now dimpled with bloody bruises. My right palm is scraped and leaking blood; I flex the wrist, tender but not excruciating. The biggest issue is my left forearm, where jagged bone pierces the flesh. Rain swills over it, forming pink rivulets, so I can't tell how hard the blood is gushing, but this is very, very bad.

In terms of problems, my ankles are a close second. I lost one boot to the ocean, but the other is still laced, pushing on my puffy flesh. I'm trembling from the cold and can't seem to untie the wet knot with my one good hand, and I curse and scream again and smack my palm on the rock in frustration, which only serves to make my fingers less agile. *Shit.*

Another peal of thunder bounces around the bay, and the rain seems to shake and scatter sideways in response. *I need to get to the shore.* I focus on the nearest rock isle between me and the island. I don't know what I'll do when I reach land—I'll be boxed in by more ocean on either side and the cliff above me—but I need to take this one step at a time. Solve one problem, then on to the next.

Keep moving. Keep moving. Keep moving.

I watch the waves, see how they bash against the rock and then heave themselves back out, mingling with the breakers behind them, creating a dustup, a choppy brawl. I have to time it right. The smaller waves hit lower, cause less of a disturbance. I need to wait for one and push off on the wave that follows. I roll onto my hip and then up onto my knees, ignoring the pain, the pain and the voice in my head screaming, *Don't you dare go back in there.*

Now. I aim for a kneeling dive but it's more of a graceless belly flop. Something in my knee snaps—another weird internal pop, more felt than heard—but I keep moving. My head dunks under; I come up coughing and spitting, eyes on fire, but I keep them open and find my target again, another sea stack, this one shaped like the head of a needle, a curving, elliptical arch.

I'm still breathing. Still fighting. *You can't take me.*

I reach the rock and cling to a narrow part of the inner arc. This one's too steep and curved for me to climb atop, so I need to keep going.

Shut up, part of me wailing and screaming and throwing a tantrum. *We don't have time for that.*

The next one is another ten feet away—craggy, with a broad, sloping top. The rain pummels it so hard that a thin layer of mist hovers over it like ghostly frosting. The surf is wilder here, beery suds slopped on top of the waves, whitecaps billowing drunkenly, crashing into each other, a mosh pit from hell.

I wait for a smaller wave, realize none are coming, each one taller than the last.

I count to ten. *Go.*

The noise, oh God, so loud it's a *scream* rushing into my ears and electrifying my entire body: churning and bub-bub-bubbles and hissing and fear, like TV static cranked to deafening levels. *Move, Abby.* My left knee scrapes against an underwater part of the sea stack, wrenching off the scab from my boat-propeller injury. Sputtering, I throw my torso forward and army-crawl onto the rock, then sit there, chest heaving.

The shore is next. So close and yet deadly far, the scariest section yet, where water thrashes from three directions: into the cliffs, rebounding off, and hurtling down from the heavens. But there's a rocky ledge at the base, disappearing and reemerging with each fresh wave, and I have no choice but to reach it. Move or die.

I plunge back in. The water feels colder, wetter somehow, heavier as it clings to my bulky shoe, flapping poncho, hair, skin, nails. I try to keep my head up but it's a wall of wetness out here too, and I gasp at the oxygen between clumps of rain. I plunge below the surface once, twice, but still I swim, my desperation a match for the sea's relentless fury.

I reach the ledge. Slide right off, just like the puddle of water on top. Groan and try again and this time I stick, I scramble on top, I'm shivering head to toe and dribbling blood into the water but I'm ashore, *land ho*, and my whoop turns into a cough.

I think I hear shouting behind me, a female voice snatched away from my ears by the wind and pounding surf. I squint at the waterlogged horizon and—is that a light? A red pinprick bobs in the distance, blinking in and out amid the waves. I flash to the bioluminescent bay, all those strobing specks of plankton. But the longer I stare, the less sure I become.

No, it's nothing. I turn back to the cliff.

And then I look up.

I flash back to that moment on Esteban's boat two days ago. All of us gawking at this very cliff as we passed. Amari turned, eyes glinting: *Pedro, tell Abby about the rock!*

It looked terrifying from out there in the water, unfathomably high and the color of yellowing teeth.

It looked sheer from the top, too, when I leaned over the edge and felt my stomach flip.

But now, as rain beats my face, as my gaze goes up, up, up like a bubble rising through molasses, it reminds me of that shot from *The Princess Bride*, an upward view of the Cliffs of Insanity.

From here, it looks deadly.

There's a scramble to the bottom, Pedro said. *Someone marked it with blue paint.* Which means there's a scramble to the top.

It's dangerous. A local boy drowned a few years ago.

A teenager in presumably peak shape in ideal conditions.

I turn to look for any blue blazes and bump my knee, and the shock of pain is so sudden and bright, a neon burst, that my vision flickers like dwindling candlelight. I suck air between my teeth and it's too much, *too much*, how the hell am I going to get out of here?

I scream, an all-out, animal sound, and my breath comes faster and faster until my vision starts to blur. I reposition myself so I'm looking out at the water. The back of my head clunks against the limestone and the storm rages, indifferent. The spume's like the frothing mouth of a rabid dog. Darkness rims my vision, pulling me down.

My eyes seal shut. I did my best. I went down fighting.

"Abby!"

My eyes pop open and my whole body freezes because it's nearby, just to my right, practically a shout in my ear.

Slowly, I roll onto my hip and swing my battered legs around.

And there, at the other end of the rock ledge, tense and drenched and very much alive, is Eszter.

CHAPTER FORTY-TWO

The silver sky sets her silhouette aflame, lighting up a shape I know so well that I could spot it in a crowd or in the distance or, hell, from space. Now she's looming above me, enormous, everything. Her hair whips in the wind and she stands stock-still for a second, and my mouth finally forms a word: "Eszter?"

She rushes forward and crouches. "Oh my God, Abby. Are you okay? What happened to you?"

Her voice. *That's her voice.* Tears sting my eyes and I lean away from her. "This can't be happening. You're . . ." I glance up and our eyes meet and *what is going on,* that's her, that's really her!

She grabs my crooked arm and I howl. Grimacing, she pokes at a few spots near my elbow and each one is like a flashbulb, an explosion of bright white pain. I push her hand away and it's real, it's solid. She's . . . *here.*

"For once, I wish I'd followed in Laszlo's footsteps," she murmurs, peering at the archipelago of bruises along my knee. "And become a doctor, I mean."

"I thought you were dead."

This stops her short. Her eyes squeeze closed. "I know. I'm sorry. It all got so . . . complicated."

"You've been alive? All this time?" *The shoes*, I think. *The voicemail.* I'm vaguely aware of my pounding heart, how it echoes in my misshapen forearm and swollen ankles and palms and knees. "What the fuck?"

The relief comes out as this big pink urge to laugh, to throw my head back and let it erupt out of me, *What the what?!* I stretch my arm toward her, crying so hard I can't breathe. *Eszter's alive.* It's like waking up from a nightmare and realizing that it wasn't real, it couldn't hurt you, you're safe and alive and whole.

But she shakes her head—hard, so water flicks off her like a wet dog. "It's not important right now. What's important is you. What's important is you getting to the top of that cliff before they find you . . . or you drown."

"Where have you been? You've been here, all along?" I'm sobbing, hysterical. The relief tips into something new: a wobbly mushroom cloud of betrayal. "How could you do that? To me, to everyone? I've been . . . I felt like my heart was scooped out of my chest, Eszter. I couldn't function."

She tilts her head. "Couldn't you, though?"

"What are you talking about? *Ow.*" Her fingers on my ankle have found another tender spot, and I scramble away from her. A wave roars as it smashes into the rocks, spitting salt water all over us.

"Sorry. It's nothing." She plants her hands on her hips, looks up. "How are we getting you out of this mess?"

But suddenly, this feels more important. "No, wait. What do you mean, 'couldn't you'? I've been a *mess*, Eszter. You have no idea how awful it's been. And all this time you've been . . . what, in hiding? Letting me think you were dead? I was paralyzed, Eszter, I—"

"You weren't, though." Her eyes widen, mirroring mine. "You weren't paralyzed. You didn't stop, even for a second."

"No. No! I could barely function, I—I'm about to get fired, I couldn't do my job, I—"

"*There.*" She straightens up. "You couldn't produce, as if that were its own tragedy, bigger than losing me." She turns away, like she can't even look at me, and then her gaze tracks up the cliff. "There's a rock scramble, right? You're going to have to climb."

I'm speechless, my mouth opening and closing like I'm a fish drying and dying on land. That's how I feel—ripped out of my life, the one that made sense, floundering on a boat dock, unable to breathe.

"How could you say that?" I finally manage. "How could you?" From far away, some vague part of me is waving its arms: *This is not pressing; you don't have time for this.* But it's getting quieter along with the pain. I can't move, can't live, until Eszter understands me, agrees I'm not this callous fiancée who felt *inconvenienced* by her death.

Another wave slams against the rocks, loud as a car crash. More mist, more cold, frothy drops.

"That doesn't matter right now," she says. "Here, do you think you can walk?"

I stare at my leg dully. "It . . . it doesn't hurt as bad now. But I'm getting sleepy." In some filmy, floaty way, I know this is bad. "But tell me. Tell me how you're here. You faked your death, right?"

She regards me sadly. "Look, I knew I didn't have long before you arrived. I . . . I had to escape the life I'd trapped myself inside—you didn't even *like* me, you just *admired* me, and if I ever stopped being impressive, I'd lose you . . . and anyway, the island taught me I could just *be*, you know? I could unclench." She demonstrates with her hand, squeezing it in and out of a fist, and what comes out of me is an animal howl.

"I *love* you, Eszter. I'd do anything for you."

She looks away, lips trembling. "I know you would, Abby. But that's not the same."

"What are you talking about?"

"You liked taking care of me."

"I mean, yeah!" A sob escapes me, strangled and raw.

She tilts her head. "Because it soothed the part of you that needed someone to take care of you."

A bellow of thunder rages as I drop my head toward my knees, sobbing. She plants a hand on my forearm. I gaze at it for a second before I realize what's wrong.

It's dry.

She pulls back abruptly. "We don't have long now." She turns to the broiling bay. The rain and waves are splashing on her but her hair's not wet now, and wasn't it wet a moment ago? She nods at the water and I follow her gaze, looking out over the blue-gray horizon. I see it again—a red flicker.

"You have to hold still, babe." She speaks toward the sea but I hear it perfectly, as if she's murmuring into my ear: "You have to stop squirming. They'll come to you as soon as you stop moving."

I follow her gaze and suddenly I see them, millions of them, tiny minnows all headed straight for us.

"There they are," she whispers. "Don't move."

Lightning blasts the whole scene in a riot of white, and my eyes squeeze shut. Thunder follows a second later, rumbling through the rock and up my spine, and with a gasp, I startle awake.

Eszter is gone.

I blink stupidly, look this way and that, slack-jawed like someone's pulled off a stunning magic trick. *You passed out, Abby.* How badly did I hurt myself to believe that that could be real? That Eszter could've been hiding out on this tiny island for the last four months?

I'll deal with that later—for now, there's no time to waste. *You'll have to climb.* Struggling, I wriggle out of the poncho, and it slides past my head with a pop. I twist the plastic into a makeshift sling to get my left arm out of the way.

My pruney fingers spread on the rock near my butt (big, bright burst of pain), and I push, trying to lift myself up into a crouching position. I can't do it, fall on my hip, almost lose my balance, and slip a few inches with the receding wave. I grunt in frustration and try to shunt a knee beneath me in order to stand and look for the blue paint, I throw all my energy behind it and shuffle and scream and start to flail and—

Eszter's words echo back, a final ghostly whisper: *You have to hold still, babe. You have to stop squirming.*

With a sudden gush of clarity, I relent. Voices are still screaming internally—*Move, Abby, time to act, no time to waste, stasis is death*—but they seem feeble now, a chorus of flibbertigibbets. *Shhh.* I relax my jaw, my shoulders. I need to stop, take stock.

Hear what the island's trying to tell me.

I ease back down to a sitting position. The rain continues pelting me, but it's white noise, a sensation I can choose to ignore. The bruisey clouds still cover the sky but there's a splinter of blue far off to the right. The waves stagger and swirl, and on top of them, a fizzy blanket quivers and rocks, jostling everything it's ensnared: a snarl of green seaweed, a curvy palm frond, the cracked skull of a mouse-brown coconut. And—

What is that?

I lean forward, squinting. It disappears behind a wave, blips beneath the bubbles, resurfaces. It's so *yellow*. And man-made, I think, about the size of a glasses case. It spins around drunkenly and my whole body lights up with the revelation:

Eszter's EpiPen.

The one that slipped over the ledge my first day here. Epinephrine, i.e., pure adrenaline. An almost superhuman wallop of energy and strength in a small, self-injecting package. This—*this* is what I need to get up the rock scramble.

It's as if one breakthrough parts the curtains for all the others. *There,* that's the first marker, a slash of blue toward the top of a stair-shaped boulder. The EpiPen—it's floating this way, and if I sit on the edge here and stretch out my good arm, I can juuuuust grab it. I know that three days in salt water could've corroded the mechanism, but I pop off the cap and all the practicing on defenseless oranges comes back to me and *hell yes,* orchestral swell, it plunges right into my thigh and power surges through my body, filling me up like liquid in a fountain drink, and I can stand, I can balance, I can clear my mind and make it to the top.

One move after the other. I place my hand before shifting my weight, deliberate, endlessly patient. I register dully that pushing off of my ankles and bare foot and puffed knee and ragged palm no longer hurts, and for now that's a godsend.

Thank you, Eszter.

I keep climbing. I'm fifteen feet from the top. I ease my waist around a bulging rock, then rest my hip against the limestone on the other side.

Ten feet from the top. It's so close now, but I know from swim meets that you can't lose focus at the finish line, can't tell yourself it's basically over and get sloppy. There's a vertical crack in the wall, just wide enough for me to wedge myself inside. I rest there for a second, every nerve on high alert. I place my booted foot against an outcropping and rise, then carefully slip out of the fissure and onto a small ledge.

Five feet from the top. *You're doing it.* A part of me splits off and watches from up above, like a security cam in the corner.

Almost there. *Easy, Abby.* I can't get cocky or rush or throw it all away now. But the last move is a doozy: I have to cross a new crevasse three feet wide and impossibly deep, and the pitch of the rock means gravity will work against me. I steel myself; *You can do this, Abby, just take your time.* I plant a hand and—*Here goes nothing*—thrust my leg forward.

I realize too late that I miscalculated—this isn't a move to be done deliberately, it takes momentum, speed, a dynamic lunge I failed to factor in. The toe of my hiking boot scrapes the lip of the rock and then skids down, and a breathy *no* escapes my lips as I automatically throw more of my weight forward, but there's no way to course-correct now and I fling my good arm above me, scrambling for something to hold on to, scraping at the sky.

Clarity cuts through me, a sharp, cold knife: *This is how it ends.*

Then—pressure on my wrist. I keep struggling and something strangles my upper arm too, and I'm no longer sinking and I guess this is what happens when you're done for, the imagination's final spasm, a wild fancy of someone—an angel, my dead fiancée, God only knows—getting me out of this.

But—but it's not going away and someone's screaming my name and grabbing my arm so hard it hurts. I manage to shove my boot against the far rock and press my hips against the side of the chasm, and when I tip my face up into the rain's steady spill, it's like the world stops, a sudden blast of silent stillness.

Lying on his belly and leaning over the top of the cliff, clutching my arm and weaving a vivid macramé of obscenities, is Brady.

CHAPTER FORTY-THREE
BRADY

Two nights ago

Vomit hits the toilet, acidic and yellow, scalding his throat. Brady spits and sits back, wiping at the sweat and snot and tears gushing out of him. Like all of his insides want out. Like even the fluids beneath his skin can't stand to be around him.

Did Abby see right through him? He started burping as soon as she dropped that bomb, and then his stomach was twisting and groaning and gurgling so loudly, he was sure the noise alone would give him away. He rushed her out of here as quickly as possible and barely made it to the bathroom in time.

Eszter's fiancée. *Of course* Abby is Eszter's fiancée, of course it wasn't a coincidence that another bright, friendly lesbian appeared on the island a few months later, eager to be his mate. *I'm wondering if you guys have any memories to share.* Did she already suspect something? And then, of course, he was so flustered, he screwed up within seconds.

And then she *came to his house*. They talked together, they *cried*. He's dizzy from the whole exchange. The living room tilts a bit when he looks at it through the bathroom door. A hot poker singes his chest from the inside and he wonders dully if he's having a heart attack, if this is the end of it.

That would be appropriate, of course. He knows he deserves it.

He never meant to hurt Eszter—that's a fact. He *didn't* hurt her, not directly. He never laid a finger on her.

He really liked her, and that's why he was so devastated when, during her second visit, she sat him down at the fonda and snapped his heart in two. *I'm going to ruin your island,* she told him, though she didn't quite use those words. *The thing you love the most—I'm going to rip it apart with my bare hands.*

She was talking about it so merrily, prattling on in singsongy excitement as she described her plan, how this was going to reinvigorate the local economy and bring in so many tourists and flood the island with funds. How this was going to change everything for her strained relationship with her father and maybe Brady should give his another chance; maybe things could be different.

That's when he knew they weren't speaking the same language, not at all. They were on different planets, really. She lived on one where an influx of tourists was a good thing and father-child relationships could be healed.

But Brady lived in the real world.

And then, her third visit. She was different that time, distracted. He assumed it was because she was elbow-deep in the redevelopment, less interested in spending time with the expats socially. Because, when he asked about the project—lightly, he thought, with all the breeziness he could muster—she made it clear she was barreling ahead.

He tried to still be friends with her; he really did. He even hoped something magical would happen when they did hoja alma together. And right after the comedown, as they all laughed themselves to tears on Amari's living room floor, he thought maybe it'd worked—something had shifted.

But then . . . Amari, who knew nothing of Eszter's plans for the place, suggested they all do a walkabout on the Paraíso Escondido ruins. And the reminder was like a pickaxe to his heart.

The next day, Eszter posed a strange question: *Can I practice something on you?* A rehearsal. The day before her fiancée would arrive. Eszter was going to have a "tricky" conversation with Abby and wanted to try saying it all aloud. He knew Abby didn't know about the hotel project yet, Eszter had admitted as much, so he figured this was it—Eszter was going to tell her fiancée about her plans for Paraíso Escondido, and then there was no going back.

Eszter asked him to hike up to the ruins with her, which cemented the whole thing: She was going to take her partner there, to the actual site, and walk her through her entrepreneurial vision. Brady felt an urgent, flapping desperation, a panicked need to say something, do something, but all he could do was pick up snacks at the grocery store—Eszter requested her favorite cookies—and meet her at the start of the trail.

They made small talk as they climbed, and Brady could barely focus; it felt like his last and only chance to stop this speeding train. Strangely, she didn't even mention Paraíso Escondido as they hiked to the top. She seemed fumbly and nervous, as if Brady really were Abby, about to hear this for the first time.

They reached the hotel ruins, where there were shiny new signs along the fence, proof change was afoot. Together, they wandered into the courtyard. For Brady, each step felt heavier than the last, like he was a death-row prisoner heading straight for the electric chair. She led them to a lichen-speckled bench at the top of the courtyard's sloped end and Brady set the snacks down on the seat next to him. Absentmindedly, they both popped orejas into their mouths.

Eszter munched as she pulled an orange notebook from her backpack. She studied a page on it, then looked up: "So. I'm going to bring Abby up here tomorrow. I want to show her how special it is. I know she'll love it, all the beauty and decay. And . . ." She cleared her throat. "I'm gonna tell her I need to apologize. For keeping everything from her. And that I did it because—" She paused, frowning, and cleared her throat again.

At that moment—even now, months later, Brady can hardly believe this—something snapped.

"*You can't do this, Eszter.*" He flung out his hands and her backpack tipped over and tumbled off the bench headfirst, its contents scattering across the ground and down the small slope. He stood and crossed his arms, stretching to his full 160 centimeters. "You can't just come here and change Isla Colel."

Eszter's throat made a glottal clicking noise. She gave her head a small, surprised shake.

Now Brady presses his cheek against the cool tile of the bathroom wall; this part was awful, this part he doesn't want to think about again. But he can't stop the scene from replaying in his mind.

Eszter *ahem*-ed again and it turned into a cough, and then a dramatic, gulping swallow. She looked down at the bag of cookies, then back up at Brady, brow pursed: "Do these have eggs or peanuts in them?"

And what washed through him first was a desire to argue, like he could make things fine again with logic: *These are the ones you always buy, and it's not like I can read the ingredient list . . .*

But he said nothing and anyway, Eszter wasn't looking at him anymore—she touched her lips, then held out her hands, staring at them, murmuring about how they'd grown all tingly.

Panic grew and grew and grew, forking through his arms, up his throat, filling his skull and clouding his vision and spreading like wildfire down his legs. No, like *frost,* because the feeling immobilized him; he felt his jaw locking up, his hands stiffening at his sides.

It was the exact same thing that'd happened when he was a kid, when he'd watched his dad morph into a monster, growling at his mom, fists shaking, about to blow. Cell by cell, young Brady had grown imprisoned in his own slight body, helpless, powerless, an ice sculpture. He knew he should say or do something—anything.

But it was like a waking nightmare, and no matter what came next, he remained motionless.

As the back of his mother's head thunked against the wall.

As Eszter stood up and swooned like a flag in the wind.

Her breath was an audible wheeze now. She staggered around the bench and lifted her overturned backpack. Its contents clicked and jingled as she dug through. Her hands were swelling, he noticed, and her arms too, with purplish welts marbling the skin. They looked to him like bruises, like his mother's jawbone or cheek or brow the day after one of his father's fits.

"Where is it?" Her voice sounded like a harmonica. Her eyes snagged on her jacket and she kneeled and reached into its pockets, her chest heaving.

He didn't answer her. His brain wasn't working, it was frozen too, all thoughts stopped, every synapse and neuron temporarily down. What was she looking for? She crawled on her hands and knees, patting the ground around them, and finally, a lightbulb blinked on: *her EpiPen.*

The thought was like the Tin Man's oil can, unlocking his joints, allowing him to move again. He dropped to his knees and began to look around too, crawling farther down the hill, and—

No. Alone in his bathroom, he feels his stomach revolting again, crumpling tight to expel whatever's left in there. His hands clench the edge of the toilet bowl. No. He won't think about this part. He can't.

But then his mind rebels. He—he *spotted* it. He could see the yellow cylinder where it had rolled on the ground, chunky as a dry-erase marker. *She needs this to survive,* he thought, his eyes burning two holes into its neon casing. *Without this, she'll die.* He stood up, heart thumping, and dashed across the ground. Paused right in front of it, ready to scoop it off the dirt.

And then . . .

In his mind, over and over, he rewrites this part of the story. He plays it out from this moment forth, the alternate universe he'd like to wormhole his way into: how he snatched up the medicine, superhero-like, and saved her life.

He's pictured it so many times that it almost feels like a memory— the auto-injector gripped in his fist, the firm plunge into Eszter's flesh, time holding still as the needle dumped epinephrine into her bloodstream. Her body seeming to slide backward in time, reversing the last few minutes, hives disappearing, airways opening. Coming back to life.

Because what really happened was . . . unforgivable. And sure, he can tell himself that he was simply too slow, that he froze up like a squirrel in the road, unable to save her.

But he knows the truth.

He knows that—while Eszter's breathing shrank to a rasp and then stopped altogether—there was a shadow in the deepest corner of his mind. An additional whisper that made him turn around and step—just a tiny bit, maybe twenty-five, thirty centimeters—to the right, blocking Eszter's line of sight. He shuffled backward and lifted his heel, then let it sink down on the slim yellow plastic . . .

The hotel. She's going to reopen the hotel.

She's going to ruin the island.

He waited a long time, too long. Finally he let out a howl and kneeled. He picked up the EpiPen and flung it a few meters away. Sobbing hysterically, he crouched and looked at her notebook splayed on the ground. He flipped it over and opened it, squinting to read the last page, and when he finished, he let out another desperate bellow.

Now he's bawling again, his sobs bouncing around the small bathroom and out into his messy living room. He's been so useless at keeping it tidy ever since that day, and it shames him enough that he hasn't had anyone over since. Until Abby. Maybe some deep part of his subconscious wanted her to know. Saw her desperation, hopefulness, trust, and ran toward it like a dog chasing a semitruck.

He can't take it any longer—he stands and fishes in his medicine cabinet, then draws out his razor. He snaps it open, plucks out the blade, and sits on the toilet seat. The whole room seems to swell and shrink with every heartbeat as he hoists up his orange pants and exposes his thigh, leaning over his skin, blade shiny and shaking.

The pain is awful and clarifying, weirdly elating. Eventually he moves on to his upper arms, then his waistline. He doesn't bother removing his clothes and stares dully at the red that drips down his limbs and pools on his sleeves and joggers and the cracked tile floor. A little crimson marsh for the crocodiles covering his torso.

He almost killed himself that night. Four months ago, as if in a trance, he sleepwalked down the mountain and came here. He strode directly into this bathroom and picked up the razor blade like a man on a mission.

But then . . . his phone started ringing in the kitchen. At first he ignored it but, blade poised, he realized he'd need to turn it off to die in peace.

As he crossed the living room, sobbing and sick, his gaze fell upon a little map on his kitchen table. Pedro had sketched it out for Brady when he first moved here, then liked it so much he made Brady a copy and kept the original, a very Pedro thing to do. Brady requested it because he loved the island, admired its moods and flaws and ferocious beauty, its dangerous tides and sheer cliffs. He wanted to know it better, like it was his new crush, and no one understood its topography more intimately than Pedro.

Brady picked up the map, and instinctively, his eyes zeroed in on Paraíso Escondido. He lifted a nearby pen and encircled the ruins in red. Eszter had *died* for this place. What good would it do to kill himself, too? So that, what—so that mourners could find her plans and erect a new resort in her honor?

The phone rang again and it was Amari, his dear friend Amari, and it felt like the sign he needed—another chance at life, a cue to keep going. He didn't pick up, didn't tell her anything. He showered and went to bed and lay there staring at the ceiling, waiting for shit to hit the fan, for an angry bang at his door. He cowered as sirens whipped by a few hours later. He tried to think of what he'd say when the cops arrived—tried to rehearse, like Eszter—but he couldn't focus long enough to finish a sentence.

And then . . . it didn't matter. No one ever showed up.

The night was eerily quiet. But that morning was like a nonsensical dream: The whole island was abuzz about the American who died in a medical emergency.

In her rental apartment.

Brady thought maybe he was losing his mind. Were they not actually together at Paraíso Escondido? Had he hallucinated that entire thing?

Or—or had he left her there, deep in an allergic reaction but not yet dead? Had she found the EpiPen and somehow managed to get herself home, and then, only then, did her throat throttle her breathing? It was too horrible to imagine.

And now, as he cowers in the bathroom, it's caught up to him. He always knew it would, the anvil hanging over him, ready to crush him alive.

Maybe the only way to actually move on is to confront it head-on, Abby said. *Face it down like it's a demon.*

For four months, he's lived with this guilt, this pain, the shadow of a guillotine blade hovering above his neck. Eszter's fiancée is here, *right here,* a few short blocks away, letting him know how much devastation he's wrought. Game over.

He sighs and lifts the blade so it winks and flashes in the dull bathroom light.

Time's up.

CHAPTER FORTY-FOUR

ABBY

Thursday afternoon

Everything grows hazy, flashes of frenetic scenes strung together by gray fuzz. Curtain up: I'm dragged like a rag doll over the lip of the cliff, back to where I started, and past palm fronds and spindly trees I stare up at the soggy sky.

Blackout.

Curtain up again: I'm airborne, levitating off the mud, and someone's holding me beneath my arms, a weirdly tickly sensation like crutches, and my heels drag over the ground and my knee buzzes with pain and we're moving, stop-start like a newborn fawn, and treetops stream past my vision as rain sloshes against my cheeks and into my eyes and then, all of a sudden, the sky gives way to a dim cement ceiling and the rain, mercifully, stops.

Blackout.

Someone's calling my name, shaking my shoulder, telling me to stay awake, and it's Brady; he looks down on me like a surgeon bending over an operating table.

Darkness, darker still, but this time I fight it—this time I'm here.

"This can't be real," I whisper. "I saw your blood."

His brow furrows in confusion, but he ignores this, touches my arm. "Shh. Help is coming. They're bringing a stretcher."

"No." I try to sit up, to drag my elbow beneath me, but lifting my head sends a whoosh of sparkles into my vision. I lie back down. "Your blood, Brady. Your bloody clothes."

"You've lost a lot of blood," he replies, like that's an answer, and I'm so confused I could scream; are we speaking the same language, what's going on? I blink hard and my setting begins to make sense, like a Polaroid developing: We're in the ruins of Paraíso Escondido, tucked inside a guest room. Rain is hammering the roof, funneling into its gaping holes, racing down the rebar and saplings that peek through the windows. And wait, I'm not on the ground. I'm on . . .

"Is this a bed?" A nest of fabric cushions my back.

He nods. "I've been sleeping here. Amari wanted me to go to the mainland, but . . ."

"Amari hurt you." Then my brain glows a little brighter: "I . . . I thought she hurt you. Because she had your clothes. Covered in blood."

He winces. "That was me."

"What?"

"I did that. Cut myself, I mean. I was so freaked out about you being Eszter's fiancée."

This doesn't make sense. I swallow. "This doesn't make sense," I announce, and it's a marvel, how my tongue is still reporting for duty. "Brady, please. Tell me what happened. Tell me what's going on."

He sits on the floor. Thunder bellows, but it's quieter now, miles away. "I've been up here since early Wednesday morning," he says. "I couldn't stand it, Abby—for months I've been in this waking nightmare, waiting for the past to catch up with me. For the other shoe to drop. It . . . it was almost a relief. You'd found me. No more waiting, no more hiding. Time's up."

Tears glisten on his cheeks. I'm silent, my heart thrashing in my chest. The realization is cracking open like an egg: *Brady* killed Eszter? *Brady* ripped my life in two with his scrawny, freckled hands?

My voice trembles: "What did you do to Eszter?"

His chin quivers. "I never meant to hurt her."

"What did you do?"

"Nothing." His voice cracks. "That's the problem."

And then he tells me the story, his voice low and halting, struggling to get the words out right.

I see it in front of me—here, *right here* on the grounds of Paraíso Escondido, Eszter's skin growing blotchy, her breath shrinking down to a rattling rasp, panic like a curling flame that fanned itself into a blazing inferno as she realized she was doomed. Some of it was exactly how I'd imagined it: gasping, clutching at her throat, frantically searching for her injector, and then, finally, collapsing.

But . . . she wasn't in her apartment. And she wasn't alone.

All the times the scene played out in my mind's eye, I never panned to where Brady was standing. Frozen. Wide-eyed. Murder by passivity.

"I didn't know what to do," he concludes between sobs. "I was such a coward. I'm so sorry, Abby. I'm so sorry."

Now we're both bawling, our cries filling the decrepit hotel room. The space is just like us: unsafe, unwell, falling apart bit by bit.

"I don't understand," I say. "Where was her EpiPen? Why wasn't it with her?"

"I don't know!" He shakes his head desperately. "It must've rolled away."

"You let Eszter die." My voice quavers. "If you'd helped her, she'd still be alive."

"You think I don't know that? Not a day goes by that I don't think about her." He hangs his head. "After you showed up, I realized I couldn't keep doing this. I almost had a nervous breakdown."

I think back to his apartment two nights ago—Brady's face turned milk-white as he grew inexplicably upset. But he blamed it on bad memories, an abusive father who knocked his mother around right in front of him. I'd been so quick to trust him—to believe that that was the whole story.

"I didn't know what to do," he goes on. "You talked to me about Eszter and I stood there frozen—*again*, just a deer in headlights, letting it crash right into me—and then you left and I wanted to hurt myself. It was that simple, kind of a relief, actually." His finger strums a series of scabs above his knee. "When I finally stopped, I sat there for a very long time. I even thought about killing myself. But then . . . I saw how unfair that was to you. So I texted you. I was going to tell you everything— I really was."

You deserve to know the truth about Eszter. Meet me at the fonda tomorrow. 9 am. Is this real? Am I hallucinating again, like the conversation with Eszter? I glance at my splinted arm, fish around for the pain I should feel. Adrenaline must still be holding it at bay.

"But then . . . then I got scared," he continues. "And I called Amari. I never told her what happened—I still couldn't do it, I was too much of a coward—but I told her I was thinking about killing myself and she was like, 'We need to remove you from this situation.' She said she'd find a boat to take me to the mainland. She wanted me to go to the mental health center in Cancún—I'd checked myself in there before. And . . . and I agreed, but then I realized I was wearing these bloody clothes and there was blood all over the floor."

My ears ring. I felt so certain I knew what the clothes meant—so certain Amari had hurt him.

"She told me to change and pack a bag and go down to the beach to wait for the boat. She said she'd come over and clean up for me. I begged her not to tell anyone. I just wanted to get away. I barely remember throwing stuff in my backpack; I walked out of the house in a haze." He shakes his head. "But then . . . I was almost at the beach when I changed my mind." He looks around. "Instead I came here."

No wonder Amari was so worried. "Why?"

"Because I knew the moment of reckoning had come." He closes his eyes and leans his head against a tiled chunk of wall, *thunk*. "Like I said, time's up. No more running. I had to take responsibility and come clean."

I almost laugh. "But you *did* run."

He hangs his head. "I was working up the courage."

I glance down at the blood pooled in my makeshift sling. It's like looking at someone else's limb. He said help is on the way, right? I remember my haunted sunset walk last night, the eerie feeling of being watched. It clicks. "You saw me here yesterday."

He gives one swift nod. "Someone else came up right after you, too. A man—I didn't get a good look."

I stare at him for a second—his answer is useless, not worth pursuing, a receipt plucked from my fingers by the wind—then grunt. "Well, you could have told me when you saw me. And then I wouldn't have almost died trying to figure out what—"

"I know, Abby. I know." He stares miserably at his hands. "And I need to show you something."

My stomach squeezes like a fist. There's more? What other way can Brady find to hurt me?

He scrabbles around and crawls over to a bag. A rustling sound, and then he turns and holds it out to me.

I let out a choked gasp. It's small and orange and I haven't seen it in months.

Eszter's notebook.

CHAPTER FORTY-FIVE

The journal feels charged, alive, like a shock of static electricity as I take it in my hand.

"Read the last page," Brady says, his voice almost a whisper.

I struggle with the notebook one-handedly and he swoops in to turn to it for me. I start to sob as soon as I see the small, neat handwriting with its gentle leftish lean.

- *Haven fell apart in Oct.*
- *Dad approached me in Oct re: Paraíso Escondido (family vacation spot). Make name for myself, do it my way, etc.*
- *After Coral Gables, needed a win (∅ scandals).*
- *I knew you would hate this idea. (WRONG to keep it from you.)*
- *Devised a plan: change Miami flights, found Isla Colel "randomly." Told myself: once she sees island + hotel → great opportunity, understand. Pictures don't do it justice; needed you to see it for yourself. (Justify to myself . . .)*

- *Always saw options: both move here, go back and forth, etc.* <u>*Want to do life w/ you.*</u>
- *YOU WERE RIGHT. No way to build here w/o disrupting ecosystem, etc. No way to work w/ Dad w/o doing it his way.*
- *Will tell Dad when we get home.*
- *I'M SORRY. Should've listened. Was about acceptance, not project.*
- *Understand if you can't forgive me but won't ever betray you again.*

My tears polka-dot the page, mingling with the ink. *I need to tell you something,* she texted.

She had so much to say.

"Y'know what? Eszter once said this place was going to save lives. The hotel?" Brady looks up at the ceiling, laced with lightning-like cracks. "And now . . . it is."

The Haven, my brain spits out. *Eszter wanted to build a haven.*

"I can't believe she lied to me," I say softly. "She got deeper and deeper and just . . . thought she couldn't tell me."

Brady shakes his head so hard his hair flops around. "Listen—she first told me about the hotel on her second visit. We talked about it a few times. When things were still . . . coming along all right." He grabs my hand. "And—and the whole time she thought it was happening, yeah, she was nervous to tell you, but she was so excited about it too. Thought you could work remotely, right? Thought it would be 'good for the relationship,' she said. There was a Hungarian phrase she used . . . it rhymed, something like, awki mare . . ."

"Aki mer, az nyer," I say softly. *He who dares, wins.*

A fresh wave of grief billows up through me. And suddenly I see it clear as day: Moving somewhere new together *would* have leveled the playing field. I met Eszter right after she arrived in Madison; in time, she slid into *my* life, into the little corners and shelves I cleared for her. She bravely got to know my friends and did her best to make me happy but oh, where was *I*, why wasn't I more concerned about how this new existence suited her? Why was it perfectly fine for her to feel uncom-

fortable while I bopped along in my long-settled life? Moving somewhere where we were *both* expats, both immigrants—it would've been a
fresh reboot.

I would have said yes. *Yes.* Yes to busting away from our old patterns
and army-crawling out of ruts. Eszter was right; I do want something
different, something more, from my job, my relationships, my life.

The gutting thing is that I won't get to do it with her.

There's shouting—are the first responders here?!—and Brady and I
snap our attention toward the doorframe.

"We're in here!" Brady cries, dashing into the courtyard. He steps
aside, and—wet and stumbling, breath heavy, eyes wild—Pedro and
Amari stagger into the room.

They rush over, and from the floor, they look like ogres: towering
over me, spookily lit, impossibly tall and matted and soaked. Amari
drops to her knees and slumps forward so her forehead reaches my shin.

"Oh, thank *God*," she gasps. "Thank God you're okay. Hang in
there, help is on the way, okay?" Her attention whips toward Brady.
"And you too, oh, Brady, I was so worried. I was praying you'd somehow
found another way off the island. Because the alternative—if, if you'd
actually gone through with . . ." She crawls over to Brady and wraps
him in a hug. Pedro watches from the corner, shoulders hunched, rain
dripping off him like tears.

My brain keeps forming the beginnings of questions and abandon-
ing them. "What is going on?" I finally say.

Amari sits back on her heels and turns to me. "EMTs are coming."
She pushes her curls off her forehead. "They should be here any minute."

I'm still so swarmed with confusion that I can't think of the right
follow-up. One emerges, a softball: "You called them?"

"Of course. My phone wasn't working, but as soon as you fell I ran
up here and used the satellite phone." She shakes her head.

"I didn't even see you," Brady tells her matter-of-factly.

Amari points toward the path. "I got a hold of emergency services,
but they said it would be an hour. So then I hauled ass back down the
mountain and found Pedro so we could look for you from *Red Rum*."

With effort, I put the pieces together. The voices in the distance. The flicker of red I saw on the horizon.

"Thanks to the storm, we couldn't get close," Pedro adds in a low voice. "With the size of the waves, we would've capsized and then we'd all have been in danger of drowning."

"You were actually halfway up the cliff by the time we spotted you climbing." Amari shakes her head. "I don't know how you pulled that off. In the rain and everything? And then we saw Brady waving and hollering from the top." She clutches her hands together. "We docked and got up here as fast as we could."

I look at Amari. "So . . . you weren't trying to push me off the cliff."

Her hair swings as she shakes her head. "I was trying to help you. You were way too close to the edge—I was gonna pull you back." She leans forward. "Abby, I'm serious—we had nothing to do with Eszter's death." *She doesn't know.*

Pedro frowns at Brady. "What the hell are *you* doing up here?"

Outside, the trunks of palm trees groan in the wind. Pedro straightens up, like he's just thought of something, and marches back outside.

Amari turns to me. "I genuinely don't know what made you think I hurt Eszter. Rita said you were sick, so I tried to go over to your place and check on you. I was very confused when I got there and you were gone. And—alarmed, honestly. Since Brady disappeared, too."

I try to work backward, to sort through the dominoes that tumbled with increasing speed. Plucking red-spattered clothes from Amari's dumpster. Her landlady's voice shot through Google Translate, a taut game of telephone. My heart nearly stopping as I zoomed in on photos I thought were from Florida, photos I'd looked at a thousand times.

Looking, but not seeing.

"Here." Pedro strides up to me, something clutched in his hands. "Sómbravid. This'll help with the bleeding." His palms brim with crushed petals, the fuchsia trampled to a bruisey purple. "Amari, help me."

She gently balances handfuls on my wounds.

"I saw Brady's bloody clothes," I say softly. "And . . . your landlady said you ran out at, like, three A.M. on Wednesday morning. So I thought . . ."

Her eyes widen. "I would *never* hurt Brady."

Brady clears his throat. "I need to tell you guys something." He takes a deep breath. "Eszter was going to reopen the hotel."

He seems to expect a shocked, dramatic beat, but Amari and Pedro just nod.

"Abby told us." Amari leans forward. "Brady, you knew?"

"Why'd you keep it from us?" Pedro narrows his eyes. "I definitely would've had some things to say."

"Oh, God." Brady drops his head into his hands. "It all got so messy. Eszter asked me to keep it a secret, and I . . . I dunno, I was so shocked I kept it to myself, like saying it out loud would make it real, right? But then . . . we were up here together when she had an allergic reaction. A fatal one. And . . . before I ran away, I looked at her notebook. And I finally realized she'd come around and was actually trying to pump the brakes on the hotel."

"You were with her?" Amari asks, at the same time Pedro shakes his head: "She died *here*?"

Brady nods vigorously. "That's why I didn't tell anyone. *I* gave her the cookie, I started yelling at her, I felt . . . responsible."

"Christ, Brady." Amari touches her fingertips to her forehead. "You ran away? Why didn't you stay with her and wait for help?"

"Because . . . because by the time I could move again, she was already gone."

"But you wouldn't have been in trouble!" Amari clutches her hands together. "All you had to say was that she couldn't find her EpiPen. It was a medical emergency death—it's not your fault."

Brady wipes away tears with a shaky finger. "No—it was unforgivable. Maybe I didn't move because, I don't know . . . maybe some part of me . . ."

"Wait." Pedro crosses his arms. "How did everyone start thinking Eszter died in her Airbnb?"

A puzzled silence pulses around the room.

"I was baffled when I heard that," Brady offers.

"Who would lie about that?" Amari shakes her head. "Why?"

A circuit connects. "That's the right question," I say. "Who would need to sign on to the lie? And who'd benefit from it? I mean, other than Brady, not that many people would've known the truth—really just the EMTs."

"And her Airbnb host," Pedro adds. "Since they said it happened there."

Something Gloria said comes back to me: "Marta stopped running the Airbnb after that. And Gloria, the grocer? She made some snarky comment about how she doesn't know what Marta's doing for money now. Do you think . . . someone could've . . . ?"

Pedro claps his hand to his mouth. "Wait—some random lawyer reached out near the beginning of the year and offered me ten thousand dollars to grant him access to PDC's database. He said they were collecting data on small-town community boards and . . . well, I didn't ask questions. I was gonna put it all into changing the floodlights to amber LEDs. For the turtles, by the beach."

"They wanted access to the database?" I repeat. He nods and I furrow my brow. "That means they'd be able to remove data that's populating the front end." Seeing their blank expressions, I try again: "They could delete posts."

"So it was a coverup," Amari says. "Control the narrative, pay off anyone who could call them out. But *why*?"

"They made me sign a pretty serious NDA." Pedro rubs the back of his neck. "Which I am definitely violating right now."

"Who, though?" I ask.

"I dunno, he was representing some construction company with a weird name."

The pieces are lining up, clicking into place. I glance at Eszter's notebook, at her tiny, tidy lettering: *After Coral Gables—needed a win (Ø scandals)*. His own daughter dying on the construction site before they'd even broken ground . . .

"Was it Izmos Construction?"

Pedro points at me. "Yes."

I shake my head, stunned. "That was Eszter's father protecting his investment. Covering his ass within hours—or minutes, who knows—of finding out his daughter was dead . . . so that he could still build the resort here."

We exchange a stricken glance. "So he had someone move the body?" Amari's voice rises to a squawk.

"Or . . . or just lie about where they found it, I guess?" I reply.

Pedro grunts. "No—they definitely found her there. Neighbors saw her taken out on a gurney."

I bite my lip. The pain in my arm is starting to come back, like a distant, ringing bell. "Marta, I guess? Like I said, it sounds like she had a windfall."

"Carlos," Brady says. "Her husband—he's an emergency responder. Maybe he found her here and . . . got a hold of Eszter's dad, somehow? Or vice versa?"

My head's spinning, and the pain—it's creeping in, tapping me on the shoulder, getting louder by the second.

"We need to tell people!" Amari says.

Pedro lifts his palms. "If I say anything, they'll sue the hell out of me."

"Well, *I* didn't sign anything." Amari raises her brows. "Neither did you, Brady."

His eyes bulge. "You want me to tell the world I was there when she died?"

"And how would we prove it?" Pedro adds.

"We don't have to." I shake my head, harder and harder. "We don't have to tell anyone about Dr. Farkas."

Six eyes narrow at me. I open my mouth to explain when—

"¿Dónde están?" a male voice cries, barely audible over the rain.

The three of them jump to their feet. My blood turns to pure acid—that better not be Carlos.

"¡Estamos aquí!" Pedro yells back, rushing toward the door. "¡Auxilio!"

"No los veo." From outside, another voice, another set of lungs, winded from the climb.

Brady sprints toward the door, surprisingly nimble. "We're in here! Do you have a stretcher? My friend is hurt!"

The pain is hitting me, looping through me in rolling waves like a double Dutch jump rope. Now that I'm fixated on it, the hurt crescendos until it's all I can see, hear, or feel, a tidal wave of agony.

Amari notices me gasping and rushes to my side. "Please hurry!" she screams. "¡Apúrate, por favor!" She clutches my hand and leans over me so I have to meet her eyes. "It'll be okay."

Reality starts strobing in and out again, flashes like the climax of an action flick as people kneel around me, firing questions I can't understand. They put an oxygen mask over my nose and mouth, and, half-delirious, I try to rip it off, and then there's a bee-sting–like pinch in my upper arm and for a curious moment my thoughts turn rubbery, and then, mercifully . . .

Sleep.

CHAPTER FORTY-SIX
CARLOS

Last night

At first, Carlos couldn't believe his luck. Twenty thousand pesos a month for *what?* When that young, blond American staying downstairs—*Eszter Farkas?* she said, like she wasn't sure—first sidled up to him in October, Carlos was sure it was a scam, or some obvious gateway into illegal activity.

In fact, it felt like this big, schlocky reveal: Their quiet Airbnb guest, so polite to Marta and tidy with her things, actually had *big* connections and *wild* plans to revamp Isla Colel . . . and she'd chosen Carlos to help. It was ludicrous, and he almost chuckled when she first explained it in her halting but determined Spanish.

But then . . . he said he'd think about it, and Eszter's father, Dr. Farkas, called to answer any questions. Carlos googled the man: a heavyset, slightly skeevy-seeming developer whose gelled hair and red, sunburned face screamed *Miami*. Dr. Farkas was persuasive, his confidence like a bulldozer. And Carlos listened. He looked over the NDA and contract. And eventually, he saw no reason to say no.

It wasn't all that strange that Eszter approached *him,* once she explained it. She and her father wanted a local to serve as general contractor. Carlos would be their boots on the ground come construction time, managing bricklayers and technicians and plumbers from the region, bringing in high-quality drywall and steel and heavy machinery. Eventually, he'd have his hands full, and they wanted him on board early to ensure a smooth kickoff.

When he spoke on the phone with Dr. Farkas, though, he realized that for now, his role was simpler: to be their eyes and ears as they quietly got their papers in order for the hotel. Both Farkases stressed the need for discretion—even Marta couldn't know. Carlos was to keep an eye on the construction site, hang up some threatening-sounding signs, listen for any chatter about the project, and report back. They wanted all the islanders to be happy when they heard the announcement.

"Now's the time to shape the narrative," Dr. Farkas said in his very capable business Spanish, as Carlos sat sweating in his shop. "I just learned that lesson the hard way." At his laptop that evening, Carlos read about Dr. Farkas's Coral Gables disaster—that must've been what he was referring to. But Eszter had assured him they'd do things the right way here. Methodically, safely, sustainably building up the economy for all Coleleños.

Ultimately, that was what made him say yes: The pocket money was a perk, and the promise of a big job was mouthwatering, but in the end, a jump-started economy was exactly what Colel needed. The end goal—a revitalized island, no longer cut off from the world—was a noble one. He pictured himself as the fairy godmother in little Camila's favorite Disney movie, turning rubble into something beautiful.

And Eszter, not her father, would be in charge—that sealed the deal. He researched her too, saw the degree she was pursuing in the States, the posters she'd presented on "green infrastructure" and "climate-responsive designs" . . . indicators she'd take this seriously and be kind to their beloved island.

For a few nights, he could barely sleep, staring at the ceiling and projecting himself into the future for the ground-breaking ceremony. The whole community would be gathered, maybe even a news station or two from Cancún, ready to cheer. Marta would be there, and Ximena, with Miguel on her hip and Camila leaning against her leg. Three generations of incredible women to remind everyone whom this was for. No way would his daughter and grandkids leave the island then. Mexico City *who*?

"Carlos, help me with the laundry!" Marta tips a basket of clean clothes onto the sofa cushion. He heaves himself out of his armchair and plops next to her on the couch. She's an amazing woman, smart and capable. She gives his shoulder a warm squeeze before settling on the other side of the pile.

At first, the arrangement seemed too good to be true. Carlos looked forward to his check-in calls with Eszter and Dr. Farkas, though he never had much to report. No one on the island bothered to hike up to the hotel anymore, so the NO TRESPASSING signs he'd hung had gone largely unnoticed. Marta didn't suspect a thing even when Eszter asked to extend her stay. All seemed to be well as the Farkases got their affairs in order.

And then . . . one evening, like any other, he made his weekly pilgrimage to the hotel grounds. It felt superfluous, checking on the site while Eszter herself was in town, but they paid him to do it, so up he went. He liked to time it to catch the sunset, even though it meant a treacherous walk home.

That night, four months ago, the sunset was a particularly nice one, peaches and reds, and he stood on the cliff with his hands on his hips, watching the clouds blush and curdle. Finally he sighed contentedly and turned to do a quick lap of Paraíso Escondido. His neighbor Sergio needed help installing new kitchen cabinets in a tricky corner, and Carlos's mind was on the puzzle, juggling all those planes, how to keep each cabinet plumb, level, and square . . .

And then he stopped short. God, it was horrible. By the time he spotted her, the light was dusky and Eszter was ice-cold; there was no chance of reviving her.

It wasn't the first time he'd encountered death, no. As an emergency responder, he'd already come face-to-face with two dead bodies—once when he cut a woman out of a tangled seatbelt, blood dribbling down her chin, and another time as he pumped numbly on the wet chest of a drowned child. Both were horrible; both showed up in his dreams.

But . . . this was different. Eszter was his tenant, his business partner. His friend, even. Eszter had just been in his home, a few meters from him. He knew then and there that his tenure as a volunteer firefighter was over.

His next thought, one that still makes his gut twist with guilt: *Dr. Farkas is going to kill me.*

So . . . he called him. Hardest call he ever had to make. Dr. Farkas was quiet for a long time, and Carlos stood there, jumping at the sound of every bug, the sudden rustle of hunting bats. Mosquitos pierced his skin like tiny lances; the rotting ruins of the resort, crumbled brick and adolescent plants, grew grotesque in the darkness.

Finally, Dr. Farkas sighed. Even in his grief, he had a plan. He retraced Carlos's steps: *Did anyone see you head up the mountain? Did anyone see* her?

And Carlos answered the best he could: *Not that I know of. Looks like she was here alone, and it's dark now.*

"I need you to do something for me," Dr. Farkas said. "Don't call it in yet. They can't find her there. They need to find her somewhere else. Not at the hotel site."

At first, Carlos didn't understand what Dr. Farkas was asking—he *did* find her, *had* found her, was his boss not clear on that? But finally, it clicked, and Carlos heard the words leak from his lips: "Well . . . she'd otherwise be home sleeping . . ."

"Yes. That's it. Wait until it's dark enough, then 'find' her at home."

The way Dr. Farkas talked—confident, like this was all obvious, like Carlos was an idiot if he didn't see why it had to be this way—made Carlos feel untethered from reality.

"I don't care who calls it in—you or your wife or someone looking in the window—that doesn't matter. Just get her there, and carefully. Look around and grab all her things—make sure there's no sign of her near the hotel." Dr. Farkas's voice kept wavering, but he cleared his throat. "Obviously you'll be paid handsomely."

That was the first time it felt like blood money. But Carlos lacked the courage to disobey orders at that point; he was already in too deep. He thought back to the articles he'd read about Coral Gables. *Was* it an accident, like the papers claimed? Or had the day laborers done something Dr. Farkas hadn't liked?

All Carlos ever wanted was a better Isla Colel. Now, sitting on the sofa with Marta, folding a mountain of kids' clothes on the cushions between them, he reminds himself that his lies hurt nobody and will help so many. More opportunities for his family, his community. A reason for Ximena to stay. His grandchildren have big futures. Miguel is already learning to read; Camila dreams of becoming a fútbol star.

"I heard a big storm might hit us tomorrow." Marta glances out the window. "Wonder if it'll affect the ferry."

His stomach twinges. The ferry must embark in the afternoon; it must take that visitor away from Isla Colel. He's been on edge all week, ever since Rita called him late Monday night. *I met someone on the beach today,* she told him. *She had the saddest story. Apparently her partner was that tourist who died here. I've heard a little about that, but never the details, and I didn't want to pry. What happened?*

Talk about irony—Rita hadn't the slightest clue she was speaking with the *one* Coleleño who knew the truth. It was morbid curiosity, he guessed, and he trotted out the lines he'd used at the time. Keeping his voice casual, he asked Rita how long this woman would be visiting. Thank God, Rita said she'd be on the next ferry out. Still, throughout the phone call, his intestines were twisting and whipping like a flag in a hurricane. This was . . . not good.

Dr. Farkas's reaction surprised him—Eszter's father thought the fiancée's claim might be a cover and this mystery woman could be spying on the Paraíso Encontrado project, seeking a way to derail it. Carlos didn't follow his logic, but he listened numbly as Dr. Farkas ordered him to check this visitor out: *See who she's working for, find out why she's really here.* He had enemies, he said, wolves in sheep's clothing. Even if she *was* Eszter's "friend," as he called her, that proved nothing: She could still be working for his rival. *Grief makes people do crazy things,* Dr. Farkas pronounced. Without irony.

Carlos met Abby on the beach the next morning, one more bit of dumb luck—on an island this small, it's hard not to bump into everyone. The encounter turned panicky when she swam far beyond the breakers, then struggled to return. He watched the horizon in horror as one wave after another plowed into her; he wasn't sure what he'd do with himself if she died, too.

This morning he watched her eat breakfast on the patio of the fonda, a cloud of unhappiness shimmering around her. Earlier tonight, he spotted her letting herself into her rental—the last Airbnb on the island, that one-bedroom on a dead-end road—and waited beneath a copse of trees.

When she was gone, he slipped inside her apartment using the keypad (he'd done a bathroom reno there years ago, and of course no one ever changed the code). Then, heart thrashing, he fumbled around for proof of . . . what? He rifled through her suitcase, glanced inside the trash and fridge, feeling guilty and foolish.

Then he spotted something on the back of the laptop; he tipped the screen down and a moan escaped his lips, because *there she was*, Eszter, tiny and happy and in love. *Screw this.* He hustled out of there so fast he tripped over a set of strappy hiking sandals, cursing and lining them back up before rushing into the street, flushed with shame.

Now he tenses as a long crack of thunder, like a distant lion's roar, rolls around the living room.

"When did you get so jumpy?" Marta sets down the pillowcase she's folding and closes the window right as the first drops hit.

Good thing the rain held off while he was on the mountaintop this evening, completing his weekly site inspection. He hates being up there now—every visit feels like a time loop, some quirk in the fourth dimension where he's cursed to discover Eszter's body again and again and again. The hotel ruins felt especially haunted tonight; he imagined the eerie crush of eyes on him, as though the forest itself were watching, alive, intent. A bird, much closer than he expected, let out a lonesome, warbling boohoo, and Carlos had to resist the temptation to sprint back down to civilization.

When he got home, Marta casually dropped one final bombshell: Apparently Abby had stopped by the house to ask about Eszter's time here. The image made his heart ache: a grieving partner, desperate to feel close to her beloved again.

Carlos is *done* keeping tabs on this poor, mourning woman. She's simply bidding farewell to her dearly departed, chatting with Eszter's friends, trying to get some closure. Let her shed some tears and leave in peace.

He's sure he won't feel so spooked by the hotel when it's finally an active construction site, full of men and machinery and a brusque, particular bustle. It won't be long until Carlos's furtive duties are over and he can become a part of the project loudly, proudly, out in the sunlight. He smiles at Marta as he sets a cloth napkin on top of her stack. This isn't the first storm they've weathered.

The ground-breaking ceremony . . . it can't come soon enough.

CHAPTER FORTY-SEVEN
ABBY

Friday morning

I wake inside a spaceship: fluorescent lights, a rattling air conditioner, the faint smell of airplane food. Then more of my brain boots up and I realize I'm in a hospital, with pale blue curtains blocking whatever's to my left and right. There's a chorus of gentle, rhythmic beeps, plus the nearby squeak of tennis shoes on a waxed floor.

I start to sit up, but my left arm is in a sling fixed to the ceiling; there's a cast around it too, and bandages on my knees and palm. I stare at it all in wonder.

"You're awake!"

I jump a mile at the voice, then twist to my right. Rita's in a chair, leaning forward uncertainly. Is this another dream? Am I hallucinating again?

"How are you feeling?" When I turn she's still there. I bite my lip and try to work out what's true. I have a hazy impression of being tied down but flying—am I making that up?

"Where are we?" I say.

"El Buen Samaritano. In Cancún. A hospital, obviously."

I peer at her. "How did we get here?"

"You took a helicopter," she says. "The rest of us plebs took a boat. You beat us by hours."

"'The rest of us'?" I repeat. "And . . . wait, how long have I been here?" There are no windows in sight; it could be any time, day or night.

"Oh, all of us. Amari didn't want to leave Brady's side. Or yours, for that matter. You've been here an entire night already." She scoots her chair closer. "Brady told me everything. About what happened with Eszter, I mean. And oh, Abby . . . I'm so terribly sorry."

"Thanks." A tear trickles toward my jaw. I try to swipe it away, then remember my hand's wrapped in gauze. I don't entirely trust Brady to tell the truth—all of it. "What exactly did he share?"

She sighs. "About how Eszter wanted to rehab the hotel, like you said. But then . . ." She looks away. "How he was there, in her Airbnb, glued to the spot. We've all had nightmares like that, being bolted to the floor. It's awful. I told him it's not his fault, but he was bawling as he told me."

My stomach churns. So he's keeping the location change quiet. I thought I'd feel better, knowing exactly what happened, how Eszter passed. But in the end, it changes nothing.

A stray bit of egg or speck of peanut. An absent EpiPen. The love of my life, with her entire bright future unscrolling in front of her—gone, because Brady let her die. Gone and nothing will bring her back.

"Oh, and I finally heard from my friend Carlos—he was a little sheepish, he was just not bothering to pick up my calls. I'm sorry I wasted your time trying to track him down." She touches my arm tenderly. "Nothing makes you think about your limited time like a life-or-death situation, right?"

Wasted time. For decades, it's been one of my top fears—not utilizing every second, being idle, standing frozen like Brady while life whizzed around me. But what floats into my mind at that moment is my company, TimeIn: the near *worship* of productivity, a laser focus on optimization so you can cram more into a day.

What if that's not the goal? What if it's about freeing up time so you have more hours to picnic on the beach or watch a sunset or share onion rings in a sticky booth? Less grinding, more grounding. It's a simple revelation, obvious to everyone I've met on Isla Colel. But for the first time, it feels true.

Then Rita says something that snaps me back: "They contacted your family."

"What?"

"Your mother. Your emergency contact."

I almost laugh. Who was the Abby who filled out the migration form from a snaking line at the Cancún airport? Since Eszter died, I've been jotting down the landline for my childhood home whenever pressed to provide a number, simply because it's the only one I still have memorized.

"Is she on her way?" Then, frowning, I answer my own question: "Wait, no, she couldn't afford that."

"I don't think anyone's flying down, no. But a nurse at the hospital called her. She said she's glad you're okay and sends her love."

Who knows if it's true, but my heart swells a bit thinking of her. "I haven't called her in months," I admit.

Rita smiles. "Well, I'm sure she'd be happy to hear from you."

I peer at her silver waves, the gentle creases around her eyes. My mother's age, yet she might as well be from another planet. When I first met Rita, I felt a vague sense of despair that I hadn't gotten a parent like her: caring, present, content to let me be me.

And then I remember: This is the first time I've seen her since I flung her passport down and bolted out of her apartment.

"I googled Petra Siegel," I say.

Her face falls. "My passport, ja? I figured that was why you sprinted off like a madwoman yesterday."

I nod.

"Right. You're thinking there must be some scandal. But the truth is, I simply disengaged from the rat race." Her face glows with earnestness. "On Colel, it's not about how much you earn or impressing anyone. And I think that's why our little group is so close."

I watch her, waiting for more.

She sighs. "I had this entire career as a, quote, 'feminist icon.'" Her fingers crook into air quotes. "I was flying around the world, prattling on and on about what young women needed to do to succeed." A shrug. "I was good at it. Young women trusted me, thought I was giving them some magic bullet. But it wasn't like that—I just listened to their problems and knew how to dispense advice in a way that made them feel seen."

Her eyes find the popcorn ceiling. "And then, one day, I was chatting with a makeup artist before going on a talk show. And she said: 'It sounds like you're telling women to act more like men.' And that was it. I finished the show, went home, and started to dissolve my company."

I frown. "But weren't you helping people?"

"I told myself that, exactly that, from the start. But suddenly, it all felt like . . . what do you call it, like when you're selling Tupperware? Only I was selling women this cheap, plastic idea of empowerment. Playing the white man's game, working myself to the bone and encouraging others to do the same. And for what? For the next gig, the next speaker's fee, the next sandwich in a greenroom and night in a soulless hotel. I was done." She looks away. "I mean, I was lucky to have the savings to leave it all behind."

I peer at her. "Why didn't you just change your approach, then? I get it, the whole 'girlboss' era was annoying, but . . . you had an entire *empire,* a huge following, all this power. You could've kept inspiring people."

She smiles kindly. "You're impressed by what I built." I nod and she sighs deeply. "I'm going to tell you something that I wish I'd known sooner: If you try to impress people into loving you, you're telling yourself you aren't lovable without those impressive things." She shrugs. "But you are! And so am I. You're enough."

I look away, blinking hard. She's hit on something so deep that it compresses in my stomach, carbon turning to diamond. I think of Eszter, too, us cheering each other on in the Sisyphean struggle to be The Best. Maybe we gravitated toward each other because we recognized that drive—two overachievers, with different fuel in our tanks, both striving toward greatness. God, even that first night on the beach with

Rita, I couldn't shut up about Eszter's accomplishments, could I? Top student and brilliant thinker and accomplished pianist and *blah blah blah blah blah*.

My hallucination in the storm, Eszter's eyes sad and lucid: *You didn't even* like *me,* she said, though the real speaker was me. *You just* admired *me, and if I ever stopped being impressive, I'd lose you.* It's clear now. By seeing myself as the sum of my accomplishments, I plastered the same conditionality onto Eszter.

But . . . but I'd have loved her even if it all fell apart. If the world crumbled and we were two lost souls amid the rubble, going for walks and making dumb jokes about otters and llamas and just being Eszter and Abby. Oh, if only we had more time. If only I could go back and make sure she knew how deep and wholehearted my love for her was.

It's hard to imagine ever feeling that way again. But if I do . . . I won't make the same mistake.

I whisk tears off my cheeks. "Do you ever miss it, Rita?" I ask. "All that . . . 'success.'"

"At times." A small smile. "But no matter what choice you make, there will be grief. Roads you didn't take, things you won't get to do. We're all choosing our regrets, aren't we?"

A beat. "But why did you change your name?"

"I wanted a fresh start. With the others here, I mean. One google and my whole past is served up on a platter. As you found." She waits for me to nod. "It was time to let Petra Siegel go. My grandmother's name was Rita, and that's the wonderful thing about Colel—we're all on a first-name basis." She turns to me. "On that note, I have a request: that you not tell the others."

I furrow my brow. They have no idea after three months on the island with Rita, while I discovered it inside of a week? It doesn't track.

But then again . . . they're all bound by a code of don't-ask-don't-tell. *We love secrets here,* Rita noted that very first night. *Everyone gets a fresh start. Even you.*

"I won't say anything," I tell her. Her life, after all, is hers alone.

———

The hospital discharges me in a wheelchair, and in the parking lot, I hobble into an Uber, compliments of Rita. It'll be a while, I realize, before I'm well enough to go to the gym, let alone to swim laps. From Madison, Mei reconfirmed my half-missed hotel reservation, and, miraculously, I'll make my original flight home tomorrow. Carshares, plane tickets—it all feels like something from another planet, another life.

The front desk calls to say I have a visitor. Amari's here—she must've gotten the address from Rita—and, pulse quickening, I send her up.

I hobble to the door and pull it open, thunking the dead bolt out to keep it ajar. I don't know where I should be when she gets here, and finally I sit on the stiff gray comforter. From the bathroom, the faucet drips a steady staccato. A muffled voice roams in from a neighboring room.

A token knock, then Amari's at the door, smiling and shy. We stare at each other for a second, and then she rushes over and wraps me in a hug. "I'm so relieved you're okay," she says into my shoulder. "And I'm so sorry about everything."

We sit on opposite corners of the bed, like two girls at a sleepover. She futzes with her key ring, squeezing the little plastic turtle between her fingers.

Something dawns on me. "Your heated discussion with Pedro."

She looks up sharply.

"On the nature preserve," I continue, "the morning after Brady disappeared." I lower my chin. "I know it wasn't about the baby turtles."

"To be fair, he did yell at Rita about it that morning." She sighs. "When Brady called me freaking out in the middle of the night, I woke Pedro up and begged him to lend me the keys to his boat—I thought I'd take Brady to the mainland myself. But then Brady didn't want anyone to know what was going on with him—he insisted I go on the boat ride with you all." Her gaze sinks to her lap. "So I found another local to take him in *Red Rum*. It was a mess: Pedro wasn't expecting to see me that morning; I didn't know Brady hadn't shown up; Esteban mentioned *Red Rum* was still at the marina, so Pedro wanted to know who had his keys . . . yeah."

I consider. "Why didn't Pedro just tell me that? When I asked him about the argument?"

"I begged him not to mention it to anyone," she says. "I mean, he didn't know I was trying to find a ride for Brady—I just told him it was super urgent and super personal. You know how the expats are. We respect everyone's privacy."

Through the window screen, a bug chitters, its desiccated rattle like a maraca.

"Did you know?" I ask. "What Brady did?"

A tear rolls down her cheek. "I didn't know he was there with Eszter. I knew he was upset after her death, but it never crossed my mind that he . . . c'mon, it's *Brady*. I once saw him cry over a rat that got flattened by a motorbike."

She looks out the window. "I mean, he and Eszter bonded. It didn't seem *that* weird that seeing you triggered him. It wasn't until . . . when you said Eszter was going to reopen the hotel, and you asked who would've wanted to stop that . . ." She shrugs. "That's the only time it crossed my mind."

"Right." A blob of sun blips through the window. "Tell me everything, please," I say. "About your time with Eszter. Start at the beginning."

So she does—she tells me about spotting her on the ferry over, helping her hitch a ride to Calle Estrella. Introducing her to Brady and the others. The three were soon a "gay-gle," having adventures all over the island—she describes the first time they led Eszter to Paraíso Escondido, how they stirred up a whole colony of bats, screamed and ran as the creatures swooped and chittered. It was only during her final visit that Eszter seemed off—and now we know why.

She clutches her hands together. "I'm so sorry, Abby. I'm so sorry you lost her."

Our eyes meet, and though I know she wasn't totally honest with me, though she watched me whip myself into a froth over Brady and still concealed details about the night he disappeared . . . I understand. *He's like my little brother,* she told me. Protective, devoted. The kind of sibling I never was to Kayla, certainly.

I believe Amari. Sitting still and letting her condolences reach me: That's the simplest, but hardest, thing.

The words I heard in Eszter's voice, words that actually came from me: *The island taught me I could just* be, *you know?* And, gazing with wonder at the world at her feet: *You have to hold still.* I had it all wrong. Stasis isn't death. Lying here, I start to see.

"Thank you." A self-conscious flick of laughter. "I, um, hate myself a little for asking this. But while we're being honest . . . did anything ever happen between you and . . . ?"

Her eyes bug. "Me and Eszter? No!" She shakes her head violently. "I mean, she was obviously stunning. But she was so, so in love with you."

I peer at her until an eerie feeling kicks in—how strange that Amari is inside that body, looking out from those eyes, her inner world as complicated as my own, laced with jagged secrets and silty-dark corners and precious memories and joys and decisions, those endless calculations about what to let out into the world.

Amari smiles sadly. "Seriously—she loved you like crazy. She was a little squirrely about your visit, but now it's clear why: She didn't want to lose you."

She lets me cry in that same kind way Rita has of holding space, without looking freaked out or impatient or uncomfortable.

"I wonder what made her change her mind," I finally say. "About the resort. I wonder what made her realize it was a bad idea."

Amari stares at me a split second too long, then shakes her head. "I have no idea." She kickstands an arm behind her and sighs. "Now we have to figure out what to do about the hotel."

"I had a thought," I reply. "One that . . . I think Eszter might've liked." Her brows lift as I tell her what to do, whom to contact. She makes some notes in her phone and hugs me goodbye.

"Get home safe," she says into my shoulder.

"You too," I reply.

———

An hour later, the front desk calls again. *Rita,* I think. Or maybe they patched through a call from my mother.

"There is a guest here for you," the receptionist says pleasantly.

"Who is it?"

A muffled question, then a clank as she recenters the phone.

"The gentleman's name is Brady."

CHAPTER FORTY-EIGHT

I stare at the wall for a second, where a framed palm-print pattern hangs crookedly. I'm not surprised, but my heart sinks with disappointment. *No more running,* Brady said. *I had to take responsibility and come clean.*

But he didn't turn himself in. After all that, he's going to bury what happened, continue letting it eat him up from the inside. Do I have a duty to tell someone? For the sake of . . . I don't know, justice? Brady's own safety and mental well-being?

"¿Señorita?" Her voice crackles in the speaker.

I close my eyes. "Send him up."

Brady looks dazed, eyes red and swollen, lips sunburned and cracked. We stare at each other for a second before I limp aside to let him in. He staggers to the armchair in the corner and sits, and I turn the desk chair to face him.

"Pedro set me up with a friend of his," he says. "A lawyer. Just for a friendly chat."

I wait.

"All the sleepless nights waiting for a knock on the door, wondering why on Earth someone changed the story of Eszter's death and what they were going to do to me if they found out . . . well, he said turning myself in would be a waste of time."

I lower my chin. "What are you talking about?"

"Apparently it's a legal quagmire, for one thing. The United States can't prosecute an Australian for a crime committed in Mexico, so it'd fall to the system here. But based on everything I told him, they wouldn't bother charging me with negligent homicide, especially since I'm not a Mexican citizen."

I look down. That's the crux of it, isn't it? Brady's failure to help her that day—is it homicide? He's at least partially to blame, but that doesn't change the fact that what ended her life was a medical emergency. Where *was* the EpiPen? Would it have made a difference if he'd found it for her, or if he'd called 911 right away?

Tears stream down his cheeks. When I look at him, I don't feel anger. Only sadness.

"I guess if her family knew, they could pursue a civil suit," he continues. "But since she died here, it's not under American jurisdiction. And Mexico probably wouldn't extradite me. And considering her dad was likely the one who wanted to change the story around her death, well . . ."

I swallow. "So you came here to, what—ask me to keep my mouth shut?"

He looks up, eyes haunted. "No, not at all. It's up to you, if you want to tell people. If you think people should know the truth."

The seconds seem to spread out. I picture them, Dr. and Mrs. Farkas, in that massive house in Florida. Calling them, clearing my throat. *I need to tell you something.*

What kind of monsoon would my words—flapping butterfly wings—set off? *I know the truth about Eszter. I know what you did . . . and what you missed.* Would they track Brady down and try to buy his silence . . . or, delirious with grief, find some way to punish him? As a corporate bigwig, Dr. Farkas is no stranger to the media—even if he couldn't hurt

Brady through the legal system, would he find a way to smear Brady's reputation?

Brady's got it even worse than me; we both have one parent, but mine never hit me, never committed violence. Instead I shouldered those quiet moments of emotional neglect, with both of us laser-focused on Kayla. Mom did her best. I suspect she's jealous of me for getting out, resentful, even, but her envy isn't really about me; it's about her own life not turning out how she thought it would. I left Elmridge behind. Brady, on the other hand, is still in hiding.

"I won't tell anyone," I say.

He can't meet my eyes. Instead he mouths *thank you* and wipes away tears. "You know you can change your mind whenever you want, right?"

I nod. "But I won't."

A beat.

He looks up. "I have a question."

"Shoot."

"I know you're leaving. But . . . do you think we can keep in touch?"

A *yes* hangs on my tongue—Brady is desperate, paunch-eyed, pitiful, the definition of a friend in need. Certainly I'd get something out of the arrangement; I'd get to feel like the bigger person, magnanimous and wise. The *together* one, stooping to his level, wielding my supposedly superior emotional intelligence to reassure him and make sure he's okay. The realization makes my stomach flip over, wringing with disgust and shame.

I think of Eszter, so eager to please, distressed at the thought of making anyone—myself included—uncomfortable, even when I was in the wrong and she damn well should've.

I picture myself in our home together in Madison . . . God, I just started calling it *our* home, as if the possessive adjective were a magic wand. Never mind that it was *my* idea, *my* stuff, *my* default paper products and disheveled shoes and quotidian rhythms, all of which Eszter adapted to seamlessly. A shadow, a chameleon. Someone I loved deeply yet pushed a tier below me out of some messed-up savior complex.

"I can't do that." Tears fill my eyes. "There's so much pain there, and for both of us . . ." *No,* no more speaking for other people. No more declaring what's best for them, thinking I somehow know their inner worlds better than they themselves do. "For *me,* I mean . . . it would be too hard."

He nods, red-faced and miserable.

I can't help myself: "You're going to be okay, Brady." I cross my arms over my belly. "We'll both be okay."

He sniffles once, clears his throat. "Thanks, Abby." He looks me right in the eye and his voice balloons with sudden certainty. "You're right."

He's almost out the door when he stops short.

"Oh. I wanted to give you this." He pauses and sets something on the dresser. He can't look at me. "Bye, Abby."

"Adiós."

When he's gone, I limp over. It's Eszter's notebook, the orange cover the worse for wear. A thousand moments flash at once: leaning over the kitchen table and helping her organize her thoughts; giggling in a dive bar while I played the role of her dad; swearing to myself whenever she approached me, broodily, notebook in hand. For the entirety of our relationship, this object had so much power. All the things she wanted to say. All the thoughts she needed to work out.

I run my finger along the spine, then drop my arm. She was protective of this notebook, and so private. I'm not sure what I'll do with it. Maybe in time, I'll work up the courage to read it. But for now, right now, I flip to the last page and revisit her tiny, slanted handwriting:

- *I'M SORRY. Should've listened. Was about acceptance, not project.*
- *Understand if you can't forgive me but won't ever betray you again.*

I pluck my laptop off the desk and drag it onto the bed. A calendar notification pops up: *Weekly tag-up with Tyler.* This is the longest I've gone without working in a while—without scanning through Python files and slamming my head against the wall, trying to fix the scheduler function. But now, after a few days away from the terminal . . . I feel different. Curious, not furious. I shrug, actually *shrug,* as I launch JupyterLab. I lean back against the pillows while my eyes coast through line after line of code—I *do* speak another language, come to think of it.

I stop. *No.* It cannot be that simple.

All the drama, the anguish, the months of stalled progress and the potential loss of my job . . . are from a dang capitalization error. I've swapped *%m,* month, for *%M,* minute, in the format codes. The module is trying to parse impossible date/time strings, scheduling events for, say, the forty-fifth month of the year. I fix the line and rerun the demo.

It works perfectly.

I open Slack to let my team know, and more notifications pile in: fires to put out, merge requests to review, a fresh set of test data to clean up and feed into the model. Something cracks open inside me—a rushing feeling, like I've opened Pandora's box.

I think of that moment at the base of the cliff, my bone snapped in two, Eszter before me, pelted by the rain. Everything she said: It came from *me,* my own wisdom. About my priorities, my grim determination to be in control.

TimeIn is such a scam—it's time management marketed as "Buy this so you can stop being such a goddamn failure!" In truth, the app has exactly one goal, and that's making its C-suite rich. I picture the wolf pack of founders—men like Tyler who sit in board meetings and go out for beers afterward and play golf on weekends while their wives are at home, on the brink of collapse, and no, no AI is going to save them. Screw more apps, more smartphones, more shiny plastic things studded with cobalt laced with the blood of child laborers. Screw Tyler. Why was I so eager to impress him? Truly, who cares?

Typing awkwardly around my cast, I write an email alerting him that I've fixed the bug . . . and that I'm resigning. I offer to give two weeks' notice but acknowledge that, given the proprietary nature of the work, I may not be welcome back; I'll pay to courier my things. I thank him for the experience and wish him all the best.

After I hit Send, I see a new email in my inbox. My heart quickens—it's from Eszter's brother.

Hi Abby,

I got your emails about Paraíso Escondido and Eszter staying on the island. I called my dad and we had probably the longest talk we've had since E passed. I knew she was on vacation there but neither she nor my father told me they were working on a development project there. My mom didn't know either, I guess they were going to surprise everyone when the permits were in place. (He asked if I wanted to help with the project going forward and I was like, absolutely not.)

Reading between the lines, I think he felt/feels a huge amount of guilt for sending her there. He cried on the phone and it's the second time in my life I've heard him cry. The project was supposed to bring them closer and it ended the most horrible way possible. He said he regrets that he didn't tell her he was proud of her, which is maybe the most emotional thing I've ever heard him say.

Anyway, he was too emotional to want to speak with you (as am I—hence the email) but he said he'd consider it, and I'm hopeful. Obviously no pressure. I'll try calling you next week sometime. How long will you be in Mexico?

Tears stream down my cheeks. I see why Eszter kept the project a secret; my attitude toward her father was basically: *F that guy.* That hasn't changed; the real shocker is that, in the end, she started coming around to my way of thinking.

But, at the same time, I never looked at it from his perspective. He wasn't wrong to dislike me—I *did* want to keep Eszter away from him. Where I saw a boundary, he saw a barbed-wire fence. It's unfair she never got the chance to tell him Paraíso Escondido was dead in the water.

I swipe at my neck as the wet trails reach my collar. I don't have a choice; I have to compute it, the snarl of jagged emotions inside me. Blame some combo of Percocet and my weird data-scientist brain, but I close my eyes and try to make sense of it all.

It takes me a second to work out what I'm feeling: It's admiration for Eszter's courage, respect for the way she was going to assert herself. I blink and my gaze falls on her orange notebook, closed and shy on the desk. I can almost hear her: *This isn't going to work, Dad. This isn't what I want to do.*

She was—no, *we* were changing at the end, weren't we? She was going to be honest with her father. She started being honest with *me*—about her need for space, for time. For this trip to paradise. For a shared life that didn't orbit around me alone. *I need to tell you something.* That something was Paraíso Escondido, sure, but also more: Eszter was going to finally, bravely tell me what she wanted.

So she craved a relationship with her parents. And though I didn't support her working with her dad, maybe I could've given her the space to decide. Another fact clicks into focus: The expats of Isla Colel are another kind of family, closer to the blood kind. Brought together by happenstance, whether they'd otherwise choose one another or not.

Eszter and I had this tension, a never-ending debate: Which kind of family is more important, one bound by friendship or by fate? And maybe my stance explains how fully I fell for the expats at first, and before that, how desperate I was to make Eszter my wife. *Look*, a small, insecure part of me screamed. *I've got a more robust family than anyone bound by blood.* Now I see how silly it is. Why should it be either/or?

I refresh my inbox and two new emails pop up. One is from Delta: *It's time to check in for your flight.* The other is from Mei, relaying that a bunch of my friends want to greet me at the airport but she'll put the kibosh on it if I don't want them seeing me all bandaged and bruised.

I smile a bit as I type one-handedly. "Let them come," I tell her. "Can't wait to see you."

CHAPTER FORTY-NINE
ABBY

May 16, 2022 (two years ago)

Her smile. That's what I couldn't stop staring at, those perfect teeth and the smirklike smile that kept playing on her lips, like she had a secret, like you'd have to earn her affection. She reminded me of a cat, watchful and calm. I, on the other hand, have always been more of a dog, smile open and wide, voice eager and loud, rushing around to put everyone at ease, all I-love-you-please-love-me.

Luckily, the first date seemed to be going exceptionally well, and Eszter appeared to be picking up what I was putting down—snickering at my jokes and jumping excitedly onto things I shared as we passed back and forth the proverbial talking stick. We had so much in common: two capital-*N* Nerds in male-dominated fields, passionate about working out (her at Pilates and yoga, me at the gym or pool), lovers of brainteasers and trivia and the ruby-colored Negronis we kept ordering.

And already, I was fascinated by our differences. She was raised in a wealthy suburb of Miami, and I grew up in a drafty rented house with a weed-choked backyard and siding slipping from the front. She moved like a dancer, and it was a miracle whenever I made it up a set of stairs unharmed. I was a proud extrovert; she identified as an introvert. Twice

I asked her a question and she was quiet for long enough that I figured she hadn't heard me and started to repeat myself—but no, this was simply how she spoke, not jumping in until she'd worked out what she wanted to say.

Gaps and all, the conversation flowed and I kinda couldn't believe it: This gorgeous woman seemed to be enjoying herself. Wheat-gold hair, pert nose, hazel eyes: She was much prettier than her photos on the dating app. Because they couldn't capture that flashing intellect, the way she spoke a little quietly and all you wanted to do was lean in and listen.

We talked and talked until, somehow, the bar was closing, and then we stood outside, sharing enthusiastic "We should do this again!"s. When her Uber arrived, she pulled me into a hug, and though I wasn't bold enough to kiss her, I felt calm about it.

Something told me I'd get another chance.

CHAPTER FIFTY
ABBY

November 17, 2024 (six months after Isla Colel)

A pearl of sweat slides down my chest. I hurry to the thermostat and turn the heat down a notch—I'd rather not arrive all red-faced and frazzled. I'm nervous enough already. But in a good way, more excited than anxious.

A clunking sound, and heat stops flowing out of the vent. Though I've been here for almost five months, I'm still in awe of this apartment—smaller than my Madison one but more open, with high ceilings and buttery afternoon light; brick fireplace in the bedroom, pretty backsplash over the kitchen sink. It's right above a darling coffee shop, Café Mona, and if I stand on my tiptoes in the bathroom, I can catch a glimpse of Lake Michigan. It reminds me of Lake Mendota—same windswept waves and crisp, crackling blue. But here, in Milwaukee, I'm on the western shore, with a perfect view of the sunrise.

But there's no time to admire the lake right now—it's almost five, and I've got about six minutes to finish getting ready and complete a ten-minute walk. I curl my eyelashes, slick on mascara. I snatch my phone up from the vanity and send a text: "Running a minute behind!"

"No worries!" comes the reply, but still, I hustle. Perfume, motorcycle jacket, quick debate over appropriate shoes. I tuck my things into my back pocket—wallet, wallet, where's that stupid wallet?—then bound into the living room, eyes on the door at the far end.

But I'm not used to these shoes, and my toe catches on the edge of the rug. I stumble forward, then catch myself, letting out a bark of laughter.

A car honks outside, and instinctively I turn to the windows. On this autumn evening, the sun's pouring through them in two silky pools. I hung a gallery wall between them, black-framed squares and rectangles of varying sizes pleasingly arranged above the gray sofa. At first, I was going to hang them haphazardly, lifting frames at random and making it up as I went.

But at the last second, I put the hammer down. I took out a tape measure and recorded the artworks' dimensions in Eszter's old orange notebook; though I still haven't read the notes wrinkling the first half, a task that might be too overwhelming for this lifetime, I picked up where she left off, jotting things down in the remaining blank pages. Then I arranged the gallery wall in an app, taking an hour to get it just right. It was painstaking work, slow going and persnickety. If Eszter had tried this at our home in Madison, I would've hovered behind her, tapping my foot. But what I ended up with is beautiful, so balanced and calm, and I smile at it every day.

There's a print I picked up in Montreal last month, a pattern of curvy minnows. A charcoal drawing of a palm frond. A cheeky ink sketch of a bare butt and legs middive, head and torso already in the water. A photo of a geometric-looking cornfield in Elmridge, and a grid of Polaroids from Mei's Fourth of July cookout, eyes and smiles floating in overexposed faces.

My gaze lingers on the painting in the center, its blue swirls and bold strokes. *Eszter.* Amari's name is in the corner, eddying into the background. I showed her the complete gallery wall a few weeks ago on FaceTime. She's in Uruguay now, in the boho town of Rocha, and she told me about the little expat community she's infiltrated there, another motley crew. She keeps in touch with Brady, who recently moved to Bali. He's closer to Australia there, to childhood friends he's confessed to missing. She hasn't heard from Pedro, who's still on Isla Colel.

Rita sends me the occasional long voice memo. There are new arrivals on the island, other nonnatives, and one by one she's taken them under her wing. I can almost picture them, sharing tequila and roasting fish on the beach, discovering the otherworldly magic of a bay that glows at night. Bobbing on a panga boat toward the north tip of the nature preserve, the spot with the scratched picnic table and occasional visits from black-and-red grackles.

In the end, those friendly birds were Isla Colel's savior. The expats agreed my idea was a good one, and a few weeks after I left, Pedro used his connections to pull in an environmental impact crew. Near the hotel ruins, they found exactly what he'd hoped for: the nesting grounds of the red-capped grackles.

Then the dominoes began to fall. Brady used PDC to organize an information campaign about the endangered birds; Silvana, the pretty waitress, started a charming TikTok account about the island's unique feathered inhabitants. Kids at the local school made posters and projects about the rare species, construction-paper creations so adorable and earnest that a Cancún news crew ferried in to film a segment. Pedro even contacted Hilde, a former expat with connections to the Mexican media—she knew Eszter, apparently, she was the pale, round-faced woman in that group photo—and with her help, they got some good publicity around the impact report's findings. The government stepped in and declared the mountaintop a "critical habitat" just days before Izmos Construction was set to break ground.

I still feel a bit torn about it; surely there were Coleleños who would've welcomed a new, economy-boosting hotel, and who are we to decide what's best? All I know is that Dr. Farkas's team pulled out, a humiliating blow on the heels of the Coral Gables fiasco.

Just as Pedro feared, birders have begun flocking to the island, but there's a cap on visitors—preregistration required, timed entry to the preserve, the whole nine yards. Marta, who apparently had a robust career in hospitality before opening her Airbnb, is running the entire operation. Eszter's best friend, Shane, is planning a trip there in January and invited me along, but I said no; my time on the island feels complete.

The painting gazes back at me. Eszter's eyes look bright, intelligent, taking things in at a level so micro, most of us couldn't even fathom it. I don't know how Amari managed to capture that. Even photos don't come close.

I pause to let the tears fall, flushing away some of that fresh mascara. I laugh aloud. God, this poor woman I'm meeting tonight—I warned her in the app that she'll be my very first date since my fiancée passed away. She, a social worker, was exceptionally kind about it and assured me she'd "hold back on the charm so you don't fall madly in love with me on day one." In turn, I promised not to turn our date (bowling, how low-pressure is *that?*) into an impromptu therapy session. "I'm excellent at boundaries," she replied. "And I accept Venmo and Zelle if that's where the wind blows."

I wipe my eyes and give the painting a gentle tap, smile brimming. I turn and scoop my keys off the hook.

Then I head out, pulling the door closed behind me.

Gloria leans against the counter to gaze out the front door. Rita turns and gives a final wave before disappearing into the sunlight. It's been a week since that tourist, Abby—inexplicably adored by Rita—caused a ruckus, slipping off the cliff in front of Paraíso Escondido and somehow scrambling her way back up in the middle of a tropical storm. Thank God that's over. The helicopter took her away, beating its choppy heart, and now the girl's back home in Wisconsin. Rita said it like she wasn't sure Gloria would've heard of it, *Wisconsin*. And Gloria played along, tilting her head: *Is that where they make all the cheese?*

In fact, Gloria was there once, as a little girl. Her school took a day trip from Chicago to visit the sprawling Milwaukee County Zoo. Her most vivid memory is of a free-range peacock ambling across the path, one iridescent tailfeather dragging behind the others.

Not that anyone on Isla Colel knows this. People here assume she's from elsewhere in Mexico, and she lets them. She's lived here for over three decades now, ever since she planned a spring break trip to Cancún with a few college friends and, bored with all the drinking, wandered over to the marina and chose a route at random.

It's funny to think about how differently her life could've turned out if she'd boarded another ferry: Would she now reside in Cozumel, Holbox, Isla Mujeres? But in this reality, she stepped off the boat onto Colel, and the island captivated her like nowhere she'd ever been. Living in Chicago felt like scuttling along a glass-and-metal canyon with the true horizon a hundred stories in the air. Here, the locals mistook her for a visiting mainlander and welcomed her ashore.

She was lucky—with a Puerto Rican mother and a knack for picking up accents, she had no trouble playing the part. A cute fisherman at the fonda took her out in his boat. He and his friends showed her the nature preserve, the beaches, the bustling hotel at the top of the cliff, and the bio bay that blinked and shimmered in the darkness. She spent three ecstatic nights here before tracking down the Yellow Pages and using it to call her frantic friends back at the hotel. They were annoying on the phone, squawking and ditzy. She decided then and there to never see them again. Better yet—to never leave.

It was like a fairy tale, and the fisherman, Esteban, proposed after just a few months. She bought the local seafood store from a hunchbacked old woman to sell some of Esteban's catches instead of passing them all to money-grubbing distributors, and after a few years, she expanded the business into a full-fledged grocery store. They welcomed a beautiful daughter, Silvana. She's so lucky she can't believe it sometimes—how precious and fragile her life here is.

Rita barges back inside and sheepishly snatches up the tote bag she left on the counter. Gloria likes Rita. It took Gloria a while to warm to her, but finally she became satisfied that the tall, gabby German lady was only interested in keeping a low profile, living quietly on this serene island.

Most of the native Coleleños ignore the immigrants, a quiet truce born out of mutual avoidance. *You leave us alone and we'll do the same.* But Gloria tries to get to know them. She slows down her speech, thickens her Mexican accent, just to keep a boundary up between her and them. But lately, she's liked the crew. Amari just wants to make art. Pedro straddles the two worlds like an acacia tree linking heaven and Earth. She was glad when Brady reappeared. He loves this island almost as much as she does.

Eszter was the first to cause problems. Late last year, the small, pretty blonde got it in her head that she could reopen the hotel—a multiyear, head-swimmingly huge undertaking. There would be contractors all over the island, public hearings to discuss the permits. Excavators, bulldozers, clanking steel and swarms of construction workers—the building process was horrible to think about. Let alone what would come after, when the hotel opened, a blinking beacon calling out to chic tourists all over the world.

And sure, some of the Coleleños would've been happy about it; they wanted jobs and updated infrastructure and those crisp bills from tourists' soft leather wallets. But they didn't know what they were talking about. There's zero doubt in Gloria's mind: If the hotel had reopened, life as they knew it would've been destroyed.

Eszter's real mistake wasn't having the idea, though . . . it was talking about it in front of Silvana.

Waitresses hear everything; they're like cabdrivers or barbers, quiet sponges for the chatter around them. When Silvana overheard Eszter sharing her plan with Brady at the fonda, she told her mom straightaway.

That's when Gloria knew she had to find a way to get Eszter off the island. She paid attention, collected information. Moved when she got her chance. Sweet Brady with his big, goofy grin: *I'm here to pick up Eszter's favorite orejas! She said you'll know the ones.*

Gloria didn't mean for her to *die,* obviously. She thought Eszter would recover at a hospital on the mainland and be too spooked to return. Gloria should've listened to the little flare of guilt that went through her as she waved goodbye to Brady, bag of cookies swinging from his hand. It's weird, isn't it? A woman dying of anaphylaxis in her own small Airbnb, unable to find her EpiPen? How could Gloria have guessed that'd be the outcome? It was tragic, but in the end, she got her wish: Isla Colel won't change a bit.

Hilde was the second liability. Hilde with her freelance writing career, her journalist's eye, the stylish Instagram account documenting her day-to-day on the island. One post said she dreamed of breaking into travel writing. Where do you think she'd send readers first? So Gloria quietly got rid of her too. She made small modifications to Hilde's grocery runs, choosing her fresh ("fresh") meat and produce carefully. Voilà: GI issues so intense, Hilde landed in the hospital more than once. Blaming the water, the girl realized her system couldn't cut it here and moved on to another place, another subject for her articles.

There are benefits to being the only grocery store in town.

Then that Abby arrived, big-eyed and smiley. Within seconds of meeting Gloria, she delivered a bombshell: Abby was *Eszter's partner,* here to set the record straight. It was unlikely Abby would trace anything back to Gloria—she was too careful, and after all, no one force-fed Eszter that cookie—but certainly, Abby seemed poised to bring international attention to the island by conjuring up her fiancée's ghost.

Gloria did her best to control the situation; she volunteered to be the interlocutor with Marta, though of course, she didn't count on Marta producing a damn *rental agreement.* After that, when it was clear Abby didn't intend to leave without answers, Gloria drank a little too much mezcal and made an uncharacteristically ham-fisted move, leaving an untraceable voicemail telling her to leave. There was a ferry coming and she wanted Abby on it. Gloria thought the call would scare her—this helpless, monolingual traveler in way over her head—but it only seemed to strengthen her resolve. A rare misstep in Gloria's methodical shadow campaign to preserve Isla Colel. It won't happen again.

Esteban tromps into the store, pausing to twiddle his fingers at the parakeets by the door. When he approaches, Gloria runs her hand through his wind-mussed hair.

"Catch any fish today?" she asks. Any trace of her Puerto Rican accent has long since disappeared.

He plants a kiss on her cheek and grins. "A few."

ACKNOWLEDGMENTS

Reader, the fact that you picked this up fills me with wonder and gratitude. Thank you so much for joining me on Isla Colel and trusting me
with your limited time, money, and/or attention. Connecting with
readers has been the most magical part of this journey, and you are the
reason I get to keep doing this. From the bottom of my heart, thank
you—yes, *you,* hi, I appreciate you *so much.*

I'm raising a glass to the book influencers, librarians, and booksellers
who invest so much time and creativity into helping people find their
perfect reads. I'm especially grateful to everyone who's read and shared
my earlier four books over the years. Your hard work and talent mean the
world to us authors.

My reps at CAA are astonishingly good and I kinda can't believe I
get to work with them. To my badass agent, Alexandra Machinist, a true
champion for my books: What would I do without you?! I'm so blessed
to have you steering the ship; thank you for always listening and having
my back! You are truly the best in the biz. Cheers to the uber-talented
Xanthe Coffman for razor-sharp feedback and behind-the-scenes work
keeping the trains running on time.

Josie Freedman, thank you for everything but especially for taking
seriously my plucky dream of writing for the screen! You're a magic-
maker and I'm beyond lucky to have you in my corner. Thank you to
Elyse Pham for being so organized, helpful, and a delight to work with.
Much gratitude to my foreign rights team and everyone who makes
CAA such a powerhouse. It's a privilege to work with you all.

This is my fifth (!) novel with the brilliant Hilary Rubin Teeman, and
I'm so honored to be one of your authors. I regularly thank my lucky

stars that you took a chance on my debut almost a decade ago. I can't fully express my appreciation for all the encouragement, brainstorming, and pep talks . . . and for trusting me to dive into my weird ideas without knowing how they'll end. I grow so much as a writer with every single book as a direct result of your deep wisdom and pitch-perfect feedback. My sincere gratitude to Elsa Richardson-Bach, a paragon of organization and sharp editorial ideas! What a team.

I'm *obsessed* with my dynamite publicist, Sarah Breivogel, who makes the whole pitching-media process fun and exciting instead of scary and soul-sucking. I have no idea how you pull off so many PR miracles, but I'm pinching myself that I get to work with you a fifth time. So much gratitude, too, to the bright and capable Angie Campusano for all the PR support. Kathleen Quinlan, thanks a ton for your creative and thorough labor getting the word out about, well, my latest pile of words. I so appreciate your enthusiasm, ideas, organization, and can-do attitude.

Bravo to Sarah Horgan for this beautiful cover, Elizabeth A. D. Eno for the book's gorgeous inside, and Eric Hanson for the chef's-kiss map, as well as the copy editors, proofreaders, and myriad behind-the-scenes heroes who helped get this book to the printer and out into the world. My deepest thanks to Kara Cesare, Kim Hovey, Kara Welsh, and everyone else who champions my books and makes me feel so supported and at-home at Ballantine.

Many thanks to my authenticity reader, Paolo M., for helping me make this book's setting, characters, and narrative all come alive. For kindly sharing their expertise in a grab bag of topics (construction, plant biology, Mexican culture, Uruguayan geography, European history, the Madison area, business school, Spanish, Python coding, and Hungarian, among them!), thank you to Diego Andree, Megan Brown, Skyler Carson, Cristina Couloucoundis, Marianne Denes, Alanna Greco, Sabrina Gillman-Basave, Amanda Leipold, Erin Pastrana, Kristina Schierenbeck, Kate White, and others. (As always, I take full responsibility for any departures from believability.)

To all the kind and generous expats I met during my travels in Mexico and elsewhere: Gracias for welcoming me into your ranks. The characterizations herein are borne out of admiration and envy; not one of you gave me murder vibes!

Thank you to the unstoppable Reese's Book Club team for championing women's stories and creating such a beautiful, resilient community of authors and readers. I'm so grateful to the entire RBC crew, including Jane Lee, Melissa Seymour, Gretchen Schreiber, Olga Khaminwa, Sarah Harden, and others, as well as all my "Reese sister" author friends—and, of course, Reese Witherspoon, the book-lover-in-chief herself. I'm blown away by the ongoing encouragement and support from all the happy sunflowers in the RBC family. Thank you, thank you, thank you.

Leah Konen, my dear friend and crit partner for what feels like decades: I literally couldn't do this without you. I'm a little verklempt reflecting on all the long walks, endless plot-doctoring, brilliant notes, and many years of friendship. Leah deserves credit for coming up with the big reveal that snapped a bunch of swirling details and side plots into place. (I'll never forget the text: "I'VE GOT IT. Call me.") Girl, you're an actual genius.

I'm in awe of Danielle Rollins and Julia Bartz, beta readers extraordinaire, for their lucid, thoughtful notes. You're incredible storytellers and I'm so fortunate to learn from you with every new batch of feedback. Relatedly, the warmth and kindness of the writing community will never cease to blow my mind. Love and gratitude to Jennifer Keishin Armstrong, Megan Collins, Saumya Dave, Jessica Goodman, Caroline Kepnes, Vanessa Lillie, Julia Phillips, Melissa Rivero, Marie Rutkoski, and others for making this wild industry feel cozy and manageable. A special thank-you to everyone who's attended one of my writing retreats or followed my newsletter for authors, Get It Write. I couldn't be more grateful for my crew.

In fact, I hit the jackpot with a whole constellation of wonderful, supportive friends, including Laura Barisonzi, Lianna Bishop, Blaire Briody, Megan Brown, Jesse Jiryu Davis, Kate Dietrick, Monica Fay, Lindsay Ferris, Ross Guberman, Michael Howard, Carl Kelsch, Leigh Kunkel, Abbi Libers, Booters Liebmann-Smith, Kate Lord, Anna

Maltby, Emily St. John Mandel, Erin Pastrana, Akshay Patil, Katherine Pettit, Peter Rugg, Katie Scott, Emily Siegel, Nicole Stahl, Andrea Stanley, Jennifer Weber, and many others. Love y'all.

Special thanks to Julia Bartz for being the best big sister and BFF a girl could ask for. I'm grateful to my entire family for their continued support and love, especially Mom and Dad, Tom and Cathy, and my grandmother, Marianne Denes. Köszönöm szépen.

To Julia Dills, my kind, funny, brilliant partner: Thank you for always being my soft place to land. I'm so lucky. Te llamo.

Finally, a message to anyone who's ever conflated their output with their value; fretted they were too much or not enough; doubted they were worth the inconvenience; or believed, deep down, they wouldn't be lovable if they stopped impressing or serving others:

You were wrong. You're whole and deserving of soul-deep, unconditional love exactly as you are, right now, imperfect and messy and still.

You're just right.

ABOUT THE AUTHOR

Andrea Bartz is a journalist and the *New York Times* bestselling author of the Reese's Book Club pick *We Were Never Here, The Spare Room, The Lost Night,* and *The Herd.* Her work has appeared in *The Wall Street Journal, Marie Claire, Vogue,* and many other outlets, and she's held editorial positions at *Glamour, Psychology Today,* and *Self,* among other publications. She lives in Brooklyn and the Hudson Valley.

andreabartz.com
Instagram/Threads/TikTok: @andibartz
Facebook.com/andreabartzauthor

ABOUT THE TYPE

This book was set in Ehrhardt, a typeface based on the original design of Nicholas Kis, a seventeenth-century Hungarian type designer. Ehrhardt was first released in 1937 by the Monotype Corporation of London.